Even If It Kills Her

ALSO BY KATE WHITE

FICTION

The Secrets You Keep

The Wrong Man

Eyes on You

So Pretty It Hurts ★

The Sixes

Hush

Lethally Blond ★

Over Her Dead Body ★

'Til Death Do Us Part ★

A Body To Die For ★

If Looks Could Kill ★

★A Bailey Weggins Mystery

Even If It Kills Her

A Bailey Weggins Mystery

Kate White

HARPER LUXE

An Imprint of HarperCollinsPublishers

HarperCollins books may be purchased for educational, business, or sales promotional use. For information please e-mail the Special Markets Department at SPsales@harpercollins.com.

FIRST HARPERLUXE EDITION

ISBN: 978-0-06-268821-7

HarperLuxe™ is a trademark of HarperCollins Publishers.

Library of Congress Cataloging-in-Publication Data is available upon request.

17 18 19 20 21   ID/LSC   10 9 8 7 6 5 4 3 2 1

To Annie Pleshette Murphy, my wonderful friend
across decades and continents

Even If It Kills Her

Chapter 1

I don't have a ton of regrets to show for my thirty-six years on the planet, but the ones that I *do* have seem to possess a determined and sneaky resilience. Every once in a while, say, when I'm working on a crime story that's particularly soul-sucking, and I've been on the road far longer than planned—holed up in Beyoncé-style luxury at a Best Western or DoubleTree Suites—one of them will resurface, like a lake snake coming up for air, raising its snout above the waterline and forcing me to stare it in the face.

I regret not knowing my father well, though there was nothing I could have done about that one. He died of a brain aneurysm while on a fishing trip with a friend when I was twelve.

I regret (grievously) the eighteen-month hand grenade of a marriage I embarked on in my twenties, though I'm not sure I could have done much differently with that one, either. Compulsive gamblers, I came to discover, don't fess up to their addiction when they begin to woo you, nor to the sordid fact that they'll soon be dipping into their work T&E (and your jewelry box) in a desperate attempt to cover their losses.

And I regret that I spent over a year of my career reporting on celebrity crimes and misdemeanors (which generally involved the hurling of a cell phone at someone's head) for one of those tabloid magazines that used to be like crack for women under fifty but are now so desperate for newsstand sales that they run fake headlines like "Kate Pregnant with Triplets—Palace Confirms." My only defense about that one is that I needed the work.

There's one regret, however, that I never had a good excuse for. When Jillian Lowe, a girl I'd become friends with sophomore year at Brown, was roused by a phone call one Friday morning during the second week of April and was informed that her parents and two younger siblings had been murdered, I did nothing to comfort her. Oh wait, excuse me. I *did* send a sympathy card, and I also chipped in on a floral arrangement for the private funeral service, one of those standing sprays that make it look like the coffin's just won the

Kentucky Derby. But that was it. And my failure as a friend ate away at me for years.

So needless to say, I was floored when Jillian showed up looking for me one Tuesday night in July, nearly sixteen years later.

I'd just conducted the final interview in a sold-out, four-part series called "Inside the Criminal Mind" at the 92nd Street Y in Manhattan. The Y's programmer had approached me a few months before, suggesting that with my crime-writing background, I was the perfect interviewer to pair with the ex-cons they'd wrangled for the program, including an infamous inside trader who'd served seven years in prison. I jumped at the chance. This would be a way to keep momentum going on my true-crime book, which was published in February.

As hoped, the series garnered a ton of buzz, and I'd sold a boatload of books. However, enabling those felons to elaborate on their crimes and fluff their feathers in public had left me feeling sullied. I couldn't wait to be done with the whole thing, and when the audience Q and A portion of the final evening was over, I bolted from the stage so fast that the female con artist I'd been interviewing had probably checked her wallet. I still had to sign books in the vestibule, but that would take only twenty minutes or so.

Jillian, it turned out, was waiting for me, off to the side of the book table. I couldn't see her face from my place at the table, but I remember being aware of someone's presence as I scrolled my signature. At signings there are always a few hoverers, people unwilling to cough up eighteen bucks for your book and yet eager to request the name of your agent or suggest that you might enjoy critiquing their six-hundred-page unpublished manuscript free of charge because "it would mean a lot to me."

I signed the last book, thanked the rep from the Y for her assistance, and jumped up to leave. Before I'd taken a step, I could sense the person over my shoulder closing in. I turned, prepared to announce that I unfortunately had to dash.

"Hello, Bailey," she said.

It took a few beats for me to realize who she was. Once I did, my mouth dropped open, as I felt a rush of both shock and delight. Neither time nor tragedy had dimmed her prettiness, I noticed, but her long blond hair was now brunette and cut to her chin, and though her skin still had that same lovely glow, there were small crow's-feet around her eyes, the kind that sprout from too much sun. Something else seemed different, too, though I couldn't put my finger on it.

"Oh, my gosh, Jillian, it's you," I said, finally wiping the blank look off my face.

"It's really nice to see you, Bailey."

"Your hair—it's different. I almost didn't recognize you."

At first she didn't seem to grasp what I meant.

"Oh, right," she said, lightly touching a lock by her temple. "I stopped coloring it a long time ago. And yours is short now, I see."

"Yeah, I chopped it off when I hit thirty, let it grow back, then cut it again just recently. I never had great hair, did I?"

"At least you're a natural blonde."

"Well, blondish brown." I smiled and she smiled back. But the pleasure I'd experienced at the first sight of her was quickly shape-shifting into awkwardness. I could sense guilt creeping around the edges of my mind, trying to assert itself. *You were a lousy friend to her, Bailey. She suffered the most horrible loss and you did close to nothing for her.*

Jillian, however, seemed genuinely pleased to see me. Nothing about her attitude hinted at lingering disappointment that spanned over a decade and a half. I couldn't believe I was actually setting eyes on her. Where had she been all this time? Had she been *all right*?

"Were you here tonight, at the event?" I asked.

"Yes, I mean, kind of hanging in the back. I've wanted to get in touch with you, but I didn't know any other way. I was afraid if I used the contact email on your website, the message would end up in some kind of black hole."

"What are you doing in the city?"

"Living here—temporarily. A sublet in Williamsburg."

I had no idea what she did professionally, or even if she worked. What I *could* surmise just from looking at her was that her clothes—cropped black pants, chunky heeled sandals, and a flowy gold-and-black top that accented her nice curves—were classy and hip and that she probably wasn't married, since there was no wedding band on the appropriate finger.

"It'd be great to get together while you're here," I told her, though the idea, even while she stood right in front of me, was difficult to imagine after so many years. "Would you have time?"

"Yes. I was actually thinking we could catch up tonight."

She said it with what seemed like an odd casualness and disregard, as if she wouldn't have expected me to have either plans for the evening or a desire to head home. But I sensed an urgency underneath. Despite the fact that I'd promised my live-in boyfriend, Beau, that I'd decompress with him tonight on the roof-deck of our apartment building, there was no way I could turn Jillian down. I wanted to know what she'd been doing and how she'd fared in life. Besides, my guilt wasn't going to take anything but a yes for an answer.

"Of course. Were you thinking of coffee, wine . . . ?"

"Either's fine."

"Um, okay. There's a café I noticed a block up on Lexington. They seem to do both, so why don't we try that?"

It took only five minutes to reach the café, and we didn't say much on the way, just an inconsequential comment or two about how nice the summer weather had been. At about five foot three, she was roughly three inches shorter than me, I realized, a fact I hadn't recalled. Her presence had always read so *large* to me.

We settled at a table at the back, and each of us ordered a glass of red wine. She then excused herself, saying she needed to use the restroom.

While she was gone, I texted Beau, telling him that we'd have to bag the roof-deck tonight because I'd run into a long-lost friend and would explain more about it later.

Long-lost friend. Did I have the right to call her that?

She certainly hadn't strayed far from my memory, nor had the grizzly crime at the center of her life. Even after all these years, the details of the murders were still vivid in my mind, as I'm sure they were for people who lived in or near Dory, Massachusetts, one of a series of towns and villages in the Berkshire Mountain region. Jillian's parents; her younger brother, Danny; and sister, Julia, a Barnard College freshman at home recuperating from mono, had been stabbed to death late one night by a teenage boy from their neighborhood, who apparently had developed an obsession with Julia.

At the time of the killings, I'd agonized over what Jillian must have been going through. Though we'd known each other for only five or six months, we'd grown close. In addition to living a few doors down from each other in the dorm, we were both in the same late-afternoon sociology class and had settled into a routine of splitting a pizza afterward while trying to decode the ramblings of our professor. I could still recall Jillian wagging a pizza slice one night and exclaiming, "That man is going to drive me into the arms of animal research." She had a magnetic confidence, as well as a wry sense of humor and a contagious, carefree laugh. It was my first realization that science majors could possess a wicked sense of humor.

I didn't see her before she took off for Dory that morning, and though I had every intention of calling her, I nervously kept putting off the task. I mean, what in the world would I *say*?

I suppose I could blame it on being twenty and having less-than-perfect social skills, yet I think it had more to do with having lost my father as young as I did. His death for me had been like falling overboard in the middle of the sea and watching the ship pull farther and farther away as I bobbed helplessly in the waves. For a long time the mere topic of death left me tongue-tied, and I was totally lame at comforting the bereaved. Though that's hardly justification.

Several days passed, and it grew harder and harder to phone Jillian. I promised myself I would make it up to her when she returned to campus.

But she never came back. She dropped out of college, and the next I heard, she was living on the West Coast. By then I was too ashamed to reach out.

Five minutes later, Jillian settled back at the table. I realized I wasn't yet used to her no longer being a blonde. She took a quick sip of wine and smiled, with warmth that I could also see in her deep blue eyes. There was still no sign that she was holding my past failing against me.

"Just so you know," she said, "I didn't buy your

book tonight because I already own it. I thought it was terrific, Bailey."

"That's really nice of you to say." The book, *A Model Murder*, explored the homicide of supermodel Devon Barr at a country house where I'd also been a guest at the time of her death. I was touched by the fact that Jillian had read it, that she wanted to connect with me again.

"Of course, at school, people were sure you'd be a writer one day, but I guess we just didn't know it would be about crime. How did you end up going in that direction?"

I weighed my words before I spoke. Though her question didn't seem loaded, we were on weird terrain, considering the tragedy in her life.

"My standard reply is that when someone in ninth grade started leaving anonymous nasty notes for me, I played detective and figured out who it was, and that gave me a love for that sort of thing. But that's only part of it. Right after Brown I got a job at a newspaper in Albany, and they put me on the police beat. One thing kind of led to another."

"And now you're focusing on books?"

"Right. I used to write mostly for magazines, I even had part-time gigs at a few, but print opportunities are drying up, thanks to the Internet."

"And you're married, right? I remember hearing once that you were."

"Well, briefly, but it didn't work out, to say the least. I'm living with someone now, though. A nice guy. His name's Beau Regan. But enough about me. I want to hear about *you*."

She cocked her head and glanced off for a moment, the expression in her eyes momentarily wistful. I found myself holding my breath. I'd googled her name from time to time over the years, but once the neighborhood kid was tried and sentenced, nothing ever surfaced, and I didn't have a clue what had unfolded for her. I just prayed that she'd found a certain peace.

"I've bounced around a bit," she said, returning her gaze to mine. "But not necessarily in a bad way. After—after everything, I went to live with family friends of ours, the Healys, who'd moved from Dory to Seattle several years before. I just needed to hide away for a while, and they took me in. Me and the cat."

"There were no relatives in the east you could have turned to?"

She shook her head. "My mother and father were both only children, and my grandparents on both sides were deceased. But the Healys—the parents and kids—were great. They did their absolute best to make me feel at home."

"It must have been so hard."

"I was a basket case for a while, longer than I wish, but I eventually found a great therapist. And I went back to school, to the University of Washington."

Something had started pawing at my brain as she spoke, but I wasn't sure what it was. Maybe I was simply feeling unsettled from thinking about her loss.

"Studying biology still? I remember you were wild about birds."

"Hmm, hm. There was a brief period when I thought of becoming a lawyer and helping other crime victims, but I realized that law school would bore me to tears. I got a degree in biology, a master's, too, and worked after that with a professor in Patagonia, studying Magellanic penguins."

"*Penguins*? How fantastic. They're birds, of course, right?"

"Yup."

"How long were you in Patagonia?"

"On and off for a few years. That's when I stopped being blond." She smiled. "They don't exactly have hair colorists in Punta Tombo."

I grinned back. "And after that? Did you return to the States?"

"Only briefly. Then I headed to Australia for field-work, studying what they call 'little penguins,' and I taught as well. It was different there from Argentina but incredible, too."

All that sun and wind explained the crow's-feet. But more important, it sounded as if things *had* been okay, that she hadn't allowed the murders to unspool her life. Though had all that globe-trotting actually been a form of being on the run?

"And now?"

"I'm considering doing a PhD program—I've been accepted into one—but for the time being, I'm taking a bit of a sabbatical. My parents had always wanted us to be self-starters, and they designed their will so that if they died young, we wouldn't inherit most of the money until we were each thirty-five, which means I recently came into a decent chunk. I thought I'd take a break. Travel, take care of some things. With New York City as home base."

"Do you ever go back? I mean, to Dory?"

"Not since the sentencing. It was just too hard."

I, on the other hand, had been to Dory a couple of times since then, while visiting a first cousin of my father's who lived in a nearby town, and on each trip, I had driven by Jillian's old house. I wasn't going to admit that, though. It would sound really creepy.

"It's just so good to see you, Jillian," I said instead. "And I hope you'll accept my apology."

"What do you mean?"

"I never reached out; I was never there for you."

She shrugged, as if I was apologizing for picking up the wrong sandwich for her on a deli run.

"It's not easy to know what to say or do in situations like that."

"I know, but I should have done *something*, tried to come see you."

"I probably would have discouraged it anyway. It was hard for me in the beginning to even *accept* sympathy, except from the Healys and a few friends I'd known for ages. There were people in town—like my father's business associates—who were upset because I didn't want to have this huge funeral service with open caskets so that everyone had a chance to pay their respects. But I couldn't bear the thought. The only way I could cope was to keep things small and private."

At that moment I finally recognized what was different about her appearance. There was a tautness to the muscles of her face that had never been there before, as if she was working hard underneath the bonhomie to stay in control, swaddling or even strapping down emotions and instincts to keep them from playing havoc with her demeanor.

"I'd love to spend more time together while you're here," I said. "Would you like to come over for dinner one night? If you're seeing someone, you can bring him, too."

"Oh that's nice. And yes, maybe sometime. But there's something I want more than that."

"Of course." I couldn't imagine what it could be. Maybe she was eager to write about her work with penguins and needed advice on how to start. People often picked my brain about becoming an author. "Tell me what I can do."

"I want you to find the person who murdered my family."

Chapter 2

Hearing her say that—*the person who murdered my family*—chilled my blood. It took a moment, though, for me to compute the words and latch on to the discrepancy. She wanted me to *find* the killer, and yet the killer was currently serving consecutive life sentences. He confessed to the murders eight days afterward.

"Wait," I said. "Are you saying that you don't believe Dylan Fender did it?"

She slipped her top lip under her teeth and bit down on it. I saw the muscles in her face tense even more.

"I'm pretty sure he didn't. There's new DNA evidence. It strongly suggests that he was wrongly convicted."

For a moment, I was speechless. "Omigod," I said finally. "So the confession was coerced?"

"It seems so. As the defense said during the trial, he'd been awake for most of the night, and he didn't have a lawyer with him. Couple that with the fact that he had learning disabilities."

"Has he been released yet?"

She bit down again, this time so hard I thought she might draw blood. "No. No, he died in prison five months ago."

Instinctively my eyes pricked with tears as the full force of the revelation hit me. An innocent eighteen-year-old boy had spent more than a decade and a half in prison and died there. The real murderer was still at large. And Jillian, who had tried so hard and for so long to build a new life for herself, was now smack back in the middle of the nightmare again.

"How did this come to light? Did you have something to do with it?"

"No, one of those innocence groups uncovered it. After years of trying, Dylan's mother convinced them to take a look at the case. Eventually they petitioned a judge to allow for a broader test on the blood samples, and they found that some of the blood smeared on the wall in the hall didn't belong to either Dylan or anyone in my family. The killer must have cut himself that night and left his blood there."

"So why was Dylan still in prison?"

"Another petition was entered, this one for a new trial, but the DA was dragging his feet. In February, Dylan contracted an infection, which turned into sepsis and spiraled out of control. I'm sure the health care in prison is terrible."

She ran a pointer finger around the wet rim of her wineglass, pressing so hard the glass began to sing. "The only consolation is that he died knowing there was a decent chance he was going to be exonerated."

For a few years, I'd kept Dylan Fender's name on my Google Alerts list, but after his appeals ran out, I'd deleted it, not wanting to be reminded of him anymore. But his face, from a class picture that had accompanied every media story about the case, was still fresh in my mind. There'd been something goofily endearing about him in that photo, so unlike the typical sullen-looking faces of teen boys who go on killing sprees. I'd cautioned myself not to be fooled.

"Oh, Jillian," I said, touching her arm, "this must be horrible for you."

"His whole life was ruined. And he died without ever being free again."

"That wasn't your fault."

"But I should have known better." Anguish bled into her voice. "He was a sweet, harmless-seeming kid, just a little quirky. It never really made sense that he could have done it."

"You can't blame yourself. It's only in the last few years that we've come to realize how common false confessions are, especially for people under twenty-five."

Again she let her finger trace the rim. Her hands, I noticed, had aged more than her face had, and were rough and wrinkled, clearly from working outside in the sun, cold, and wind.

"I need to make this right," she said. "For Dylan's sake. And I need to make sure the real killer is caught."

"Have the cops reopened the investigation?"

She scoffed. "I don't think so. Though the DA agreed to the additional testing, he apparently isn't convinced Dylan was innocent, and he's made no move to vacate the conviction. I've at least been granted a meeting with him to air my views. It's set for Friday morning in Massachusetts. Not Dory, thank God. Pittsfield."

My mind was racing, processing everything she'd shared. "Now that you believe Dylan wasn't responsible, any thoughts about who could have done it?"

She pulled a breath. "Someone who wasn't a stranger."

"Because?" After all this time, some of the details were fuzzy to me.

"From what they surmised, my sister was downstairs fairly late that night, still dressed, and she turned off the security alarm at around eleven, obviously to let the person in. She would never have done that for a stranger. That always lent support to the assumption that it was Dylan. His family lived down the street, and Jules would have definitely opened the door for him. She would have thought there was a problem at his house or that he'd locked himself out when his parents weren't home."

"Were there ever any other suspects?"

"Not that the cops shared with me."

"Wasn't there something about your father's business partner?" I said, the memory suddenly dislodging. Her father had been a prominent real estate developer.

She shrugged. "In the very first days, before they arrested Dylan, my father's partner, Bruce Kordas, was mentioned in a story or two as a possible person of interest. I mean, a business partner would be a natural suspect. And when the Healys came east, Mr. Healy told the police that he sensed my father hadn't been very happy with Bruce in recent months. But I don't know if they ever seriously considered him. They were so laser focused on Dylan from the minute they set eyes on him."

"Would your sister have opened the door for Bruce Kordas that late?"

"Probably. She might have thought there was an emergency on a site."

"Gaining control of the company is a pretty strong motive. Do you know if he's still in the area?"

"Yes, and he still runs the business, though of course my dad's share went to the estate."

Her gaze tightened, her eyes imploring.

"I need your help, Bailey," she said. "You have to find the person who killed them."

She'd said that a few minutes before, but I saw now that she meant it not in some figurative sense but *literally*. She wanted me to play investigator and determine who the real murderer was. I felt a swell of sadness. That idea made little sense, and I was going to have to tell her that.

"Jillian, I want to be there for you this time, but if you don't trust the cops to take action, your best bet would be to hire a private investigator, someone with real expertise."

She scoffed again. "I looked into a couple of them in the area, but they specialize in stuff like insurance fraud and finding out whether an ex-wife should have her alimony revoked because she's got a live-in lover on the down low. You've actually solved murders, Bailey. You found out how that model died."

"Okay, there've been times when I've been able to

get to the bottom of a crime, but I'm not a real investigator. First and foremost, I don't have any forensics training, and in light of the new evidence in the case, you'd want someone who could interpret that for you."

"I wouldn't expect you to give me a report on blood spatter. What I want is someone with your reporting skills—who can talk to people, dig up stuff that's been buried or that other people would miss. And once I have that, I can go to the police with the new evidence and press them to do more."

"But reporters only have so much access. It's going to be tough to find anything out, especially sixteen years after the fact."

I hated the way that came out of my mouth. Reducing the slaughter of her entire family to "the fact."

"But certainty there's *something* that could be dug up after all this time. I just can't bear the thought of not trying."

She seemed determine to go ahead, and I could hardly blame her. And if the killer really *was* someone familiar with her family, there might be a few old threads to inspect and ponder over, threads the police had missed in their rush to judgment.

"I'll pay you, of course," Jillian said before I could answer.

I almost flinched. "Don't be silly."

"Trust me," she said, her tone rueful. "It's been a long time since I've known how to be silly. *Of course* I'd have to pay you for your time. I'd be paying an investigator if I hired one."

"But it's not about money, Jillian. I'm just afraid that as a civilian I wouldn't be of much help. And though the police may not want to get off their asses in terms of the case, they're going to be annoyed if they discover that someone else is tramping on their turf."

Jillian didn't say anything right away, just recomposed her face, tightening up all those muscles again.

"There's one more thing I could offer," she added. "I know you must be thinking about writing another book, looking for a new topic. I'd give you an exclusive."

Interestingly, she'd intuited the fact that I *was* eager for a topic. When I'd sold the idea for *A Model Murder* to my publisher, they'd given me a two-book deal, and so far I'd been hopelessly stumped on an idea for the second one. This case was definitely worth a book, but it could hardly be my motivation for getting involved.

"Would you be willing to let me think about it overnight?" I asked. "I'd have to go to the Berkshires with you and stay for a bit. Let me take a look at what obligations I have this month, and also consider whether there might be a better strategy for you."

"Sure." She looked dubious.

"I'll help you, Jillian. One way or the other, I promise."

Out on the sidewalk a few minutes later, after she paid the check against my protests, we'd exchanged contact info and she pulled out her phone to request an Uber for the trip back to Brooklyn.

"Jillian, there's one thing I need to stress, regardless of whether we work together on this. Looking into the case could be dangerous. There's a good chance the killer isn't in the area anymore, but he *could* be. And he could have heard the news about Dylan Fender."

"I understand. I just can't let it go, Bailey—the fact that he's still out there, *free*. I'll do anything to make sure he's caught."

It took only a minute for her Uber to arrive.

"I'll call you tomorrow, okay?" I told her.

"Thanks, Bailey."

"One more question," I said as she stepped off the curb. "Is this whole turn of events the reason you came back to the US?"

"I was already back when I heard about Dylan. I started to miss the States, and to be honest, I wanted to see if I could finally live a normal life here."

"And do you think you can?"

"Hopefully." A wry smile formed on her face, a hint of the old Jillian. "Though I do feel a little like a penguin out of water these days. The best I can do at times is waddle up the hill or slide along on my belly."

A few seconds later the car shot into the summer night. Her parting words hung in the air, squeezing my heart. Some grief *did* diminish greatly with time, but not the kind that had been foisted on Jillian.

I opted for a cab home since one came barreling along a second later, and by the time I let myself into the apartment, it was after ten. Beau was already in bed but wide-awake, with his iPad on his lap and his new reading glasses perched just below the bridge of his nose. At thirty-nine, he was on the young side for reading glasses, and they annoyed him to death, but *I* liked them on him. Though Beau and I had been living together for around two years—my first attempt since my divorce at a major commitment—there had always been a slight air of mystery about him, about those deep brown eyes and hawk nose. It was a mystery that I occasionally found disconcerting.

The reading glasses nicely undermined that. I mean, people in reading glasses always seem refreshingly normal and transparent to me. *You know everything there is to know about me,* the glasses seem to say. *That I like to devour books and peruse menus, and I'm so lacking in vanity, I don't mind the way these make my hair look like early Dolph Lundgren when I push them on top of my head.*

"Oh, hey, didn't hear you come in," he said, looking up. "How'd it go?"

"Pretty good. Nice crowd."

"Did you sell a lot of books?"

"Not as many as the other nights, but there were quite a few repeats in the audience and they may have already bought one."

Beau shoved the glasses on top of his head, spiking his dark brown hair. It was actually a cute look on him.

"And how about the con artist? What was she like?"

"All con and no artist, as far as I could see. She claims prison made her a new woman, but I don't buy it."

I kicked my shoes off, plopped down on Beau's side of the bed, and kissed him on the mouth. Most nights he slept bare-chested, but this evening because of the AC running, he'd pulled on a T-shirt. I couldn't help but admire the way it stretched over his pecs.

"How did *your* thing go?" He'd been planning to attend tonight's event but had been forced to cancel in order to meet with a potential investor for the next documentary he was slated to shoot. I'd felt a prick of disappointment when he broke the news, then quickly let it go.

"He might cough up a little dough, though right now he's being noncommittal. I can't believe I had to miss your thing just for that."

"Don't worry. You can come to the next one if I can stomach doing it. The Y's already talking about a second series for next year."

Next year. A funny thing to consider in relation to Beau. The only time we ever discussed the semi-distant future was while making vacation plans. When I'd first set eyes on Beau, I'd been struck by the thunderbolt of a thought that I was going to marry him one day, and yet that concept had grown blurry over time. Not that I didn't love him. Rather we just tended to ground our lives very much in the present tense.

"So who's the friend you bumped into?" he asked. "Anyone I've met?"

"No, actually not."

I told him then about Jillian, not only her tragic history—as well as Dylan Fender's—but also my failure to be much of a friend in the aftermath. For the time being, I kept quiet about Jillian's request. I figured it would be best to give Beau a chance to sit with her story for a few minutes first. I knew he was proud of my work, and the success of my book this year, but over the past several months he'd begun to sound skittish about some of the stories I was drawn to. I half expected him to say I shouldn't take an assignment unless I was willing to wear a Kevlar vest.

"That's heartbreaking stuff," he said, when I'd finished. "And the poor guy. Are the cops trying to find the real murderer?"

"Jillian's worried they're not, that they're still convinced the right guy was convicted years ago."

"God, that's crappy."

Okay, here was the perfect entrée for me and sooner than I'd anticipated.

"I know. . . . She begged me to help her out on this. She wants me to go to Dory, ask questions, try to dig up information about the past, thinking it might point to the killer and she can relay it to the police."

There was a beat before he replied.

"What did you tell her?"

Careful, Bailey, I warned myself. *Proceed with caution.*

"I didn't commit to anything yet, said I'd think it over. But it would be great to be able to help her after screwing up all those years ago."

He pursed his lips, clearly considering.

"Could you write about it? That way you wouldn't feel as if you were compromising your work by spending time in—what did you say the place was? Dory?"

"Yeah. And funny you should mention that.

Because she said I could write a book about the process if I wanted."

Beau cocked his head. "That would kind of kill two birds with one stone. You'd clear your conscience and have a topic to write about. I know you've been anxious to figure that out."

Ahh, *very clever*, if I did say so myself. I was expecting Beau to flinch and urge me to turn Jillian down because of the inherent danger in looking for a killer. Perhaps he was trying a new tactic, having determined that his previous attempts to discourage me didn't work. Of course, I realized, I might have underestimated him. Maybe he could see that this was something I really needed to do.

"I still want to think it over, and then I'll let her know tomorrow."

"When would you have to leave?"

"Probably Thursday. She has an appointment up there the next morning."

"We'd be leaving about the same time then. I have to fly out early Friday morning."

Beau had a shoot to do in Miami. As a documentary filmmaker, he often traveled for work.

"Let's do something fun tomorrow night then. We could even venture out of Chelsea."

"Sounds good," he said. "You coming to bed now?"

"I think I'll decompress for a bit and consider my next steps. It's been quite a night."

I kissed him again, a longer one this time, then padded out into the living room in my bare feet. When the two of us had decided to live together—after close to a year of dating—it made the most sense for me to move into Beau's place in Chelsea because it was roomier. He'd made a couple of accommodations with the decor and reconfigured his home office back into the small dining room it was meant to be. He'd set up a real office for himself in his nearby studio.

At the time we met, I was living in a small but cool one-bedroom I owned (thanks to a tiny trust fund from my father) on the corner of Ninth Street and Broadway, where the East Village meets the West, and there was never any talk of me letting go of it. As a full-time freelance writer, I needed a quiet place to work, and my apartment, with its insanely low maintenance, perfectly fit the bill—and was a smart investment to hold on to.

I still found it hard at times to switch into work mode in the Chelsea apartment, but I forced myself that night. I typed the pertinent details into the search bar and began to read through everything I could find about the Lowe murders, the very same articles I'd pored over years before.

There'd been a ton of coverage initially—newspapers, TV, even *People* magazine—but it had trailed off after about a month, spiking again briefly during the short trial and sentencing.

Julia, age nineteen, had been the first to die in the Lowes' spacious home, her body found inside the library, which, based on a diagram in one article, was off the left side of a large center hall. As Jillian had reminded me, her sister had apparently let the killer into the house. She sustained nearly two dozen stab wounds to her head, torso, and arms, as well as to the palms of her hands, from a futile attempt to defend herself. The killer had used a butcher knife of some sort, possibly one from the household; there had been such an eclectic mix of knives in the kitchen, it had been impossible to be sure if it had come from there. The weapon was never found.

Claire, Jillian's fifty-one-year-old mother, was discovered dressed in a nightgown at the base of the staircase. According to police, she'd most likely been killed on the landing between the first and second floors. She may have been awakened by the sounds of the struggle below and had hurried from the master bedroom to investigate. The killer, perhaps hearing her footsteps, had apparently ascended the stairs and confronted her. He took the knife to her face, head, and neck, severing her jugular. It was evident from certain bruising on her body—and all the blood on the walls of the staircase—that once he'd finished stabbing her, he'd hurled her body down the steps.

Next, it seemed, he entered the master bedroom. Jillian's father, Carl, though only fifty-three, had lost most of the hearing in one ear and had evidently not been awakened by the noise downstairs. He was stabbed a dozen times in the head, neck, torso, and also his legs, as if the killer had just wielded the weapon up and down the body. His jugular had also been severed.

And then there was poor little Danny, age twelve. Unlike his father, he'd clearly discerned that something was horribly wrong because he was found dead in his closet, suggesting that the killer had come upon him cowering in fear. Tragically, he might have survived his small number of stab wounds if he'd received immediate medical attention, but the carnage was not discovered until the next day, when Carl Lowe's secretary arrived at the house, concerned because he'd missed an important meeting.

Only the family cat had survived, and was found the next day, hiding in a guest bedroom.

According to Dylan's confession (later recanted), he had murdered Julia because he felt slighted when she shied away from his attention during her recovery. He killed everyone else simply to cover his tracks.

Though Dylan might have been innocent, it was possible that a similar scenario had played out that night. Someone could have gone to the house targeting Julia specifically, and after waking up Claire with the noise, had decided that a murder spree was his only option. Of course the killer might have been after Carl instead, or Claire, or even Danny, and the others had ended up as collateral damage.

Or the killer had always intended to murder everyone. He may have hated what they represented—unity, happiness, wealth, a picture-perfect family.

I'd hoped that in rereading the coverage, a detail might leap out and present me with a nugget worth pursuing, but there was nothing like that. Within days all the coverage was focusing on Dylan. As Jillian had pointed out during our conversation, one article suggested that the police were eyeing Bruce Kordas, Carl's business partner, but there was nothing to suggest he'd ever been considered a suspect.

For a while, I simply studied the photos, as I'd done on numerous occasions after the murders. Many of the articles and TV reports had featured the same posed family shot, clearly taken during a summer vacation, along with candid shots of Danny and Julia, as well as Jillian, the sister who'd been spared.

They were a stunning family. Carl had the chiseled features and silvery hair of someone who could have run for US president if he wasn't busy being a successful real estate developer. Claire was gorgeous, her thick brunette hair still worn long. I knew from some of the coverage that she'd been an ER nurse for a time but had left her job when her two daughters were young.

The girls were both beautiful, too, though Julia was more slender and somewhat fragile-looking. I remembered Jillian saying that her sister had been seriously ill as a child. I'd never thought the two looked much alike, but now that Jillian's hair was brown like Julia's had been, I could see a resemblance.

And then there was Danny. Totally endearing. It was hard to fathom that anyone would have targeted him specifically, though I'd once read about a family who'd been killed by two fourteen-year-old boys because those boys had disliked the son, a schoolmate of theirs.

I'd read all I could handle in one night. I closed my laptop and switched off the table light next to me. The city twinkled outside the tenth-floor windows.

Okay, true-confession time. There was something about which I hadn't been totally forthcoming with Jillian tonight. When she'd asked why I'd become a crime writer, I'd told her I'd been inspired by an incident in high school, and that's true to some extent.

But her family's murder had played a role, as well. I'd devoured every word I could find about the crime and felt haunted about it for years. Those tragic deaths had ended up fanning my early fascination with crime into something bigger and far more fierce, leading me to plead for a job on the Albany paper's police beat. Crime writing, I realized, wasn't just about informing the public. It could be about opening eyes, nudging law enforcement, and making sure the guilty were caught and punished.

A few minutes later, I slipped into bed beside Beau, spooning his sleeping body with mine. My decision was made. In fact, I'd probably made it back in the café on Lexington Avenue. I'd head to Massachusetts this week and start digging into the murder of the Lowe family. I owed that to Jillian in more ways than one.

Besides, every part of my being was desperate to know who the real killer was.

Chapter 3

Two days later, Jillian Lowe and I were tucked into the front seat of my Jeep Cherokee, pointed toward the Berkshires of Massachusetts. We'd hit the road later than I would have liked, but at least we'd arrive before dinnertime.

There was no way for me to miss the irony of us barreling along the Taconic State Parkway together, dressed in T-shirts, jeans, and sandals. Just a couple of days before Jillian's family had been murdered, the two of us had hatched a plan for a road trip to Cape Cod in early May. We were going to stay with a cousin of hers at the family's summer home and spend our time walking the beach together, eating clams and lobsters, and studying for finals.

Now, these many years later, we were finally on a

journey together. But there would be nothing fun and beachy about this one.

I'd spent the day before ensconced in my office on Ninth Street, tying up loose ends, rearranging my calendar for the next week, and doing as much prep work as I could for the trip ahead.

The first call I made in that department was to the lawyer from the innocence group who had worked on Dylan's behalf, and he confirmed what Jillian had shared. I also phoned Bonnie Peets, a forensics expert I frequently consulted with, and asked for her thoughts on how a smear of blood from the killer might have ended up on the wall. She explained that he could have accidentally cut himself when the handle of the knife became so wet with blood that it caused his hand to slip onto the blade. It wasn't, she said, an uncommon occurrence.

Finally, I did an online search for anything on Bruce Kordas. I found nothing from years ago that hinted at any problems at Lowe/Kordas Development; in fact, I turned up very little about Kordas or the company.

Before heading home, I popped over to say hi to my dapper seventy-plus-year-old next-door neighbor, Landon, filling him in on the case. We'd met when I first moved into the building almost ten years ago and had become close friends after my divorce.

That night, Beau and I had eaten out, as planned, and I woke the next morning, antsy to get moving.

Jillian's original plan for her part of our trip had been to spend, max, forty-eight hours in the Berkshires. That would allow time for the meeting with the DA and also dinner at the home of a high school friend named Mamie Allard, whom she'd stayed in periodic touch with. Then she was going to beat a fast retreat out of town.

And yet as much as it was going to pain Jillian to be in the area again, I needed her there for longer. She'd not only be able to give me the lay of the land but also answer, in real time, the questions that popped up as I conducted my research.

So I pressed her during a phone call to make her stay at least three days. After a few seconds of silence, she agreed. Her one restriction: she couldn't stay in Dory itself, which I completely understood. I booked us into the Briar Inn in Ferndale, about twenty-five minutes southwest of Dory, figuring that we'd be able to keep a low profile there, which was key. We didn't need the media finding out Jillian was back—and we certainly didn't want the killer learning that, either.

The killer. As I'd relayed to Jillian, there was a decent chance he wasn't around any longer. Unless he was a total and complete nut job, it would have been troubling for him to stay so close to the crime scene. If, however, he'd had serious ties to the area—as in a very successful real estate business—it would have been tricky to leave.

Of course, no matter where he was at this point, he probably kept tabs on things. The new DNA finding had to be his worst nightmare come true.

"I have an idea for my cover story," I announced after we'd managed to clear some traffic. "I hope you'll be okay with it."

"Sure, try me."

"The first person I need to focus on is Bruce Kordas. Even if Mr. Healy hadn't been suspicious of him, he'd be at the top of the list based on possible motives. If I call him out of the blue, though, and say I'm researching the murders, he may feel threatened and refuse to see me. What if I told him I was helping you write a memoir and that you'd suggested I speak to him?"

I shot a glance across the front seat. She didn't look happy.

"I'd never write a memoir, though," she said. "Never."

"I know. But this might be the way to convince him to talk to me."

Jillian touched a little hollow spot on her neck. "Okay," she said softly. "It's probably smart to have an excuse like that. He was always a slick guy."

"Point noted. And then who else should I zero in on? Before they arrested Dylan, was there anyone else who occurred to you, even for a millisecond?" I hated the sound of my voice tossing out that question so matter-of-factly, as if I were asking her to make a choice between Thai or Mexican food for dinner tonight. But I had to go there.

"The police asked me that, of course, but absolutely no one came to mind. People loved my family—or at least I thought they did."

"Did your dad ever mention any problems with a client or someone he did business with? Or with a work colleague other than Bruce?"

"No. As far as I knew, he got along with everyone. And I don't think Jules would have let anyone from his work in besides Bruce. She would have called my dad downstairs first."

"Let's start from that end then. Who would Julia have let into the house at that hour?"

"I suppose she would have opened the door for a close friend of my parents, though it's hard to say for sure. I just don't know."

"Did Julia have a boyfriend?"

"She wasn't seeing anyone at the time."

"You sure?"

"Yes, she would have told me. . . . There was a guy she dated her first semester at Barnard, he went to Columbia, but they stopped seeing each other before Christmas. I know the police checked him out and didn't find anything. The guy's roommate said he was in the dorm all night."

"And you're certain she didn't start dating anyone when she was home recuperating? Maybe an old boyfriend who was still in town?"

"No, she was housebound from the mono. Besides, she'd been kind of a loner in high school. I don't know if you remember my telling you this, but she was pretty sick as a kid. She developed something called cardiomyopathy, probably from a virus, and it led to congestive heart failure. She was one of the lucky ones who recovered, but for many years she was awfully frail. She mostly hung out with me—or by herself. She would read, write music, that kind of thing."

"Do you think it was hard for her to be in your shadow?"

Not exactly a pertinent question, but I couldn't help be curious. I'd picked up from our pizza dinners years ago that Jillian had been popular in high school, one of those girls who'd been a triple threat—varsity athlete, gorgeous, *and* an academic star. It couldn't have been fun to attempt to live up to that.

"Maybe at times. But she had her own successes, especially as she got healthier. Like me, she was a science nerd, and she won a bunch of prizes. And she played solo violin all through high school."

"Okay, let's go at it from one more angle. Had anything odd or disruptive happened to your family in the weeks before that night? Had they mentioned anything to you, even something that seemed fairly insignificant at the time?"

I had my gaze flicking back and forth between the road and the rearview mirror, keeping an eye on a royally obnoxious tailgater, and it took me a moment to realize Jillian wasn't answering. Finally I had a chance to glance over. Her expression was grim.

"Jillian?"

"Sorry," she said at last. "In some ways that's the hardest question of all."

"Why?"

"I hadn't talked to my parents in almost two weeks," she said, nearly choking on the words. "It still tortures me. I mean, to think I hadn't heard my mom's voice for so long before she died."

"Were you upset with them over something?"

"No, it was nothing like that. I used to check in by

phone with my parents every Sunday, when I knew they'd both be around. I generally called the landline, since my mom was a mess on her cell. She didn't really like it, and she used to do that awful cell-yell thing, so that you have to hold your phone about a foot from your ear. When I called this one Sunday, Danny answered and he said my dad was golfing and my mother wasn't around, that she'd had a fight with Julia and had left the house crying. I don't think he ever gave her the message because she didn't call back and I got busy. We emailed once that week but it was just a little thing, my asking her to mail me a few of my spring clothes . . . And then it was Friday, and they were all dead."

By now my pulse had kicked up, as if I'd just been roused in the middle of night to the sound of a window sliding open.

"Do you know what it was about?"

"What?"

"The fight."

"Something to do with school, Danny said."

"You mean Julia's grades, how she was doing?"

"No, no. He said Jules was upset about the school, that she'd been yelling at my mother about the principal, and it made my mother cry. I asked him to put Jules on the phone, but he said she was in her room and wouldn't come out."

"So it was related to high school?" I said, confused as to why there'd be an issue after Julia had already graduated.

"No, Danny just didn't understand. Julia had been home sick for a few weeks by this point, and I think Barnard may have pressed her to drop the term rather than come back and try to play catch up with all her course work. I'm sure that was sending her into a panic. She wouldn't have wanted to forfeit a whole term. Danny heard her yelling about school and must have assumed she meant high school."

"Hmm."

"Do you think it could be significant?"

"I think we need to look at *everything*. Is there anyone around Dory who could give me a snapshot of what your family's life was like at that time? A friend of one of your parents?"

"My mom had a close friend named Jocelyn London. We've exchanged a few emails over time. Nothing lately, but I know she's still in town."

"Okay, good. If you wouldn't mind doing an email introduction, it would be helpful to talk to her. And what about any kind of papers from that time? I know most records would have been on the family computers, but there must have also been paperwork. Was any of it saved, do you know?"

"Paperwork?"

"Notes, letters, bills, calendars even. I'm sure the police carted lots of it away; I'm wondering if there was stuff that didn't end up as evidence."

"Um, yeah, maybe," she said after a couple of moments. "There's a storage unit in the area—Uncle Jack's, it's called—where some stuff is stored. Jocelyn helped with that actually. There are a few pieces of antique furniture I wanted to keep, and she filled boxes with odds and ends she found lying around. I never went through any of it myself."

But she had the key to the unit on her keychain, she said, and the passcode for entering the gate to the facility. I suggested that if it was okay with her, I'd make a trip to Uncle Jack's myself after we arrived in the Berkshires.

"Sure," she said. "Though I doubt you'll find much in the papers. There was nothing really valuable, just things Jocelyn didn't feel comfortable tossing."

"It won't hurt to look, though."

"Is there anything *I* can do, Bailey?"

"Definitely. I'd love for you to talk to Mr. Healy and ask if he remembers anything specific your father told him about his relationship with Bruce Kordas. As I start delving into research, I'm going to need you to answer questions, brainstorm with me, and perhaps introduce me to other people besides Jocelyn. I know it's going to be hard to be in the area, but it will really help."

For the next two hours, I concentrated on driving, and Jillian mostly stared out the window. The final part of the trip was on a rural highway that twisted through mountainous countryside, dotted with everything from expensively refurbished farmhouses for weekenders to run-down trailer homes. We stopped briefly at a small general store to pick up coffee. As we climbed back in the car, I finally realized what had been tugging gently at my brain since Tuesday evening.

"Remember that road trip we were going to take to Cape Cod?" I said, firing up the engine.

"Oh, yeah. Vaguely, I guess. No offense but that whole term is now a total blur for me."

"We were supposed to visit a cousin of yours. But the other night you mentioned that your parents were both only children."

"Oh, it was the Healys' daughter, Chloe, we were going to see. Our families were so close, we always thought of their kids as our cousins."

"Got it. My boyfriend, Beau, has family friends like that, too. He even calls the parents aunt and uncle."

"I'd like to meet him one day."

"And you will for sure. He's eager to meet you, too."

"Did he mind you coming away like this?"

"Oh, he's used to me traveling for work," I said, dodging the need to answer specifically. "What about you, Jillian? Is there a special person in your life right now?"

She smiled ruefully.

"Not at the moment. I was seeing someone in Australia, a guy I met on the penguin project, though he was really from Johannesburg. As much as I loved him, I knew I couldn't live halfway around the world forever."

"That's gotta be tough to leave someone you love. Have you been able to meet guys in the city?"

"A few. I've been invited to a couple of—quote—epic rooftop barbecues, but frankly the best thing at each of them was the view."

"There'll be someone else for you, Jillian. It's probably hard to concentrate on that now with everything going on, but one day . . ."

Finally, at about six thirty, we pulled into the inn, a pretty, white clapboard building with black shutters and flower boxes bursting with red geraniums. It was small, not much more than a bed-and-breakfast, but that was just fine. From the driveway I could see a deck running along the back.

After parking in the small lot, I glanced toward Jillian. She looked totally drained. Though we were a good twenty-five minutes from Dory, her hometown was clearly exerting a force-field kind of pull on her.

I reached out and laid my hand on her arm.

"You okay?" I asked.

"Yes, thanks," she murmured. We grabbed our bags from the back and took the short stone path to the house.

Inside, the inn turned out to be clean, warmly decorated, and mercifully short of tchotchkes and needlepoint pillows featuring beagles, pugs, or West Highland terriers. Seconds after we entered, the proprietor emerged from a small office that jutted off the parlor and introduced himself: Rod, about sixty-five, I guessed, polite enough but awfully dour for a guy who worked with the public every day. But what did I care? I wouldn't be posting a review on Trip Advisor.

Rod checked us in, ascertained that we didn't need help with our bags, and then described where our rooms were located. I was in the Violet Room on the second floor, and Jillian was one flight above me in the Rose Room. The two of us agreed to take thirty minutes to freshen up and then meet downstairs again. Before making my way to the storage facility, I was going to drop Jillian off at the veterinarian clinic Mamie and her husband owned. He was a vet, Jillian had said, and Mamie, the manager. Their house, where Jillian planned to eat tonight, was apparently out of the way and hard to find even with GPS, so Mamie had suggested Jillian meet them at the clinic in Blackbrook, one of the bigger towns in the area, and the one my father's cousin Candace lived in.

The car ride had left me feeling as grungy as a yak, so I took a short shower, savoring the feel of hot water on my muscles. While simultaneously toweling off and checking my phone, I noticed that Jillian had already done an email intro between Jocelyn and me, though I was dismayed to see that she'd mentioned the name of the inn. Clearly I hadn't made a strong enough case to her that people outside of Mamie and her husband shouldn't know where we were staying. Nothing I could do about that now. I sent my own email to Jocelyn, stressing how eager I was to speak with her.

As I was changing into a fresh T-shirt, Jillian called my cell to say that Mamie was running late—something about emergency surgery on a dog with a badly torn ACL—and we needed to delay our arrival by thirty minutes. I glanced out the window. At the rate we were moving, I'd be lucky to make the storage facility by nightfall.

Finally we were back in the car, en route to the clinic, about a fifteen-minute drive southeast of where we were.

"Were you and Mamie pretty close growing up?" I asked once I'd programmed the clinic's address into the GPS.

"Fairly close. We played four years of field hockey together and we palled around on weekends, but we never really had much in common. Under ordinary circumstances, we probably wouldn't still be in touch, but I feel I owe her. She was so good to me after—after everything."

Yeah, unlike *some* people we know.

"Have you met her husband?" I asked, figuring the answer was probably no, since Jillian hadn't been back to the area.

"Yes, Blake, though I haven't seen him in a zillion years. He was in our class in high school and we had a few dates back then. I had a pretty intense crush on him, but I was never his type. Not like Mamie is."

Well, regardless of their personal chemistry, it looked like Mamie and Blake knew what they were doing when it came to catering to the medical needs of house pets. The clinic turned out to be huge, made of limestone and wood, and it felt like we were pulling up to the clubhouse at a fancy golf course. Even at this hour, there were about ten cars in the parking lot. A woman dressed in hospital blues with her black hair in a ponytail stood right outside the entrance reading something on her phone.

I heard the intake of Jillian's breath.

"That's her," she said. I maneuvered into a parking spot, and we both stepped from the car.

Mamie appeared absorbed in whatever she was reading on her phone, oblivious to even the sound of our footsteps.

"Mamie," Jillian said softly.

Finally, she lifted her head, and her dark brown eyes glistened.

"Omigod, it's really you." She threw her arms around Jillian and hugged her tightly. "It's so great to set eyes on you."

"You, too." Jillian introduced us, and Mamie gave me a hug as well. She seemed like a huggy kind of girl.

"How's the place you're staying? Is it okay?"

"Yes, fine," Jillian said.

"If you change your mind, you're more than welcome to bunk down at our place."

"That's really sweet of you, but I think we're all set."

"Okay, well why don't we go." She turned to me. "Are you sure you don't want to join us, Bailey?"

I told her thanks but that I had a few things to take care of, and I'd grab a bite later. Though Mamie might be a friend of Jillian's, the fewer people who knew what I was up to, the better.

I bade them good-bye and watched Mamie lead Jillian off to a black SUV. It was after eight by now, and I cursed out loud as the twilight seemed to fade before my eyes. It would mean tackling the task ahead after dark. The last thing I was angling for right now was some *Silence of the Lambs*-ien experience that involved me, a creepy storage unit, and a flashlight clamped between my teeth.

Still, despite my misgivings, I decided to stick with the plan. Surely the place would be well lit, perhaps even guarded. And if I didn't follow through, there'd be nothing to show for the evening.

By the time I entered the parking lot, the sky was dark and stars had begun to pop into view. There was a small brick administrative building in front, closed at this hour, needless to say, and a shiny black wrought-iron gate just to the right of it. The place was indeed well lit, and though there was no guard on duty, a sign indicated there were plenty of security cameras.

I nosed my car up to the gate, stepped out, and peered through the metal bars. From where I stood, the place seemed to go on forever. I punched in the code Jillian had provided, and the gate slid slowly open.

After jumping back into the driver's seat, I eased

the Jeep through and began following the signs toward unit number 407. There were endless rows of attached units, their fronts featuring rolling aluminum shutters. I hadn't expected the place to be booming at this hour, but I'd assumed *someone* might be around, maybe a girl pissed as hell at her live-in boyfriend and busy hauling a lumpy old mattress out of storage. But Uncle Jack's was absolutely empty.

Despite the sodium lights, I had to squint to see the unit numbers, and it became clear after a minute that I'd overshot the correct row. A U-turn wasn't possible, so I had to drive around one of the blocks and circle back. Finally, I pulled the car up to 407.

I killed the engine and emerged into the summer night. I was at the edge of the facility, and just beyond the metal fence there was a field with hundreds of fireflies, blinking on and off in a magical performance.

Things on my side of the fence weren't nearly as enchanting, however. I glanced around, taking in my surroundings. The facility, I suddenly realized, had the feel of one of those towns you see in postapocalyptic horror movies—the kind four or five survivors stumble upon as they travel cross-country, desperate to learn whether anyone else besides themselves is still alive. At first all the buildings appear abandoned, but five minutes later, hordes of zombies hurl themselves out of hiding and start tearing the survivors' faces off with their teeth.

Just put your ass in gear and get out of here, I told myself. I wasn't overly timid about snooping around places, but spending half the day with Jillian and talking so much about the murders had left me vaguely unnerved.

To my relief, gaining access to the individual unit was easy enough. The padlock didn't fight me, and the shutter rolled up without a hitch. After a few seconds of fumbling, I located the light switch and everything burst into sight.

Though the space smelled a tiny bit musty, the contents appeared unmarked by time, and they were decently organized. The antiques Jillian had mentioned—a couple of chairs, mirrors, a few framed prints and paintings—took up the bulk of the space. Along the right wall, however, was a stack of large plastic storage tubs, most likely the boxes I was looking for.

I stepped toward the stack. The words *Claire and Carl* had been scrawled in indelible marker across the lid of the top one. After wiggling the edge of the lid, I managed to pop it open. I peered inside.

It was just as Jillian had thought: random paperwork. My guess was that Claire's friend Jocelyn had hurriedly rounded up anything she'd found lying on counters or stuffed into drawers and dumped it into the best that Rubbermaid had to offer.

I secured the lid back on and eased the top tub toward me enough to see what was written on the one beneath: *Julia.* I figured the tub at the bottom probably held Danny's stuff.

Though I hadn't asked Jillian for permission, I decided to load the three tubs into the car and lug them back to the inn. I certainly wasn't going to take the time to go through them here. Instinctively I glanced outside into the empty "street." It wouldn't take more than five minutes to complete the job and then I'd be out of here.

I set down the flashlight I'd brought from the car and loaded the first tub into the back, then did the same with Julia's tub. The tub at the bottom was indeed marked with Danny's name. Though I was anxious to split, something made me pry off the lid and look inside. It was brimming with books, a box of Magic cards, Marvel comic books, and a spiral notebook. Written in ballpoint pen on the front, in handwriting that could only have belonged to a twelve-year-old boy, were the words *My Summer.*

It felt as if someone had pinched my heart.

I replaced the cover and was about to press it back into a locked position when I heard what I thought were footsteps, the scuff of shoes on gravel. I cocked my head toward the sidewall, trying to listen. Was someone out there?

And then, from behind me, another sound, this one a mix of roar and rattle. I spun around and watched the metal shutter come rolling downward.

Seconds later, it hit the ground with an angry clang.

Chapter 4

What the hell just happened? Had the shutter rolled down on its own, dragged by gravity?

Or had someone yanked it down on purpose?

I took a couple of steps forward and listened. For footsteps, or—please, no—the sound of the padlock being locked on the outside. All I could hear were my shallow breaths.

I ran my gaze over the frames on either side of the shutter, searching to see if there was a latch I should have used, a way to secure the aluminum shutter. There was nothing like that, which indicated that the shutter was supposed to stay up on its own.

The fact that it had closed meant someone had probably lowered it. *Why?*

Grabbing my flashlight—the only thing I had for protection—I stepped toward the shutter and pressed my ear against the metal, straining to hear. There was no sound of movement. Steeling myself, I reached down for the handle and yanked upward.

To my relief, the padlock hadn't been locked, and when I finally had the shutter over my head, I could see that I was alone. The only things visible besides my car were endless storage units, and the fireflies flashing in the field next to me.

Still, I felt spooked and decided to beat it fast. Danny's box was still at the back of the unit, and I made a quick dash for it. After loading the tub in the car with the others, I dragged down the shutter and quickly secured the padlock.

One last glance around and then I jumped into my car. Three minutes later, I was at the front gate. Before climbing out to punch in the passcode, I twisted around in my seat, making certain no one was lurking nearby. The sight of the security camera posted on the top of the gate drove home the point that if anyone had come in after me, there would be video of it. I would check with the company tomorrow.

Even once I was back on the highway, my heart continued doing a nervous jig. Perhaps, I told myself, I'd let my nerves get the better of me tonight. Yet part of my brain kept insisting that the shutter couldn't have come all the way down on its own. I began to wonder if someone had followed me to the facility in order to give me a scare, a warning to back off. But who would even know I was in town, let alone at the facility?

There was one thing I *was* sure of. I wasn't going to tip off Jillian about the incident tonight. That might alarm her unnecessarily. And I certainly wasn't going to report the news to Beau. He'd probably go all Petey Panicky and urge me to return to the city.

Once I was back at the inn, I lugged the rubber tubs, one by one, to my room, as well as a fried-clam platter that I'd picked up at a roadside restaurant.

I'd just wolfed down dinner when I heard a car ease into the driveway. Peering out my window, I saw the back end of what I guessed was Mamie's black SUV, illuminated by a light mounted on the building. I bolted downstairs, wanting to catch Jillian before she disappeared into her room.

By the time I was outside, Jillian was headed up the path to the inn, but Mamie, and a tall strapping guy who I assumed was her husband, continued to hang in the driveway. Maybe they were waiting to make sure Jillian made it safely inside.

"Everything okay?" I asked Jillian.

"Yeah, I was grabbing something I brought for

Blake to read—a paper I did in grad school about penguin behavior."

I nodded, and as she continued up the path, I made my way toward the couple.

"Bailey, this is my husband, Blake," Mamie said. She bounced a little in place and offered one of her beaming smiles.

"Hey, nice to meet you," he said, reaching out a hand. He was almost a foot taller than his wife, with dark blond hair, gray eyes, a strong jaw, and a hawk-like nose not unlike Beau's. At first glance he seemed easygoing, the kind of guy who never minded having to stick his finger up the butt of a dog or cat when the need arose.

"I'm so sorry you couldn't join us for dinner," Mamie said. Her hair was out of the ponytail now and flowed in waves around her shoulders. "I would have loved to have shown you our barn."

"Do you keep horses?"

"No, no, we live there. We converted it a few years ago."

"Maybe another night while we're here." I turned to her husband. "How did things turn out with the dog? The one you were operating on."

"Oh, the terrier," he said. "The little guy did great."

Jillian reappeared, hurrying down the path with a

sheaf of paper in hand, and Blake strode toward her to accept it. After glancing at the cover, he flicked to the first page and studied it intensely. I returned my attention to Mamie.

"I was really impressed by the look of your clinic," I told her. "Do you treat mostly cats and dogs?"

"Thanks, and yes, primarily cats and dogs, but we also see a few types of exotic pets—like ferrets—and also birds. Mostly it's to clip their nails." She rolled her eyes and smiled. "Owners *hate* doing that."

"And you manage the clinic?"

"Uh-huh. Though I'm a licensed vet assistant now, so I can help out on the clinical side, too, if we're short-staffed." She smiled again. "I've trimmed a lot of cockatoo nails over the years."

"Would either of you have any interest in the kind of fieldwork Jillian's done?"

"With *penguins*?"

"Or any type of animal."

"Nah. When Blake was in college he did one of those January plans in Brazil—to study monkeys—and he came down with malaria really badly. I think we'll play it safe and stick to cats and dogs."

Briefly her gaze shifted to where her husband and Jillian were chatting. Jillian seemed to be describing something to him—"It's called slender walking,"

I heard her say—and Blake was nodding in understanding, a light smile on his face. Mamie glanced back at me.

"Were you and Blake high school sweethearts?" I asked.

"People assume that, but no, we were just passing acquaintances then. I didn't get to know him until after he was done with all his college stuff. He'd graduated from Wisconsin and stayed there for vet school, but moved back here after his dad was diagnosed with cancer. Living in the boonies isn't everybody's cup of tea, but we like it. We've got a nice life."

"Jillian tells me you've been a wonderful friend to her."

Mamie sighed. "I've tried, though there have been stretches when she hasn't felt like talking. So I don't push."

I lowered my voice a little, not wanting my words to carry in the night. "Were you surprised to learn that Dylan Fender wasn't guilty after all?"

Mamie shrugged. "I want to be supportive of what's happening now, but frankly, I have my doubts about this new theory. From everything I heard at the trial, Dylan was *obsessed* with Julia. He'd been kind of sickly as a kid, just like her, and he thought they were soul mates."

"There's pretty good forensic evidence suggesting he was innocent. Do any other suspects come to mind? Someone who might have been angry at a family member that night?"

She shook her head, making her hair dance a little. "Sorry, no. I'd been over to Jillian's house in high school, of course, and I knew the rest of the family enough to say hi to, but she was the only one I really had much contact with."

I heard Blake thank Jillian for the paper and he promised to read it soon. Then he strode back toward the SUV, his long legs covering the distance in a few strides. We said our good-byes, and as soon as the car was out of the driveway, Jillian asked if I'd found Uncle Jack's okay.

"Yes, and the key still worked," I told her as we headed in.

"Did you find anything worth looking at?"

I explained I'd discovered three tubs of personal papers and had taken the liberty of lugging them back with me. If it was okay with her, I was going to start going through them tonight.

She winced. "Of course. I'd volunteer to look through them with you but I'm not sure I could bring myself to. If there's anything you find that needs to be explained, just ask me."

Her grief was palpable; it seemed I could almost reach out and touch it.

"Will do," I said. "Tell me about *your* evening. How was dinner?"

"Nice." She shrugged. "I guess I should have expected it, but we had kind of a hard time finding things to chat about. At least when Blake showed up, we could discuss animal research a little bit."

"I hear you . . . Are you all ready for tomorrow?"

"I think so. I'm going to bed early to be at the top of my game, whatever that means."

We were in the first of two parlors now, where the only sound was the ticktock of a grandfather clock.

"I'm sure you'll handle it perfectly. . . . Jillian, there's one thing I need to ask you." I lowered my voice. "How many people have you told we're staying here?"

I was thinking about the shutter crashing down at Jack's.

"Um, just Jocelyn, in that email I sent to both of you. Why, was that a bad move?"

"Probably not, but I just think that the fewer people who know where we're staying, the better. So she's the only other person who's aware you're in town?"

"Well, Bruce Kordas knows. When we got here, I left a phone message for him on his office phone and he called back when I was at Mamie's. But he has no idea where I'm staying."

"You called Kordas?" I said, taken aback. In the car I'd had the impression she had zero desire to connect with the guy again.

"I realized that the only way he'd ever meet with you was if I opened the door, so I just picked up the phone and did it. He's willing to meet you tomorrow around midday, but he's going to confirm the time and location in the morning."

"Thanks, I'm glad you did that. How did he sound?"

She looked off to the far corner of the room in that manner I was getting used to. "All charm. That was how he always acted whenever I saw him."

"And you definitely didn't mention the inn?"

"No, I'd never want him to know where I was."

We climbed the stairs to the second floor, and as we parted at my door, I touched Jillian's shoulder.

"If there's anything I can do to make this whole thing easier, just let me know, okay?"

"Sure," she said, and I could tell what she was thinking. Nothing on earth would make this easier. She turned to go and then looked back, offering a wan smile. "Thanks, Bailey, it's good to have you here."

"I'm really glad I came. . . . By the way, what's

slender walking? I overheard you use that phrase with Blake."

She chuckled a little, and I had my second hint of the fun girl I knew years ago. "It's what penguins sometimes do when they have to walk by other burrows to reach their own. They don't want to provoke a fight, so they make themselves tall and skinny."

"Ah, smart of them. Well, good night. Want me to call you in the morning?"

"Yes. But use the room phone. I don't seem to have cell reception here at the inn."

It wasn't till I was inside my room with the door closed that I grasped the full ramifications of her last comment. If her reception was bad here, she must have used her room phone to contact Kordas. Which meant that Kordas would have been able to see the number the call had come from and could have used reverse directory to determine that it belonged to the inn. He could have driven over here and seen the two of us climb in my car. And tailed me to the storage facility, slamming the shutter closed in an attempt to scare me off.

It was a stretch. How would Kordas have gained access to the facility? And there was still a chance that the shutter had simply come crashing down on its own.

Whatever way I looked at it, the scare had been a worthwhile lesson, reinforcing the fact that both Jillian and I needed to act more cautiously. No more after-dark runs to desolate places. No more blabbing about our whereabouts. It was time to act like penguins and engage in some serious slender walking.

After stripping down to a T-shirt, I moved the plastic tub marked with Julia's name from the desk to the bed, and, taking a deep breath, peeled off the lid. I'd mentally prepped myself for the potential jolt of setting eyes on her possessions, but what I wasn't ready for was the smell. Or scent, I should say. It was vanilla, with a trace of maybe patchouli. Gosh, I thought, it must be the fragrance Julia wore, lingering after all these years on her belongings. Despite the fact that I'd never known her, my eyes pricked with tears. It seemed as if I'd released a trace of her essence in the room.

Inside the tub, it looked at first glance like a mixed bag of papers—all probably cleared from the desk, dresser, and bulletin board in Julia's bedroom. Did this include the items that had been left behind in her dorm room? There was no way to tell.

It seemed like the best tack was to just dig in. I lifted a small batch of material out of the tub, sorted through that handful, and then repeated this procedure over and over. I could see quickly enough that most of the contents were pretty mundane, slice-of-life stuff—a ticket stub for an event over the Christmas holidays;

printouts of several term papers; sheet music; fashion and beauty tear sheets; a postcard from a girl named Becky who seemed to be at college in Denver and who reported suffering from a hangover so severe that she'd been forced to dim the screen of her computer while studying for a midterm; a catalog of fall classes; and a MasterCard bill for March of that year, the first month Julia had been home. Obviously Jocelyn London, the family friend who'd had the grim task of wading through Julia's belongings, hadn't had time to triage the material.

I took a minute to peruse the credit card bill. It showed very little activity, clearly reflective of the fact that Julia had been laid up at home during the second half of the month. The only charges of note appeared to be for clothes. A $102 charge from J.Crew and two smaller ones from a place called Two Boots, which I assumed was a shoe store. All three were in late March. It was possible back then that she'd made purchases online from her sickbed or she might have felt well enough to do a minimum amount of shopping in person.

Midway through the tub, I stumbled on a bundle of get-well cards, seven in all and only a couple with envelopes. I stripped off the rubber band and opened the cards one by one.

All the senders wished Julia a speedy recovery from

her mono, with a few people joking about the fact that she'd caught "the kissing disease." Since most of the envelopes had been tossed and the cards were signed with only first names, it was impossible to know if the people who'd sent them were local or from college. Except for one card, which *did* have an envelope and was clearly from her Barnard roommate.

Julia
  I'm keeping your side of the room clean. Hurry back!

xo
Amber

The return address was topped by the name A. Tresslar. I would need to track her down.

Two cards, I noticed, were from guys—Kevin and Jake—but their brief scribbles implied they were probably buddies, not boyfriends. I made a mental note of the fact that Julia seemed to be less of a loner in college than she had been at home.

I restacked the cards and tugged the rubber band back around them.

It wasn't until I reached the bottom of the tub that I found something that quickened my pulse. It was an official letter, dated March 31, from the dean of students at Barnard, confirming that the college was approving a medical withdrawal for Julia and that the dropped courses could be made up, tuition-free, either by adding one class each term going forward or by completing a ninth term at the end of four years. And even more intriguing was the message handwritten on a thick white notecard clipped to the letter:

Julia,

I understand your decision, and I think it's a smart one. Now you can focus totally on your recovery. Let me know if you have any additional questions or if I can be of help in any way.

Lillian Mara

The letterhead on the card indicated that Mara was the freshman dean.

So Julia had decided on her own to drop the term, without, it seemed, undue pressure from the college. Contrary to what Jillian had surmised, it didn't appear that her sister had had any reason to be pissed at Barnard. Which left me wondering what Danny had meant by his comment on the phone to Jillian—about Julia being upset with the principal.

When I was in my first job after college, at the *Albany Times Union*, I sat one desk over from another police beat reporter, an old and grizzled guy named Buddy, whose white nose hairs were so long they showed up at a crime scene about a minute before he did. I still lived by some of the aphorisms he'd shared.

"Sometimes," Buddy used to say, in that gravelly, pack-and-a-half-a-day voice of his, "you gotta take things absolutely *literally*."

Maybe that's what I had to do in this instance. Take Danny literally and accept that Julia had indeed been referring to the high school principal. Something negative might have happened to Danny at school, the details of which Julia was privy to because she was home, and it had angered her. Hopefully the principal was still at the school and I could convince him or her to share the information—if that person could even recall it.

I didn't have to look at my watch to know how late it was. My eyes were bleary, and frankly my heart hurt from pawing through all of Julia's things. I returned the items I'd extracted from the tub, trying to create a little order this time.

As I was about to replace the lid, my glance landed on a three-by-five photograph I'd missed in the clutter. It was of Jillian, face forward and posed alone against a dark building, dressed down in an unzipped black leather jacket, jeans, and suede booties, but as gorgeous as ever, her long blond hair fanning around her shoulders and arms.

There was a small hole, I noticed, in the top border of the photo, obviously from where a pushpin had been inserted at one time. Julia must have hung the photo on a wall or bulletin board. She clearly had cared for her sister and admired her, even if at the same time it might have been tough to live in her shadow.

It was after midnight when I tucked myself into bed.

I was the first one at the breakfast buffet the next morning, which was served in a large window-lined room at the back of the house. Over coffee and yogurt, I used a black-and-white composition book to scribble down a to-do list for the day. First on the agenda was a reengagement with Operation Rubbermaid, followed by the meeting with Bruce Kordas, tentatively set for midday. Ideally, Jocelyn London would respond to my email, and I'd be able to speak with her today as well.

And somehow I was going to have to track down a woman named Eleanor Mercandetti, who had been the former principal of the regional middle and high schools. A quick Internet search before breakfast had revealed that Mercandetti had retired fifteen years ago and had been replaced by a man named Ray Haberman, who was still in the job. I planned to drop by the school at some point today to try to score contact info for Mercandetti.

Jillian arrived at breakfast at eight, dressed in a light pink short-sleeved sweater, a black pencil skirt, and black open-toed pumps. Clearly she had gone the extra mile to dress for the appointment with the DA.

"Wow, you look great," I said. "Are you nervous at all?"

"A little," she said solemnly. "Not about meeting with him per se. I—I just don't want him to tell me anything I don't want to hear."

"About Dylan?"

"No," she whispered. "About *them*. I'm afraid I'll learn something about their deaths that I've never heard before."

Inside, I cringed, thinking again of how hard this must be for her.

"If he starts to go down a road you don't like, put up a hand and ask him to stop. Tell him you're there simply to be reassured that they're reopening the investigation."

I'd planned to bring her up to speed this morning about the letter from Barnard, but in light of how preoccupied she was, I decided to hold off. We chatted a bit more about Kordas and what I might expect from my meeting with him. She promised to text me once he'd confirmed the time.

Though I'd assumed I'd be giving her a ride to the municipal office, Jillian said she was requesting an Uber and would do the same for the return trip—that way I would have the car totally at my disposal.

As soon as she was gone, I refilled my coffee mug and headed back to my room, where I peeled off the top of the tub marked with Jillian's parents' names.

It was packed more densely than Julia's, though nothing seemed to be of any real significance—just batches of random mail, notes, a few credit card bills that I would go through later, a couple of stray take-out menus.

My spirits soared when I spotted the calendar. It was spiral-bound and from the Rhode Island School of Design Museum, with a shot of an Asian textile on the front. My guess was that Jillian had bought it in Providence for her mom. It was the type of calendar that featured a week on every page, with only a very small box for each day. Thumbing through I saw that though the space was limited, Claire had definitely used it. Most boxes, in fact, had some kind of penciled notation in them, stuff like, *pick up prescription*, *Danny/Scouts*, and *haircut*. I spotted the name Jocelyn in a bunch of boxes.

Holding my breath, I paged through to the second week of April, the week of the murders. *Julia/doc* had been scribbled in the box for Monday along with *post office*. Tuesday was blank. On Wednesday, there was *art class*, on Thursday, the day of the murders, *Danny/ swim*, and on Friday *oven repair*.

I replaced the lid, feeling a disconcerting blend of sadness and frustration. Anything of real importance would have been on the family's computers, but those were probably still in police custody or else buried in a landfill somewhere. So now what?

The answer seemed to come out of the blue, but I guessed it had probably been forming in my mind for the past couple of days. I needed to go to Dory and check out the Lowes' former house. Maybe setting eyes on the home again would help jolt my brain into seeing the situation from a fresh angle. There was a chance, too, that the residents would be out at work or school, and I could even peek in the windows. That wouldn't be nearly as helpful as viewing the crime scene photos, but it was better than simply using my imagination.

I needed, of course, to be poised and ready to meet with Kordas, but I could probably drive to his house just as easily from Dory as I could from the inn.

The trip took me along a winding road, banked on one side by a small mountain, and then, like someone springing out before me, there was Dory, with all its charms on full display. The downtown area along Main Street consisted of a couple dozen well-kept white clapboard buildings with shops and cafés on the ground floor, set across from a small park. American flags on several of the buildings snapped in the early-morning breeze.

The Lowes' house was located several streets off Main, and I managed to find it solely from memory. I pulled up in front and killed the engine.

The place had most likely been built in the early 1800s and was as big and stately as I recalled—and still painted yellow with white shutters. Despite its grandness, it somehow also managed to look inviting, perhaps because of the screened porch off the right side and the rambling addition jutting out on the left side toward the rear. It was the kind of house whose exterior hinted at coffee tables laid with board games, chair arms draped with library books, and sofa cushions smudged with dog hair.

No hint at all of the grisly night that had transpired there.

It took me a moment to notice the sign in the front yard, swinging gently from a white post. FOR SALE, it read. O'BRIEN REALTY.

For sale. How many times over the last sixteen years

had a sign like that been posted in the yard? Maybe living in this house was just too unsettling for people. Maybe they told themselves they could handle the fact that nearly an entire family had been slaughtered inside, but then, during the night, whenever the house groaned and creaked, they had the crap scared out of them.

I glanced back at the house, and as I took it in, a thought hit me. Since the residence was for sale, I had a more than decent chance of maneuvering my way into seeing it. I'd just have to fake that I was in the market for real estate—and rich enough to afford this particular property.

I slipped out of the car and trotted over to the sign. As I was taking a photo of the contact info with my phone, I heard the front door swoosh open. Glancing up, I spotted a middle-aged woman, with a messenger bag worn cross-body, stepping onto the large front stoop. The lady of the house, I assumed, on her way out for an appointment or to run an errand.

"Can I help you?" she called as soon as she noticed me.

"I'm just making a note of the real estate agent's number," I replied.

The woman hesitated briefly and then strode in my direction, the messenger bag bouncing against her hip.

By the time she reached me, she seemed moderately winded and she nudged a lock of blond-gray hair off her face. There was a trace of skepticism in her eyes, and I wondered if she thought I was actually out playing Pokémon Go.

"You're house shopping? I'm with O'Brien Realty."

Okay, I was in even more luck than I'd realized, and I needed to play it smart.

"Yes, I am. My fiancé and I have had our eye on this house for a while. I'm thrilled to see it's actually for sale now."

The lie had been the first thing I could think of—since a single woman my age wouldn't be in the market for a house this size. And yet saying the *f* word felt weird, as if I'd just discovered myself speaking in tongues.

"Are you from the area?"

"We're actually from New York City, but we're planning to relocate here."

I caught her gaze flick over my navy poplin, zip-front dress, which *I* thought couldn't be cuter but was probably advertising the fact that the house was *soooooo* out of my price range.

"My fiancé runs his own hedge fund, which means he can work from anywhere," I added.

"What a shame you didn't know about the open

house last night. I was dropping by to make sure I'd tidied up well enough."

"Do you have a card? I'd love to arrange a time to see the house as soon as possible. I'm headed back to the city in a day or so."

She sighed, but not in annoyance. She was clearly fighting a thought that had popped into her mind.

"I'm supposed to be someplace, but I could give you a short tour now if you'd like."

"That would be wonderful," I said. Again, I couldn't believe my luck.

"I'm Ginger, by the way. Ginger James."

"Bailey Weggins."

With me a half step behind her, Ginger retraced her footsteps across the lawn, pumping me for more information as we walked—what I did for a living, why we'd picked the area, and how soon were we hoping to move in. I kept my answers as vague as possible, saying I was a journalist and that we wanted to move that autumn.

"Once you see inside, you're going to adore the house even more," she said, swinging open the door. "It's an ideal residence for entertaining, but also perfect for a family if that's part of your plan."

Did she know about the murders? I wondered. Sixteen years ago was a long time. But *of course* she did. Even if she hadn't been around when the Lowes were killed, someone from the realty office would have filled her in.

"After you," she said.

I stepped into the hallway.

It was large and elegant. The gleaming, wide-planked wooden floor in the front hall was partly covered with an Oriental runner that stretched toward a grand stair-case. My stomach clenched. That was *the* staircase—the one Jillian's mother had been heaved down, her body riddled with stab wounds.

And to the left, behind the closed double wooden doors, must be the library, I realized. The room where Julia had died.

What kind of monster was responsible for such car-nage? And where the hell was he now? Goose bumps shot up along my arms, and I felt icy all over. Though I didn't know why, an answer formed in my head, as if a wraith had whispered in my ear.

He's still *here*, I thought. Living not far from Dory. And he must know that his freedom is now in jeopardy.

Chapter 5

Is everything okay?" Ginger asked, clearly curious why all the color was now bleached from my face.

"Yes, sorry. I'm just kind of blown away by the house."

"Jaw-dropping, isn't it? Why don't we start this way?" She gestured toward the living room on the right, and as she raised her arm, I noticed the wet sweat stain that had spread amoeba-like on her blouse. Maybe being in the house unnerved her, too.

I followed her across the threshold. The room was lovely, though the furnishings appeared thinned out. A few items looked like they might actually be staging furniture, pop-up pieces used by real estate agents to help fill near-empty houses, stuff you never want to sit on because you would come crashing through on your ass.

"The fireplace is limestone, and the floor is the original oak," Ginger announced. "A magnificent room for a party."

"I take it the owners have already moved out?"

"Yes, to Cleveland. They hated giving up the house, but he had a job offer he couldn't refuse."

"Were they here long?"

"A couple of years . . . Let's take a look out here."

After a quick view of the screened porch, I trailed her back through the living room, into a formal dining room, the walls covered with murals of pink dogwoods, and then into a bright white kitchen that opened onto a family room. As if on cue, Ginger began tossing out phrases like *Carrara marble*, *high-arc faucets*, and *subway-tile backsplashes*.

"Wow, two dishwashers," I said feebly. I knew I should be fielding a ton of questions and comments, but I still felt shaken from the creepy sensation that had overwhelmed me in the entrance hall. I was doing the best I could to keep up.

From the kitchen we looped back toward the front, going along the other side of the house this time. I heard a ping from my phone in my handbag and, sneaking a glance, I discovered that Jillian had texted me with

Kordas's home address and the fact that he could meet me there at exactly noon. No mention about her own meeting.

We passed through a space my guide called "the morning room," and were now back in the entrance hall. Ginger pointed to the closed double doors ahead on her right now. "Wait until you see *this*."

As she swung open the doors, I found myself holding my breath, half expecting to spot a terrible vestige of Julia's death, a faded bloodstain on a floor plank, for instance. But of course there was nothing like that.

The room was entirely wood-paneled, with rows of bookcases on two sides, the walnut gleaming brilliantly in the sun. The shelves, I could see, were filled with what appeared to be faux book spines, more staging for the benefit of potential buyers.

The only pieces of furniture were a desk, a wooden library table across the room, and a hunter-green love seat just inside the door. I cringed as I recalled a detail from one of the articles I'd reread about the murder: Julia's body had been found lying in front of the sofa. I was staring at the spot where she'd died.

A thread began to wiggle in my brain, but I couldn't catch hold of it.

"Mind if I snap a few photos?" I asked Ginger as I aimed my phone at the library.

"Of course, go right ahead. And we have a big selection of pictures online if you want to show your fiancé."

There was still the upstairs to tour. There turned out to be six bedrooms in all, and though one was clearly the master, it was impossible to tell which one had been Danny's or recognize the closet he had cowered in.

By the time we were back on the first floor, I felt numb and oddly detached, as if my mind couldn't metabolize one more impression from this sad, sad place. I managed to summon a few more mundane questions for Ginger, like, "Do all the fireplaces work?"—in the hope that she would be assured that I was a real prospect and would allow me back in the house for a second look if I needed it.

Once we were out on the wide front stoop again, we exchanged cards—I crossed my fingers that Ginger wouldn't google me—and then drove off at the same time. A couple of blocks away, I pulled my car over to the side of the road. I needed a chance to think, and to seriously decompress.

Being in the house had unsettled me much more than I'd anticipated, perhaps because the opportunity had presented itself out of the blue and I hadn't had a chance to ready myself emotionally. Though perhaps no amount of readying would have done the trick.

It had been so easy to picture the Lowes in those

rooms—Jillian and Julia lounging in the family room; Danny eating pizza at the kitchen island; Claire in the so-called morning room, her eyes tugged to the window by a robin bobbing in the yard or the first flakes of a snowstorm; Carl at his desk in the library.

And of course Julia, also in the library, her hacked and bloodied body lying sprawled on the floor.

The question just out of reach in my brain finally asserted itself: Why had Julia been killed in the *library*? She had presumably opened the front door to the killer and invited him into the house. But if he was intent on killing her, why not do it in the entrance hall?

Perhaps she'd stepped inside the library to speak to the killer, to better ascertain the reason for the visit without waking the others in the house unnecessarily—and of course she probably had no clue at that moment what horror was about to befall her.

Sixteen years ago the police had concluded that Dylan Fender came to the house to murder Julia because he was obsessed with her. Though Fender wasn't the killer, Julia still might have been the main target. She was the one with the greatest number of stab wounds, after all. Jillian had stressed her sister was a loner and wasn't dating anyone. Could the murder have been related to what Julia had been fighting about with her mother?

I opened my phone to the photos I'd taken of the library and noted once again that the couch, at least this staged one, was just inside the door. It was possible that she'd ended up in the library not because she'd invited the person into the room but because she'd staggered there after first being stabbed. Perhaps to the killer, Julia had been nothing more than an obstacle in his attempt to reach someone else in the house. I had to stay open to the fact that one of the other family members—even Danny—might have been the primary target. Or the entire family could have been.

One thing seemed particularly odd. If the killer had used a butcher knife from the house, how had he convinced Julia to allow him to enter the kitchen? Maybe he had brought the knife with him from his own home.

I glanced at my watch. I had two hours before my meeting with Kordas and if I hustled, I'd have enough time to drop by the regional school the Lowe kids had attended. According to the online calendar, summer school was in session, which meant a handful of people from the administration would be around.

What I wasn't going to be able to squeeze in today was a visit to my father's cousin Candace. As much as I wanted to see her, that would have to take a backseat for now.

The school turned out to be not too far away. It was

set on an attractive campus dotted with fir trees as well as oaks and maples. I spotted at most ten cars in the parking lot, and about seven yellow buses. I parked and headed for the entrance.

The front door was unlocked, though once I stepped inside the large foyer, I spotted a set of double doors that surely required a buzzer to open. To my right was a long counter, with work space behind it and then beyond that a row of offices, which probably belonged to members of the administration. Sitting at the counter was a man who could have played Gramps in any movie requiring a crusty but bighearted old-timer in a supporting role. Something told me he was a summer fill-in.

"Good morning," I said, stepping closer. I then launched into the cover I'd formulated—about working on a memoir of a former graduate and needing a few minutes of the principal's time.

"I hope you didn't drive a long way today," Gramps said, with an expression that said he was sure I had. "Because Mr. Haberman isn't here. He's on vacation."

"I see. Though I actually don't need to speak to Mr. Haberman himself. Just someone who can provide me with a number for the former principal, Eleanor Mercandetti."

He scratched the side of his neck. "She's been gone

a dozen years. Actually, more than that. And I don't think anyone's in touch with her. Moved to California, I hear."

"But her info may be in the files. Is there someone else in the administration I could speak to?"

"Unfortunately, young lady, you're flat out of luck today. The assistant principal, Mrs. Campbell, is out with a head cold. Not planning to come back until Monday."

I felt a big, fat prick of annoyance.

"What about the principal's assistant? I'm sure that person would be able to help."

"Well, yes, she's here—but she wouldn't be able to release any information without checking with Mrs. Campbell first."

I nodded, giving him the sweetest smile I could muster. "I *have* driven a long way. What would you suggest I do?"

Gramps scratched his neck again, his mouth scrunched. At least he seemed to be giving the matter a soupçon of consideration. "You know who might know actually?" he said at last. "The former administrative assistant, Penny Niles. She worked under Mrs. Mercandetti."

"She's not here now, though?"

"Gosh, no. She retired a few years back. But she lives in the area, in Carversville."

"Wonderful. Can I get a number for her?"

Gramps chuckled, as if I were a little kid who'd just asked if there was really a pot of gold at the end of the rainbow.

"I'm afraid I can't do that. But I'd be glad to try to get a message to her."

Damn, I thought, that might take days.

"Okay, if that's the only option." I pulled out a business card, handed it over, and thanked him enthusiastically for his help. There was a chance, after all, that I would be back if I didn't have any luck on my own.

As soon as I was in my car again, I went to work on Google. It took only a couple of minutes to find a Penny Niles on Braxton Street in Carversville, another Berkshires town. No phone number, though it would probably be best to make my case in person.

It was finally time now to come face-to-face with Bruce Kordas, whose home was out in the countryside, about ten minutes back toward Dory. I liked to be super-prepared for interviews—it's the only way to guarantee the chance of walking away with *something*—but even after additional searching, I'd found basically squat about Kordas online. Atypically for a successful busi-

nessman, he didn't seem to be involved in local charities or organizations, which suggested he liked flying
below the radar.

When I'd probed at breakfast, Jillian hadn't been
able to provide much info beyond what she'd shared on
the car ride. After all, until yesterday she'd had no contact with Kordas since the funeral service. Everything
to do with the business and her profits from it had been
handled by lawyers.

The one tidbit she *did* offer up was that Kordas had
been married at the time to a woman named Lynne.
No kids, though the wife had a son from a previous
marriage.

I arrived with only seconds to spare. I was expecting
a house not dissimilar in style to the elegant, historic
one Jillian had grown up in, but I'd guessed wrong.
Kordas's home was totally modern, a huge, stunning
edifice made of glass, cement, and steel, and so unlike
most residences I'd glimpsed in the area.

It was set far back off the road, behind a black
wrought-iron fence with a gate that featured a keypad
and intercom. The gate was open, which I took to mean
I should drive in. I headed up the cypress-lined gravel
drive and parked in front of the house.

I half expected the bell to be answered by some
type of thoroughly modern manservant decked out in

a fitted white shirt and tight black pants, but it was a woman who swung open the door. She was about sixty-five, dressed in slinky beige pants and an elegant silk tunic a half shade lighter than the pants. Her long, platinum-blond hair was thin but had been teased into gossamer, like a swirl of spun sugar on top of a cupcake.

"Come in," she commanded, and ushered me into a huge center hall with rooms shooting off in three directions.

"Hello, I'm Bailey Weggins," I said. "I'm here to meet with—"

"I know. I'm Bruce's wife. Lynne."

Now that I had the chance to focus on her, I saw that she'd been fighting time with the same determination the Ottomans had mustered during the siege of Constantinople. Her face clearly had been buffed, Botoxed, dermabrased, and Juvédermed into something that looked natural only if you were squinting at it.

"Why don't you take a seat," she said. "Bruce will be with you in a minute." I figured she'd show me to the living room, but she simply pointed to a sleek, cushioned bench in the hall.

"Great, thank you," I said, without really feeling grateful. Her tone suggested she'd placed me on par with a delivery guy from Domino's Pizza. Though, actually, she didn't look like much of a pizza eater.

Lynne ran her gaze over me for a second time and then turned and walked away, her tunic fluttering. Fragrance wafted off her, a woody scent with perhaps a touch of amber. Maybe she envisioned herself as Diana, goddess of the hunt.

I expected Bruce Kordas to appear momentarily, but minutes passed. I rose and paced the gallerylike entrance space, studying two huge abstract paintings that adorned the walls. I didn't recognize the artists, but I suspected that the work had cost a pretty penny.

Finally I heard the sound of footsteps and looked up to see a man with short silver hair, tufted a tiny bit in front, enter the room from the left. Bruce, I assumed. But as he drew closer, I realized that it couldn't be him after all. Despite the silver hair, this guy was, at most, in his early fifties. It was obvious not only from the smoothness of his face but also from the athleticism of his body, shown off by the fitted dress shirt and slim, cream-colored pants. Could this be the stepson, I wondered, sent to run inference? No, too old for that.

"Good morning," the man said from halfway across the hall.

"Hi, I'm Bailey Weggins. I'm here to meet Bruce Kordas."

He reached where I was standing and offered the kind of too-firm handshake meant to show who's boss.

He waited a beat before delivering the next line, his eyes locking with mine.

"Well, I'm Bruce Kordas."

I tried to will my face not to betray me but I felt my lips part in surprise, as if they had a mind all their own. If this was Bruce Kordas, it meant that he was married to a woman who was, at the very least, ten years older than him, possibly fifteen.

Just as noteworthy was the glimmer of amusement in Kordas's eyes. It was clear to him that I'd been taken aback—and he was getting a kick out of that.

"Thank you for your time," I said quickly. "As Jillian mentioned, I'm helping her with a memoir and I'd love to ask you a few questions."

"Of course. It's a nice day, so why don't we sit outside."

It actually *wasn't* that nice of a day—at least for talking outside. Walking across the drive, I'd noticed that it was already over eighty and humid.

I followed Kordas through the perfectly cooled house out onto a stone patio. Just beyond us was a long, rectangular black-bottom pool, and in the distance, a vista of undulating blue-green mountains. Kordas gestured for me to have a seat at a wrought-iron table that looked like it weighed at least a thousand pounds.

He was handsome, that was for sure, with light green

eyes, sharply arched brows, and a strong, prominent nose. His mouth wasn't quite wide enough for his face, but his lips were full and sensuous, more than making up for the deficit. It was clear now that he'd probably been no more than thirty-four or thirty-five when his business partner had been murdered, and probably only in his twenties when he'd joined the firm.

"So tell me," he said, leveling his gaze at me. "How *is* Jillian? It was a pleasant surprise to hear from her after so many years."

"She's doing pretty well, all things considered." I reached into my bag for my notebook and pen. "She's had a very interesting career so far, researching penguin colonies."

"Ah, that doesn't surprise me. From what C.J. used to tell me, she always had her nose in a science book. . . . I assume she's married by now."

"Actually no, not yet, anyway. How old was she when you first started working with her father?"

"About twelve I'd say, maybe thirteen."

"And you were pretty young then yourself."

"You could say that. C.J. and I went into business when I was only twenty-seven, but I'd been doing real estate since I was eighteen."

I was trying to picture it. Carl Lowe in his forties, dreaming up projects with a twenty-seven-year-old.

Maybe the partnership worked as a kind of father-son thing, one that possibly became strained over time. It wasn't hard to imagine the younger one beginning to challenge his mentor, perhaps considering some of his ideas out-of-date.

"How impressive."

"I had a passion and I ran with it," he said bluntly, not taking his eyes off me. "It's not any more complicated than that."

Jillian had mentioned that Kordas was loaded with charm, but he was being stingy with it in my case, like someone hinting he had a hot piece of gossip but wasn't about to share.

"Not everyone runs with their passion," I said.

"True enough . . . So, you're helping Jillian write a memoir. That can't be easy."

"Writing it?"

"No, remembering—on her part. I've spent a good chunk of my life trying to chase thoughts about that year from my mind."

"She doesn't want to focus on the crime but rather on how she put her life back together afterward. Could you tell me a little bit about the family?"

He leaned back in his chair, his hands pinned loosely to his sides.

"C.J. and I spent a great deal of time together professionally, but we didn't socialize. Any observations I had of the family were from a distance. They certainly wouldn't be of much help to you, would they?"

"Oh, even little things can matter. How did they seem to you?"

"Pretty special, just like everyone said. And despite the money, the kids never acted spoiled."

I resisted the urge to fill the vacuum with a comment or other question. I wanted to see what Bruce might add unprompted.

He looked off for a moment to the mountains in the distance, and then let his gaze drift back to me. "I mean they weren't perfect. But what family is?"

"How do you mean not perfect?"

"Oh, I don't know. The usual stuff."

"Jillian wants the book to be as honest as possible, so any insight would be valuable."

"They seemed very tight as a family unit, and yet C.J. and Claire never appeared particularly close. They were warm with the kids but somewhat cool with each other. I didn't see a lot of passion there."

"What about Jillian and her sister? How did they seem to you?"

"Fond of each other, from what I heard, but as I believe I said, I really didn't socialize with the family."

I shifted in my seat a little so I wouldn't stick to the

chair. The hot air seemed trapped under the portico. Kordas had not even offered me a glass of water, which made me assume that this was all a power play on his part. I bet the guy used a lot of those.

"When Julia was home with mono, did you see her at all?"

"What does that have to do with anything?" he asked, arching his right brow even more.

"I'm curious about what she might have been up to. Jillian is trying to fill in the blanks about that time period because she wasn't at home herself."

"No, I didn't see her, but C.J. discussed it. He was concerned at first, in light of Julia's previous health issues, which I assume you know about. But though mono can be serious, she seemed to be recovering nicely. I remember him saying at one point that she was no longer contagious but still pretty fatigued."

"Sounds like you and C.J. were close, that you confided in each other."

"Of course, we were partners. His death was devastating to me, as I'm sure you can imagine."

"Have you heard the news about Dylan Fender?"

"Only what was in the local paper."

"What's your thinking on that?"

"You mean do I believe he should be exonerated?" A shrug. "I'm really not privy to the details."

He shot the cuff on his left hand and checked his watch.

"Look," he said, "I wish I had more time to share with you, but unfortunately I need to get on with my day."

"Of course." But I felt irritated. We'd barely been talking ten minutes. All I was going to have to show for my effort here were some overactivated sweat glands.

"Just one more minute if you don't mind. If Dylan Fender didn't do it, any thoughts on who might have?"

A pause.

"I'd say that's a job for the authorities, wouldn't you?"

"According to Jillian, they don't seem super-eager to investigate. It would be great if they could be motivated to do so."

"Unfortunately I don't have any fresh ideas . . . just what I told the police at the time."

I'd been taking notes, but as his words registered, my hand paused instinctively.

"What do you mean?" I asked.

"There was a man who came to C.J.'s office one day not long before the murders. And he was mad as hell."

Chapter 6

O kay, he really had my attention now.
"When exactly was this?" I asked.

"It was about two weeks prior. I never actually saw the guy, just heard the raised voices."

"What were they arguing about?"

"No clue. The door was closed, and the guy didn't stay long. Later, I asked C.J. if everything was okay, and he brushed me off. But I could tell he was shaken. And he was in a funk for days afterward."

"Maybe Carl was having an affair," I suggested, "and the guy who showed up was a pissed-off husband."

After all, Kordas had pointed out that the Lowes' marriage lacked heat, and Carl might have strayed. Perhaps the cuckolded husband had turned up at the office—and weeks later at the Lowe home with a butcher knife.

Kordas shook his head slowly, as if he was still considering the question as the words spilled from his mouth. "C.J. was fairly glum that winter. He didn't act like a guy in the throes of lust."

"What about money troubles?" The word *gambling* had just darted across my mind. Maybe the stranger had shown up to collect payment. A bookie. I knew firsthand from my former marriage how threatening bookies could be if you fell behind on your debts.

"Doubtful. The company was in great shape when C.J. died. Jillian would know that. I'm sure she's benefited very nicely from the proceeds."

There was something the tiniest bit snarky in his tone. Why *shouldn't* she do nicely from her parents' estate?

"Do you think the police looked into your information about this guy?"

"I'm not sure because within days they zeroed in on Fender. Why so interested? I thought you were focusing on Jillian putting her life back together again. Penguin research and all that."

"True, but I can't ignore the death of her family. And, of course, both of us are concerned that the real killer is still at large."

"Sounds like what you're really writing is part memoir/part crime story. Am I right?"

"Not really. As you said, it's best to leave that to the police. Have they contacted you, by the way? It would show they actually *are* investigating."

"Not yet." He rose from his seat, making it clear this was wrap-up time. "I'm sorry but I really *do* have to end this."

He led me back through the house, where I briefly savored the crisp, cool air. There was no sign of the goddess Diana.

"Please tell Jillian I'd love to see her," Kordas said, swinging open the door. "Though I can understand why it might be difficult for her to meet up with her father's old partner."

"And you're still in real estate development, correct?" This was my last chance to probe about him and C.J.

"That's right."

"I was just curious because someone mentioned that you and Mr. Lowe had talked about parting ways that winter. I thought maybe you'd decided to try something else."

It was a trick I'd learned years ago, probably from Buddy. One of the best ways to flush out information from a person was to present them with a detail that wasn't true, thus forcing them to comment on it. Kordas kept his gaze leveled at me, but I saw his eyes widen ever so slightly, and the rims began to pulse like a jellyfish.

"Now who in the world would have told you that?"

I raised my eyes to the left, as if trying to think.

"I actually don't recall. Is it true?"

"Hardly. C.J. and I had no intention of parting ways. Good day, Ms. Weggins. As I said, please give Jillian my best."

I lingered after the door closed behind me, deliberating about the last exchange. He'd been defensive. Was it simply because Kordas didn't like the idea of an unfounded rumor floating around, or was it because I'd come close to the truth?

Back in my car I took a minute to both review my quickly scribbled notes and flesh them out. In the end, I'd come away with more than I'd anticipated. The detail about Carl Lowe's mystery visitor—two weeks before the murders—was extremely significant, and I'd have to figure out how to learn more. It was also interesting, and a little discouraging, that the cops hadn't reinterviewed Kordas, suggesting that they definitely weren't hustling to find who had left the unidentified DNA at the murder scene.

Before starting the engine, I checked my phone. Still

no word from Jocelyn London. And still nothing from Jillian on the meeting. I shot her a text, asking for an update. I decided that since Penny Niles's house was on the way to the inn, I'd stop there to see if she was home before heading back to check on Jillian.

Pulling out of Bruce's driveway a minute later, I ended up blocking another car attempting to approach. The driver accommodated me, backing out onto the road and giving me the right of way.

I thanked him with a wave when I passed his car, and he nodded in response. He was extremely blond and looked to be in his late thirties or early forties. Based on the coloring and age, I wondered if it might be Bruce Kordas's stepson. I quickly did the math in my head. If it *was* the stepson, and he was indeed fortyish, he would have most likely been in his mid-twenties at the time of the murders. Now *that* was interesting.

It seemed too much to hope for that Penny Niles would be home at the moment I arrived, but there she was—or who I assumed to be her—watering a border garden beneath the windows of her small, two-story house.

As I parked across the street, she glanced once in my direction and then resumed her task. It wasn't until I was headed up her path that she let the hose sag in her hand and took me in, obviously curious. She was in her early seventies, I guessed, with short, curly gray hair. She was dressed in a short-sleeved blue blouse, high-waisted, mom kind of jeans, and a pair of sneakers so white they could have triggered snow blindness.

"May I help you?" she asked. The tone was friendly and no-nonsense at the same time. That had probably worked well for her in her career, especially with kids who had a tendency to lay on the bullshit. I bet she had called some boys *Mr.*, as in, "Don't you have some-place to be, Mr. Talbot?"

I stepped closer and, offering a business card, gave her a slightly different version of my spiel—I was in the area helping a former student research a memoir and the student had recommended I speak to her.

She accepted the card with one hand and shut off the hose with the other, though a few drops of water continued to drip onto the flower heads. She wasn't what you'd call a pretty woman, but her pale skin was soft and her face pleasant-looking, and her eyes a lovely blue.

"I see," she said, slightly guarded. "And what former student would that be?"

"Jillian Lowe. She thought you might remember her."

In an instant, Penny Niles's expression turned sorrowful.

"Of course I remember Jillian. How *is* she? Many of us were eager to stay in touch with her, but once she moved cross-country, it seemed she preferred leaving everything from the past behind."

"She's pretty good, all things considered. It might seem that a memoir would be hard for her, but she's hoping it will enable her to deal with some of the residual grief."

"I can see that. But I can't imagine how I could help. I knew all three kids, of course, and their parents, too, yet only in the context of school."

"Jillian's just hoping for a little background."

She bobbed her head gently a couple of times, as if weighing the idea, and tossed the hose in the yard.

"Why don't you come in then? I have a few minutes to spare."

The foyer was tiny, and two steps later we were in the living room. The house was sweet inside, like a country cottage.

"Won't you have a seat?" she said. "And let me get us both an iced tea."

"That would be wonderful." How refreshing not to be subjected to the withholding-all-liquids power play that Bruce Kordas had pulled on me.

The five minutes she took in the kitchen gave me a chance to look around, though there wasn't a lot to see.

The room was what could be called grandmotherly in style, with its chintz-covered sofa and blue La-Z-Boy recliner, but as I scanned the space with my eyes, my sense was that she *wasn't* a grandmother or even a mother. The mantel above the blocked-off fireplace featured animal figurines, candles that had never been lit, and only one photo, a shot of Penny Niles sporting her bright white sneakers and holding a huge teddy bear at a carnival. It looked like it might have been taken this summer.

There were built-in bookcases on either side of the mantel and they held an eclectic assortment of books—mysteries by Agatha Christie and Sue Grafton, romances by Danielle Steel, and about ten volumes on the Civil War. One more photo was nestled in with the books, a shot of Penny—looking a little younger—standing in front of the Eiffel Tower with another woman. Either Penny didn't like displaying photos, or she'd spent a lot of time on her own. After all those years of keeping an eye on kids, I wondered if there was anyone to keep an eye on her.

"I see you have an interest in the Civil War," I said, as Penny returned from the kitchen with a tray bearing two glasses of iced tea and a tiny bowl of ridged potato chips.

"Yes, I'm quite the night owl, and I love reading history books in the evenings." She settled onto the couch. "So how did you and Jillian end up working on the book together?"

"We were friends for a while at Brown, when she studied there, and she knew I'd become a writer."

"I can't tell you how grief-stricken we were about what happened. It couldn't compare to the pain Jillian suffered, but it stayed with everyone at the school for so long afterward."

"I'm sure . . . I don't want to take up much of your time so let me get to the questions."

There was only one I really wanted to ask, but I needed to maneuver my way there carefully.

"As I mentioned, my association with the Lowes was only through my job, but I'll do my best to answer."

After accepting a glass of iced tea, I wrestled my notebook out of my purse. I started by asking her to share any memories she had of the three kids in school, and she went on for a bit, pointing out that they were all terrific students and extremely well behaved and conscientious.

"I couldn't say a bad thing about any of them," she added, "though Jillian, in particular, was such a star. Besides being an excellent student, she was a varsity athlete and involved in school politics. And she played the piano beautifully."

"Oh, I wasn't aware of that," I said, surprised by the revelation. "I'd heard that Julia was musical, but I never realized Jillian was, too."

"I hope she still plays. Music can be such a powerful healer."

"Tell me, was that hard for Julia, do you think? Having such an accomplished sister."

Penny took a sip of iced tea, her brow wrinkled in thought as she drank. She had pretty hands, I noticed, with long, slim fingers.

"It probably *was* hard, yes. Julia was extremely talented, too. Smart, an accomplished solo violinist, and she had a gift for science. But she'd had heart issues as a child, as you're probably aware, and though she recovered, she was a bit fragile and shy, as well. Jillian, I must say, was very protective of her sister, always looking out for her."

"That's lovely to hear. What about the parents? What were they like?"

"Very nice people. They weren't the kind of *helicopter* parents you see nowadays. The mother volunteered at the school for many years, though that trailed off after a while. The father was active in the community; I believe he was with the Boys Scouts—or Cub Scouts. I'm not sure which."

I could tell that Penny had begun to relax with

me, and if I was going to strike, this seemed like the moment.

"Just one more question if you don't mind. It's not so much for background, but to solve a mystery for Jillian, something she's always wondered about."

I watched her draw a breath, expectant, it seemed, maybe a little nervous.

"I'm not much of a mystery solver, I'm afraid."

"The week before the Lowes were killed, Jillian called home from college and Danny told her that Julia and her mother had just been in an argument that left her mother in tears. He said Julia was angry about something the principal had done. Do you have any idea what it could have been?"

Her eyes widened in alarm, and not just any kind of alarm. She looked as if I'd just handed her a note that read, *I have a bomb in my bag, and I'm about to blow up your house.*

"I wouldn't know," she said, finally forcing the words out.

But clearly she *did* know.

"You hadn't heard about any kind of issue? Something that could have upset her?"

"Julia was in college then," she said, her voice betraying her unease. "What issue could she possibly have had with the school?"

"Maybe it had to do with Danny, and Julia was trying to look out for him, since she was home. Was he being bullied, do you recall?"

She shook her head quickly.

"We never tolerated bullying. Not even for a second."

I went the pregnant-pause route, hoping that might help tease out the truth, but she sat there dead still.

"Perhaps something will come to you in a day or two," I said. "If it does, will you give me a call?"

"Of course, but I can't imagine it will. That was such a long time ago."

"By the way, I'd love to talk to the former school principal—Eleanor Mercandetti. Would you happen to have a forwarding number for her?"

"No, I'm sorry, I don't. We lost touch a number of years ago."

Penny walked me to the door, and I thanked her for her time. As I heard the door close behind me, I could almost sense her body sagging in relief that I was gone.

Clearly I'd pricked a nerve, and yet I had no clue what she was holding back on. Maybe I'd hear from her, but I doubted it. What I needed to do, I realized, was track down the principal and see if she would be more forthcoming.

As soon as I was in the car, I checked my phone.

Jocelyn had finally responded, offering to meet tomorrow at eleven at a café in Dory. Good. But not so good was the text from Jillian. The meeting had been a bust, she said. No details.

Back at the inn, I found her sitting on the rear deck, changed into jeans and a T-shirt. Though there was a book in her lap, she wasn't reading it, just staring off across the yard. I climbed the steps to her.

"Tell me everything," I said, plopping down next to her.

"When I arrived, I was told that my meeting had been switched from the main guy to the first *assistant* district attorney," she said angrily. "A woman named Belinda Bacon, who turned out to be a nightmare. First, she kept me waiting for forty-five minutes. And when I was finally summoned into her inner chamber, she told me that any kind of exoneration is highly unlikely."

"Why?"

"She says it's because there isn't compelling enough evidence that Dylan didn't do it. He confessed; he didn't have an alibi."

"But what about the new blood sample, which clearly didn't belong to Dylan?"

"She said he might have had an accomplice."

"Does that make any sense at all to you? Was there anyone he palled around with that you're aware of?"

"From what I remember, he was a complete loner. That's why he was so happy whenever Julia was nice to him."

"Even if the police believe the accomplice theory, it means that person is walking around free today. Did she say anything about trying to find him?"

"She claims the police are looking into it, but who knows if that's true?"

"From today's meeting, I found out they haven't re-interviewed Bruce Kordas."

"How did that go, anyway?" she said, raising her eyes to meet mine.

"He didn't give me much time, but enough to insist that things were fine between him and your father, that there was no discussion about dissolving the partnership."

"I heard back from Jim Healy, by the way. He said that there was just one comment my father made to him about Bruce on the phone that winter. He told him, 'I'm really not sure how I feel about the guy anymore.' So, that doesn't really point to anything."

Maybe not. Or maybe it did.

"What's the deal with his wife being so much older?"

"Lynne?" she said dismissively. "That's a relation-ship for a shrink. I once heard my mother say that Lynne had been left millions when her first husband died."

I pictured Kordas's stunning home, those paintings that had obviously cost a mint.

"There's one more thing I need to run by you," I said, "but first I want to set some ground rules." On the way back from Penny Niles's, I realized that Jillian and I needed to establish certain criteria, which I actually should have addressed on the drive to Massachusetts. "What if I find out details that might be unsettling or disturbing to you? Do you want me to curate the truth or share it all?"

"I want to hear everything, no matter how ugly it is," she insisted. "I should have pushed harder for the truth years ago and realized that Dylan couldn't pos-sibly be guilty."

"Understood." I then shared what Kordas had dis-closed about the visit from the angry mystery man and her father's glum mood.

"That's *important*," she exclaimed. "It's exactly what the police need to be following up on now."

"I know. But since we're not sure they'll contact Kordas or that he'll take the initiative to speak with them, why don't you bring up the visitor to the inno-cence group that contacted you."

"Okay—but I don't understand. Why did you think that information might be upsetting to me?"

"I wondered whether the man confronting him had been a cuckolded husband, that your dad might have been having an affair. Do you mind my asking? How was your parents' marriage?"

"It could have been better," she said quietly. "When my father was around—which wasn't a ton—they got along well enough, but there didn't seem to be a lot of affection there."

Her words echoed what Kordas had conveyed.

"Do you think your father might have been cheating on your mom?"

She glanced off in that way I was becoming familiar with and then brought her eyes back to mine.

"No, I think it might have been the other way around. That my mom was cheating on my dad."

Okay, wow.

"Tell me why."

"She'd seemed distracted over Christmas break and a little secretive. Jules noticed it, too. You know how I told you my mom didn't really love her cell phone? Well, I walked in on her a couple of times using it, and she jumped off the call right away."

"But you don't have any idea who it could have been?"

"No, none."

If I was lucky, Jocelyn might know if there'd been someone in the picture and be willing to confide the truth. But even if she'd been looped in, that still left the problem of the angry man's identity. Perhaps he was the one Claire had been having an affair with, showing up for a confrontation with his competition.

"Your father had an assistant, right? Do you recall her name?" I should have thought to ask Kordas.

"Heather. Heather something. I don't remember after all this time."

"I have another job for you then. Can you try to find out so I can reach out to her?"

"Sure."

"There's something else important I found." I told her about coming across the letter from Barnard, then about my conversation with Penny and her weird response to my question.

"Wait, are you saying that the argument Jules had with my mom actually *did* involve the high school principal?"

"Sounds like it might have. First of all, Julia didn't seem to have any reason to be pissed at Barnard. And second, I clearly touched a nerve with Penny. Can you think of anything in the world that might have happened with Julia that involved the school? Maybe an incident involving Danny rather than her directly?"

Jillian wrinkled her face in confusion. "Gosh no, I can't. It's even hard picturing her having a fight with my mom. Julia worshipped her."

"Maybe Jocelyn will know."

"But—but even if she does, what does it matter in the grand scheme of things?" She touched the hollow spot in her neck. "I mean, I don't see how a problem with the high school could have had anything to do with what happened."

"You're probably right, but I don't want to leave any stone unturned. As I said on the drive here, we need to view everything as possibly significant."

We were interrupted by the sound of a car pulling into the driveway behind us. Instinctively I turned, and though bushes blocked the view, I heard doors open and luggage being hoisted from the trunk. Best to keep our mouths shut with people around. When I turned back to Jillian, I saw that her eyes had brimmed with tears.

"Let's table this for now," I said. "It's a lot to deal with."

I suggested we head out to someplace nice for a late lunch, maybe one of the bigger inns nearby, which would be filled with tourists rather than locals, reducing the likelihood of her being recognized. Jillian begged off, saying Mamie and Blake had invited her to spend the rest of the afternoon at the clinic, observing a surgery, and that Mamie would be picking her up.

"I hope you don't mind," she added. "I really need the distraction."

"I don't mind at all. . . . Besides, I've got plenty to focus on today. By the way, Penny Niles mentioned you played piano beautifully. I noticed one in the parlor if you feel the urge."

Jillian smiled ruefully. "Thanks, but I don't really play anymore."

After parting, I drove to another inn for lunch, happy in one respect to have the time alone to think. As soon as I was seated, I dug out my notebook and began to noodle over the notes I'd taken. In many regards it had been a fruitful half day, with me coming away with more than I'd anticipated, and yet it had also led to more questions than what I'd started with. Hopefully Jocelyn would be able to answer some of them tomorrow.

On my return from lunch, I made a stop at Uncle Jack's, hoping Jack—if there really was one—would be willing to check the security cameras for me. There was no longer a Jack, it turned out, but the receptionist said a guy named Harry could probably help me, except for the fact that he was off-site for the rest of the day.

I took advantage of the trip to take a look at the facility in broad daylight. The fence was at least eight feet high, with spears at the top, but there wasn't barbwire, and therefore someone agile could have scaled it, snuck up on the Lowe unit, and dragged the shutter down.

Once I'd returned to the inn from Jack's, I set up shop at the desk in my room. My first effort was a text to my friend Jessie Pendergrass, a former colleague from my stint at *Buzz* magazine, asking if she'd provide contact info for Amber Tresslar, a fellow Barnard alum. I needed it, I told her, for an important story I was working on. Jessie would know that she could trust me with the number.

I spent the next hour futilely trying to track down Eleanor Mercandetti. Based on the meager tidbit Gramps had tossed my way, I knew she might be in California, but at least according to what I found online, there was no one by that name owning property there or in Massachusetts. It seemed odd that she wouldn't own property at this stage of her life, though, of course, if she was married, she may have kept her own name and the home was under a husband's name, not hers.

There was also no sign of her on Facebook, LinkedIn, Instagram, or Pinterest. That seemed odd, too. What I knew from observing my mother and her friends was that older women, particularly those who had moved a lot or worked for a variety of companies, loved certain types of social media because it was an easy way to stay connected with the myriad people from their pasts. So why wasn't Mercandetti using it? Didn't she have at least one potato salad recipe she wanted to share on Pinterest?

Next, I turned my attention to the final Rubbermaid tub, the one belonging to Danny. It was chock-full of the kind of heartbreaking items I'd glimpsed at the storage facility: comic books, Magic cards, notes from friends, a note from his mom saying how proud she was of him for getting an A in English, his goals for the year written in boyish block letters on a piece of construction paper.

There wasn't a single indication that he'd had any sort of trouble at school. Though that was hardly proof that there hadn't been.

Now and then I checked my phone for messages, mainly to see if Jessie had texted back or if Beau had been in touch. I'd contacted him late yesterday afternoon, saying we were settled at the inn, and he texted back, wishing me luck. But since then I hadn't heard from him. I'd call later.

At close to eight, I flopped back on the bed and closed my eyes, weary. The morning had been so productive, but I had nothing to show for the second half of the day. And the conversation with Penny kept gnawing at me. What secret was she holding back?

I didn't mean to but I ended up dosing off. When I woke, the room was pitch-black. I fumbled for the bedside light and checked my phone—9:03. There was no text from Jillian asking about dinner, so I assumed she'd eaten again with Mamie.

I knew I should grab food myself, but something weighed on me even more. I realized I wanted to try again with Penny Niles, especially in light of the fact that I'd been unable to track down Mercandetti. Perhaps the best tactic would be to come clean about my real mission and plead for her help.

I grabbed my purse and scurried downstairs, scooting by two other guests on the stairs. I drove as fast as I could to Penny's. She'd mentioned in passing that she was a night owl, and I was praying she hadn't turned in for the night.

To my relief, the lights were on in Penny's living room, and also the room right above, which I assumed must be her bedroom. I parked the car and stepped out into the quiet summer night. It was almost nine thirty by now.

Once I reached the top of the stoop, I noticed, to my surprise, that the front door was partly ajar. Maybe she'd left it that way to better circulate the air on a hot night.

I found a bell to the right of the door and rang it. The sound pierced the silence and the *dong* hung on, finally mutating into a hum. I waited for a rustling sound or footsteps but none came.

I rang the bell again, waiting. The house was so small, there was no way she hadn't heard it. I wondered if she might be sitting in the backyard, savoring the evening. And yet, it seemed odd that she would be there at this hour and leave the front door ajar, even in a small town like this. A tremor of unease rippled through me.

"Ms. Niles," I called through the opening. *"Hello?"*

Not a sound.

I pushed the door open further and stepped inside.

"Hello?" I called again. From the rear of the house, I thought I could hear the drip of water. Plopping into a sink.

I started down the short hallway, listening, my whole body on alert. After passing through the living room, I made my way down another hall to the kitchen. Only one light was on, above the window over the sink. The view was to the backyard, which was swathed in darkness.

And then I saw her. She was over to the right, by

the door to the outside, kneeling on the floor with her head leaning forward. She's washing the floor, I realized, but I couldn't understand why. Who would wash the floor at this hour, and in such dim light?

"Penny," I said, inching closer.

I jerked backward, my surprise morphing into horror. There was a scarf knotted around her neck and the ends extended behind her, taut.

Penny Niles had hanged herself from the knob on the back door.

Chapter 7

I let out a cry and rushed forward. *No,* I thought. *No, no, no, please don't let this be happening.*

For a split second I considered that Penny might still be alive, but as soon as I reached her, I could tell she wasn't. One eye was shut, and the other one was open and vacant, and the tip of her tongue protruded between her lips. The scarf around her neck—a silky blue-and-yellow one—had been double knotted in front, obviously to guarantee it did its gruesome job.

My stomach roiled. *Why?* Why had she done this?

Though I knew Penny was dead, I reached for her wrist anyway and felt for a pulse. Nothing. Her skin was barely cool, so she may have died less than an hour before. My first instinct was to untie the scarf so she wouldn't have to hang there indignantly for one more second, but I knew I shouldn't. That was for the police to handle. I stepped back, rifled through my bag for my phone, and called 911.

"A woman is dead, a suicide, I think," I said to the operator. "Please send someone right away."

"Is there any chance she's still alive?"

"No—I don't think so. I couldn't find a pulse. And she's hanging from a scarf."

She asked for Penny's name, my name, the location, whether I was talking on a cell or landline, and what my relationship to Penny was. I quickly explained I was a writer, interviewing her for a project.

"Please do not touch her again. The police are on their way."

Based on the size of the town, there were probably only one or two patrol cars on duty tonight, and it could take anywhere from five to twenty minutes for one of them to arrive.

I forced my eyes toward Penny again. The sight of her body tore at me, filling me with anguish. Was I somehow *responsible* for this? After all, I'd alarmed Penny with my last question. Was she afraid I was intent on prying the lid off a box she never wanted open? What secret would impel her to kill herself rather than see it exposed?

Or was it all a bizarre coincidence, my visit unrelated to her desire to end her own life?

I glanced around the room, my eyes searching frantically. Though I knew suicide notes were less common than books and movies made them out to be, about 30 percent of people did leave one behind. There was no note on the small kitchen table, nor anything on the counter. I stepped backward, turned, and hurried into the living room. I didn't find a note there, either.

Grabbing a breath, I reentered the kitchen. As soon as I stepped onto the linoleum, I was struck by a detail I'd noticed when I first entered the house: the sound of water dripping. I glanced toward the faucet in the sink. A drop at the tip blistered, fell, and plopped into the basin; a moment later another began to form. I wondered if it was simply a drippy faucet—or whether Penny poured herself a glass of water before knotting the scarf around her neck.

If she *had* killed herself. My blood chilled as I considered another possibility. Someone may have done this to her.

I thought I heard the whir of a car coming down the street, and I knew I needed to hurry outside. This was an unexplained death and I shouldn't be mucking up the scene any more than I already had.

But before leaving, I forced my eyes toward Penny Niles one last time, as if another glimpse could possibly explain the scene before me. And then I did something I knew I shouldn't do but felt I *had* to. I used my phone to snap a few pictures of her body, and a few more of the room. I wanted to look at them later with more time on my side. The flash going off unnerved me even more, as if there were a presence in the room with me.

I backed out of the kitchen again, nearly tripping this time, and after snapping a couple of shots of the living room, I stumbled onto the small stoop. Whatever car I'd heard hadn't belonged to the cops because the street was empty now. Though it was muggy and warm out, I shivered with fear.

I needed to call Jillian, I realized, needed to make sure she was okay. There was a chance this death was connected to her somehow. She didn't pick up until the fifth ring, and by then my dread had mushroomed.

"Jillian, where are you?" I asked.

"At Mamie's," she said. "We're just having a glass of wine. I sent you a text but never heard back."

"Look, something's happened. Something terrible."

"What? Are you *okay*?"

"Yes, but I'd like to pick you up tonight and take you back to the inn myself. Can you hang there for a while?"

"What's going on?" she demanded. Being vague, I could see, wasn't going to help matters.

"Penny Niles is dead. It looks as if she's hung herself."

"Oh my god. But *why*? Why would she do that?"

"I don't know. I have to be interviewed by the police and then I'll swing by for you. I'll call for directions when I'm close."

"But what about—"

Another car was approaching. This one might actually belong to the cops, and it wouldn't be good for them to catch me on the phone.

"I better go. We can talk when I get there. I'll probably know more then anyway."

Which actually wasn't all that likely, but I needed to ease Jillian off the phone. Before signing off, I heard her blurt out a few words to someone beside her, obviously starting to fill Mamie in.

"All right," she said distractedly back into the phone.

"See you in a bit."

I had just enough time to drop my phone into my handbag when a patrol car lurched to a stop in front of the house. Not far off I heard the haunting, summer-night wail of what I thought was an ambulance.

Two uniformed police, both women, sprang simultaneously from the car and rushed up the path to the house.

"I'm Bailey Weggins, the person who called 911," I told them. "She's in the kitchen."

"Is anyone else on the premises?" the older of the two asked.

"No. I've been here only once before, but I believe she lived alone."

"Please stay with Officer Aitkens," she said quickly. "Someone will take a statement from you shortly."

"Why don't we step down to the car?" Aitkens said after her partner had entered the house. This is what police called "controlling the witness." They wanted me removed from the premises stat. If someone was dead inside, I might have played a role in it.

By the time Aitkens and I had reached the sidewalk, an ambulance had pulled up right behind the police car, cutting off its siren mid wail. She directed the EMTs into the house. Neighbors, a few in jammies and housecoats, began spilling out into their yards, craning their necks. A minute later, a bald-headed guy from the house next door suddenly barreled across his lawn in our direction.

"Please, sir," Aitkens called out. "I need you to stay on your own property right now."

"Is she okay? I mean Penny. What's happened?"

"Sir, I'm not at liberty to say. Please remain in your home."

Once she'd ushered the guy back to his own turf, Aitkens returned her attention to me, asking for my name, contact info, and what had brought me to the scene. I explained that I'd stopped by to ask Ms. Niles a follow-up question to an interview I'd conducted and found her body in the kitchen. Putting everything into words made me feel the shock even more intensely.

"Why were you interviewing her?" Aitkens asked.

"For a memoir I'm ghostwriting. In collaboration with a former resident from the area." No need to mention the Lowe name at this point.

"You just walked into the house like that, without anyone letting you in?"

"I rang the doorbell first, but no one answered. I noticed that the front open was open, and that seemed odd to me. I wanted to make sure she was okay."

Her look suggested she didn't love my answer, but she said nothing else. It would be a detective's job to drill down.

Moments later another patrol car pulled up to the house. After instructing me to wait, Aitkens approached the two officers for a short confab, addressed someone briefly on her walkie, and then hurried back to me.

"We're going to need a formal statement from you, Ms. Wiggins," she said, being about the seven hundredth person to botch my last name in my lifetime. "I can take you to the station now and bring you back later to pick up your car."

I nodded, knowing I had no real choice in the matter. It would have been so much better if I could have waited for a while at the scene, observing the action and overhearing whatever I could. But that wasn't in the cards tonight.

Aitkens opened the back door of the patrol car and I slid inside. People gawked. Hopefully no one was videotaping the scene with the idea of posting it on Facebook.

The ride to the station was mercifully short. I warned myself to stay calm, since I'd need my cool for the interview, but it was hard to tamp down the nauseating distress I was experiencing. I'd stirred a pot today and now, hours later, a gentle, decent woman was dead.

With the cruiser parked, Aitkens ushered me out of the vehicle and into a side entrance of a large brick building that appeared to be the town hall, with the police station at the rear. After greeting the beefy desk sergeant, she led me to a small, nearly bare interview room.

"Would you like some water?" she asked. "Unfortunately, it may be a wait. You're going to be interviewed by a detective from the state police, and he's coming from a couple of towns over."

The fact that I'd be talking to the state police didn't cause me any extra anxiety. Small-town police often relied on either the state police or the area sheriff's office, or sometimes both, for backup to help with a serious crime. But I had a particular challenge in this instance. I felt obligated to tell them about the question that had triggered the alarm bell in Penny Niles—in case it had played a role in her death—but I couldn't let on that I was investigating the Lowe murders.

The wait ended up being close to forty minutes. At least it gave me time to think. I tore my mind away from the heartbreaking scene in the kitchen and forced it back to my earlier encounter with Penny, trying to conjure up what might have occurred between my first and second trips to the house. Let's say my question about Julia really forced her to reflect on a secret she was guarding from years ago. Had it really been so painful or dangerous that she decided to kill herself because of it? According to what Danny had blurted out to Jillian, the secret had involved the school principal, so how big of a role could Penny Niles, a former administrative assistant, have actually played?

The principal. I wondered if, despite what she'd conveyed to me, Penny had stayed in touch with Eleanor Mercandetti all these years and had contacted her after I left. Penny may have reported that I was poking around in stuff they didn't want to see the light of day. But then what could have happened after the call?

I shifted gears momentarily. It could be, of course— just as I'd considered earlier—that Penny's death was a coincidence, or a partial one. She may have been depressed already, contemplating suicide, and I'd pushed her over the edge by bringing up the murder of the Lowes.

The door swung open, jerking me from my thoughts. A commanding, fiftysomething-year-old man strode into the room.

"Ms. Weggins? Sorry for the delay. I'm Detective Greg Maynard with the state police."

He was tall and in good shape, with full, coarse gray hair that he wore slicked back on the sides and a thick, droopy mustache. Handsome for his age, and though his outfit consisted of a dress shirt, jeans, and a pair of super-pointy, scuffed cowboy boots, he gave off a sophisticated vibe. I wondered if he might have once been a big-city cop who'd moved to the Berkshires for a major change of pace.

"Not a problem," I said. I offered a polite smile but made sure my guard was seriously up. I'd been interviewed more than I'd liked by cops following a violent death and it had never been a pretty experience. If you're on the scene of a homicide, they assume, at the very least, that you may know more than you're volunteering, and, at the most, that you're the killer.

"So tell me about tonight," he said. "What brought you to Ms. Niles's house? You a friend of hers?"

His tone matched his laid-back cop-meets-cowboy style of dress, but I knew better than to buy it. I was sure he'd already been informed of what I'd shared with the patrol cop.

"No, I didn't know her," I said. "I'm a writer, and I'm helping a college friend of mine put together a memoir. She'd attended the high school where Ms. Niles used to work and thought it would be helpful for me to speak to her for background."

Maynard tapped his pen, head first, on the pad a couple of times, the way guys did with cigarettes in black-and-white movies from the 1940s.

"Kind of late for an interview, wasn't it?" he said, still keeping his tone light, as if we were two work colleagues batting around the pros and cons of an idea.

"Yes, probably." It seemed smarter to be forthcoming here, since that might help my credibility factor. "We'd actually spoken earlier in the day, but there was something I wanted to follow up about, so on the spur of the moment, I drove back there. She'd mentioned she stayed up late."

"And you went into the house on your own?"

"Only because the door was ajar. It seemed strange that it would be open at night, and I was worried something was the matter."

"Nice of you to be concerned about someone who you didn't really know."

"Well, she was older and I had the feeling she probably lived alone. I think most people would have been concerned."

I expected that he might change the tone, start pressing me, but he nodded as if my explanation made sense. It was probably part of his technique, a way to ease my guard down.

"Okay," he said. "And did you touch the body at all?"

"To take her pulse, yes. From what I could see, she was dead, but I wanted to be sure."

"And that's it?"

I nodded. I had a brief, irrational fear that the words *Yes, but I took pictures of the body and they're right here in my purse*, might suddenly come flying out of my mouth like bats from a cave at twilight.

"What did the two of you talk about?"

"I'm glad you brought that up. I mostly asked basic questions about my friend and her family, but one question seemed to rattle her, and I don't know why."

I told him then about Jillian, about her family being murdered several towns away, and the comment Danny had made on the phone that Sunday before their deaths, which suggested there'd been a problem with the school.

"I sensed Ms. Niles was withholding something," I said in conclusion. "I went back tonight to see if I could convince her to open up."

Maynard was taking notes, and I saw his eyes flicker as he clearly began to fit the pieces together.

"Your friend is Jillian *Lowe*?" he said. "From Dory?"

"Yes, that's right."

He took a moment to fully digest this.

"Don't people in your line of work call that burying the lede?"

"You could say that, I guess. But I figured you'd first want to hear about what happened tonight."

"So you're not just a writer, you're a mind reader." He grinned with half his mouth, but he wasn't amused. I was no mind reader in his view, though something told me the words *possible troublemaker* had popped into his brain.

"I'm sorry, I was just trying to be helpful."

"And you're writing about what happened to Jillian's family? The murders?"

"No, like I mentioned, it's a memoir," I said, probably too quickly, though at least there didn't appear to be flames shooting out from my pants. "She wants to focus mostly on her life since then. But the book will have to contain background about the crime. It shaped her life. And if I find anything relevant, I'll of course pass it on to the police."

He didn't comment on my offer, and I took his narrowed eyes as the warning they were meant to be. *You better not be butting into police business.*

He circled back to Penny with his next round of questions: What had her mood been when I'd first arrived at the house? How was she when I left? Had I noticed anything that seemed different when I entered the house the second time? I assumed he meant anything other than her body hanging from the back door.

I mentioned the dripping faucet.

After we were done, he shepherded me into the squad room and led me through everything all over again, with him typing the notes on a desktop computer. I knew cops often worked this way, talking semicasually with you before taking your real statement. It was a technique to suss out liars.

Maynard escorted me to the front, the clomp of his boots echoing through the nearly deserted station, and explained that he might have to speak with me again. If he had concerns that I'd been less than forthcoming about what I was up to, they were bound to intensify when he performed a Google search and found that the two books I'd written were titled *A Model Murder* and *Bad Men and Wicked Women*. That would make clear that I had about as much experience writing memoirs as I did performing as a trapeze artist for Cirque du Soleil.

On the drive to the Allards, I realized I felt drained and wired at the same time. When I reached the turn-off to the property, I phoned Jillian, who handed the phone to Mamie so she could direct me during the last leg of the trip. Finally, up on the right I spotted the building—a big red barn with light pouring from both a row of windows and a large cupola on top.

No sooner had I flung open the car door than two dogs bounded from the barn, a golden retriever, its muzzle gray with age, and a Boston terrier.

"This is Butternut and Tammy," Mamie called out, trailing them outside.

"I'm sorry to be so late. You guys are probably desperate to get to bed."

"Don't worry about it. What we're really desperate for is news."

She ushered me inside and shooed the dogs in as well. The barn had a large, open floor plan, and I spotted Jillian on a kind of shabby-chic sofa, cradling a nearly empty wineglass, and Blake at a long kitchen counter, with half a sandwich on a plate in front of him. As I crossed toward the couch, Blake, dressed in a T-shirt and medical scrub pants, grabbed his sandwich in one hand and joined us.

"Did you find out anything more?" Jillian asked, her eyes wild with worry.

"No, nothing. My guess is that she died about an hour before I arrived."

"She's the woman we used to get passes from, right?" Mamie said. "I can still see her at her desk."

"You must be reeling," Blake said, turning to me.

I nodded, appreciating his concern.

"It was pretty awful to see."

"And she *hung* herself?" Blake said. "I thought that was mostly a male thing."

"True, but some women do resort to that method. It was a short-drop hanging—from a doorknob."

"Could someone have *done* it to her?" Mamie said, her hands flying to her mouth as the idea took hold.

"Let's not get ahead of ourselves," I advised. "For now it looks like suicide, and we'll have to wait until they release the preliminary autopsy results."

"But why would she have killed herself?" Jillian said. "Was it because of that question you asked?"

"What question?" Mamie demanded.

"Why don't I fill everyone in tomorrow?" I announced. "I'm spent, and I'm sure you two have an early morning."

I sensed Blake and Mamie were churned up enough to want to continue the discussion, even if it would entail mostly useless speculation, but Jillian appeared eager to split. She collected a cotton sweater from the couch, hugged Mamie, and thanked both of them for the afternoon at the clinic.

Though Jillian was adept at swaddling her emotions, she wasn't doing such a good job tonight. The second we pulled out of the driveway, she squeezed her head with her hands as if she feared it might explode.

"I can't believe it," she said, her voice ragged. "I've been here less than two days and already there's another person dead. I never thought this would put anyone else's life in danger."

"We don't know for sure there's any connection. It could be that I simply ended up visiting Penny on a day when she was overwhelmed by depression. And yet, it does seem like an awfully big coincidence. I think we have to at least consider that Penny's death might be related to my interview with her."

"But how?"

"She may have killed herself because she was afraid of a secret coming out, and that secret would have to be big. Information that could affect people's lives, their reputations."

"I can't imagine what it could be."

"I'm going to have to keep digging. And let's keep this between us as much as possible."

"Is that why you didn't want to say anything to Mamie about the question?"

"Yes. Even when you trust people and they swear they'll keep information in the vault, they let stuff slip sometimes. If I've learned one thing in life, it's that there *is* no vault."

She nodded, and out of the corner of my eye, I saw her hands clench.

"Tell me about your afternoon," I said, trying to shift the subject. "Did you shadow Mamie at the clinic?"

"Not her, but Blake and another one of the vets. I observed a cystectomy on a dog—that's when they remove bladder stones. After the dog is under anesthesia and they've made an incision through the abdominal wall, they actually lift out the bladder, open it up, and removed the stones."

"Would you ever think of becoming a vet yourself?"

"I'd probably feel too cooped up being in a clinic all day. But it was great to see Blake in action. He's a dog whisperer and a cat whisperer and even a rabbit whisperer. He's actually pretty interested in birds, too. He studied them in Brazil one winter during college."

There was something that sounded a bit like hero-worship in her tone, and I found myself glancing over to read her expression, but she had turned to stare out the window.

After seeing Jillian to her door at the inn, I made my way down the quiet staircase to my own room, and immediately texted Beau.

U up? Can u talk?

It was close to one and I didn't really expect him to reply. He'd been up since the crack of dawn to catch a flight. Still, I longed to hear his voice.

Ten minutes passed without a return text. Probably for the best. I needed to think how I was going to break the news to him about Penny. If he thought I was in any danger, he wouldn't be happy.

I stripped off everything but my underwear, threw on a T-shirt, and slipped into bed with both my phone and laptop. Steeling myself, I opened the photos I'd taken at Penny's and emailed them to myself so I could view them enlarged on my laptop. God, I thought, if Detective Maynard knew I had them, he'd aim one of those pointy cowboy boots at my butt and launch me all the way back to Manhattan, preferably into the East River.

I started by studying the shots I'd taken of the kitchen and living room. Maynard had queried if anything had appeared different to me between my first visit and second, and based on my brief observation, I'd answered no. Now, looking more closely, nothing contradicting my statement jumped out.

Finally I clicked on the shots of Penny. My heart nearly broke at the sight of them.

I searched the photos slowly, trying to take everything in, despite how painful it was to stare. There was no bruising above or below the scarf, nothing suggesting she had been strangled before and then attached to the doorknob to make it appear like a suicide. But it can take hours for certain bruises to bloom after death.

Eventually my eyes landed on Penny's hands. I'd noticed them earlier, how pretty they were and what good care she took of them. Oh, Penny, I thought. Did I say something that sent you spiraling into a state of despair?

A second later, as I peered at the screen, my whole body tensed.

Penny's nails, I noticed, were painted a bright peachy pink, a shade that probably had a name like "Oh So

Pretty" or "Flirty Girl" stamped on the bottom of the bottle, as if your whole essence could be transformed by wearing that hue.

But something didn't make sense. I was positive that when I'd noticed Penny's hands during our conversation, her nails had been bare, just lightly buffed. Which meant she must have given herself a manicure or gone to a salon for one shortly after I'd seen her.

Would a woman really take the time to paint her nails—a bright and happy color no less—right before she killed herself?

Chapter 8

I didn't fall asleep until close to three. Instead I lay in bed, my nerves ragged, unable to think of much more than Penny's hands—her fingers grasping the garden hose, passing me the glass of iced tea, and then later, laying limp and lifeless on the floor. Something wasn't adding up. It didn't make sense to me that she'd go to the trouble of polishing her nails and then hang herself.

Which could only mean that someone else had tied that noose around her neck, a thought I'd briefly considered in the kitchen. But *why*? Had I set off a gruesome chain of events with my question? When I woke just before seven, the fragments of a nightmare lingered in my mind, and my stomach felt thick with dread.

I squinted at my phone, bleary-eyed. No text from

Beau. Maybe he hadn't checked his phone yet this morning.

After showering, I flipped open my composition book and scratched out an attack plan for the day. At eleven I was due to meet Jocelyn, but there was plenty to tackle before then. For one, I still needed to find Eleanor Mercandetti, and it would mean ratcheting up my online search efforts.

I also wanted to drop by area nail salons once they opened, which I figured would be about ten, and ascertain if Penny Niles had treated herself to a professional manicure at one of them yesterday. If I lucked out, it would not only be proof that I remembered correctly, but I might be able to come away with a read on Penny's mood yesterday.

What I needed to do right now, though, was to make a call to a psychiatrist named Karen Rosen. It needed to happen before her first patient showed up this morning.

"It's Bailey," I said when she answered. "Sorry to phone so early, but I really need to pick your brain."

"Sure. Just give me a minute to grab my coffee."

Like Jillian, Karen had been in my class at Brown and we'd become friends our junior year. She was now a respected psychiatrist in DC and generous enough to occasionally provide me with background information for my work. When I was researching an individual who was clearly sociopathic or homicidal, I turned for guidance to a couple of ex-FBI profilers I knew, but Karen was an ideal source for insight on issues more normal people faced. They have demons, too, just not the kind that might sway them to strangle their spouse and run the body through a wood chipper.

"Everything okay?" she asked after a brief delay.

"Not totally. Last night I dropped by to see a woman I'd interviewed earlier in the day, and I discovered her hanging dead in the kitchen. It looked at first as if she killed herself—though now I'm not so sure."

"Oh, Bailey, that's got to be upsetting. What did she use to do it?"

"A scarf tied to a doorknob. Which seemed odd to me."

"How old was she? Had she been depressed, do you know?"

"Early seventies, I'd say, and I don't know anything about her recent state of mind."

"Hanging's not the most common means for women, as I'm sure you know. The number one method is drugs, and second's gunshot. But it's not out of the ordinary. What makes you skeptical?"

"When I was at this woman's house the first time, I noticed her hands and she wasn't wearing any nail polish. But sometime between my interview with her and the time she died, she painted her nails pink. Would someone do that if she were going to kill herself?"

A couple of moments of quiet ensued as Karen obviously contemplated my question.

"I'd say it's a possibility if she were only *attempting* suicide, meaning she didn't really mean for it to work, but was hoping for attention."

That didn't gel with the little I knew about Penny.

"On the surface, at least, she didn't seem like the needy type."

"Then I'd say your instincts are right: it doesn't fit. If you're depressed and consumed with a desire to end your life, you're probably not going to take time out for a mani. That said, in some female suicide cases, the woman may want to make sure she looks good in death—but then she'd take pills, not hang herself."

I exhaled slowly, letting the full impact of her words register.

"Are you thinking she was murdered and the killer tried to make it appear as a suicide?" Karen asked into the silence.

"Yes, that's exactly what I'm thinking."

"It's certainly been done before."

"Look, I'd better let you get back to your breakfast. Thanks so much for your help, Karen."

"Call me later if you need to talk, okay? I'm free after seven tonight."

For the next few minutes, I sat on the edge of the bed, staring at the violet-colored walls and trying to imagine what might have unfolded in Penny's life after I left her house early yesterday afternoon. If this was indeed a murder, it stood to reason that she'd alerted someone to my visit, to the fact that a nosy writer was poking around, asking questions, and that a long-held secret was in danger of being exposed. Maybe the person on the other end had suggested that he—or *she*—drop by Penny's house so they could hatch a plan for handling me. Or the person may have simply shown up without warning at the house after the call, catching Penny off guard and overpowering her.

Regardless of how it had played out, it would mean that Jillian and I were in danger. I swallowed hard. I knew when I agreed to help Jillian that I might be putting myself in potential jeopardy, but I'd never imagined things escalating this quickly and with such ugly force.

Though I knew he'd be less than pleased to hear from me, I needed to connect with Detective Maynard and let him know about the nails. But I decided to wait until I'd dropped by the salons and confirmed whether Penny had been a customer.

Rising from the bed, a new question tugged at my brain. Could someone have followed me on my first trip to Penny's, realized what I was up to, and then returned later to kill her? I was having a tough time picturing that, however. Before entering the house, Penny and I had spoken for a couple of minutes out front and not a single car had cruised by.

I suddenly felt desperate for both breakfast and caffeine. I grabbed my laptop and headed downstairs.

There were already a few tables full of guests in the dining room/sunroom, people getting an early start on the day. The deck was empty, though, so I took my coffee and yogurt out there. I'd no sooner sat down than my phone rang. Beau. I felt a rush seeing his name on the screen.

"Hey there," I said. "You all settled in Miami?"

"Yup. And needless to say it's hot as hell down here. Sorry to miss your text last night. I put on the TV in my room and the next thing I knew I was out like a light."

"No problem. I remembered you had an early flight and figured you must be zonked."

"How's it going up there?"

"Good. Well, that's probably the wrong word. It's such a sad case, but at least I seem to be turning up information. Whether it will point to anything significant is another story."

I decided in bed late last night not to tell Beau about Penny until I had more information. Why alarm him unnecessarily if it really *was* a suicide?

"How's your friend Jillian handling things?"

"It's tough for her to be here, but she's doing her best."

"Is she the same person you remember?"

A good question.

"In some ways. She's still smart and beautiful. And I admire her so much for how she's survived everything that happened. But I'd be kidding myself if I didn't admit I miss the old Jillian. I'm not sure if that girl is gone for good or if it's just hard for her to emerge so close to Dory."

"Yes, around nine," he said.

"What?"

"Sorry, I was saying something to one of the PAs."

"You're shooting already?"

"About to."

"I'll let you go then."

"Okay, let's talk more later. Love you."

"Love you, too."

Okay, good. He hadn't tossed out a question like, "You're not in danger, right?" or "The people you've interviewed aren't hanging themselves with scarves from doorknobs, are they?" which meant I hadn't been forced to tell an out-and-out lie.

And yet, as I lifted my coffee mug slowly to my lips, I realized that something about the conversation had seemed funny to me. Maybe it was the fact that Beau had sounded slightly distant. Or because he *hadn't* asked any specific questions, other than the ones about Jillian.

There it was again, that *mystery* thing about him, the sense I had that I couldn't totally read him. It wasn't anything outrageously alarming—I mean, I didn't think he was, like, secretly selling arms on the black market—but there were still, after three years of knowing each other, moments, like this one, when he puzzled me.

I'd barely set the phone down when Jillian stepped out onto the deck, cradling a mug of coffee.

"Hey, how you doing today?" I asked.

I could surmise the answer with a mere glance at her. Though she'd protectively tightened up all those muscles in her face again, like someone securing the lid on a jar, there were blue-gray circles under her eyes, suggesting that she'd had a fitful night as well.

"I'm okay, I guess. I'm trying not to worry about Penny Niles. Like you said, it's best to wait for what the autopsy shows and not get ahead of ourselves."

Of course, if the autopsy confirmed my theory, it might propel her into a tailspin.

"Exactly. Are you going to shadow at the clinic again today?"

"Maybe later," she said, pulling up a chair. She was wearing white cropped pants and a yellow halter top, which showed off what good shape she was in, and she had her hair pushed back off her face with a stretchy band. "I'm going to spend the morning here. I'm still trying to get a lead on the name of my father's secretary."

"Good. I'll be meeting with Jocelyn at eleven. Do you have any plans to see her yourself?"

"No, not really."

Her answer surprised me. I wouldn't have wanted her tagging along with me on my meeting today because it might inhibit Jocelyn, but I would have thought she'd want to connect at some point with her mother's best friend.

"Are you worried it would be too painful?"

"Not that," she said, after looking off for a moment. "It's just . . . Jocelyn and I were never close. Not even after everything that happened."

"I thought she helped out a lot."

"She did, I guess. I was such a zombie at the time that I couldn't manage anything, so she oversaw the stuff being packed up for storage, and she worked with the Healys to arrange the estate sale for everything else. But she was never very comforting, and I know I wouldn't have much to say to her now."

"Did you find that odd—that she couldn't be comforting?"

"It seemed *selfish* to me, as if she considered her own grief to be on par with mine. There was one day when I actually felt like shaking her and saying, 'Being someone's coffee buddy is not the same as being her fucking daughter.' But I had the Healys and Mamie and some other friends from Dory to lean on, and I didn't think much more about it at the time."

I couldn't help but feel a fresh twinge of guilt, though I knew she hadn't meant to trigger it.

"Well, I'll fill you in on how it goes. And—and what if we had dinner together tonight? We don't have to go out. I'll pick stuff up and we can eat out here on the deck."

"That sounds nice," she said.

We'd actually spent little time together since we'd been here, and there was still a clunky feel to our encounters. I was hoping an evening together could start to smooth out the rough edges. Maybe our friendship would never be like it was in college, but there was potential for us to forge a new kind of connection.

After Jillian had returned to her room, I popped open my laptop, planning to work out on the deck rather than be cooped up in my room. The first thing I did was check the regional newspaper, *The Berkshire Eagle*. There was an item reporting that Penny Niles, age seventy-two, had been found dead in her home, an apparent suicide. Thankfully, it pointed out that police were still investigating.

Next, I sent a nudge-y text to my friend Jessie, reminding her I needed contact info for Julia's college roommate, and another text to the forensics expert I'd consulted before coming here, inquiring whether she could give me another ten minutes on the phone. I also finally emailed my father's cousin Candace, telling her I was in the area for a story and I hoped I might drop by after lunch to say hello. She wrote back almost immediately and asked me to come for lunch instead. Right now that sounded like heaven on earth.

With those tasks out of the way, I intensified my hunt for the elusive Eleanor Mercandetti. This time I paid a fee to dive deeper on the Internet. I turned up zilch.

Maybe it was my tendency to always go to the darkest explanation, but I couldn't help wonder if the former principal had *chosen* to be off the grid.

At nine forty-five I kicked off my tour of nail salons within a reasonable distance to Penny's home. A Google search had turned up three pretty close, one of which was in conjunction with a small spa. I started with the salon nearest to the Briar inn, announcing that I was reporter doing a story on a local woman who had died last night and may have been a customer earlier that day. Without even checking the schedule, the manger shook her head and said she'd never heard of anyone named Penny Niles. I stopped at the spa next, knowing it was a long shot because Penny hadn't seemed like the spa type, and sure enough, the receptionist claimed she'd never heard of her, either.

But the last spot, Lucky 6 Nails, a salon right in Carversville, proved to be true to its name. When I gave my spiel to a woman who I thought was the manager, hovering around the front of the establishment, it was clear from her expression—and the lack of surprise in it—that she knew both who Penny was and that she was now deceased.

"What kind of story?" she said, her back stiffening defensively. What did she think? That I was going to try to bust the salon by reporting that Penny may have died from inhaling toxic fumes from nail solvents?

"Simply a human-interest story. I heard she might have come in for a manicure yesterday."

She hesitated, clearly weighing whether it would be a mistake to open up to me.

"Yes, she was here," she said at last. "She came in every two to three weeks. A very nice lady."

So it wasn't a standing appointment. Maybe Penny hadn't liked to splurge on weekly manis and had stretched hers out as long as possible.

"Is it possible for me to speak to the woman who did her nails?"

Her eyes darted to the left and then quickly back. I realized she was wearing colored contact lenses, which gave her a *Children of the Corn* kind of stare.

"I'm afraid she isn't here today."

You're a lousy liar, I thought. I doubted the manicurist had anything to hide; the manager just didn't want me poking around.

"Um, that's a shame. I'd really like to touch base with her for the story. But you interacted with Ms. Niles yesterday, right?"

"Yes, for a minute."

"Did she seem like her usual self to you?"

"Maybe a little quiet. But she was never a gabber."

"Thanks, I appreciate it." I turned to go, then swung back around. "Just one more thing. When did Ms. Niles make the appointment?"

"She didn't make an appointment for yesterday, she dropped in. That's the way it usually worked with her. She came by when she was out doing errands."

It was such a small detail but an important one, and I sat for a few minutes in the car chewing it over in my mind. Penny had dropped in to have her nails done while running errands, which suggested that it was an ordinary kind of afternoon for her, and that she wasn't waiting around the house in despair, brooding about ending her life.

So maybe there *was* a killer out there, someone who felt threatened by the potential of Penny divulging a long-held secret. I felt my breath catch a little as the next thought formed in my mind: It might be the same person who had murdered the Lowes.

Time to alert Detective Maynard. I tapped on the number, which I'd already programmed into my phone.

"Maynard," he said bluntly.

I ran through the statement I'd rehearsed—that last night, after I'd decompressed a little, I recalled the discrepancy about Penny's nails. And not wanting to waste his time being wrong, I'd stopped by the local salon this morning to confirm that my observation was correct.

"*Whoa*, hold on just one minute," he said before the last words were barely out of my mouth.

Considering his tone, I was surprised he hadn't added *Little Missy* at the end. As expected, he hadn't liked what I'd been up to.

"Okay."

"Let's take this one step at a time. You're telling me you just happened to remember—hours later—that Ms. Niles's nails were different than earlier."

"Yes. I probably should have realized it at the time but I was pretty rattled."

He let that hang awkwardly in the air before his next comment.

"And then you went and interviewed someone on a matter of police business?"

"I only wanted to confirm my suspicions before I contacted you."

"The *police* do the confirming up here, Ms. Weggins. Is that understood?"

"Yes, yes it is."

I wondered briefly if I'd been stupid to go to the salons, but if I hadn't received confirmation on the manicure, Maynard might not have believed me. As always, better to beg forgiveness than ask permission.

Maynard demanded the name of the salon and then signed off with a blunt good-bye. I didn't have time to stew because my phone rang in my hand and I saw that Bonnie Peets, the forensics expert I'd left a message for, was returning my call.

"You still got stab wounds on your brain?"

"I'm still on that story, yes, but there's been a new

development." I described the scene I'd stumbled upon last night and asked if she thought it could have been faked.

"For sure. A perpetrator might have strangled her with the scarf or something else and then staged it to present as suicide. Anyone with a motive?"

"Yeah, maybe."

"Just be aware that short-drop hangings can seem unusual for suicide, but people choose that method for a reason. It's less painful than regular hanging. The ligature compresses the jugular veins, which are closer to the surface and softer than the carotid arteries. Blood continues to pump into the head through the carotids but can't get out because the jugular veins are closed. The pressure builds up in the head and the hypoxia causes a euphoric feeling. Eventually you black out and die."

"I hear what you're saying, but it still seems suspicious. There was no indication the victim had been depressed."

"Here's something else I've got to ask you. The technique for short-drop hanging is the same for something called autoerotic asphyxiation, which people used to enhance orgasm—you've heard of that, right?"

"Yes, but trust me, I've never tried it personally. And I don't think this woman was the type, either."

"The ME should be able to make a determination easily enough. For one thing, if this lady was murdered, there won't be any fibers from the scarf on her hands."

I thanked Bonnie for her help and signed off. It was finally time for my interview with Jocelyn, and I could feel my pulse picking up in anticipation.

She'd suggested a coffeehouse on Main Street in Dory, just a short drive from where I was at the moment. Entering the white clapboard building a few minutes later, I saw that it was part café, part bookstore, selling what a sign called "gently used" volumes. In the front of the space was a cluster of saggy, cracked leather armchairs, already occupied, and in the rear, about a dozen white wooden tables.

The only person alone in the back room was a woman in her early fifties, her expression solemn. I figured she was too young to be Jocelyn—it would have meant she was probably only in her late thirties when she knew Claire—but she raised her chin in a kind of signal as she saw me searching.

"Yes, I'm Jocelyn," she acknowledged when I inquired. Not even a hint of a smile. "Why don't you sit down? My husband is picking me up in a half hour but I have until then."

"I appreciate the time," I said, slipping into the chair across from her and pulling out my notebook. "And so does Jillian."

She was super slim and straight-backed, with shoulder-length brunette hair that curled a little at the ends. Elegant looking. Attractive, too, though her features were sharp and not what you'd ever deem pretty. She wore a gray silk blouse, and, from what I could see beneath the table, a pair of flowy black pants. An unexpected choice, it seemed, for a lazy weekend morning, and yet it fit with the overall sophisticated vibe she gave off.

"Frankly, I was surprised to learn Jillian was writing a memoir," she said. "Why go over such painful ground again?"

Nothing about her tone suggested the least bit of sympathy. Jillian was right about her.

"It's actually been therapeutic for her to go through the process, and, who knows, in the end she may not even try to publish it."

Jocelyn shrugged. "Well if it works for her, who am I to judge?"

"She tells me that you and her mom were great friends."

"Yes, Claire was a wonderful friend," she said,

though there was little warmth to her tone. "The best anyone could ever hope for."

She had, I could see, one of those resting bitch faces, or maybe what you'd called a resting *grump* face, the expression in repose of someone who'd had her share of dreams denied or thwarted. Her clothes and her level of poise suggested she had money, but that clearly hadn't been enough.

"How long had you known each other?"

"About three years."

"Oh. I assumed it must have been longer than that."

"I'd only lived here for a year when Claire and I met. My husband and I had moved from Boston. The Lowes had been here longer, of course. About a dozen years at that point."

"Oh, I wasn't aware Jillian wasn't born here. We haven't talked about the early years yet."

"They moved here from Virginia, from just outside of Washington. Carl was in real estate development in that area as well, but from what Claire told me, the market softened and he thought there was more opportunity in this part of the country. They decided to make the move before Jillian needed to start school."

"I take it Claire was a very loving mother."

Jocelyn took a drink from the nearly empty cappuccino cup that sat in front of her, and when she finished, she dabbed lightly at her mouth with a napkin, aiming at foam that wasn't there.

"Claire was devoted to her kids," she said, fixing her dark brown eyes on me for the first time. "She missed working—she'd loved being in the ER—but because Julia had so many health issues early on, she decided it was best to be home. What I admired about her was the fact that she never put the other two kids in the backseat, which can happen when one child has any kind of issue."

"You have kids yourself, right?"

"Yes, two girls. My oldest was in Danny's grade."

"Is that how you met? Through the kids?"

"Our kids didn't interact much. Claire and I became close through volunteering at the school."

I'd planned to work my way to the subject of school, but good, we were already there.

"Speaking of school, maybe you can help solve a mystery for us. Jillian believes there may have been a problem with the school, something very upsetting. Julia got wind of it that final winter."

The last time I'd covered this terrain with someone, her response had startled me, and less than ten hours later she was dead. I waited on alert, my gaze locked on Jocelyn in anticipation.

She lifted her torso slightly and I saw her nostrils flare.

"Oh, there was a problem all right," she said. "It's amazing how evil some women can be."

Chapter 9

I felt my heart jerk as the word *evil* spilled from her lips.

"Are you talking about the *principal?*" I asked.

Jocelyn narrowed her eyes, clearly confused by the question. "The principal? No, not her. Though she certainly didn't help the situation."

"Please, tell me then."

"I'm talking about two women who made Claire's life miserable. When I first joined the parent liaison committee, it was run by Claire and made up of about twenty other women. We worked really nicely together, dealing with the kind of things you'd expect—bullying, cell phone use in school . . . Claire, by the way, was also chair of the fund-raising committee, and she helped raise a ton of money for the school."

"She was at the school a lot?"

"Yes. She worked her butt off, but she loved it, and since Julia was stronger by then, she had more time for it. About a year after I became involved, two new mothers joined the group. One was from Manhattan and the other, I think, from Boston, both charming and extremely wealthy, and they'd managed to bond together by the time they started coming to meetings, probably over their taste in Bottega Veneta handbags. Before long, they began exerting themselves, like a couple of alpha females. For everything we suggested, they had a *better* idea, and some of their suggestions were outright ridiculous. At one point they advocated that everything sold at the school bake sale had to be *home-baked*, as if it was a crime for a working mother to buy cake from a shop if she didn't have time to make one from scratch."

"This upset Claire?"

"It upset *a lot* of us. At first Claire tried to be diplomatic, make them see that everyone's opinion mattered. But those two were sly. They started inviting some of the other mothers to fancy brunches, winning them over."

"And then something happened?" *Please*, I thought, *tell me.*

"Yes. The two ringleaders completely muscled Claire out of her leadership role in our committee, and her fund-raising efforts as well. They took it over for themselves."

She had started to lose me. I didn't see what all this was adding up to.

"And the principal? She didn't do anything?"

"I don't think she liked what was going on, but she told Claire and me that to a large degree, her hands were tied. She didn't feel it was appropriate for her to intervene with a parent committee."

"But did something *happen*? Was there ever any kind of showdown?"

"No, nothing like that. Claire would never have made a scene. She pretty much withdrew from volunteer work and wasn't involved with the school after that, except superficially."

This surely couldn't be what I was looking for. It apparently had occurred months before Jillian's phone conversation with Danny.

"Could there have been something else, Jocelyn? Something involving the school in the weeks right before the murders?"

"Not that I was aware of."

"Nothing with Danny? Did anyone ever mention another kid bullying him?"

"Danny? My lord, no. He was one of the most popular kids."

I wondered if she'd heard about Penny and whether I should raise the topic but quickly decided not to, knowing it might muddy the conversation. I realized at that moment that the waiter had never dropped by to take an order from me; I let that go, too.

"What about in other areas of Claire's life?" I asked.

"I thought this was supposed to be for a memoir about Jillian's life in more recent years. How she's coped."

"Yes, that's true, but she wants the book to address some of the unanswered questions she has. I imagine you've heard about Dylan Fender? That there's good reason to believe he was innocent."

"I've heard, yes," she said grimly. "I feel dreadful for him if that's the case, but of course, in the end, it changes nothing about what happened that night."

I doubt Dylan Fender's mother would share that sentiment.

"No, but it means the real killer is still out there."

"I don't think I can be of any help to you. I was in Maine when Claire died—I'd been there since the first of April, helping my sister through her early rounds of chemo. Claire and I spoke on the phone a few times but only briefly, so if there was a problem, I wasn't aware of it."

"Carl's old business partner told me that Carl had

seemed bothered by something during the weeks leading up to the murders—and that he'd had an argument
with a strange man in his office. Does any of that ring
a bell?"

"No." She lifted her chin ever so slightly. "And besides, I wouldn't necessarily believe everything Bruce
Kordas has to say."

From near my feet, I heard my phone buzz in my
purse. I knew the call might be important—perhaps
Detective Maynard following up—but I ignored it,
worried about interrupting the flow, what there was
of it.

"And why is that?"

"He always seemed so *slick* to me. Claire said that
Carl considered him a real asset to the business—a
total rainmaker—but she found him more charm than
smarts, and she hated the way he pressured Carl into
letting his stepson come on board. The whole thing
was absurd. A thirty-five-year-old man with a stepson
just a few years younger than he was."

"Wait—the stepson worked for the business?" I said,
taken aback. I flashed on the nearly platinum-haired
dude I'd seen pulling into the Kordases' drive, who
I'd figured would have been in his twenties sixteen
years ago.

"Only for a short time. They had to let him go."

"When *was* this?"

"I'm not sure exactly. But it was definitely that winter."

"Did—"

"Look I really don't think it's my role to be rehashing old gossip," Jocelyn said, not disguising her exasperation. "This is really a matter for the police."

Her gaze shot from my eyes to a spot just above my head.

"Besides," she added, "my husband's here to pick me up."

I turned, almost without thinking, and looked back through the doorway into the front room. A tall, stocky man had his hand raised in greeting.

"Please, just one more question, for Jillian's sake," I pleaded. "Was Claire Lowe having an affair at the time of her death?"

The question had come out more bluntly than I'd intended, and Jocelyn's back stiffened again.

"Where did you hear that?" she said, her voice nearly in a whisper.

"Jillian had her suspicions. She remembers her mother seeming secretive over the holidays."

"If you're asking me if there was another man in Claire's life, the answer is no, absolutely not. That wasn't Claire."

"Is it something she might have kept from you—because she was ashamed?"

"Asked and answered."

Heavy footsteps approached, and seconds later Jocelyn's husband sidled up to the table, with the sure but understated force of a powerboat nosing its way into a slip. The guy was even burlier than he'd seemed from a distance, not exactly overweight but with a barrel chest and thick legs that let him own any space he stood in. And not what I would have imagined as a romantic match for Jocelyn. In fact, she didn't even offer him a smile.

"Bob London," he said, shooting out a hand the size of a catcher's mitt for me to shake. His clothes—dark slacks, dress shirt, and navy blazer—were on the dressy side, just like Jocelyn's, which suggested they were off somewhere a bit fancy from here.

I gave my name and started to rise, but he motioned for me to stop.

"Please, sit," he said, and glanced at his wife with his droopy, kind of hangdog brown eyes. "Do you ladies need a few more minutes?"

"We're all set," Jocelyn announced coolly before I could take him up on his offer.

"I was hoping Jillian might be here," Bob said. "How's she doing anyway?"

"Fairly well. She's worked hard to build a new life for herself."

"Well, please tell her that she's still in our hearts and prayers. . . . You ready, honey?"

Nodding without expression, Jocelyn rose from the table, black clutch in hand. Bob loosened a ten and a twenty from a silver money clip and tossed it on the table, saying he thought it should be enough.

Jocelyn's demeanor was slightly warmer when she said good-bye, and she asked that I give her regards to Jillian, though she hadn't asked a damn thing about her. I watched as her husband pressed a beefy hand against her back and guided her out of the café.

It was only when I stooped to pick up my purse from the floor that a waitress finally materialized.

"Oh, sweetheart," she said. "Sorry, I never swung by to take your order."

I told her it wasn't a problem, though by now I felt in dire need of caffeine. Since there was enough cash on the table to cover it, I ordered a cappuccino to go.

Back in my car, with the drink parked in the cup holder, I quickly fleshed out the notes I'd scribbled down during the conversation, making sure I left nothing out. I took a few more minutes to try to digest them, but I didn't feel I ended up with a good read on Jocelyn. Though she'd been forthcoming at moments, she was, for the most part, stingy with information, and I wasn't sure why. As Jillian had mentioned, she came across as emotionally stingy, too, a cool, uncomforting creature—though that flew in the face of her professed closeness with Claire.

And then there was her comment about Claire's fidelity; I wasn't buying it. Her denial, along with the stiffened back, had been more than defensive, a perfect candidate for the thou-doth-protest-too-much category. I sensed she'd been privy to something but wasn't about to confess. It occurred to me that part of the reason she'd overseen the storage-unit operation years ago might have been so Jillian wouldn't stumble on anything she wasn't meant to see.

It was all worth further exploration, though I wasn't sure where to start. Sixteen years had passed, and the trail to an old lover would probably be stone-cold. I could see if there were other friends of Claire's I could talk to, but from what Jillian had indicated, no one had been as close to her mother as Jocelyn.

It would make sense, I realized, to scour Claire's calendar again. If she'd strayed, she may have noted her assignations in an abbreviated manner, or even a code that I hadn't picked up on the first time I looked through.

There was one thing, though, I *did* have to show for

my efforts, and that was the tidbit about Kordas's stepson. There was more than a chance he'd held a grudge
over being terminated, and it was also possible Julia
would have allowed him entry into the house because
of his relationship to her father's business partner.

This was another reason I needed to speak to Carl
Lowe's former secretary. She might be able to provide
insight not only on the angry mystery man but also on
the stepson's brief tenure at the company. Hopefully
Jillian had managed to turn up contact info for her.

Though the conversation with Jocelyn had opened a
door about the stepson, it had proved to be a dead end
in terms of what I was most hungry to learn: what had
happened with the principal close to the time of the
murders. I needed to talk to Mercandetti directly. On
Monday, I'd return to the school and hopefully the assistant principal would be over her head cold.

Before taking off, I checked my cell phone. The
missed call had been from Jessie.

"Hey, sorry it took me so long to reach you," she
said after I'd dialed her back. "I was out of town someplace with shitty cell service."

It was good to hear her voice. Jessie and I had hit it
off from the moment I started at *Buzz* magazine, but in
the nearly three years since I'd left, we'd become even
closer.

"No problem. Do you mind looking up the info?"

"I already did. I'll text it to you."

"You found her then?"

"Yup. She lives in Manhattan and works for a PR company here, though the contact number in the alumni directory was for a cell. You working on a big story?"

"Sort of. I'm in the Berkshires right now. Why don't we grab a drink when I'm back and I'll fill you in?"

"Sounds good."

"Where were you this week? I thought your vacation wasn't until September."

"I ended up going with Jason to the Adirondacks for a few days, to a fishing camp his parents have up there. Finally got to meet them."

"Wow, the parents. How was it?"

"Kind of like a scene from *Survivor*. Muggy, lots of black flies. The parents are nice enough but super L.L. Bean types. The kind of people who wear fishing vests even when they're not fishing. When I told them I was working on a Taylor Swift story, they had no clue who she was."

"Well, the last time I had dinner with Beau's parents, his mother asked if my work gave me nightmares."

"That woman is a piece of work. Speaking of Beau, I saw him roaming around midtown right before lunch yesterday. I yelled to him, but he was too far away to hear me."

"Oh, that couldn't have been him. He's in Miami. He left yesterday morning."

"His doppelgänger then. Call me when you get back, okay? I'll text you the info right now."

"Great. I owe you one. And needless to say, unless she resorts to waterboarding, I'll never tell who spilled the number."

After hanging up, I waited for the text and immediately dialed Amber Tresslar's number. I'd already decided to use a straightforward approach with her, thinking that would serve me better in this instance, and besides, there was no reason to disguise my true objective. I reached her voice mail and left a message explaining that I was a good friend of Julia Lowe's sister and that I was hoping we could speak.

Next I checked in with Jillian to see how she was faring. She said that she spent the morning at the inn, but was definitely going to shadow Blake again in the afternoon.

It hit me at that moment that I needed to reevaluate whether I ought to be encouraging Jillian to stick around. Yes, it was good to have her at the inn, but I hadn't delegated as much research to her as I'd anticipated, mainly because her only remaining contact in the area was Mamie.

And, more important, if Penny's death was indeed a homicide, Jillian's life might be in danger. It was probably best to send her back to New York and check in regularly by phone.

"Good," I said, "I know you enjoyed that. By the way, any leads on your father's secretary?"

"Unfortunately, no. I looked through some old notes on my computer to see if I might have it—or the name of anyone else who once worked there—but I came up empty-handed. Even if I turned up her name, it might not do any good. I remember now that she was engaged back then, so she might use her husband's name these days."

"Okay, we'll have to try another approach. Speaking of your father's company, do you recall Bruce Kordas's stepson working there for a while?"

"What? I mean, I know he has a stepson, but I never heard anything about him working for the company. When was *this*?"

"Jocelyn said it was that last winter, and only for a brief time. Then he was let go."

I heard an intake of breath. "Omigod, he had a motive. Do you think it's him?"

"There's no major reason to consider him a suspect at this point, but he has to be checked out."

"There was always something *creepy* about him. His name is Trevor, I think, but Julia called him Vlad because his skin was so pale."

"She knew him?" The thought made my pulse quicken.

"I don't think so. I mean, at least not any more than I did. But we saw him at things from time to time—like the holiday party. He was just a little older than we were. Bailey, what if he did it?"

"Like I said, I need to check him out. He might have been really pissed about being canned."

I reminded her of our plan for dinner and promised to meet her on the deck around seven thirty.

The call over, I sensed how tense I now was. It was partly from nearly mainlining the cappuccino but also from considering the words I'd heard in conjunction with Trevor, particularly *creepy* and *fired*. That was a combo often attached to people who went postal.

So how was I going to find anything of value about Trevor? Call Bruce Kordas, I told myself, though I'd have to proceed carefully in regard to his stepson. A second conversation would also offer the opportunity to ask about Carl's secretary.

To my surprise, he took the call, answering after the second ring with a brusque "Kordas."

"Mr. Kordas, it's Bailey Weggins. Jillian was very appreciative of the time you gave me this week, but I had a few follow-up questions. Can we meet briefly today?"

"Not possible, I'm afraid. It may be Saturday, but I've got back-to-back meetings."

"How about tomorrow?"

"I have a few social engagements, and then I have to run out to one of my new sites."

"What if I dropped by the site?" I said, pulling the idea out of my ass. "I promise it will only take a few minutes, and it would mean so much to Jillian."

I was probably overplaying the Jillian card, but I couldn't let him blow me off.

"All right," he said finally, his voice tinged with minor frustration. "I'll be through around six. The site's called Foxcroft, and it's about fifteen miles from where my house is, off Route 519. I'll text you directions."

"Can I just drive onto the site?"

"Yup. I'll meet you in front of the first group of houses you spot once you've entered there. Look for my car. It's a Baltic-blue Porsche."

Well, wasn't *that* special.

"Got it. See you then."

For the time being I was in a bit of a holding pattern—waiting to hear from Amber, waiting for the school to open up again on Monday, waiting for my meeting with Kordas. A perfect time for lunch with Candace.

The thought of finally seeing her filled me with pleasure, and not simply because I found her so engaging. She was the last living relative on my father's side, and being around her always made me feel connected to him.

The two of them had been in no way alike. My father was an engineer, kind and charming in his own quiet way but often lost in his thoughts, and sometimes brisk in manner, unless he was sitting in a rowboat with you on a summer day and waiting for the catfish to bite.

Candace, on the other hand, was very much an earth mother, vivacious and spirited, forever eager to hear details about any dragons you might be facing and then offering guidance on how to slay them. Though she was in her late sixties, she still wore her blond-gray hair long and favored flowy skirts and tank tops that nicely played up her full figure. She was almost always tanned. For years she had worked in management at one of the famous inns in the area but was now retired.

Despite their differences, she and my father had been extra-ordinarily close. Their families spent summers together at my grandparents' lake house in New Hampshire, a place my two brothers and I later came to adore.

Candace had never married. She'd been engaged back in her mid-twenties, but her fiancé had been killed in a car crash, hit by a drunk driver while en route to their rehearsal dinner. In time, Candace seemed to find joy in life again, but she never became seriously involved with anyone else, at least to my knowledge. Deep down I suspected she still longed for the man she had hoped to marry.

When I walked up the front steps of her gray cedar-shingled house, I saw that the front door was open in anticipation of my arrival. The sight unsettled me. It was all too much like yesterday, with me standing by the open door to Penny Niles's house.

"Come in, come in," Candace called from within the house. "I was just finishing up a call."

As I stepped inside the foyer, I heard her coming through the living room, the swish of whatever colorful skirt she had on that day.

Her appearance was a total shock. She weighed easily twenty-five pounds less than when I'd last seen her, and her hair was cropped incredibly short, almost like a man's. My first ridiculous thought was that she'd decided to reinvent herself, and then a smarter part of my brain foisted the truth on me: she'd been ill.

We hugged hello and then I stepped back.

"Okay, what's going on?"

"Oh, sweetie, I love the way you never beat around the bush."

"Candace, please, what is it?"

She shrugged. "It's a story even I can't put a fresh spin on. Breast cancer. They recommended the trifecta, which I went for: mastectomy, chemo, and radiation. So far the news is all good."

"But why didn't you saying anything?" I said, feeling my stomach turn over at the news.

"I know it sounds slightly counterintuitive, but I honestly discovered that the less I spoke about it, the better I felt. My hope was that if people did manage to find out, they'd understand my reticence."

"And not even my mom knows?"

"No, I didn't want to trouble her."

I wondered if that last line was code for *I wouldn't have told your mother something like this anyway.* For a reason unbeknownst to me, my mother's relationship with Candace had cooled over the years.

"Okay, I'm going to honor your wishes and not discuss it."

"Good. Have you had lunch? I've got homemade chicken salad and early tomatoes from my own garden."

"That sounds divine."

I followed her through the house to the kitchen, a total delight for the eyes. Cherries overflowed a wooden bowl on the table, tomatoes lined the windowsill, and gauzy white curtains rustled in the breeze. The air was redolent with the scent of lavender. Though the room had more charm than Penny's kitchen, the size and shape were similar, and I found myself dragged back to that other space, to the chilling sight of Penny on her knees. I had to do everything in my power to banish the image.

Once Candace had served the salad, I had a chance to catch up on her life. Lately she'd been busy gardening and taking long walks. Now that she was done with chemo, she was planning to travel again. And she sometimes filled in at the front desk of the inn, just to give herself something to do.

"But enough about me, for God's sake," she said, topping off our glasses with more sparkling water. "You said you're up here on a story. Tell me about it."

I took her through the broad outlines of the tragedy, the wrongful conviction, and the role I was playing under the flimsy guise of memoirist.

"That was such a horrible case," Candace said. "People still speak of it."

My ears pricked. "Anything of note?"

"No, mainly they wonder how the surviving sister fared. She obviously inherited a great deal of money but that could never begin to compensate."

Before I had a chance to respond, my phone rang from the spot where I'd laid it on the table. A number with a local area code appeared on the screen.

"Do you mind if I grab this?" I said, and stepped into the small dining room off her kitchen before answering.

"Ms. Weggins?" The voice was female and firm. "This is First District Attorney Belinda Bacon. You've been quite a busy lady, haven't you?"

Oh great. Detective Maynard, he of the "I-am-the-Walrus" mustache and kick-some-ass boots had clearly squealed on me.

"I'm not sure what you mean exactly," I said.

"What I mean is that you've been trotting around the area playing detective, which is *not* your job."

"I did turn over some information to Detective Maynard, but I was simply trying to be helpful. I thought it was odd that Penny Niles's nails were freshly painted and I wondered if she might not have actually committed suicide."

"Is that right? I think the two of us should have a little talk later today."

Why the need to see me in person? And on a *Saturday.* I wondered. Maybe she was the kind of official who derived her kicks from watching you grimace as she administered a verbal spanking.

"I'm happy to drop by. Is there anything specific you want to discuss?"

"I'm in Pittsfield, at Forty-Four Beech. On the third floor. See you at four."

Okay, I got it. Something was up; I could feel it. Maybe she just wanted to call me in for a face-to-face reprimand for going on a nail salon crawl without permission, but it might be more than that. As soon as I hung up, I searched the *Berkshire Eagle* website for any update on Penny. And there it was.

According to an insider tip, Penny Niles's death was being ruled a homicide.

Chapter 10

My breath froze in my chest. So Penny *hadn't* committed suicide. I felt no satisfaction from having guessed right, only a twinge of nausea at the news. Someone had overpowered Penny, terrified her, choked her to death—and I might be partly to blame. I resumed reading the short item and the last detail caught me by surprise. It stated that death had occurred during the commission of a burglary. Jewelry had been stolen and her wallet was missing from her purse. *Huh?* Had someone simply staged the burglary?

I didn't mean to but I sighed audibly as I walked back into the kitchen.

"Is everything okay?" Candace asked.

"Something isn't making sense to me, but maybe it will in time."

"Will one of these help?" Candace asked, offering a plate of brownies.

"Beyond belief."

"You've talked about your work, but give me an update on the *rest* of your life."

I shared what my two brothers were up to and the fact that my mother was teaching two college business courses in Nigeria this summer, a detail Candace wasn't aware of.

"And how about that guy of yours?" she asked.

"Beau's doing well. We seem to have a pretty good thing going."

Her lips parted and I flinched inside at what I assumed was coming next, some variation of "Are you two thinking of getting married one day?" That question always irritated the hell out of me, even when coming from people as lovely as Candace, because it assumed that relishing life together in a nice apartment in Chelsea was not enough.

"That's wonderful, Bailey," she said instead. "*Savor* it."

There seemed to be so much packed into those two little words. I wondered if the sentiment sprang from her past tragedy and was another way of stating "You never know what fate has in store, so cherish every minute you spend together."

"I will, I promise."

"What?" She obviously had seen my brow wrinkle as I'd spoken.

"Oh, nothing earth-shaking. But Beau seems a bit frustrated with my work these days. I'm apparently scaring his pants off."

"Isn't that a good thing?" she said, smiling.

"Ha, yes, in some circumstances. But I hate feeling apologetic about what I do."

Candace looked off and chuckled. "You know, Bailey, I suddenly have this vivid memory of you from the days when we were all at the lake house. You were about eleven then. While most of the kids liked hide-and-seek, you loved the game sardines—the one that starts with one player hiding, and as each person finds him, they hide in the same spot, too. The last person is the loser. Remember that? You told me once that you got such a rush out of searching and coming across a whole pack of kids squeezed together in a hiding place."

"You think I should suggest a game of sardines to Beau?"

She laughed. "No, but he has to understand that about you. You've always loved searching. That's who you are."

I nodded, weighing her words. That *was* who I was.

I finished my brownie and glanced at my watch. I had only an hour before I was supposed to meet with Belinda Bacon, and I wanted a little time to suss out what I could about her. I explained to Candace that as much as I hated to split, I had an appointment I couldn't be late for.

"Of course," she said. "It was wonderful to spend this much time with you." She nodded at the stainless steel Rolex on my wrist, her expression suddenly wistful. "You still wear your dad's watch, I see."

My mother had given it to me after he died, rather than one of my brothers, because she knew I'd associate the wonderfully durable and waterproof watch with all the hikes and fishing trips my father had taken me on.

"Yeah, it's practically glued to my arm."

Candace walked me to the door, and I promised that before I left the area, I'd drop by again or grab coffee in town with her.

"And please," I said, "if there's any change in your health, would you be willing to make an exception and let me know?"

"For you, Bailey, yes," she said warmly.

As soon as I was in the car, I reread the *Berkshire Eagle* article on Penny. I could feel the word *huh?* forming once again in a thought bubble above my head. This news wasn't making sense to me.

I tapped on the photo icon and scrolled through to the pictures I'd snapped in Penny's kitchen. With the exception of the horrific disruption in the room created by her dead body, there was no other hint of disarray, at least in the kitchen. Of course, the jewelry would have probably been in the bedroom upstairs, and so that room might have been a mess. Still, this whole theory wasn't sitting well with me—for a bunch of reasons.

First of all, from what I knew from research, most burglars have zero interest in encountering a home-owner. That's why they generally break in during the day, when people are working, or in the middle of the night, when the residents are asleep and less likely to hear a window being punched out or a screen slit with a knife. If someone had wanted to rob Penny, why would they do it in the *early* evening? Her house was small, and a burglar could have easily seen her through the front window and known that she was up and about.

Second, why would a burglar feel a need to kill her? She hadn't looked like the kind of woman who would want to kick serious ass if confronted with a home inva-sion. She would've probably cowered and encouraged the thief to take whatever he wanted.

Last—and most significant—why would the killer go to the trouble of staging a suicide, especially since he'd apparently left evidence that he'd absconded with her jewelry and cash?

Were we supposed to believe that this was some crazy brand of house burglar/sadist killer? It seemed more likely that someone had murdered Penny, staged it as a suicide, and then, in a frantic moment, tried to make it also appear to be a burglary to confuse the hell out of law enforcement.

Regardless of what was really going on, I needed to update Jillian on this new development. I shot her a link to the *Berkshire Eagle* story, adding that I had my own thoughts and would share over dinner.

I was still parked in front of Candace's house, and suddenly my gaze was drawn to her front door like a force field. Despite my misgivings about what the police were reporting, they had far more to go on than I did, and they could very well be right about the burglary. If someone was breaking into the homes of older women in the area, Candace was at risk.

I jumped out of the car, bolted across the lawn, and jabbed at the bell.

"Did you forget something, sweetie?" she said after swinging open the door.

"No, but there's news I need to fill you in on." I told her about the death two towns away and advised her to be extra cautious. The information clearly disturbed her, but I didn't regret sharing what happened. I hugged her for the third time that afternoon and promised to check in later.

The GPS indicated that the trip to Pittsfield would be about twenty-five minutes, and that left me enough time to grab a cup of coffee at the McDonald's drive-through and chill with it for fifteen minutes in the municipal building parking lot. It was an older building that looked like it had been around for at least a century. I wondered if they kept a vat of hot oil boiling in the basement for troublemakers like me.

While I sipped my coffee, I did an Internet dive on Belinda Bacon, turning up not only several news items about cases she'd prosecuted, but also four or five YouTube videos of her at press conferences. Three facts became clear immediately.

1. The woman liked to talk tough.

2. She wore mostly dark suits, with the collar of her blouse layered over the blazer collar, a fashion trend that, from what I knew, was last popular in the 1970s, and embodied primarily by John Travolta in *Saturday Night Fever.*

3. She seemed about as much fun as a bone saw.

I would need to mind my p's and q's today.

Bacon unfortunately didn't do much to help in that regard. After speaking to me briefly, she kept me waiting for close to half an hour in the empty reception area, the same move she'd pulled on Jillian. Since the ancient-looking AC window unit had the cooling effect of a snap-on fan, my top was damp with sweat by the time I was ushered into Bacon's inner sanctum. And I was feeling the tiniest bit snarky.

My bad mood was intensified by the fact she didn't even apologize for the delay.

Her appearance was pretty much the same as it was in the videos, though she'd cut her brunette hair a few inches and added henna-like highlights, which made it look like she'd rolled her head around on a clay tennis court. She was wearing a dark blue shirt today and, in typical fashion for her, had layered the collar over her dark gray suit jacket. The color combo gave her the appearance of a giant bruise—though the set of her mouth suggested that if anyone were going to be smarting when we finished, it would be me.

"Have a seat," she commanded.

I slid into the chair directly across from her and waited for her to lob the first ball.

"So you're a *mem-oir-ist*," she said, drawing out

each syllable in a mocking way. "Who else have you collaborated with?"

"This is the first memoir I've worked on, actually. Mostly I report on crime and human-interest stories." I added that last part knowing that she had probably already checked me out and was only feigning ignorance.

"Switching gears then?"

"Jillian Lowe is an old friend and she asked me to work with her on it. I've been interviewing people from Jillian's past, like Penny Niles. Is it true what the paper says—that Penny Niles was murdered?"

She didn't answer, just bore through me with her eyes.

"So tell me. Why would a *mem-oir-ist* feel the need to go to a nail salon and confirm that a dead woman had been there earlier in the day prior to her death?"

"As I mentioned on the phone to you, there was an odd discrepancy I felt I should alert the police to, but before I called Detective Maynard, I wanted to be a hundred percent sure I was remembering correctly."

"Is that so? You didn't think the police were capable of going to the salon?"

"I was just trying to do the right thing. It was nothing more than that."

Bacon drummed her fingers on the desk.

"More important," she said, "why would a so-called

mem-oir-ist show up to interview someone at ten o'clock at night, particularly after she'd already been there once that day?"

Careful, I told myself. I'd be walking a fine line here. I didn't want to give any indication I was looking into the Lowe murders, and yet on the other hand, I wanted to be sure she had all the relevant information in relation to Penny's death.

"Just for the record, it was actually nine thirty. Something about my earlier interview with Ms. Niles really concerned me, and I couldn't get my mind off it. Jillian Lowe had told me that during the week prior to the murders, her mother and sister were apparently upset about an issue regarding the school, but she didn't know what it was, and when I asked Penny Niles if *she* knew, she became alarmed but didn't say why. I decided to drive back and see if I could convince her to tell me."

Bacon had one elbow on her old wooden desk and she rested her head on her fist, staring hard at me. "Sounds to me as if you're trying to investigate the Lowe murders. Wearing your famous crime writer cap."

"Jillian just wanted the mystery about the school solved. She's been pulling thoughts and memories together about her life, trying to make sense of everything." I paused, picking my words. "But if I stumble onto anything about the murders, what harm would there be in that? I might be able to offer you valuable information."

"The harm would be that it's not your job to investigate those murders, which by the way resulted in a conviction that still stands. Nor should you be meddling into the investigation of Penny Niles's death. Am I making myself clear?"

She'd lowered her voice slightly to deliver the last line, which I assumed was a trick she'd devised over the years to make statements all the more intimidating.

I knew she was simply doing her job, and that as a first assistant district attorney, she had to play it tough. Plus, once she'd discovered that I was a crime writer, she'd clearly pegged me as a possible nuisance, someone who might disrupt the investigation. But what I didn't get was why, as I sat across from her acting perfectly cooperative and looking about as subversive as a pair of mom jeans, she had to take her hard-ass act to this level.

But I couldn't let her work her way under my skin. My focus had to be on reinforcing the idea that I wasn't meddling in a no-meddling zone, while at the same time somehow encouraging her to look deeper into Penny's death and not dismiss it as the result of a burglary.

"Yes, of course," I told her. "I can understand your concerns. I shouldn't have gone to the nail salon, and I apologize for that."

She gazed at me expectantly, shrewd enough to sense I wasn't finished.

"Do you mind me asking a question?" I said. "Assuming the newspaper is correct and Penny Niles was actually murdered during a burglary, I'm curious if there have been any other burglaries involving older women in the area?"

"Why should that matter to you if you're not playing amateur investigator?"

"Jillian was very upset about the death, as I was. Initially we assumed it was linked somehow to her family, because otherwise it's a very odd coincidence. If there *have* been a string of burglaries—or there's nothing in Penny's phone records indicating she made any significant calls after I visited her—we'd be eager to hear, just to put our minds at rest."

I saw Bacon's nostrils flare. Clearly I was irritating the hell out of the woman.

"Ms. Weggins," she said, straightening up in her seat and smoothing down her blazer with both hands, "if you interfere again with official business, I'm going to have the police issue a ticket citing you for obstruction of justice."

So she was threatening to ticket me simply for asking questions. That pissed me off.

"You're speaking about the Niles case, right?" I said.

"I'm speaking about *both* cases. About what transpired last night *and* the murder of the Lowes."

"From what I've heard, the Lowe case is still closed," I said rising from my seat. "So there's actually no police business to interfere with in that regard. . . . Have a good day."

As I turned on my heels, I could almost feel Bacon bristling behind me, and I was afraid if I turned around, she might try to set my hair on fire with her gaze.

Buckling my seat belt a few minutes later, I realized that my parting shot wasn't going to help a thing, but at least I'd managed, during the course of our brief conversation, to drop a hint about checking Penny's phone logs—on the off chance the police hadn't already done that. If she'd been murdered in relation to the secret about the school, she must have called someone.

On the drive back, I picked up cheese, bread, olives, salami, and homemade hummus at a fancy farm stand and a bottle of Chianti at a wine shop.

Things seemed to be bustling at the inn when I arrived. Several couples, who looked to be in their sixties or seventies, had congregated in the parlor, and as

I passed down the hall I could overhear them swapping details about the antiques they'd haggled over that afternoon.

After returning to my room, I stuffed the more perishable food into the little fridge, and paced the room. I still felt agitated from my meeting with Bacon, but even more from the story in the paper. Why would a burglar leave evidence of his presence but then stage a suicide?

There was also the coincidence factor to consider. Buddy, my old reporter pal with the epic nose hairs, had an interesting view on that subject. "Coincidence my ass," he'd say profoundly whenever someone tried to suggest one was in play. Like me, he would have found it far-fetched to believe that Penny happened to be burgled just hours after my fraught interview with her—and he would have considered the police stupid for thinking so.

But maybe I was underestimating the cops. Maynard, for one, seemed like a smart guy, and the police could have leaked the "apparent burglary" line to force the murderer's guard down, to make him think his ploy had worked. I could only hope so.

Weary of pacing, I trudged to the bathroom and drew a bath, not even bothering with the lavender bath gel on the counter. When the water had filled the tub,

I lowered myself in, with my body practically moaning in gratitude. I was more wiped than I realized.

Despite the pleasures a hot bath had to offer, I could feel regret finally sneaking up on me, like a kitty cat creeping through the grass. I should never have mouthed off to Bacon. I couldn't make that mistake again.

I also realized it was time for a shift in focus. The school issue that Penny had been unwilling to disclose might indeed be a bombshell, but there was a chance it had nothing whatsoever to do with the deaths of Carl, Claire, Julia, and Danny. I still hoped to speak to Mercandetti—and on Monday I'd try to convince the assistant principal to provide me with the number— but I had to prevent myself from ending up in the weeds.

Tomorrow I'd have the chance to speak with Kordas again, and that would ideally provide me with insight into the stepson and possibly a lead on Carl's secretary. I'd hopefully hear back from Julia's former roommate, Amber, and if not, I'd keep phoning till I reached her.

Spelling out my game plan in my head left me wondering what came afterward. I was counting on one of these steps leading somewhere else—that, for instance, by snagging a contact number for C.J. Lowe's secretary, I'd learn more about the angry mystery man and why the stepson had been canned.

But what if they were all dead ends? Then what? I needed something substantial enough to turn over to Jillian, who could then present it to either the innocence group or the cops. There had to be *something*. I couldn't help feeling that there were connections between things that I just wasn't seeing yet.

I hauled myself out of the tub. It was now close to seven thirty and before going down to claim a table on the deck, I wanted to check in with Beau. My call went straight to voice mail, but less than a minute later, as I was slipping into a T-shirt and jeans, he phoned back.

"Hey there," he said.

"Hey there to you, too. You done shooting today?"

"Yeah, we ended up breaking a little early. How are things on your end?"

"Up and down. I got bullied by the first assistant district attorney today. She told me to mind my own business."

"You tell her that nobody puts baby in a corner?"

"Ha, I think she would have ordered me Tasered if I'd said something like that. I have to steer clear of her going forward. . . . Hey, by the way, you have a doppelgänger."

"In the Berkshires?"

"No, back home. Jessie swears she saw someone who looked just like you in midtown yesterday."

"That probably *was* me, actually. I had to make a crazy last-minute run to B&H Video."

"But—" I found myself squinting as I thought. I was sure Beau had told me his plane was leaving around nine. "But you had an early flight."

"I know, but when I realized one of my lenses was cracked, I had to switch to a later one, which of course meant paying the ridiculous change fee."

I kept squinting, remembering the conversation between Beau and me yesterday morning, replaying it in my head.

"You still there?" he said after a few seconds.

"Yeah, I'm just a little confused. When we spoke, you told me you'd been bushed the night before and I said I'd known you had to get up early for your flight. You didn't say anything about deciding to leave later."

"I *had* gotten up early. I just ended up flying a few hours later. There didn't seem to be any reason to go into the minutia."

"Um, okay," I said.

We chatted a few more minutes, mostly about a friend of ours who had called to ask us to his house on the Jersey Shore later in the summer and Beau wanting me to block the date on my calendar. We signed off, promising to talk tomorrow.

Beau's revelation bugged me. He wasn't the kind of guy to bother me with minutia but needing to change flights was the couples-share-this-kind-of-boring-crap detail he normally *would* have divulged. One of the bonuses of a relationship was being able to bitch to your partner about the little miseries in life that would make someone else's head explode.

Of course, when we'd spoken yesterday, he'd just started shooting. People were probably waiting for him. Let it go, I told myself. Besides, I felt a twinge of guilt thinking about how much I'd hidden from *him*. At some point I needed to cough up the news about Penny.

I packed the food from the fridge back into a shopping bag and lugged it downstairs. Luckily it looked like Jillian and I would have the deck mostly to ourselves. There was a couple at the far end, but they were all dressed up—her in crisp pants and him in a navy blazer—so they'd probably be heading out soon to a restaurant.

It was actually a perfect night to be eating alfresco. The temperature had cooled slightly, and the sky was a beautiful denim blue. As I was laying out the food for a tapas-style meal, someone inside the inn snapped on the row of tiny white lights strung along the rear of the deck and they twinkled magically in the twilight.

I'd just uncorked the Chianti and poured myself a glass when a text came in from Jillian, saying she would be arriving back from the clinic in less than two minutes.

And in exactly that amount of time, I heard a car pull into the driveway. I descended the wooden steps to meet her. I was just starting to round a hydrangea bush when I spotted an SUV through a cluster of leaves and flowers. Blake was in the driver's seat and after putting the car in park, he climbed out and walked around the front of the vehicle, meeting up with Jillian as she emerged.

"You all set?" I heard him say.

I took a step forward, but then instinct made me pause. I stood frozen in position, peering through the pink hydrangeas.

"Yes, all set," Jillian said. "It was an awesome day, Blake. I can't thank you enough."

She smiled, reached up, and clasped his arm. She kept her hand there as her eyes lingered on his face.

It wasn't a good look for her to be giving him. In fact, it was the kind you gave someone when you wanted to be much more than friends.

Chapter 11

I took a step backward, trying not to rustle the leaves, and positioned myself so that there was little danger of being spotted, but I could see through the branches. Though it was creepy to spy, I needed to figure out what was going on.

Jillian still had her hand on Blake's arm, and she tilted her head so that a stretch of her neck was exposed, smooth and white as candlewax. Her lips parted slowly, as if she intended to say something but was first gathering her thoughts or her nerve. Her eyes didn't leave his face.

Blake looked uncomfortable. He raised his other arm in an awkward-wave good-bye and stepped back, so that Jillian's hand slid down his arm.

"Glad it worked out," he said. "Let us know if we can do anything else."

Interesting that he chose the words *us* and *we*. It seemed to be his way of saying, *Let's not forget, Mamie, all right?*

"Have a nice night," Jillian told him.

I turned and beat it back up the steps to the deck. Thirty seconds later I heard the vehicle pull out of the driveway, and I expected to see Jillian round the shrubbery, but she didn't materialize. Moments later she shot me an email announcing that she was back at the inn but was going to take a few minutes to freshen up before joining me.

I indulged in a long sip of Chianti and considered the scene I'd witnessed in the driveway. There was little doubt in my mind that Jillian had been flirting with Blake. I'd read enough about nonverbal communication to know that when someone's infatuated, his or her body language often reveals, on an almost involuntarily level, a desire to submit. Jillian's parted lips and tilted head were giveaways. Plus, as a member of the same sex, I recognized a come-on when I saw it.

Maybe I should have expected it after the kind of gaga way Jillian had spoken about Blake the other night. That stuff about him being a dog whisperer and cat whisperer and a ferret whisperer or whatever . . .

Yet it surprised me that she'd actually flirted with the husband of a woman who, in her words, had "totally been there" for her. Fortunately Blake hadn't taken the bait and flirted back. If I'd learned one thing in life it was that flirting can lead to *dirty* flirting, which can quickly lead to fucking, and that certainly would be disastrous in this case.

I decided, though, to cut Jillian some slack. She was under extraordinary stress being back in the area, and perhaps that stress had imprinted itself, in the form of infatuation, on the first attractive male she encountered, like something out of a fairy tale or *A Midsummer Night's Dream*.

Jillian surfaced ten minutes later. She was wearing the same clothes—jeans and a V-neck cotton sweater—but she smelled almondy, as if she'd taken the time to wash up a little. She'd hijacked a battery-operated candle from a table inside and set it on our table.

"This looks great, Bailey," she said, pulling out a chair. "I really appreciate you doing this."

If she was bothered by Blake pulling his arm away, she wasn't showing it.

"I figured we both could use some good food and wine after the past forty-eight hours." I poured a glass for her and handed it over. "How did the shadowing go today?"

"Fascinating. By the way, thanks for letting me know the latest about Penny Niles. Mamie heard a mention of it on the radio right after you texted but they didn't offer any specifics. This means her death didn't have anything to do with your interview, right?"

"It seems that way. But until we know more, we both need to be really careful, okay?"

I knew my comment would be unsettling, but I didn't want her lowering her defenses.

"Okay, understood," she said, her expression grim. "So how was your meeting with Jocelyn?"

"I see what you mean about her. Not exactly the warm-and-fuzzy type. Her husband, Bob, showed up at the end, and I didn't like him much, either."

"Neither did my mom. I don't think my parents ever did things as a foursome with them."

"At least Jocelyn was willing to talk. She said she had no idea what problem could have existed at the school during that time period. Of course, it might have been an issue your mother didn't feel comfortable sharing with Jocelyn."

"Or maybe there wasn't an issue with the school at all." Jillian had a piece of *sopressata* dangling between her fingers, as if she was about to take a bite, but instead she set it back on her paper plate. "It just seems that Danny must have been talking about something with Barnard. Jules had been out of high school for almost a year, so what problem could she have had with anyone there?"

"You could be right, of course, though I know my question hit a nerve with Penny. There's one revelation from Jocelyn that I think you'll be glad to hear. She was absolutely adamant that your mother wasn't having an affair."

Jillian rested her chin lightly on her hands as she considered the comment. Then she shook her head a little, as if not buying it.

"Maybe it wasn't an affair, but there was *something*. I felt it. As you said, my mother might not have shared everything with Jocelyn."

I took a sip of wine, letting my thoughts wander.

"Do you think your mom might have been experiencing a health crisis? That could have entailed phone calls she wanted to keep private."

Jillian's face pinched with concern.

"I suppose so, though Jules would have probably picked up on that when she was home—and she would have let me know. She and I didn't keep secrets."

"I plan to go back through some of the stuff in the boxes to see if I spot any details I didn't notice before."

"What about Trevor?" Jillian asked. "Shouldn't he

be one of the main people you're focusing on now that we know my father canned him?"

"Absolutely. I'm meeting with Bruce Kordas again tomorrow at one of his sites to see what I can learn about Trevor's stint at the company. And I'm hoping he can give me contact info for your father's secretary. I'm sure she'd be able to clue us in. And she might also know whether the relationship between your dad and Kordas had soured."

"All right," she said. She turned and glanced out across the yard. Instinctively I followed her gaze, though it didn't seem to land on anything in particular. The twilight would soon turn to dusk.

"LBI," I said as I saw a bird shoot from one tree to another. By the shape I could tell it was a woodpecker, though I wasn't sure what kind—downy or red-bellied.

"What?"

"'Last bird in.' It was a phrase my dad made up for around this time of day. He was always intrigued by whatever bird had the nerve to be the last one in for the night."

Jillian smiled. "That's so enchanting. In all my research with birds, I've never heard anyone say that. Was your dad a birder?"

"Yeah, though not manic about keeping lists. He just loved looking at them."

"How did he die anyway? I'm sure you told me years ago, and I'm sorry not to remember."

"He had a brain aneurism on a fishing trip when I was twelve."

"Oh, Bailey, that's so sad. I know this is a crazy question, but do you think losing your dad so young influenced the kind of men you've been attracted to?"

"Funny you should say that. My ex-husband was a lawyer, only a few years older than me, but he seemed mature for his age, and I remember wondering if I was drawn to that maturity because of losing my dad. Unfortunately he turned out to have a huge gambling problem, which makes him totally unlike my father, who was a really steadfast, reliable guy."

"What about Beau? What's he like?"

"No indications of a dark side, thankfully. But very different from my dad. More social, for one thing. And I guess you'd call him the creative type—he makes documentary films—whereas my father was an engineer. What about you? Do you think you've looked for your father in some of the men you've dated?"

As open as we'd been with each other in college, I don't think we'd ever talked so intimately. It felt both thrilling and vaguely dangerous at the same time.

"To be honest, and it hurts to say this, I don't think I really knew my dad very well. He was always, *al-*

ways working. Some of his projects were a few hours away—like in New York State—and so he was gone quite a bit."

"You were close to your mom, though, right?"

Jillian dabbed a finger at the hollow spot on her neck.

"Yes. We were close—and she would have done anything for me. But in some ways she always seemed closer to Julia because of how sick she was when she was little."

"Was that hard on you?"

"I guess early on. But I grew to accept it as just the way things were, though I told myself that when I got older, it might be *my* turn." She shrugged in such a sad way it made me wince inside. "Overall I had a great life as a kid, and yet—gosh, I don't think I ever told this to anyone before—I always had this weird restlessness, a yearning really, for something I couldn't define."

"Any idea what caused it?"

"I've sometimes wondered if it's because, deep down, I wanted my family to be more like the way we presented ourselves to the world on our Christmas cards. It's not that we were unhappy or there was ever any ugly drama. We just weren't as tight as people thought we were."

"Jocelyn mentioned you actually moved here from

Virginia when you were about to go to kindergarten. Maybe being uprooted created that restlessness and yearning."

"Possibly, though I don't remember being bothered by the move."

"She said it was because of your father's work."

"Yes, partly, though Jules was four then and showing signs of getting better, and my mother said she didn't want to live in our old house anymore. Too many reminders."

She drained her wineglass and set it with a plunk back on the table.

"Want more food?" I asked, nodding toward the paper plates of makeshift tapas I'd fashioned.

"No, I'm good. I may head up now."

I sensed something was on her mind. Though maybe she simply felt uncomfortable from having shared so much. Or the encounter with Blake was indeed weighing on her.

"Sure," I said. "I'll stash the leftovers in the fridge in my room. If you're hungry later, feel free to stop by for them."

As Jillian rose from the table, I realized that, as unfair as it was, I really *did* miss the girl she used to be—funny, irreverent, so easygoing. I had a sudden memory right then of her leaning across the table at the pizzeria we frequented and stating solemnly, "Bailey, I need to tell you something, something I've never said to another person before. . . . You have a huge hunk of tomato sauce stuck in your bangs."

Still sitting, I reached out and gave her hand a squeeze. "I'm going to hang here for a while longer. Call me if you need anything. . . . Oh, wait, there's one more thing I have to tell you. I ended up meeting with the charming Belinda Bacon today."

"*What?* About Dylan?"

"No, about the Penny Niles murder—though you and your family came up in the conversation, of course. She heard I'd been asking questions, that sort of thing. In a nutshell she told me to butt out, and she even threatened to ticket me for interfering with a police investigation."

"I don't believe it," Jillian exclaimed.

"I know. She should spend less time swaggering, and more time trying to dig up the truth."

"No, that's not what I mean. I spent my first day here trying to ingratiate myself with the woman so she'd be more inclined to want to clear Dylan. And now you've got her pissed at you, and probably me, too."

I felt more than a twinge of guilt at her words. I knew she was right. I'd already realized I had played it wrong. Still, I didn't want Jillian to be annoyed with me.

"I know, I'm sorry. I've considered the research I need to tackle over the next couple of days and I'm pretty sure there's nothing Bacon will get wind of. And if she's really a good prosecutor, she won't let her annoyance with me discourage her from doing what's right."

Jillian folded her arms across her chest, and let out a long sigh, her eyes on the floor of the deck.

"I'm starting to wonder if this was really such a good idea anyway."

"What do you mean?"

"Bacon doesn't seem motivated to help in any way. And now that I'm back, I realize how hard it's going to be for you to find stuff out when so much time has passed. I know we've been here only two days but we've turned up so little."

I'd been aware of how tough it was for Jillian to be back, but I'd failed to pick up on her frustration.

"I hear you, and I know how maddening investigations can be because, at least initially, they often move at glacier pace. But I do think we've turned up a few valuable *threads*. Those often lead to other threads, and eventually to answers."

"Threads besides the school issue?"

"Yes, and don't worry, I'm not going to get sidetracked on that. There are other areas to explore."

She nodded, seemingly relieved. "I just wish there were more ways for me to help. I've been pretty useless so far. The only thing I have to show for my time here is that I can now describe how to perform a tooth extraction on a cat."

I flashed on the thought I'd had earlier. Maybe Jillian should return to New York. Leaving would not only help ease her frustration, but it would also tamp down any crush she was developing on Blake.

"First of all, it's been really good for me having you here because you've been able to provide info and make introductions, so don't feel that you've been useless. That said, I've been wondering if it might be time for me to start doing this solo."

"You mean for me to go back to the city?"

"Right. I could take over from here and call you when I need any insight or answers."

She lowered her head, obviously thinking, and then lifted her gaze back to mine.

"No, I want to stay, Bailey. If only for solidarity's sake."

"Okay, but if you feel the urge to go, let me know."

She nodded, wished me good night, and left the deck. As the door to the inn closed behind her, I poured another glass of wine.

I could hardly blame Jillian for her frustration. In addition to the trauma of reliving everything again, she was now having to deal with the fact that her father—or mother—might have had an affair, that Penny Niles had been murdered, too, and that the person who killed her family was still at large, perhaps not more than a stone's throw away.

But as I told her, we now had certain threads in our possession, and there was a chance they would lead us to answers.

I picked at the food for a few more minutes and guzzled the rest of my wine. Finally, I trudged back to my room. There was stuff for me to do, but I decided to hit the sack early and make a fresh start in the morning.

I was up by about six, and after grabbing coffee downstairs, I set to work on Claire's calendar. I began with the first week of January and perused every single page. Still, nothing jumped out at me. I'd hoped that if Claire *were* having an affair, I'd be able to pick up hints here and there. But there was nothing. Just as I'd observed previously, each notation seemed to be about a routine activity in a busy mother's life.

Finally, I reached the second Thursday of April,

the day of the murders, and as I did I realized how stupid I'd been when I'd looked through the calendar previously. I'd stopped at this page, as if nothing written after the date mattered a damn. But, of course, it might.

So this time I kept going. The notations turned out to be similar to what had come before, though, as expected, they gradually thinned out. One detail, however, caught my attention. On every Wednesday from mid-April to June, the words *Danny/Scouts*, written in pen, had been crossed out.

It appeared he'd dropped out of the program. Why? I wondered. Penny had mentioned that Carl had been a Scout leader, and it was more than possible that he led his son's troop. Had Danny simply grown tired of camping and writing secret messages in invisible ink or whatever Boy Scouts did? Or had there been a problem of some kind? I needed to investigate.

Next, I went back through the random credit card receipts and statements that had been tossed in the same tub. Nothing seemed weird, though out of context, most of it was meaningless. What I didn't find were any hotel bills that screamed "Somebody's been stepping out on her husband!"

As I was checking my phone afterward, I noticed an email from Jillian.

Bailey,

Gonna mostly hang here today. Might have lunch with Mamie. Sorry about last night. I was just feeling frustrated. I really want to stay, and if there's anything I can do, please let me know.

J

I told her thanks and reminded her that I'd be meeting Kordas at his new site, one called Foxcroft. I also asked, knowing that the chances were slim, if she might remember the names of any friends of Danny's—or their parents—and particularly any kids who'd been in Scouts with him. She quickly replied that she didn't offhand, but would give the question some thought.

It was after nine by now, and though that might be early for a Sunday, I decided to take another stab at reaching Amber Tresslar, Julia's roommate at Barnard. When I first started as a reporter, the fact that someone didn't return your call probably indicated they didn't care a rat's ass about speaking to you. These days, however, it often meant nothing more than they were crazy busy or lazy, and you had to keep trying.

This time Amber answered.

"I'm sorry I didn't call, but I had to work this weekend," she said. "What's this about, anyway? And how'd you get my number?"

I ignored the query about the number and briefly recapped the news regarding Dylan Fender, explaining that, confidentially, I was helping Jillian look into the case.

"Oh man," she said, clearly taken aback. "You mean the real killer's been free all this time?"

"Yes, it looks that way. Can you tell me anything about Julia's life that in hindsight might seem significant?"

"Gosh, it was so long ago—and we were still getting to know each other. There was the mono, of course. And the fact that she had to drop out that term."

"Do you recall if she was angry with how the school handled her leave?"

"*Angry?* Gee, I don't think so. She was pissed she had mono, and had to go home, but she didn't blame the school. I talked to her once on the phone and she seemed cool with the way things had been resolved. She was coming back in the fall and we were going to live together again."

So there it was. More indication that she probably *wasn't* ticked at Barnard.

"When you talked to Jillian on the phone, did she bring up anything that was going on at home?"

"*Jillian?*"

"Sorry, I mean Julia." The sisters' names were easy

to transpose. I'd come close more than once using the wrong one in conversation.

"She said she was mostly reading and watching TV."

"Not seeing any friends?"

"Not that I know of. She'd always said she'd been pretty shy in high school. Oh, I do remember her saying that once she felt a little better, she was going to use the time to finally get her license."

"Her driver's license?"

"Yeah, she'd never taken the test for some reason."

"Did she mention any problems at home, anything that might have been troubling her parents?"

"Um, not really. I mean, there was one little thing, but it probably doesn't mean much."

My heart skipped.

"You never know."

"Okay, she made a dismissive comment about her mom. I can't recall now what she said, but at the time it surprised me. At the start of the year she'd acted as if her mother walked on water."

So there was *that* again, too. Julia having a problem with Claire.

"You definitely don't remember the comment?"

"No, sorry."

"I have a few more questions, if you don't mind. Jillian didn't think her sister was dating anyone new, but could there have been someone? You can catch mono a bunch of ways, but kissing is still a common culprit."

"As far as I know, she hadn't started seeing anyone new yet, even casually. And she was pretty sure she got mono from a girl she shared Chinese food with, who also came down with it."

"And you weren't aware of any trouble brewing in her life, or problems she was facing?"

"No, in fact, from what I could tell, everything was good for Julia, except for the mono. She'd gained part of the freshman fifteen but it looked great on her, because she'd been pretty scrawny back in September. She was less introverted, too. She really seemed to be coming into her own."

"If anything else occurs to you, will you let me know? I really appreciate your help. And Jillian does, too."

"How is she anyway? Tell me that she's okay."

"As well as to be expected," I said. "I'll send her your regards."

After hanging up, I sat on the bed, mulling over the conversation. Based on what Amber had shared, I was even more convinced that the issue angering Julia years ago involved the high school principal—exactly as Danny had stated. Though it might not connect to the Lowe family murders, I was determined to find out what it was.

There were still a few hours to kill before I was due to leave for the development site. I drank more coffee, took a long speed walk to remind my muscles of what it felt like to be in motion, glanced through Julia's and Danny's tubs once again, in case I'd missed anything the first time, and picked at the leftovers from yesterday's dinner.

At five I finally took off, itchy for my next meet-up with Kordas. I was giving myself more time than I needed, but I wanted to arrive fifteen to twenty minutes early in order to scope out the area. After my scare at the storage facility, I wasn't going to take any chances and put myself in a vulnerable position.

When I was nearing the location, my phone pinged, and after slowing the car down, I saw Kordas had texted to say that he was running late and needed to move the meeting to seven.

Fortunately it would still be light out at seven, though the time switch aroused my suspicions. It was even more important now for me to get the lay of the land in advance.

I detoured to the closest town and bought an ice cream cone, just for something to do. At close to six thirty I set out again for the development, following a two-lane road through landscape that soon shifted from rural to suburban in feel. The old farmhouses, barns, and silos I passed gave way to a rolling landscape dotted with newly built homes and trees freshly sprung from nurseries.

Even with Kordas's directions, the place wasn't a cinch to find. Finally, I spotted the sign: FOXCROFT, in fancy, hunter-green script on a white background. I turned into the property, on a road called Bear Hollow. It was clearly a luxury development. After a quarter of a mile, I spotted a cluster of handsome-looking clapboard-and-stone houses down a road to the left, this one called Deer Run Lane. They were really working that woodland creature angle here. I bet if I drove around the site long enough, I'd come to Little Beaver Drive.

I swung left and headed up the road toward the houses. There were half a dozen all together, each with peaked roofs and dormers, obviously styled to look as if they'd been around for over a hundred years. Though the setting was attractive—a big stretch of woods unfolded in the rear—the houses were bunched close together. Wasn't privacy one of the perks that came with being affluent?

I didn't see the Baltic-blue Porsche, or for that matter any Porsche, but there was a silver SUV parked ahead of me, nuzzled up to a cluster of trees. It meant that Kordas wasn't here yet, or he'd driven another vehicle. I pulled up near the trees, killed the engine, and surveyed the area from my seat. No sign of Kordas, in the SUV or elsewhere. And no sign of anyone else. Frankly, I didn't love how deserted the area was. Somehow I'd let myself imagine there'd be more action around.

I swung open the car door and stepped outside, glancing cautiously around. The houses appeared completed but unoccupied. I wondered if Kordas was inside, perhaps inspecting them. Far ahead and off to the right I suddenly noticed another development under construction, at least seven or eight huge houses, and these spread much farther apart from one another. The breeze carried the sound of a hammer pounding, and few seconds later, the whine of a buzz saw. People working on a Sunday, probably being paid overtime to finish a job behind schedule. At least I had company reasonably close.

I turned back toward the houses and, taking a few steps, studied them. Each one, I realized in surprise, had *two* garages, one at each end, and then it hit me. These were a type of town house rather than single-family homes, which explained why they were so close together.

I retreated to my Jeep and rested my butt against

the back, biding my time for Kordas's arrival. Despite the name of the road, I didn't notice any deer darting around the area, but suddenly a brown rabbit appeared in the grass, as if conjured by a magician, and then hopped silently into the woods. If Kordas needed any more names for the roads in his development, I had a suggestion: Cottontail Lane.

The time for the meeting came and went. Then it was 7:10, 7:15. The air went still, the saws and hammers quieting almost in unison. The temperature, I noticed, had cooled off as the sun sank lower in the sky. Where was Kordas? I started to feel a little weird.

My phone pinged with a text and I dug it from my sweater pocket. It was from Kordas.

Kordas: You coming?

I wrote back, confused.

Me: I'm here, right in front of the houses.
Kordas: So am I. Don't see you. Wait, are you at the town houses?
Me: Yeah, think so.
Kordas: That's not the right spot. Stay there. I'll come down to you.

Maybe he'd meant for me to meet him farther up the hill, where the larger houses were. A normal enough mix-up, but an alarm went off in my brain. Better to wait in the car, I thought. I pushed off and took two steps.

From the left, near the woods, a movement caught my eye, a flash of something dark and going fast, and then there was a sound, sharp and explosive. I turned my head in that direction. It was a dog, huge and black and charging toward me, its teeth bared as it barked ferociously. My heart leaped into my throat.

I threw myself closer to the driver side door, thrusting out my hand to grab the handle. But I wasn't in time. The dog hurled itself at me like a torpedo, nearly knocking me off my feet.

I righted myself and reached again for the door, my heart pounding fiercely but it was too late. He sunk his teeth into my left forearm, tearing through bare flesh.

Chapter 12

The pain was like an electric shock, ripping the air from my lungs. I tried to wrench my arm away but the dog bit again and clamped down like a vise.

Frantic, I caught a breath, lifted my leg and rammed it as I hard as I could into the dog's side flank. It was like trying to kick a tank away, and enraged, the dog dug his teeth in even deeper. *Freeze*, I screamed to myself, a directive buried somewhere in my subconscious. I forced my arms and legs to be still.

Mercifully the dog froze, too, but he didn't loosen its grip. With his mouth still on my arm, he snarled furiously, his dark lips coated with foamy saliva.

"Help," I yelled, my voice nearly strangled. For a split second the dog released my arm and then bit down

once again. The pain was searing and the pressure unbearable, as if my limb was being crushed by the wheel
of a car. *Concentrate*, I commanded myself. *Try not to
hyperventilate.* I glanced around desperately for a stick
to beat him off with, but there was nothing.

I heard a noise then, above the growling. A car coming, so fast it sprayed stones from the road, and finally
lurching to a stop.

"Stay still," a man's voice called out. Next came the
sound of car doors being flung open. A trunk popping.
Heavy footsteps.

"Help me," I pleaded. I tried to turn my head enough
to see, but the car was directly behind me.

"Just stay still," the man called again. "Don't move
or yell."

Moments later he appeared behind me to my left.
It was Kordas, armed with a plank of wood. The dog
went wild at the sight of him and shifted direction, but
Kordas rammed the dog in the chest with the wood.
Finally, the dog released my arm. Then another man,
slim and pale blond, carrying what seemed to be a
bungee cord, darted toward the dog from behind. In
one quick motion he looped the cord around the dog
in a chokehold, jerked both ends tight, and yanked the
animal away from me. The growls turned to yelps and

finally to whimpers. And then the dog dropped to its feet, motionless. For the first time I realized it was a German shepherd.

Kordas flung the plank to the ground and rushed toward me. Out of the corner of my eye I saw the blond man looping part of the cord around a post in the ground.

"Thank you," I said, barely able to stand. "I—"

"Let me see your arm," Kordas said. He raised it gently with his hand. "Jesus, that's brutal."

I glanced down. My forearm was clearly mangled but I couldn't see details because the whole area was smeared with blood. It was seeping from the wounds but at least not gushing.

"She needs to get to an ER stat," Kordas shouted.

"We'll take her to Beacon," the other guy said. He was younger than Kordas, though not a lot.

"No, not there. Berkshire Medical. Ride in the back-seat with her and put a bandage on. I've got a first-aid kit in the car." Kordas looked back at me. "Can you handle a twenty-five-minute car ride?"

"Yes," I said, though I felt light-headed suddenly, dizziness fighting the pain for attention. "But—but please get my purse. In the car."

As the blond guy flung open the front door of my Jeep, Kordas led me to his Porsche, ushered me into the backseat, and strapped the belt on for me. Seconds later, the blond guy was beside me, my purse in hand. Seeing him up close, I realized he wasn't much older than I was. A business associate of Kordas? Or maybe the guy I'd seen as I'd left the Kordas house. The stepson?

Kordas started the car and jerked into reverse, while the blond guy began to wrap strip after strip of gauze tape around my arm. I knew he needed to stop the blood flow, but the bandage meeting skin made my arm throb even more. So did every bump the car hit as we exited toward the main road. It felt as if I'd been stabbed with an ice pick and lye had been tossed into the wound as a bonus.

I closed my eyes, trying to slow my breathing. A wave of nausea washed over me and then another. I felt the man tuck a sliver of gauze inside the end of the bandage in order to secure it and then he gently lowered my arm onto the seat.

"Do you feel like you're going to pass out?" he asked. "You should probably put your head between your legs. I'm Trevor Hague, by the way."

So it *was* the stepson.

"Thanks, I think I'm okay. It just really hurts." I opened my eyes and glanced over. "How did you know to do that?"

"The bandage?"

"No, subdue the dog."

"I saw someone have to do it once to a guard dog on a construction site."

"Is that what it was? A guard dog?"

"Maybe. It had a tag, which means someone owns it. Try to rest now, okay? You're going to need all your energy."

"Okay," I said weakly. "The dog—is he dead?"

I have no clue why I freaking cared. That hound from hell had nearly torn my arm off, but I needed to know.

"No, just unconscious, I think. We'll have to let someone know he's still there."

The next minutes were a total blur. I closed my eyes again and rested my head against the door. From the front seat came the sounds of Kordas making a call to the ER, letting them know to expect us. After a while I found myself needing to take Trevor's advice, lowering my head between my legs because it seemed like I would faint. When I finally raised my head again, I saw why the car had slowed. We were in a city, and pulling into the driveway of a large, gray-colored medical center.

Kordas helped me out and led me around the car.

"Go with her," he snapped at Trevor.

"And what do *you* plan to do?"

"I'm going to park the car, for God's sake."

Trevor walked me into the triage area, then helped me extract the insurance card from my wallet and explain the situation to the triage nurse. By now the pain was so intense it was tough to talk.

Within a few minutes I was sitting on a bed in a curtained area with a nurse named Tom peeling the gauze from my arm. He tried to do it gingerly, but every little touch was agony.

"I'm sorry," he said. "That's gotta hurt."

I stole a glance at my arm again. It looked as if parts of the flesh had been put through a food processor. I quickly closed my eyes, fighting off another wave of nausea.

"Don't worry, we'll take care of it," Tom said. "The PA will be in shortly to clean it and we'll give you something for the pain."

"Will I need stitches?"

"Not stitches, but I'm going to hook you up to an IV now. Don't worry, I'll use your right arm."

"Why won't I need stitches?"

"We generally don't close up animal bites because there's a high risk of infection. This might be little consolation, but cat bites are even worse in that regard."

He was right; it *wasn't* any consolation.

As soon as the nurse departed, I heard someone pull back the faded curtain and Kordas poked his head in. Trevor was sitting just behind him, on a folding chair.

"Do you need me to call anyone for you?"

"Yeah, Jillian. She's gonna be worried. Um, she doesn't get cell reception where we're staying; you'll need to call her room. It's the Briar Inn."

"Okay, I'll do that. And Trevor's going to stay here with you, to make sure you're okay. Unfortunately I have to take off for something I can't rearrange."

"What am I supposed to do about a car?" Trevor said.

"Keep mine for now," Kordas told him bluntly. "Lynne is picking me up."

He handed over the key, and with that he was gone.

I didn't have the time or the energy to focus on the tension between the two men. The stinging and throbbing in my arm suddenly intensified, as if the wound had a mind of its own and refused to be ignored. After a wait of about ten minutes, the PA arrived and introduced herself as Sasha Oliver. Pretty, African-American, dressed in scrubs, with her long black hair tied back in a ponytail.

"The good news," she said after examining my arm, "is that there doesn't seem to be any serious damage to either the blood vessels or the muscles, which would have required surgery to repair. And thank God, he picked this spot. Any lower and he might have hit an artery."

She explained that she was going to apply a topical anesthetic followed by an injection of lidocaine. Then she was going to do, in her words, a copious amount of irrigation and a debridement of dead tissue.

That would make for great conversation back in New York:

How was your stay in the Berkshires, Bailey?

Pretty good. I finally had a chance to try debridement!

Oliver added that the nurse was going to administer a painkiller through the IV and give me a tetanus shot, since I'd told the triage nurse that it had been at least a dozen years since I'd had one.

Even with the topical anesthetic, the lidocaine shots were a bitch because they came so close to the bites. Without warning my eyes pricked with tears. *Just breathe,* I told myself, *and for God's sake, don't blubber.* I felt utterly miserable, both from the blistering physical pain and my sheer unluckiness. How stupid I'd been to agree to meet Kordas in the middle of nowhere. And why had that dog chosen *me* to inflict its rage on? Would I even be able to drive? That question brought my car to mind. It was still at the development site, unlocked and with the key in the ignition.

After a few minutes, the painkiller began to kick in. Relief came in waves, seeping through me like fog as I lay on the bed. I began to feel a little loopy, as if I was partly underwater, but I still seemed to be coherent. Or at least I thought I was.

The procedure took longer than I expected and, groggy, I let my eyelids close. In my foggy state, other questions gurgled up in my mind, and then floated off. Where had the dog come from? The woods? Or somewhere on the site of town houses? Was it there to guard against trespassers? Finally, I felt the PA dress the wound with fresh gauze and heard her roll the cart she was working from out of the way. I opened my eyes.

"I'm going to give you scripts for an oral painkiller and an antibiotic," Oliver announced. "And we'll give you meds to take during the night and tomorrow morning. It's essential that you follow through with the antibiotic. As for the wound itself, it'll need to be looked at again tomorrow."

"So I can leave now?" I asked.

"No, no," she said, her eyes widening. She looked as if I'd just inquired if it would be okay for me to bowl later tonight or hurl a discus around. "The attending physician, Dr. Kahn, needs to come by when he's free to take a look at you. We're also waiting to hear from the animal-control people. They're retrieving the dog now."

"You're not going to make me ID him in a lineup, are you?"

Oliver chuckled. "I'm glad you haven't lost your sense of humor. No, it's because they need to see the dog tag and contact the owner. That way we can be sure the dog has had all its shots."

I thanked her and the nurse, and before they even departed, I had my head back on the pillow. I wanted to call Beau and let him know what had happened, but I felt myself drifting off to sleep.

When I stirred awake later, it took me a few moments to unstick my eyes and recall, to my dismay, where I was.

"Trevor?" I called out quietly. *"Trevor."*

A moment later an older women in scrubs tugged a small section of curtain open. "You looking for your friend?"

"Uh, yeah. Is he around?"

"He said he had to run out for a little while but to tell you he'd be back."

"Um, okay. And what about the doctor? Do you know how much longer it will be?"

238 · KATE WHITE

"Let me check for you."

After she departed, I raised myself up from the bed and managed to reach my purse on the nearby chair. After digging out my phone with my uninjured arm still attached to the IV, I tapped Beau's number. To my dismay, the call went straight to voice mail. He was probably shooting late. Not wanting to freak him out in case he called back and I wasn't able to pick up, I left a message asking him to call when he could and that it was kind of important. While there was nothing he could do from Miami, I knew that simply hearing his voice would help.

For the next ten minutes I lay on the bed, just waiting and listening to the endless ER noises outside the curtain: the beeping and pinging, the sound of trolleys bumping along the floor, and people calling out things like "Stat," "He's in X-ray," and "You want burritos tonight?"

Where the hell was Trevor? I wondered.

Finally, I heard the curtain part.

"How you doing?" It was him.

"Better. They gave me a pretty intense painkiller. What time is it?"

"About ten fifteen."

"Did Bruce reach Jillian, do you know?"

"Yeah, but it took a while. She was apparently downstairs at the inn, waiting for you to come back, and so, needless to say, didn't pick up the phone in her room. He finally had the manager find her. She was upset at the news, he said, but he told her not to worry and that you were in good hands."

"Is she coming to get me?" I'd figured she'd arrange for Mamie to drive her here and the two of them would transport me back to the inn.

"She wanted to, but since it's not clear when you'll be leaving, I volunteered to drive you back."

Now *that* was ironic. I'd arranged the meeting with Kordas in part to extract a few details about his stepson. Now I had the guy all to myself—though I wasn't in shape to do much with the opportunity.

"Thank you. . . . How 'bout my car? I've got to pick it up somehow."

"Bruce arranged for some workers to retrieve it and drop it off at the inn."

"Oh wow, that's great."

It was the first time I really had the chance to look directly at Trevor and process his appearance. He *was* pale, though not to the Draculean degree that Jillian had insinuated. It seemed that the whiteness of his skin was intensified by the fact that his eyebrows, the same platinum-blond color as his hair—and his mother's hair, too—were nearly invisible. He was roughly six feet two, well built, and obviously strong. He'd neutralized the hound from hell, after all.

"What happened to the dog? Was it still unconscious?"

"The guys who went for your car said the dog was no longer there. My guess is that animal control already picked him up." He offered a wry smile. "You think you'll ever be able to look at another German shepherd again?"

"Not without my heart stopping. . . . You said it might have been a guard dog. What was it doing there?"

He shrugged. I noticed for the first time that his slim-fit chinos and pale pink polo shirt both had smears of blood on them. Mine obviously.

"I've been wondering about that," he said. "It's possible it wandered over from a quarry that's not far from the site. I'd heard they had problems with people sneaking in and carting off stone, and they may have brought in a dog for security."

"It wasn't guarding the houses I was standing by?"

"Definitely not. The town houses are part of Foxcroft, and there aren't any dogs used there. By the way, just so you know, Bruce had meant for you to meet him at the bigger houses up the road, and you ended up at the town houses by mistake—though it's all part of the same development."

It sounded as if he was working with Bruce. So at some point in time, his job had been reinstated.

The curtain made a swishing sound as it was tugged open again. A fortysomething man, probably of Indian descent and dressed in a white coat, ventured into the area. Trevor lifted his hand in a wave, indicating he'd let me have my privacy, and stepped outside.

"I'm Dr. Kahn," the man said, smiling. "Tough night, huh?"

"Yeah, but everybody's been great."

"Glad to hear it. As the PA told you, we're giving you a couple of prescriptions. Try to transition off the painkiller as soon as you can, and start taking regular Tylenol. Someone's going to come by in a minute and have you fill out a form about the bite. It's a state requirement."

I nodded, indicating I understood on all counts. Ideally the next statement out of his mouth was going to be, "You're free to go," because all I wanted now was to crawl into bed at the inn and rest. But Dr. Kahn appeared hesitant. In fact, a tiny grimace formed on his face, and I had the funny feeling that a bombshell was about to land at my feet.

"There's another matter we need to discuss," he said. His tone was making me nervous. "Unfortunately animal control was unable to locate the dog. Your friend said the dog was unconscious when you left but it apparently came to and managed to escape. Since we have no way of knowing whether the dog has been vaccinated, you're going to have to have the prophylaxis for rabies."

"You mean those *shots*?" My heart skipped a couple of beats. I'd never been a wimp about shots, but I'd read that the injections used to protect against rabies involved needles that were as long as a selfie stick and were excruciatingly painful.

"Don't worry, it's not what you think," he said. "Years ago a person had to have over twenty of them, and they were administered in the stomach. We'll give these in your arm, and only four shots are necessary. You'll get the first one tonight along with something called rabies immune globulin. And then you'll need a series of follow-up injections over the next two weeks. We'll give you a pamphlet that explains it all."

"And they're not painful anymore?" I was sounding like a four-year-old, one who was going to expect a lollipop when it was all over, but by this point I was having a hard time putting on a brave face.

"They hurt a bit more than regular injections, and

have to be administered near the bite. But tonight at least you're already numbed up."

"Where do I go for the follow-up shots? I'm not sure how long I'll be the area. I live in New York City."

"Not a problem. I'll write you a prescription and you can probably arrange to have the other injections at a walk-in clinic."

I nodded. What choice did I have?

It was close to eleven by the time I emerged from the ER, with Trevor guiding me by my good arm. The shots hadn't been fun, but I hadn't screamed for mercy, either. Trevor had me wait briefly in front of the hospital as he brought Kordas's Porsche around and then helped me into the passenger seat. I flopped my head back against the leather.

After the PA had given me the shots, she'd mentioned that I might end up with soreness, redness, or swelling around the injection site, but it was going to be hard to distinguish any of that from the misery created by the bites. Right now, at least, the area didn't hurt—the painkiller from my drip still seemed to be doing its job—though my arm felt heavy and weird, as if I was lugging around a limb that belonged to someone else. And I still felt loopy from the medicine.

As we drove, I did my best, even with a foggy brain, to get a bead on Trevor. The guy had managed to put a choke hold on a dog that weighed at least seventy pounds, which seemed like a kind of weird skill to have, but I wouldn't have described him as creepy, the word Jillian had tagged him with. He seemed pretty together, coolheaded.

Still I had no reason yet to remove Trevor from my list of possible suspects. As a fired employee, he had a motive for the Lowe murders. Plus the more distance I was gaining from the dog attack, the more I could see that the whole chain of events at the site—me waiting in the wrong spot, the dog coming out of nowhere—was suspicious and troubling.

"I really appreciate this, Trevor," I said to him as the car exited Pittsfield. "I ended up ruining your whole evening."

"In all honesty, the only thing I had planned tonight was catching up on emails. And I did that while I waited."

"Would you mind running me through what happened earlier? I just want to have it straight in my mind."

"You mean with the dog?"

"Well, before that. How did you know I was in trouble?" I could still hear the sound of Kordas's car spraying gravel.

"We didn't at first. I was meeting with a colleague

at one of the houses, and Bruce was farther up, talking to his crew. He called my cell to say you'd gone to the town houses by mistake and that he was heading down there. And as we got closer, we saw the dog mauling you. I told Bruce to keep the dog busy while I grabbed the bungee cord from the back of my SUV."

The silver one parked by a cluster of trees.

"I can't thank you enough for that. I was sure the dog was going to tear me limb from limb."

"Yeah, he looked like a mean son of a bitch—literally *and* figuratively."

Wait, I thought. Something didn't make sense.

"You had planned on coming to the meeting, too?"

"No, Bruce was just going to drop me at my car. I'd left it at the town houses and walked up to the other area. Bruce is my stepfather, just FYI."

"Right, I figured that out earlier."

There were other questions I would have liked to ask but couldn't: "Why did Carl Lowe fire you?" "On a scale of one to ten, how mad did that make you?" "Where were you the night of the Lowe murders?" I would have to figure out how to get at those another time.

When we pulled into the driveway of the inn, we found the building dark, with the exception of a few exterior security lights and one lone lamp burning in the parlor. After retrieving the keys from my car, which was now parked in the small lot off the driveway, Trevor handed them to me and walked me up the path, even took the inn key from me and unlocked the front door.

"Bruce says you're helping Jillian Lowe write a memoir," he said, as he pushed the door quietly open. "Will you be in the area for a while?"

Interesting question.

"Probably a few more days. Beyond that I don't know."

"Here's my card," he said, quickly snapping it from his wallet. "Let me know if I can help further. And if I learn anything about the dog, I'll let you know."

"Do you mind one more question?" I asked. My thinking had cleared up just enough for me to realize that because of the incident tonight, I'd lost my opportunity to ask Kordas for a key piece of information. "I need to find Carl Lowe's old secretary, but I don't know her name. Do you recall it by any chance?"

"Heather Pleshette, I think."

"Is that her married name?"

"No, actually that would be Todd. She worked for Bruce for a little while after Carl died, and moved to Manhattan not long afterward. She'd fallen in love with a broker the company did business with from time to time. He was with a firm called Harrow Realty in Manhattan."

"Is—"

"Look, you should get to bed. Call me tomorrow if you need any more information."

Once inside, I staggered up the stairs. In my room I managed to find my notebook and jot down the detail about the secretary, and then collapsed on the bed. My body had begun to tremble a little and my stomach was cramping. I remembered the PA mentioning that the injections could cause headache, abdominal pain, and muscle aches. Before I could even form the words, *this sucks,* I was out cold.

I woke hours later in a haze of pain, dim sunlight nudging its way into the room. My head hurt, my left arm throbbed, and my stomach felt all twisty. As I struggled to a sitting position and checked the time, I became aware of a tapping sound on the door.

"Bailey, are you okay?" a voice called from the other side. "It's me, Jillian."

"Uh, hold on, okay?"

I somehow managed to force my ass out of bed and stumble toward the door. When I eased it open, I was surprised to see not only Jillian standing there but also Mamie and Blake.

"What time is it?" I asked, bleary-eyed.

"It's about seven thirty. I hated to wake you but I was so worried. And I thought Blake might be able to help."

"You poor thing," Mamie exclaimed. "Is there anything we can do?"

"Tell us what happened," Blake said. "But first, sit down. You must be fried after last night."

As I settled on the edge of the bed, Mamie and Jillian took seats on the tufted window seat and Blake pulled out the desk chair for himself. I gave them a quick overview of the whole ugly experience and described what treatment I'd receive at the medical center.

"The dog just bounded out of the woods?" Mamie said. "You never saw the owner?"

"There was no one near the dog, but Kordas's stepson saw an ID tag on it. He thinks it must have been a guard dog that managed to get loose from its location."

"That's horrible," Mamie said. She turned to Blake. "Honey, can you check with animal control and see if they've had any luck finding the dog? . . . Honey?"

Blake didn't say anything for a moment, but he appeared to be listening intently, his brow furrowed.

"It doesn't sound like a guard dog that attacked you," he said finally.

"Then why did it come after me that way?" I asked. "Do you think it could actually have rabies?"

He shook his head. "It's probably not rabid. That's pretty rare, though the hospital was required to give you the shots just in case. Did the dog ever try to bite another part of your body?"

"No, only my arm. It let go a couple of times, but would then chomp down again."

Blake's face clouded even more in concern.

"It actually sounds like a personal-protection dog," he said.

"How is that different than a guard dog?" Jillian asked.

"Guard dogs are trained to be easily agitated and to fiercely protect a certain domain. They attack anyone who enters the area, and they'll go for any part of the body they can reach, including the head. Personal-protection dogs, on the other hand, are generally very social—unless the owner is threatened. And they're trained to latch on to an arm or a leg rather than anyplace else."

I saw the distinction, but I didn't understand how it really mattered.

"How does that relate to what happened to me?" I asked.

"A personal-protection dog will only attack if the owner gives a command."

"Wait," I said. My heart started to hammer as his words sunk in. "You mean that dog wouldn't have bitten me on its own?"

"Right," Blake said grimly. "It sounds like someone may have signaled for it to go after you."

Chapter 13

Before I could react, Jillian sprang from the window seat.

"Are you saying someone *planned* for Bailey to be mauled?" she exclaimed.

"All I know is that it seems suspicious," Blake said. "There's a chance that the dog was naturally super aggressive and attacked out of the blue, but the latching-on part says it's probably been trained to attack on command."

This was scary, heart-in-mouth scary. I'd been targeted. And if Kordas hadn't come to my rescue, the dog would have kept chewing away at me, possibly severing an artery. I might have bled to death.

Jillian glanced at me. "It's because of the research you're doing," she said, her voice panicky. "Someone wants to hurt you because you're trying to figure out the truth. God, maybe Penny's death is actually related to all of this."

If someone *had* set the dog on me, it seemed likely that it was the person who'd killed the Lowes—because he sensed I was closing in on his identity.

"She's right," Mamie blurted out. "You're in real danger—and so is Jillian." She glanced fearfully at her husband, and I could tell what she was thinking but didn't want to say. *And we might be, too.*

"We don't know for sure that the attack was planned," I said. "And if it *was*, it means we've probably smoked out the killer, which is a good thing."

Blake had risen from the chair and begun to pace, his fist pressed to his mouth.

"Why don't I at least give animal control a call, as Mamie suggested, and see what they have to say," he said. "Maybe they have the dog in custody by now and we'll learn more."

"Could the dog really have recovered enough from the choking to skulk off?" I asked.

"Maybe, but there's also a chance that the owner came to collect him. That way there'd be no evidence."

"If the dog is alive but injured, he might have been taken to a vet," I said.

"I can ask around," Blake said. "Make some calls."

"Shouldn't you call the police, Bailey?" This from Mamie. "The detective you talked to about Ms. Niles?"

Blake cocked his head and studied me, waiting for a response.

"Um, I'm not sure that would be a good idea right now," I said. I was doing my best to pull thoughts together, but the throbbing in my head wasn't helping, nor was the pulsing pain in my arm.

"But why not?" Jillian said. "What reason would there be for *not* telling him?"

"If the dog isn't located—and something tells me it won't be—it'll be hard to convince them that someone planned this. Plus, I've been told to stay away from the investigation or else run the risk of being ticketed. I don't really want them to know what I'm up to."

"But you can't keep doing research if it's going to get you killed," Jillian said. She'd moved closer to Blake by now and she reached out and squeezed his arm. "Blake, please. Talk some sense into Bailey, will you?"

The air around us seemed to chill instantly. Not simply because of Jillian's gesture but also because of how she'd spoken Blake's name, drawing it out in that way you do with a person you know almost as well as yourself. It was like stepping into a room without announcing yourself and seeing something you weren't meant to see and damn well wished you hadn't.

Instinctively I drew my gaze away, and in doing so, I noticed Mamie posed motionless on the window seat, staring at her husband and friend. Her dark-brown eyes had widened in awareness, as if she'd been told a secret that shocked her but also made perfect sense.

Jillian let her arm drop quickly, clearly only now realizing how suggestive her gesture had been.

"Let me mull it over after I feel a little better," I said, hoping to shift the mood in the room. "I don't want to be stupid about this. But right now I can't even think straight."

"Understood," Blake said. "You need to rest, and later you can let us know what you intend to do." He glanced at his watch. "Mamie and I need to head to the clinic. You're not planning on leaving the inn today, are you?"

"I have an appointment with the doctor at noon, but other than that, I'll be here. In light of everything, I think Jillian ought to stay close to the inn, unless she wants to shadow at the clinic again."

Mamie slid off the window seat with a look of what seemed like resolve on her face.

"Unfortunately it's going to be an insane day," she said. "We have students from the vet school at UMass coming to observe, and we don't really have space for anyone else in the rooms. Why don't we stay in touch during the day so we know you're both okay."

Clearly whatever concern Mamie had about Jillian's well-being was being scooted aside at the moment, as she considered the need to sandbag her marriage against a possible threat.

I let my eyes glide over to Jillian. She was tightening those muscles in her beautiful face right before my eyes.

"Sure, that makes sense," she said. "I'm just so appreciative of all you've done. This way, though, I can keep an eye on Bailey and take her to her doctor's appointment."

Blake turned once more to me.

"Promise us you'll be careful, all right? Maybe the dog attack *was* random. Until we find out for sure, you shouldn't take any chances."

I nodded, not so much in agreement, but because I was seriously hurting now and didn't have the strength to flap my lips anymore. Mamie and Blake made a move to leave, and Jillian volunteered to walk them downstairs. She was trying to fix things, pretend everything was exactly as it should be, but I was doubtful it would work. Mamie was a take-care-of-business kind of girl and no pushover. She didn't seem like the type who'd wait around to see if her instincts were wrong and an old friend didn't really have the hots for her husband.

After they were gone, I secured the chain lock on the door, stumbled into the bathroom to pop a pain-killer, and then nearly crawled on my belly to the bed. I realized suddenly that I'd never heard back from Beau. With my good arm I fished out my phone from the bag and discovered that he'd attempted to reach me this morning at seven. I must have been in such a comatose state that I'd slept through the call.

I punched his number, eager to hear his voice, but the call went straight to voice mail again. I left another message, trying to make my voice sound something other than pitiful, but I knew I came across as a kid who'd accidentally left her favorite stuffed animal, Mouser, on a plane that was now in midair, bound for another city.

I flopped back on the bed and just lay there, staring at a long, thin crack in the ceiling. Despite how useless my brain felt, I tried to fit the pieces together.

If the dog attack had been planned, it meant that the owner had probably tailed me to Foxcroft, with the dog in tow. He may, in fact, have been stalking me for a while, had even been responsible for the dropped shutter at the storage facility. I dragged through my memory. There'd been a fair amount of traffic on the road to Foxcroft—and yet not a *ton*. It seemed I would have noticed if someone had been following.

Which meant I had to consider whether the dog and its master were already at the site. But the only one who knew I was going to Foxcroft was Jillian.

And Kordas, of course. What if he'd *meant* for me to show up at the town houses, so that he could have someone who worked for him hide in the woods and sic the dog on me? And then Kordas had raced to my rescue because he wanted me scared but not dismembered.

There was also Trevor Hague to consider. Kordas might have told him I was coming to Foxcroft and he arranged for the attack himself, only to have the plan foiled by Kordas. This scenario was a bit harder to fathom, though he and Kordas might have worked in concert, squelching their friction long enough to attain a mutual goal.

And they each would have had the opportunity to retrieve the dog—Kordas when he left for the "something" he couldn't rearrange and Hague while I was dozing in a medicated stupor. I'd slept for at least an hour, probably long enough for him to make the drive to the development site, drop the dog someplace, and return to the ER.

There was one other detail to factor in. Neither

Kordas nor Trevor had any apparent connection to the school. If either one was the Lowes' murderer, he probably hadn't killed Penny. Maybe her death really *wasn't* connected to the Lowes. Or maybe it was, and Kordas and Trevor were nothing more than my rescuers.

My head hurt even worse from thinking so hard.

I closed my eyes and rested my head on the pillow, hoping for a second wind. Soon, though, I was drifting off again, into a sleep that felt like I was sinking to the bottom of the sea.

When I woke the next time, I was in even worse shape. My symptoms were vaguely flu-like, including feeling feverish. Part of my problem, I realized, was that I'd had no caffeine—or food for that matter—since late-yesterday afternoon. As much of a bitch as it was going to be, I needed to force myself downstairs.

I checked my phone—9:47. If I were lucky, there might still be scraps on the breakfast buffet. At this point I'd settle for one of those single serving–size boxes of Frosted Flakes.

After dunking my face in cold water, I made my way to the breakfast room. I had the place to myself, and fortunately there were still muffins in the basket and a container of yogurt in a bowl of mostly melted ice. I filled a coffee mug and carried it with my food out onto the deck. The day was muggy, but it was a relief to be out of doors.

I knew I had some serious deciding to do, but for the time being I gave all my attention to devouring the blueberry muffin and directing caffeine through my system. Within a couple of minutes I felt marginally better. And even better when my phone rang and I spotted Beau's name on the screen.

"Hey, good to finally connect," I said.

"Same here. Everything okay? Your message sounded a little weird."

"I got bit really badly by a dog last night. It was like being trapped in a sequel to *Cujo*."

"Bailey, that's awful. Where?"

"At a ritzy housing development about thirty minutes from where we're staying."

"No, I mean where's the bite?"

"On my left arm."

"Damn. Did you need stitches? Can you use your arm?"

"Apparently they don't generally do stitches with dog bites. They cleaned it out and bandaged it up, though it still hurts like hell. And believe it or not, I have to have a series of rabies shots."

"Jeez. Are—are you sure you're getting the right medical attention up there?"

"Yeah, the ER was great."

"But wouldn't it make sense to go back to the city and be treated there?"

I'd made the decision last night to come clean with Beau, no sins of omission. I took a deep breath.

"I'm giving it some thought, but not because of the bite per se. There's a possibility that someone sicced the dog on me, that it was an intentional attack. I may have kicked the proverbial hornet's nest while asking questions up here."

"Are you saying that someone's trying to kill you?" His voice was almost hoarse with concern.

"Maybe, or at least scare me silly. In addition, a woman I interviewed was murdered Friday night, and though the police say it's related to a burglary, I'm not so sure."

"Bailey, you need to get out of there."

"Uh, I'm still trying to figure out my next move. This could be an important turning point in the case."

Things went deadly quiet on the other end.

"Beau?"

"I don't know what you want me to say, Bailey. I'm in Miami, totally unable to help you, and you're refusing to leave a place where you're clearly in danger."

"I'm not refusing to leave. But there are important

things to consider. I may be close to figuring out who killed the Lowes."

"Would you ever think of considering *me*? I'm going to be spending these next days worried sick about you. . . . I should have known this would happen."

"What do you mean?"

"The *story*. You go on the hunt for a murderer, so why *wouldn't* you end up in trouble?"

"But you actually encouraged me to come here—or are you forgetting our conversation?"

"What choice did I have? Every time I act concerned, you think I'm overreacting."

"Beau, this is what I do for a *living*. You knew that when you met me. You can't write about crime without coming across criminals."

"I get that it's your job, Bailey, and I admire your dedication. But there's this sense I have lately that you don't know when to back off and protect yourself."

"Whoa, hold on a minute. It sounds like you're accusing me of being reckless."

"Do you not see it? That some of the stories you like to pursue are the equivalent of trying to bolt across a six-lane highway."

"Well, what do you want me to do? Get my massage license and switch careers?"

Even as I spoke, I could hear an internal voice warning me: *Step away from the vehicle, Bailey.* His comments were pissing me off and that, combined with the miserable way I was feeling, might make me say something I'd later regret. I had a dangerous tendency when mad to bite my nose off to spite my face and absurdly enjoy the experience.

"Bailey, please. A lot of what you're hearing in my voice is really just concern. I don't like what happened to you, and I don't want you to be at risk."

I felt myself soften a little. But I needed to jump off the phone call before things went from bad to worse.

"I'm sorry to alarm you like this. I just need to figure some stuff out. I'm waiting right now for additional information. Why don't I call you later when I have a game plan?"

Long sigh on his part, which amped up my annoyance again.

"So when you say later, what do you mean?" he asked. "Later this morning?"

"Later *today*, by this afternoon for sure."

"Okay, I'll have someone hold my phone while we're shooting and be sure to answer it."

"Thanks. Talk to you later."

"Bye. And let me know, too, if there's anything I can do."

Wow, so much for the comfort of someone's voice. All the call had done was make me feel even lousier. I had myself partly to blame, of course, from holding out on Beau the past few days and reporting the category-five shit storm to him all at once. But he'd forced me to walk on eggshells about my work. And now he was piling on the pressure when I needed to keep my head clear.

I set my elbow on the table and rested my face against my hand, trying to slow my breathing and curtail the renewed throbbing in my head.

Now what? I couldn't deny that the dog attack had left me scared, but scared wasn't a reason to quit, especially when the truth was starting to feel within reach. And was searching for the truth really *reckless*, as Beau had implied? I hated his choice of words.

The ideal situation for me and everybody else would be to turn things over to the police, but I was sure that without a dog as evidence, they wouldn't buy that the assault had been planned.

I summoned a momentary burst of energy and staggered upstairs. Before Jillian had left with Blake and Mamie earlier, we'd agreed that she'd return to my room at eleven fifteen to drive me to the doctor, allowing for a run to the pharmacy beforehand. Her knock came right on time.

"Are you doing any better?" she asked.

"I think so," I said, though I was pretty sure any relief I felt was due primarily to the latest pain pill. "Thanks for playing chauffeur."

"Of course. I couldn't imagine letting you go on your own."

I handed her the keys and we headed out to my Jeep. She took a moment to adjust the seat for her height before maneuvering out of the parking lot. I twisted around and peered out the back window, just checking.

"Bailey, you have to tell me," Jillian said after we were on one of the main roads. "Do you think someone really set that dog on you?"

I could hear the fear in her voice and I shifted my body to grab a better look at her. I'd been so busy wallowing in my own misery after the bite, I hadn't focused much on Jillian. She had to be badly freaked by what had happened to me. If someone wanted to hurt me, it had to be the person who'd slaughtered her family, which meant he was right here, maybe only minutes away from us, and he probably wanted to hurt her as well.

"I'm not sure, but the more I think about it, the more the dog attack feels like yet another incident that can't just be random. I interview Penny and she's murdered that night by a burglar. I go to meet someone and while

I'm waiting, a personal-protection dog not associated with the site bounds out of the woods after me."

"You think it's the murderer doing it?"

"I'd say it's likely, yes."

"I guess I always knew something like this was a possibility, but I never let myself picture it happening Have you decided what to do?"

"I want to wait until after we hear from Blake about animal control, and whether they've located the dog. Until then we'll both have to be extremely careful. But, Jillian, as scary as this is, it's also a good thing. It means we might really figure out who killed your family. And we'll get Dylan cleared."

"Okay," she said after an extra-long pause. "One more question I have to ask. Do you think Bruce Kordas set up the dog attack?"

"He could have—but I don't have a clear feeling on that. First things first. Let's wait to hear what Blake turns up."

The trip to Pittsfield went smoothly enough and Dr. Kahn took me right away. It was the first chance I had to really study the wound, or I should say wounds, because I could see now that it was an ugly grouping of short, straight incisions, as well as three large, gaping, half-moon-shaped lesions, which echoed the shape of the dog's jaw. There would be scars for sure.

"It's already starting to heal," Dr. Kahn assured me. "Just be religious about your antibiotics and go off the pain meds as soon as you can tolerate it."

Returning to the waiting room, I found Jillian gnawing at her thumb. She seemed to be fretting even more than before. On the way home we made one quick stop at a food shop and grabbed premade sandwiches. As Jillian pulled onto the road, I checked behind us. Nothing suspicious.

"You're a good driver," I said as she maneuvered along the twisty road.

"Thanks. I really miss having a car in the city."

"By the way," I asked, my mind tugged back to a question that had been lingering, "why didn't Julia have her driver's license?"

"How'd you know that?"

"Her college roommate mentioned it."

"It was my mom babying her, I guess, because she'd been sick as a kid. So she drove her places, or she tagged along with me. But Jules wasn't happy about it. She was determined to get her license before she went back to Barnard in the fall."

My chills had started up again, and I pulled the cotton sweater I'd worn tighter around me. It didn't help. What I needed, I realized, was to crawl under the covers again and go completely comatose. But there was still another topic to cover with Jillian, one I had to be sure ended up on the table. I waited until she had pulled into the parking lot at the inn and switched off the ignition.

"Jillian, there's something I wanted to ask you about before we go in."

"Sure."

"Is there anything going on with you and Blake?"

"You mean *sexual*? Of course not."

"There seemed to be an awkward vibe in my room this morning, and I think Mamie noticed it, too."

"There's nothing going on."

"Are you attracted to him, though?"

"I've always liked and respected him, and I'm really interested in the work he's doing now. It's been a nice distraction for me to shadow him."

Call me cynical, but I didn't think she was being honest with me. Yes, she might like and respect Blake, but the way her hand had lingered suggested more than that.

"I just worry that Mamie may be picking up on something and it's making her uncomfortable."

"To be brutally honest, I could use a little distance from Mamie's cheerfulness. It's starting to wear on me."

"But you don't want to upset her, do you?"

As we'd been speaking about Blake and Mamie, Jillian had kept her gaze from me, but now she snapped her head in my direction, so fast I heard her neck crack. She leveled her deep blue eyes at me.

"Are you *lecturing* me, Bailey?"

Her tone caught me totally by surprise.

"No, definitely not—and forgive me if it came across that way."

And I meant it. Jillian had been through hell, and who was I to judge her?

"It sure sounds like that's what's going on."

"I just wanted you to be aware that Mamie may be reading things a certain way. We wouldn't want to lose the only allies we have up here. Besides, as you said, Mamie's been a good friend. And Blake is her husband."

Jillian snickered, taking me aback.

"Oh that's rich, Bailey," she said. "You're going to tell me how to treat people, and what the better thing to do is. *You*, who couldn't even bother to pick up a phone and call me after my entire family died."

The words were like a slap in the face. She'd convinced me days ago that there'd been nothing to forgive, that she understood that it had been tough for me to reach out. But my failure *had* troubled her all these years, and still did.

"Jillian, you're right, and I'm sorry," I said. "And I'm sorry about what I said. I know you'll do the right thing and I shouldn't have suggested otherwise."

She didn't reply. My achiness had intensified, and I would have loved to bag the lunch for now. But that, I knew, might only add to the awkwardness between us.

"Shall we eat on the deck?" I asked.

"I think I'll take my sandwich to my room, if you don't mind. I need to make a phone call." The snarkiness was gone from her tone, suggesting she'd accepted my apology. And I was grateful to be able to skip the deck.

"No problem. I may take a nap now anyway."

"By the way, I've made a decision. It sounds sudden but I've actually been mulling it over since last night. I think it's best if we both packed up and left."

My jaw dropped in surprise. I'd read her frustration yesterday evening, of course, and her fear today, but I'd never guessed she'd seriously want us to back down.

"Jillian, wait—"

"I have a friend from U Wash who's in Boston, and she wants me to come see her. I'll take the bus or an Uber or something. And you should go home to New York—where it's safe."

"Please, Jillian. You're welcome to leave, and that's

probably a smart idea, but I think I'd like to stay for a little while longer, at least until I know more about the dog. I might end up talking to the police after all."

"I don't want you investigating on my behalf anymore. It's too dangerous."

"But we're so close. Can we just think this through?"

"I *have* thought it through," she said. "When I'm in Boston, I'll update the innocence group and they can pass along the information to the cops. . . . Do you need help getting to your room?"

"No," I said feebly. "I think I'm just going to sit here for a minute."

I waited until she entered the inn and then trudged upstairs a couple of minutes later, floored by the conversation in the car. She wasn't simply afraid—she was pissed at me.

I popped a pain pill as soon as I was in my room and flopped on the bed. The second my eyes were closed, my phone rang, and thinking it might be Beau, I grabbed it and peered at the screen.

It was my friend Landon.

"God, it's so good to hear from you." My voice came out like a little mouse squeak.

"What's going on? You sound horrible."

I blurted out the top-line info—Penny's murder, the dog mauling me, the rabies shots, Jillian's change of heart. And the fact that she was headed to Boston with no apparent concern about how I'd get back to New York.

"Omigod, is Beau coming to get you?"

"No, he's in Florida," I moaned. I'd missed the right window for the painkiller and both my arm and head were throbbing in unison now, like they were part of the same dance band. "I have no clue what I'm going to do."

"Well, I know what *I'm* going to do," he said. "I'm coming up there to get you."

Chapter 14

No, no, I won't let you," I said. "Uh, besides I have my car with me. I can't abandon it here."

"I'll figure it out, Bailey. Tell me where you're staying."

"Um, let me think for a second. I'm not up for driving but there may be a way for me to get back on my own."

I couldn't believe that I was now considering beating a retreat to Manhattan, and yet what choice did I really have? I wasn't all that functional, Jillian had told me to cease and desist, there was only a slim chance the dog would turn up, and if it did, the police—and that mood bomb Belinda Bacon—would be even more irked with me than they already were. There was also the obnoxious little fact that someone seemed to want me dead.

"Maybe I *could* leave my car here and come back for it in a week or so. I could take a bus back to Manhattan." Though based on how flushed I looked, I might be thrown off as a possible Ebola carrier.

"A *bus*? God forbid, no, I won't hear of it. Now give me the name of the inn and town where it's located."

I coughed it up without further protest.

"Thank you, Landon," I said before I signed off. "I can't tell you how much this means to me."

I fell into another deep sleep after that, and when I woke at four, I discovered that my cell had nearly blown up with texts and phone calls, none of which I'd heard in my stupor. Beau had called once and texted twice, begging me to make contact. Both Hague and Kordas had texted to check on my condition, ironic in that one of them might be responsible for it.

There was also a text from Landon—from fifteen minutes ago—saying he'd arrive in two hours to transport me home, though no hint of how. I just prayed he hadn't arranged for me to be medevacked by chopper or something else totally extreme.

After texting Beau to say I was heading back to the city and would be home by this evening (and resisting the urge to add, "There, happy now?"), I lurched toward the bathroom and managed a five-minute shower, holding my bandaged left arm out on the other side of the curtain. The hot water did an excellent job of soothing my miserable muscles. By the time I toweled off, I felt vaguely human again. I could see now that my physical discomfort was going to come and go in waves, partly due to the timetable for taking the medication, but also because that's how the rabies vaccine seemed to play with my system.

It was a few minutes later, as I was tossing clothes into my duffel bag, when I noticed the envelope lying on the floor, a few inches from the space beneath the door. I picked it up and tore the flap back. The note, as I'd surmised, was from Jillian, written on stationary with the inn's name at the top and the sketch of a bunny in the corner. I'd about had my fill of the animal kingdom at this point.

> *Bailey,*
> *Thank you for all you did. I've paid for both our rooms, including yours for tonight, in case you decided to drive back tomorrow instead of today.*
> *Jillian*

Though she'd certainly seemed concerned about my dog bite earlier, it was clear she had no clue how impaired I was. But I couldn't bring myself to hold that against her. This trip had been traumatic for her. And rather than help her find closure, our stay had only added to her distress.

My gaze drifted across the room and settled in the corner, on the three plastic tubs shoved back there. *Shit.* I'd completely forgotten about them. The storage facility was in the opposite direction of New York and there was no way I could make Landon stop there tonight. I would have to lug the tubs back to the city with me and return them on a later date, in conjunction, perhaps, with a visit to Candace. I still had the key to the unit.

After packing my bag, I ordered a burger from a diner I found online. As I waited for the delivery in the breakfast room, I texted Trevor and Kordas, thanking them for their concern and saying I was on the mend, which felt about as close to the truth as me announcing I was about to start a German shepherd–fan site. I emailed Candace, as well, explaining that I'd been called out of town unexpectedly but would be in touch soon.

There was another text, I noticed, from Beau.

So relieved you're headed back. Let me know if you need anything.

I couldn't help but feel a jumble of emotions: annoyance that he had such an issue with my work but also pleasure at his concern for me.

Landon arrived forty-five minutes later, by Uber-BLACK it turned out, which I realized must have cost him a bloody fortune. I offered him the best half hug I was capable of. Not only had he come to my aid, but by taking Uber one way, he was going to be able to drive my car back to the city. While I took charge of my duffel bag and laptop, he proceeded to haul the tubs downstairs and load them into the back.

"Oh man," I said when we were finally on our way. "I feel like Helen, and that you've stormed the gates of Troy to rescue me."

Landon was over seventy now, and with his cropped silver hair and slim physique—to say nothing of the fact that he was wearing a peach-colored Ralph Lauren polo shirt and pale khaki pants—he didn't exactly resemble a Greek warrior, but he looked like a hero to *me*.

He chuckled and glanced over at me. "I guess I should ask then, 'Is this the face that launched a thousand ships?'"

"And the answer to that would have to be *not on your life.*"

"Well, not tonight at least. No offense, Bailey dear, but you look like hell."

"No offense taken. I saw for myself in the bathroom mirror."

"Do you need food? We could stop someplace."

"I'm okay for now. It's just so good to be here in the car with you."

"Do you feel up for talking? I'm bursting with questions."

I could sense a new wave of achiness cresting in the distance. For now, though, I seemed okay. I fleshed out what I'd told him on the phone, covering the most important points from over the past few days.

"What a saga," he said when I'd finished. "It doesn't take a genius to figure out that you've probably made someone very mad and if so, it must be the killer."

"Exactly."

"Is there anything you can do from New York?"

"I've been wondering about that. I mean, I certainly don't need Jillian's permission to keep investigating, and yet being offsite is a real handicap. I'll check with Mamie and Blake—Jillian's high school friends—to find out if the shepherd turns up, and I'll probably call the detective who interviewed me. I want to tell him about the attack, even though he may think it's unrelated." I snickered. "And since I'll be out of range, he can't kick my ass."

"And what about Jillian? What's next for her, do you think?"

"Gosh, I don't know. It's awful that things ended

so awkwardly between us. I feel as if I'm almost back where I started with her."

"It sounds as if she kind of snapped."

"Yeah, I know, I was thinking about that over dinner. Five days ago she was so gung ho about my being involved and said she would do anything to find the killer. Then suddenly she wants me gone. Of course, she's justifiably freaked about everything that happened, but I'm wondering now if there's more going on."

"Like what?"

"No clue, though I had a weird feeling when we were talking Saturday night. It felt like something was on her mind, something she wasn't willing to disclose."

"Maybe she'll tell you in time."

"Yeah, maybe." Though I wondered if Jillian would even bother staying in touch.

We were off the rural roads now and on the Taconic, the sky black. Fatigue finally nailed me. I muttered a comment about needing to rest and drifted off to sleep.

By the time I woke again, we were closing in on Manhattan. I fished out my phone and texted Beau, letting him know that the city was in sight. I asked Landon if he'd mind dropping me off in Chelsea and parking the car in the garage in the building on Ninth Street, where he lived and I worked every day.

"I have a better idea," he announced. "Your old bed's made up, right? Why don't you stay there tonight and I can fix you breakfast in the morning. With Beau still out of town, you need someone to keep an eye on you."

It took me only a second to decide. It would save Landon an extra stop tonight, and, beyond that, his cooking would definitely be a partial cure for my aches and pains. After parking in the garage, we hurried to the lobby and boarded the elevator to the fourteenth floor, leaving the tubs in my Jeep. Landon kissed me on the cheek good night and told me to simply knock when I was ready for breakfast.

Despite my nap in the car, I had no trouble summoning sleep that night, though it felt weird to be in my old bed. I'd stayed in it only once since I moved in with Beau—on a night when I'd been working really late, he was shooting out of town, and snow was coming down hard.

When I woke around eight the next morning, the total silence confused me, and then I realized where I was. From Beau's tenth-floor apartment, I could sometimes hear muffled car horns and the occasional manhole cover blowing off. This apartment, on the other hand, faced away from the street, and there was rarely any noise from below.

For a time I lay very still, trying to decipher what my body was telling me. I was definitely less achy than yesterday, and though *perky* was way too strong of a word to describe my energy level, the lard-ass sensation was gone. Maybe this was only a reprieve until I received the next dose of vaccine, but I'd take it.

There was, however, no escaping the mental hangover I was experiencing. I felt even more frustrated and regretful than I had last night, perhaps because now that I was miles away from the Berkshires, the truth had finally sunk in. I was technically off the case.

While this might solve my immediate problem with Beau, it just didn't sit well with me. I didn't like giving up and slinking off. This way I'd never be able to clear Dylan Fender's name, never learn whether my visit to Penny Niles had precipitated her murder, never discover what bastard tried to turn me into a chew toy. And never know who killed the Lowes.

I considered for a moment what I'd told Landon in the car. I didn't need Jillian's permission to keep digging. But I wasn't sure what I could do from New York that would add up to much, even with a hint of my mojo back today.

After forcing myself out of bed, I rifled through my duffel bag for the pain medication, taking only half a pill this time because I wanted to begin weaning myself off them. As I was tossing the container back into the bag, my gaze fell on the composition book I'd been using to take notes over the past few days.

Glumly, I withdrew it from the bag and thumbed through the pages, scanning my entries. On the final page were the nearly illegible words I'd scribbled Sunday night: the name of Carl Lowe's former assistant and the real estate agency where her husband worked. In my nearly delirious state, I'd still managed to record the info after Hague had dropped me off.

I texted Landon and asked him to give me at least a half hour before I showed up at his place for breakfast. I showered, a longer one today than yesterday, during which I managed a shampoo with one hand. The results weren't perfect, but it was better than walking around looking like my hair had been hosed with motor oil.

Once I was dressed, I called Beau.

"Hey, so there you are."

"Can you talk now or are you already shooting?"

"No, this is good. We haven't started yet today. . . . You got in pretty late, I guess."

"What do you mean?"

I didn't mean it to sound challenging but it kind of came out that way.

"I had Sam go by our building a couple of times last night to check on you and see if you needed food." Sam was an old pal of Beau's. "He said that even at ten, no one answered the buzzer."

"Oh, that was sweet of you. But I'm staying on Ninth Street. Landon drove me back to the city and it was just easier this way. Plus he said he wanted to make me breakfast."

A couple moments of silence. Was he weirded out by the fact that I'd bunked down at my old place?

"Okay, that makes sense, I guess. Look, Bailey, I'm really sorry about how I launched into you yesterday—when you were clearly dealing with so much."

"Thanks, I appreciate that."

"It's just—"

"Beau, can we please table this till we're face-to-face? I don't want to end up in a conversation like the other one we had."

I was eager to hash it out, but not over the phone.

"Sure, you're right."

"Are you still coming back on Thursday?"

"I'm hoping to."

"Hoping to?"

"We've had trouble with another interview subject, but I'm trying to work it out."

It seemed ironic. I'd hightailed it out of the Berkshires, not at Beau's insistence but surely with his insistence in the back of my mind, and yet he had no idea when he was coming home.

"Okay, well I guess I'll see you whenever."

"Bailey, look, if there's any chance I can make it earlier—"

"Don't worry about it. I'll be fine."

"I'll call you tonight."

Ten minutes later, I was sitting in the dining area of Landon's apartment, a place he'd remodeled brilliantly by tearing down the walls to a second bedroom and creating a lovely, loftlike space with pale, pickled wood floors, light gray sofas and chairs, and dark antiques. While I dug into an exquisite chive-and-goat-cheese omelet, the first food I'd been able to relish since Sunday morning, I filled Landon in on what was happening with Beau. His cold feet about my crime writing.

"Do you think he's always had a problem with your work and you never saw it?" Landon asked.

"If he did, he kept it tightly under wraps. When I had any type of trouble in the past, he might have wigged out for a bit, but then he'd let it go. Mostly he seemed totally intrigued by my assignments."

"When did things shift?"

"Six or seven months ago. It's like a guy who starts

dating a woman he's seen perform at a strip club and then suddenly pressures her to keep her clothes on."

Landon chuckled. "Well, I wouldn't put it in exactly the same category. Maybe Beau's simply become more concerned as his feelings for you have grown over time."

"Aren't *you* the hopeless romantic?"

"You don't think that could be it?"

I looked off, my mind knitting pieces together. "I don't know . . ."

"*What?*" Landon narrowed his light brown eyes.

"It's not simply his attitude about my work. His—his schedule seems less predictable lately—more canceled plans, that sort of thing. He had to bail on seeing my final interview at the Y because something came up at the last minute. It's odd."

I realized suddenly that this revelation had probably taken vague shape weeks ago and had been sneakily growing and adding muscle without my being fully aware of it until now, like one of those pet baby alligators that gets flushed into the sewer and eventually emerges full-grown, ready to devour every small dog within a mile radius. It wasn't until Beau mentioned needing to stay in Miami that it crystalized for me.

"You're not thinking Beau is cheating on you, are

you?" Landon asked, his voice hushed. The words made me cringe.

I shook my head slowly.

"God, no, I hope not. I don't have any reason to think that. And yet what does it mean when a guy's plans seem as hard to nail down as Jell-O? And something else weird happened lately. He ended up taking a later plane to Miami than he told me about, and I only found out by chance."

"Days later?"

"Hours. But it was odd for him not to alert me. Out of character."

Landon wiped his mouth with a crisp white napkin and laid it back on the table.

"You've always said that Beau has an air of mystery, so maybe that's all this is."

"Yeah, I guess."

"Or perhaps you're still skittish because of that cad you were married to."

"I thought I'd put all that behind me when I decided to move in with Beau."

"Talk to Beau when he gets back, see what he says."

"Do guys ever come clean about cheating?"

"No, but then again women don't, either, from what I know."

I thought suddenly of my conversation with Jocelyn London.

"Speaking of cheating, I forgot to mention yet *another* twist in the whole Lowe saga. Jillian thinks her mother might have been having an affair, and, of course, any lover of hers would belong on the possible suspect list."

"Any idea who it could have been?"

"There were no hints in her calendar. And when I asked her friend about it, she gave me this really fierce denial. Though maybe *too* fierce."

"What did she say exactly?"

I'd noticed the comment when I was thumbing through my notebook earlier. "She told me that if I was asking if there was another man in Claire's life, the answer was absolutely not. She said Claire wasn't *capable* of something like that."

Landon had been sipping his coffee and as he set down the cup, a sly grin spread across his face.

"What?" I said. "You think she was protesting too much?"

"No, not that. Let me ask you: Did you ever hear that riddle about the kid in the car crash who ends up in the ER?"

"Uh, yeah, vaguely. Remind me."

"A man and his son are in a terrible crash. The father dies and the son is rushed to the hospital and into surgery. The surgeon takes one look at the boy and says, 'I can't operate on him. He's my son.' And the question is, 'How can that be?'"

"Oh, yeah. It turns out the surgeon is the mother, right?"

"Exactly. Apparently, even now people can't figure it out, or they say, 'Oh, he had two fathers.' Which, as a gay man, warms my heart, but it proves that we're still so programmed to think of surgeons as male."

"But what does that have to do with Claire Lowe?"

"Her friend's comment makes me think of that old riddle. The way a certain choice of words can be used to deceive. She told you there was no other *man* in Claire's life."

I dropped my mouth open in surprise.

"Omigod. You mean the affair might have been with a woman?"

"Just a thought."

But a good one, and I felt dumb for missing it. I could still hear the way Jocelyn had bitten off those words, as if she had contempt for the notion of her friend with a man. In fact, if the affair had been with a woman, that woman might very well have been Jocelyn.

And I knew how I might learn more.

"Look, I hate to eat and run," I told Landon, "but I have to check something out. I'll call you later, okay?"

I hugged him good-bye, nearly flew out of his apartment, and rode the elevator to the garage level. After locating my Jeep, I dug out Claire's calendar from the tub with her and Carl's names.

Back upstairs I parked myself at the table. Up until I moved in with Beau, I used to work in a Lilliputian home office that had once been a walk-in closet, but more and more these days I set up shop at my dining table by the window. The view was to the west and a series of redbrick and yellow-limestone apartment buildings, topped by enchanting wood-shingled water towers.

I opened the calendar at the very beginning and began paging through for the third time, reading what was scribbled on the boxes for each day. And with a fresh perspective, I saw something that hadn't registered before—just how many times Jocelyn's name was in there. When I'd gone through on the two other occasions, I'd been so focused on looking for red flags and possible codes for assignations that I hadn't noticed what was right under my nose: All year long, except for early April—when Jocelyn had told me she was with her sister in Maine—there were two, three, sometimes even four scheduled get-togethers a week for her and Claire. That seemed like a lot, even for best friends.

If there had been an affair—and, of course, this was hardly proof of it—I wondered how long it had been going on. And I wondered if Bob London, he of the barrel chest and tight grip on his wife's elbow, had discovered it. Something told me a guy like that wouldn't have taken the news well.

That made Bob London a possible suspect. Though Jocelyn had supposedly been out of town at the time of the murders, there was no reason to think he was. He might have set out to confront Claire and, in his fury, had taken down the entire family.

I needed to figure it out—this and other unanswered questions. And somehow I was going to have to do it from New York City.

Chapter 15

I opened my laptop and did a search on Bob London. According to what I turned up, he ran a company called COT Technologies, which apparently did a lot of work remotely and had been in operation for at least twenty years. It appeared Bob was probably about eight or ten years older than Jocelyn. Unlike Bruce Kordas, London wasn't off the grid when it came to the community. He supported local charities, took part in golf tournaments, and was on the board of a country club.

And interestingly he'd been charged with a DWI fifteen years ago. *One year* after the murders. Had something been eating away at him then? Eating away at the Londons' marriage?

When Bob London had come to collect Jocelyn that day at the café, I hadn't sensed any chemistry or affection between them. Based on quick math, I figured she'd been only in her early- to mid-twenties when they married. Perhaps she'd been too young to see that Bob wasn't the right fit for her—on more than one level. In the years that followed, she may have been intimated by him—he gave off a bully vibe—and unsure of how to extricate herself, as well as worried about the impact a divorce would have on her daughters.

If Jocelyn really *had* been Claire's lover, it could possibly explain why she was so emotionally stingy with Jillian. The whole Lowe family might have been, in her view, an impediment to her relationship with Claire.

I did a search on Jocelyn next.

Not a ton came up, but a couple of details jumped out. Though the mean Bottega Veneta mommies had muscled her out of school activities, she was still doing volunteer work, now as a board member of a local theater. She showed up in a bunch of photos from events supporting the theater, and in a couple of them, the same woman appeared by her side. It didn't necessarily mean anything. But it left me wondering: If Jocelyn *had* loved Claire beyond friendship, did she later go searching for someone to replace her?

Also of note: an obituary from five years ago for a man named David Tagg stated that he had been survived by "a daughter, Jocelyn London (Robert), and a son, Carter." No mention of the sister in Maine. Did that mean Jocelyn's sister had passed away from the cancer?

I didn't have a cell number for Jocelyn, and though I located a landline number for her through the White Pages online, I was reluctant to use it in case Bob answered. I sent her an email instead, saying I had a few more questions and was hoping to speak to her by phone. It was hard to imagine her coming clean with me, but I was eager to see how she reacted when I returned to the topic of Claire's fidelity.

While I had my computer open, I did a quick search online about personal-protection dogs, comparing them to guard dogs. The difference was just as Blake had described. I made the mistake of also checking out a few videos of Dobermans, German shepherds, and pit bulls attacking trainers in protective gear, and within seconds my heart was pounding hard.

I took a break then, stretching my legs on my terrace and replying to a text from Beau asking for an update on my condition. It was sunny out, the temperature in the mid-eighties, with a light, pleasant breeze. Summer was hurtling by, I realized, and I was barely paying attention. That was okay. Right now I had something that interested me more than balmy weather.

I returned to the table. There was another lead

I could tackle from New York, I knew, and that was tracking down Heather Pleshette Todd.

I started with a Facebook search for both Heather Pleshette and Heather Todd. More than a handful of women with both names turned up. The most likely candidate was a redhead with the last name of Todd, who appeared to be in her late thirties. Her privacy settings prohibited me from seeing any more than her name and her profile picture.

Facebook, I realized, probably wouldn't be the best way to connect with Heather anyway. She would surely check out my Facebook author page and, discovering that I wrote true crime books and articles, might suspect I'd spun the friend-of-Jillian story in order to snag an interview.

What I needed was a more direct way to reach her, and that might very well be through her husband, if, that is, they were still married. I could try to make my case with him, hoping that he would put me in touch with Heather.

I pulled up the Harrow Realty website. It seemed to be a fairly big outfit, one that handled plenty of luxury properties. The navigation bar had a tab for agents and after clicking on it, I found one with the last name of Todd. Kensey Todd.

From the accompanying photo—which, of course,

might have been dated—he appeared to be in his mid- to late-forties. That made sense. It would have meant he was in his mid-thirties or so at the time he met Heather Pleshette. He was not only handsome but also dashing-looking, with dark eyes and hair. Possibly half-Asian, I guessed. It wasn't hard to imagine a woman from a small town falling for him when he blew into her boss's office one day.

I called the number listed for Todd, clearly a cell, and after reaching voice mail, left a message saying that I was a good friend of Jillian Lowe's, was calling on her behalf, and was hoping to be able to speak to him today.

I checked my watch. Much of the morning had already flown by, enough time surely for Blake to have made contact with the animal-control people. I texted Mamie, using the number Jillian had given me at one point, and asked for an update.

"As you probably know, I'm not in the area anymore," I added, wondering if she'd even been informed of this fact. "But I'd love to stay on top of this."

I didn't have a lot to show for the morning, but I felt good. I was back in action, *doing* something. I wasn't naive enough to think I was going to solve the case on my own from my old wooden dining table, but I had a few new threads to play with, which might end up turning into information that could be passed to May-nard. If Jillian discovered I was probing, she could hardly object. I wasn't the least bit in danger.

It was now close to noon and I was eager to show up at the clinic for my second rabies vaccine, which I'd arranged by phone. I knocked on Landon's door, since he'd insisted on accompanying me, and we walked the short distance.

"You didn't get bitten by a bat, did you?" the PA asked.

"Don't I wish," I said as I rolled up the sleeve of my shirt. "Dog."

Back in my old apartment I braced for impact, but for the time being at least, I felt vaguely normal and also hungry for the salad I'd picked up with Landon on the way home. As I was devouring it at the table, a text came in from Mamie.

Hope you're better. Unfortunately nothing on the dog. Blake's called 3x. Wlyk if news.

Damn. The chances were slim and yet part of me had remained hopeful. Since the dog hadn't been found by now, I doubted it would ever turn up. Which meant the owner retrieved it before animal control could show up or the dog had skulked off in the woods to die with the bungee cord still around its neck.

For the rest of the afternoon I was in a holding pattern, waiting to hear from both Jocelyn and Kensey Todd. Neither made contact.

And neither did Jillian. I hadn't expected her to call for a gabfest, but I thought she at least might text to see how I was faring or ask if the dog had been located. I ended up sending her a text saying I was back in New York and I'd love to touch base this week if possible.

Landon cooked up lamb chops for dinner, and I tried to enjoy them, but the muscle ache and head throbbing had boomeranged back. I decided to stay at Ninth Street again and crashed early after thanking Landon profusely for all he'd done. Though I pleaded to reimburse him for the UberBLACK, he wouldn't hear of it.

Beau called again that night to check on me, and reported that it was definitely looking as if he wouldn't be back until Thursday. It wasn't his fault, but I felt irritated by the announcement. I couldn't tell how much of that was me and how much was the vaccine. I had enough sense, however, not to let my irritation leak over the phone.

Later, in bed, I found myself wondering about Jillian, whether she was still in Boston or possibly en route back to Williamsburg. Did she have any regrets about pulling the plug? I wondered. Would I even hear from her again?

Early the next morning I ordered an Uber to take me to Chelsea. After being dropped at a deli near my building, I picked up a few supplies, knowing there'd be little in the larder at this point. It felt weird when I stepped into the apartment, as if I'd been gone for weeks, not days. The only sign of life was a pair of Beau's shoes lying haphazardly on the foyer floor. I wondered briefly if he'd made it home, but quickly realized he'd probably chucked the shoes out of his suitcase at the last minute before dashing out the door.

For the flight that was later than the one he'd originally booked.

I dropped my bags in the foyer, put the food in the kitchen, and after turning on the AC, made a beeline for the couch in the living room. The side effects from the second dose of the vaccine had really kicked in and I was having little luck ignoring them. I rested there for a while, begging for a second wind and hoping for responses to the two inquires I'd made.

By eleven, still nothing. I shot Jocelyn another email, explaining I really needed to speak to her. If I didn't receive a response by the end of the day, I would consider trying her landline tomorrow at a time when her husband would most likely be working.

The fact that I hadn't heard from Todd yet was more worrisome. The guy was in sales, which meant he was a people person and someone not shy about jumping on the phone. It was possible that he and Heather had left the murders squarely in the past and didn't want to revisit anything involving the Lowes. Or maybe he was super busy. I told myself to be patient and give it a few more hours.

In hopes of a distraction, I padded back out to the foyer for my tote bag. I dug out the thick and raggedy folder I'd lugged from Ninth Street, the one I'd stuffed over the years with both newspaper clips and down-loaded articles about noteworthy crimes. I'd already thumbed through the folder a couple of times during the past months, praying that a particular case would stir me enough to consider writing a book on it. Now it was time to peruse the contents all over again. When I'd agreed to help Jillian, a small part of me was hoping that the case might prove to be the topic I was search-ing for. But even if I managed to dig up a few facts from New York, I couldn't imagine Jillian wanting anything to do with a book project anymore.

I needed a new book topic—*fast.*

And it wasn't simply because my publisher would be on my case if I didn't put my ass in gear. If I intended to be a crime writer for the undeterminable future, books were going to have to be the main ticket for me, since there was little opportunity in magazines anymore.

For the next hour and a half, with my legs stretched out on the couch, I waded through the clips. Though there were a few compelling cases, absolutely nothing spoke to me. When I reached the last, tattered page, I felt like I'd just spent a chunk of the day sorting through a big, twisty heap of clothes at a sample sale, trying futilely to find items in the right color or size.

Next I returned to my laptop and headed down the rabbit hole of the Internet, trolling through various links to see what I'd stumble on. Eventually my head hurt and I couldn't tell if the pain was mostly due to the vaccine or to the fact that reading about forty or fifty grizzly homicides in one sitting was too rich for even my blood.

Just for the hell of it, I pulled up Kensey Todd's photo once more and stared at. "Why won't you *call* me?" I demanded.

And then suddenly I had an idea. Maybe it was time to start shopping for real estate again.

Todd might be reluctant to return a call, but if I

could position myself face-to-face with him during an apartment showing, I might be able to make my case and convince him to put me in touch with Heather.

I would have to use a different name. And rather than call his cell again and try to alter my voice, it would be smarter for me to set up a viewing through his assistant. Did real estate agents *have* assistants?

I scrolled through his apartment listings until I found one for a small Tribeca loft that fit the price range of someone who sounded like me, meaning a woman who was clearly not a pop singer, a Kardashian, or the daughter of a Russian oligarch.

This time, I phoned the main number and asked if Mr. Todd had an assistant I could speak to.

"Have you tried his cell?" the receptionist asked.

"Yes, and I've spoken to him," I lied, "but I thought he mentioned the name of an assistant he wanted me to follow up with."

"Maybe he meant one of his associates. Amy Burden is the key person on his team."

"Yes, that sounds right."

"Let me give you the number."

As soon as I was off the phone, I called Burden and she answered with the high energy only someone in sales could totally master. I explained that a friend had recommended Mr. Todd and I was hoping he could show me the Tribeca loft as soon as possible. Was that something she could arrange for me?

"Of course," she said. "It's a terrific property, by the way. And your name is?"

"Jessie Pendergrass," I said, knowing she wouldn't mind me hijacking her name for the moment.

The perfectly peppy Amy asked for my contact info, and I ended up giving her Jessie's email and *my* cell number. I was pushing it, I knew. I'd just have to alert Jessie later and plead emergency conditions.

"How about four today?" Burden said after pausing to take down the information.

"Perfect. Shall I meet Mr. Todd in the lobby?"

"Actually, I'll be showing you the apartment."

Oh, great. I should have seen that this was a possibility.

"No offense, but I promised the friend I'd connect with Mr. Todd. I feel a little guilty leaving him out of the loop."

"Unfortunately he's very busy with a major open house this week and won't be available for any showings. But I'm on his team, so working with me is basically the same thing. I can tell him a friend referred you."

The last thing I wanted to do while feeling, quite literally, like dog meat, was traipse around an apartment

I had no interest in, with a woman who couldn't be of any service to me.

"Oh, gosh, let me check with my friend, okay? I just want to be sure I'm doing the right thing."

"Sure," she said pleasantly enough. In her line of work she probably had a high tolerance for flaky people.

I was back to square one. Due to the open house, there'd be no chance of meeting Todd for a showing.

Then maybe, I thought, I needed an open house on my schedule, too.

I found a link for "open houses" on the Harrow site, and a whole bunch popped up. The one being hosted this week by Kensey Todd was tomorrow at five, on West Sixty-Second Street. I would be there with bells on. I took a risk and registered with my own name, but I figured there was a decent chance he wouldn't bother going over the names in advance.

Without warning, a tsunami of fatigue threatened to drag me out to sea and, forgoing lunch, I staggered into the bedroom for a nap. I could smell the scent of Beau's musky cologne emanating from his pillowcase.

I missed him. And I wanted things to be okay with us. I would have to make him see my side of things regarding my work so I wouldn't feel stymied. At the same time, I had to get to the bottom of the issue I raised with Landon—Beau's schedule shifting more these days, his seeming distant at times. Though as Landon had theorized, I might simply be experiencing residual paranoia from my divorce. The gift that kept on giving.

I wasn't sure how long I slept but I awoke with a start. A noise had roused me, I was sure of it. I froze, listening, feeling my pulse pick up. I had no reason to be seriously alarmed. Our apartment door, after all, had adequate locks on it, but my nerves were still on edge from the Berkshires.

I'd almost convinced myself I'd imagined the noise, when I heard a faint but unmistakable sound from one of the other rooms. Someone was inside the apartment. I tore back the covers and tiptoed out of the bedroom. Turning down the hall, I saw him.

Beau Regan, mystery man, was standing in the middle of the living room.

"Hey, I hope I didn't startle you," he said. "The plans changed and I grabbed the first flight I could. I dropped the equipment off at the studio and then headed straight home."

"Nice to set eyes on you," I said.

We covered the distance between us and embraced, with me warning Beau to please steer clear of my left arm.

"Is the bite still really painful?"

"Yeah, but it's more the side effects from the vaccine that are giving me problems. Achiness, that sort of thing."

"Can I see it?"

"Uh, I have to change the gauze later today. I'll show you then if you really want."

As good as it was to see Beau, there seemed to be a clunkiness to our conversation.

"Can I make you dinner?" he asked. "We don't have a ton of food, but I could whip up an omelet."

"That would be great. I picked up tomatoes and lettuce earlier, so we could have a salad, too."

"Okay, just let me wash my hands first."

"I'll set the table."

"Don't you dare. You're off duty."

Beau ended up serving us dinner on the couch, which made it so much easier for me. While we ate, he shared a little news and gossip about his shoot, and how the weather had miraculously cooperated after threatening not to. Then it was my turn. Over espressos I went into more detail about my experience in and around Dory, including Penny's murder and the dog attack. I knew I wasn't helping my case with such ruthless candidness, but I'd decided that being cagey or secretive wouldn't do me any good in the long run.

When I'd finally wrapped up, Beau exhaled loudly and shoved his hands through his hair. Here it comes, I thought, expecting him to begin harping again on the risks I was subjecting myself to.

"So this German shepherd," he said. "Would it have killed you if the two guys hadn't shown?"

"I'm not sure. I did a little research on protection dogs, and in general they're trained to latch on to an arm or a leg from now until the end of time rather than maul you to death."

"But—"

"Look, Beau, I'm trying to be as honest as possible. I don't actually know how much danger I was in."

"I'm simply asking. I was really worried about you, and I want to know the details."

"But I get the feeling you also want to make your case, like you did on the phone the other night."

"I don't want to make any case tonight. You're sick and you're tired, and you need to rest. We can talk about all this another time."

I didn't actually *want* to postpone the conversation. It was essential, after all, to clear the air on the subject, but considering my condition, I knew I might end up saying something super crabby.

"Okay, let's table it for now."

"Good," he said, and leaned down to kiss me tenderly on the mouth.

"I think the vaccine is working," he said afterward. "I didn't hear you snarl when I kissed you."

That earlier clunkiness had dissipated, and Beau seemed truly happy to see me. Had I only imagined him being remote at times?

We were in bed by ten and up early the next day. I ate bagels with Beau in the small dining room. He said he'd be back for dinner at around six thirty and would pick up groceries.

I felt marginally better but hardly ready to rock and roll. For most of the day I hung around the apartment, answering emails about work stuff—which included saying yes to a couple of talks in the fall about *A Model Murder*—and biding my time for the open house.

No word from Jocelyn yet, but I decided to hold off calling her landline until I saw what progress I made with reaching the Todds.

And still, I noted, no response from Jillian.

Finally, at four, I grabbed a cab to the West Sixties, dressed in a long-sleeved blouse, slim skirt, and open toe pumps, figuring I needed to look the part—and that included not displaying a gauze bandage oozing blood. The building turned out to be at least forty stories, with a huge, double-height lobby of rich wood and obviously imported marble, the kind of place that could make you wonder if there were a few kings or popes buried under the floor. Upon entering, I spotted a young woman standing with a clipboard that read Harrow Realty on the back. After checking in with her, I was handed a fancy-pants promotional packet and directed to take the elevator to 34C.

It was only when I was in the elevator, glancing at some of the material, that I realized that I would not be viewing an apartment that was actually for sale but rather a model for one in a building still under construction. But what did I care? I was here only with the hope of meeting Kensey Todd.

Todd, it turned out, looked exactly like his photo, and I spotted him the moment I emerged from the large, gallery-style foyer into a humongous living space. He was dressed in a nicely cut suit, no tie, standing against an entire wall of floor-to-ceiling windows. There was a couple talking to him, a man and a woman in their late thirties perhaps. The guy seemed super alpha, and I pegged him as a hedge-fund type, someone with money to burn.

There were at least thirty other people milling around the living space or drifting in and out of rooms flowing off from both sides. Some chatted together as they checked out the apartment, and others simply admired the breathtaking view. Beyond us, the Hudson River gleamed, and the sun, preparing for its descent, was a bright, fiery ball in the sky.

I spent a few moments pretending to eye the apartment, but then nosed toward Todd and the couple, picking a spot to stand just outside the circle. Mr. Hedge Fund was describing how they'd recently seen a town house with Hermès leather walls, but he was looking for something "sun-drenched and more authentic," whatever *that* combo could entail. Todd told him to check out the fabulous master suite and he'd follow up later.

"Mr. Todd?" I said as soon as the couple had moved off.

"Yes, but please call me Ken. And you are?"

"I'm Bailey Weggins. I left a message for you yesterday, but I thought it might be better for us to speak in person."

He blanched.

"What's this about?" he demanded, lowering his voice to just above a whisper. His smile had vanished in a heartbeat.

"It's about Carl Lowe and his family," I said. "It's urgent that I speak to your wife. Would you be willing to give me a phone number for her?"

Todd clamped his mouth shut, which suggested the conversation might be over, but then cocked his chin toward an empty corner. "Why don't we step over there," he said.

Once we were sequestered in the corner, I collapsed everything into as short an explanation as possible. Dylan Fender, now deceased, had *not* murdered the Lowes, he had died in prison before being fully exonerated, and Jillian had recruited me to help find the real killer since the police didn't appear to be taking action.

It was clear from Todd's expression that he hadn't heard yet about Dylan, and that the news had thrown him.

"This is terrible," he said, his voice still low. "Heather's going to be really upset about it." He glanced away from me and out into the room, obviously checking whether our tête-à-tête had aroused any curiosity.

"I can imagine. But as I said, I'm eager to speak to Heather because I believe she may have information of real value to us."

Todd shook his head. "I'm sorry, but there's really nothing my wife can contribute."

"But I think there may be if I could only speak to her."

"It won't do any good. Until they arrested the boy, she had no clue who could have been responsible for that monstrosity. She went through all the questioning with the police years ago."

He was really digging in his heels. My only option, I decided, was to appeal to his sense of justice and hope that broke down his resistance.

"Please, Ken," I implored. "An innocent young man spent years in prison for a crime he didn't commit and the person who murdered the Lowes is still at large. I think Heather may possess information that she never realized was significant. All I'm asking for is five minutes of her time to ask a couple of questions. I could even do it on the phone."

Todd pinched his lips together again and, after a moment, let out a sigh.

"I have responsibilities tonight and I need to get back to them, but I'll call my wife and ask her. And then I really need you to leave."

He abruptly walked away and ducked into what I guessed was the powder room. Three minutes later he emerged looking grim. My stomach sank.

"My wife is joining friends for dinner at a restaurant called Orsay in the East Seventies. She will meet you at the bar in twenty minutes. And I've assured her you'll be quick."

"All right, good. How will I know her? Does she happen to be redheaded?" That was the woman I'd seen on Facebook.

"Yes, she's hard to miss." He turned to walk away.

"Thank you," I called after him. "Thank you so much."

This was even better than I'd hoped for. Surely I would end up with answers before the night was over.

Chapter 16

In the interest of time I ordered an Uber, paying a ridiculous surge price, but it still took over twenty minutes to travel cross town to the restaurant. From the doorway I was able to survey the entire bar area, and I groaned out loud in frustration. The only people hanging there were two clusters of middle-aged men.

I grabbed an empty stool at the zinc bar and ordered a Perrier. The restaurant was one of those wood-paneled French bistros with amber-tinted wall sconces and intricately tiled floors designed to make posh Upper East Siders feel as if they were on the Left Bank for the evening. I glanced behind me into the main part of the restaurant to see if Heather might already be at a table. The only redhead in sight was a middle-school-aged boy chowing down with his parents.

But then, like a ghost materializing from a wall, she was by my side. Slender and pretty, with lightly freckled skin, green eyes, and hair styled in a modern, intentionally messy French twist. I wondered if she might have been waiting quietly in a corner until she could take a measure of me.

"Heather, thank you for agreeing to this," I said.

"What's going on exactly? Ken said you told him Dylan Fender didn't do it."

"That's right. New DNA evidence indicates that someone else was the killer, and I'm trying to help Jillian Lowe figure out who it was. There's something I really need to ask you."

"I swore I'd never speak about this again," she said, and then, instinctively touched her freckled fingers to her lips. From her appearance, I guessed she'd only been in her mid-twenties at the time of the murders.

"I'm sure it's still very painful, but it would mean a great deal to Jillian."

She let out a ragged sigh. "I was never close to C.J., but he was *more* than a decent boss, and his family was lovely. I can't believe what happened to them. And I was the one who found them." She had nearly choked on those last few words.

"You wondered where Carl was that morning?" I said, remembering that, according to news reports, she'd gone by the house.

"Yes, when he didn't show for an eight-thirty meeting—and didn't answer his phone—I knew something was wrong, so I drove to Dory. I—I saw Claire through the window by the door, lying in all that blood. I was shaking so hard I could barely call 911."

"I heard that not long before the murders, a man came by Carl's office and confronted him. Do you remember that?"

"Who *told* you that?" she said.

"Bruce Kordas. He claims he informed the police and assumed it wasn't relevant once Dylan was arrested. But maybe it *is* relevant. Do you remember the episode?"

Heather's mouth sagged open and she cast her gaze downward.

"Yes, I remember. It was a couple of weeks before."

"Did you know who the man was?"

"Oh God, I can't believe you're asking me this."

Something big was coming. I could tell by her tone and the look on her face.

"Did you know him?" I asked again.

"His name was John Denali. His son was in the Boy Scout troop that was led by C.J."

I didn't have to hear anymore to make goose bumps happen. A young boy. A middle-aged Scout leader. Please tell me this wasn't going where I thought it was.

"Did you overhear any of the conversation?"

"Yes. I could tell the man was angry, and I eavesdropped after the door was closed. I wanted to be sure that C.J. wasn't in any kind of danger."

"And did you figure out why this guy was so angry?"

"It was horrible," she said, her voice barely above a whisper now. "He accused Carl of abusing his son."

My body went limp. As I'd contemplated what might have angered someone enough to show up at Carl Lowe's office, unannounced, I'd considered everything from an affair to gambling debts, but never this. It was heartbreaking. It also might explain why Danny had dropped out of Scouts. Carl probably insisted on it after the accusation.

I was also looking at a motive for murder.

I reached over and touched Heather's hand. "Thank you for sharing this. I know it wasn't easy, but it was the right thing to do."

"I've never breathed a word of it to anyone, not even Ken."

"And not the police then?"

Heather shook her head. "No, though I would have if they hadn't made an arrest. But as soon as they accused the neighbor, I decided there was no reason to. I—I feel so guilty now."

"At this point there's no evidence that the man who came to see Carl—this John Denali—is guilty, but I want to look into it. Do you have any idea if he's still living around Dory?"

"I have no idea because I haven't been to the area in years. My mom's in Florida these days, and we have no other reason to go back. I was dating Ken by the time everything happened, and when he offered to take me away from it all, I said yes in two seconds flat."

"But you worked for Bruce for a period after, right?"

"Yes, for a short while. Everyone was reeling from shock, and I wanted to help out and do what I could at the time."

I thought for a moment, picking my words carefully.

"Here's the toughest question of all, Heather. Do you think there's a chance John Denali was right?"

This time she pressed her fingers even harder against her mouth, as if she was worried about what might escape from her lips.

"I—I don't know," she said finally. "I was so naive back then, and for a minute I didn't even understand what the man was getting at. He kept saying, 'You ruined my boy,' and I thought C.J. might have accused the son of doing something wrong in Scouts and humiliated him in front of the other boys—or didn't give him a badge he thought he deserved. Then he finally told C.J. he was going to make sure the whole world knew he was a pedophile."

"Carl must have been pretty shaken afterward."

"I'll never forget it. You know the expression about blood being drained from someone's face? It was like that. He spent the rest of the day in his office with the door closed."

"Were there any other warnings that Carl might have had a problem like that?"

"No, never—at least from what I could tell. He wasn't the warmest person in the world, but he seemed, well, *normal.* As I told you, though, I was really naive at the time and I might not have noticed something that another person would have picked up on."

"You said the family was lovely. Did you know them well?"

"No, not well. I saw them from time to time, like when I had to drop papers off at the house for C.J. And I got to know Jillian a little during her winter break that last year. She helped out in the office because we were short-staffed then. She was so poised and pretty and fun. I was a few years older but still a little in awe of her."

Something over my right shoulder caught her eye

and she raised a finger in the "give me one minute" signal. I turned to see two women about Heather's age eyeing us from the maître d' stand.

"My friends are here," Heather said. "I need to join them."

"Just one more minute, okay? Was there any trouble between the two partners? Someone suggested that Carl might have been disenchanted with Bruce."

"Oh, I don't think so," she said, clearly surprised by the question. "Not from my vantage point, at least. I must say, though, that in those last months, there seemed to be a bit of distance between them. When I first started, C.J. acted like a mentor to Bruce, almost a father figure—there was such an age gap, you know—but there didn't seem to be much mentoring at the end. I just assumed it was because Bruce was becoming more sure-footed. Business was booming, and it was as much due to Bruce as C.J. He had a way with people. He was always suave and charming."

Of course, Bruce might have wanted that booming business all to himself.

"But what about—"

"You said just one more minute." It was clear that the conversation had wearied her and she wanted it over.

"Sorry, I promise I'm almost done. What about

Bruce's stepson? I hear he worked at the company briefly."

Heather scoffed. "Oh, *him.* Yes, he worked with us that last February, maybe early March. I remember because Jillian had already gone back to school. I could tell C.J. wasn't thrilled about the hire, but he went along, knowing that Bruce's wife had probably pressured him. The guy was clueless, and lazy, and they had no choice but to fire him."

If Bruce thought Trevor was such a loser, why had he hired him again?

"How long was he there?"

"No more than a month."

Which would put the termination just weeks before the murders.

"Do you recall how he took the news?"

"I believe Bruce told him at home, so I never saw how Trevor—I think that was his name—reacted. I really have to stop now. My friends are waiting, and I can't bear to discuss this anymore."

"I understand," I said. I would have loved even a few more minutes with her but it wasn't in the cards. "Thank you so much for all your time." I quickly drew a business card from my purse and asked her to please reach out if anything significant occurred to her.

She slid off the barstool and I could see her trying to

recompose her expression. I doubted she'd be having much fun with the girls tonight. She started to move off and then turned back to me.

"How's Jillian?" she asked.

"Pretty good," I said. "She'll be a lot better if we can solve this."

She nodded, her expression sober, and hurried away.

I was feeling really drained myself by this point, my body nearly pulsing again with that weird achiness. It would have helped to recharge my batteries with a cappuccino before I split, but I didn't want to disturb Heather by hanging around. As I slunk out of the restaurant, I noticed her friends quizzing her, obviously trying to figure out if something was wrong, but Heather raised a hand and shook her head. She clearly wasn't going to discuss the situation with them.

During the cab ride home, my stomach wouldn't stop twisting over the revelation Heather had shared. The idea that Jillian's father might have been a pedophile made my skin crawl. If it was true, Danny could have been a victim, too. And it meant that John Denali had possibly killed the Lowe family in revenge.

There was something else to consider, I realized, as the cab nudged through a snarl of traffic on Lexington Avenue. Pedophiles are always on the lookout for victims. If Carl was guilty, he might have targeted boys at the school, as well, even friends of Danny's. Was that the secret Penny didn't want me to know?

As soon as I was in the apartment, I did a Google search for John Denali. My breath caught at what popped up: an obituary.

It turned out that John Denali, of Lyle, Massachusetts, had died two years ago, at the age of fifty-three, of a "long illness." Which meant that though he may have murdered the Lowes, he wasn't the one responsible for the havoc that had been wrecked during my stay near Dory. I raced through to the end. He was survived by two brothers; a daughter, Mandy of Bakersfield, California; and a son, Keith, of East Lyle, Massachusetts. I checked a map online. Lyle and East Lyle were only a short drive southeast of Dory.

If Keith Denali had told his father about his abuse— and how else would the father have known?—he may have been aware that his father had confronted Carl Lowe. It's possible that after the murders, he worried that his father was responsible and was relieved when an arrest was made. He may have learned of the attempt to exonerate Dylan Fender and decided to do all he could to prevent the truth coming to light. That, of course, would have entailed somehow discovering that I was in Dory and tailing me places—to the storage facility, to Penny's, to Foxcroft.

I googled Keith Denali next. In terms of links, only the father's obituary turned up, though I managed to find an address for him in East Lyle.

So now what? If I was going to learn anything more about Denali, I couldn't do it sitting on my butt on the couch in my living room.

"You doing okay?" Beau asked when he arrived home shortly afterward. He followed his comment by sitting down on the edge of the couch and kissing me hello. Despite our recent friction, I felt a swell of pleasure from his sheer presence.

"About the same."

"Would a glass of wine help—or make it worse?"

"Why don't I give it a try and find out," I said, smiling. "I finished with the painkillers."

"I hope you don't mind, but I ordered Chinese. I ran too behind to cook tonight."

"No, that's fine. Better to save your culinary skills for when I can fully appreciate them."

Beau brought me a glass of Spanish rioja and I stretched out on the couch, nursing it. I heard the buzzer from downstairs go off and a few minutes later, Beau returned with the food, plates, and cutlery.

I studied him as he set up the coffee table, his brown eyes doing a final perusal to make sure he hadn't forgotten anything. Maybe I shouldn't be concerned about a man who had not only just spooned chicken and broccoli onto my plate but also made sure I ended up with the crispier spring roll.

As we ate, we caught up on stuff we hadn't had a chance to discuss yet: a dinner invitation from a couple we knew; a drip in the kitchen sink that needed to be fixed; and details about a museum show we wanted to see. Beau also mentioned that his parents had told him they'd be at their vacation home in the Hamptons for only one of the two weekends that bookended our ten-day stay there in August.

Good, I thought, about the last piece of news. I liked his father a lot, but his mother seemed secretly judgy of me in ways that occasionally leaked out into broad daylight. I knew she liked the fact that I'd gone to Brown—*that* at least fit with the standards she'd determined for any love interest of Beau's—but deep down she wished that I was a banker or pediatrician or even an entrepreneur, and not the type of person who hung around crime scenes, wrote about homicidal maniacs, and ended up mauled by wild, possibly rabid dogs.

"So who's John Denali?"

"What?"

I'd let my mind wander as Beau discussed his parents' change of plans and now realized that his gaze had landed on the article on my laptop.

"This obit for John Denali. He's not a friend, is he?"

"No, just someone whose name came up in relation to Jillian's father. I was curious about what happened to him."

"Well, I guess this answers your question."

"More or less."

"What's the less part?"

"John Denali is dead, but his son still lives in the Berkshires. There's a slim possibility he's behind some of the bad stuff that happened up there."

"Are you going to tell the police?"

"Based on what I turned up today, I'll probably have to clue them in to one critical detail." They would need to know about the abuse accusation because it might be tied to the murder. "But I need to get a better handle on the situation before I make that call."

"How are you going to do that?" he asked. His tone had turned wary.

"Not sure."

Beau stretched his long legs out in front of him and appeared to study the Chukka boots he was wearing.

"I thought Jillian didn't want you poking around anymore."

"Jillian doesn't really have a say about whether I look into this. And there's no danger in doing research remotely."

"But what's the point in continuing? She's moved on; you're not getting paid. As you pointed out last night, it's not like you can do a book on it now."

Really? Was he actually asking me this question, the guy who'd once said, as a compliment, that I was like a dog with a bone when I worked on a story?

I shrugged. "I guess it's like that line in *All the King's Men*—'You have to open the envelope, for the end of man is to know.'"

Beau, I'd come to realize, didn't love it when I went all English major on him, quoting lines, but I hadn't been able to resist. The irritation I felt during the phone conversation the other night had started creeping back.

"You mean *All the President's Men*?" he said.

"No, *King's*. It won the Pulitzer Prize in the 1940s."

He just stared at me, clearly biting his tongue. Beau had lived in Asia for three years, meditated every day, and unlike me, didn't do snippy.

"I'm sorry," I said. "That was a cheap shot. It's just that we seem to be circling the topic you said you wanted to table, and maybe it's time to get it out in the open."

"You honestly think it would be good to discuss it right now? Considering how you feel."

"Yes. Because otherwise we'll be trying to ignore something we can't ignore."

"All right. Though I don't think there's much to add to what I said on the phone, Bailey. Your job freaking scares me."

"But why have you never raised this before? I thought you were fascinated by what I did."

"I am and I don't have an issue with you being a crime writer per se. It's all the jeopardy you seem to end up in. I guess I initially assumed that it wouldn't be a regular thing, but it hasn't gotten better. I feel at times as if I'm living with a member of SEAL Team Six or one of those people who fight wildfires, waiting to see if you make it back alive from a mission."

I took a breath and tried to see it from his perspective. My life *had* been threatened on more than one occasion, and it certainly made sense that he'd be concerned. Maybe I'd put him through more than I'd realized.

"I hear you. There've been a few hairy times for me, including this past week. But those have mostly been when I was helping out a friend and ended up in the thick of things. It's not always going to be like that, especially when I'm simply reporting a story."

He shook his head.

"I'm sorry, but I find that hard to believe, Bailey. Regardless of what kind of situation you're covering, it seems you're always opening doors no one else wants to open. It's like you don't know when to stop."

Okay I didn't like where this was going. "Are you saying I *purposely* place myself in treacherous situations? That I derive a certain thrill from it?"

He didn't respond, just studied me.

"Wait, is that it?"

"That's definitely what it looks like to an outside observer."

"God, Beau. You make it sound like I'm an adrenaline junkie, that if I weren't doing this I'd be bungee jumping off the GW Bridge. I don't *seek* danger. But I also don't believe in turning away from tough situations. I thought you *got* that about me."

He threw a hand up, as if he didn't know what to say next. For the first time I wondered if that funny thing I sensed about him lately was connected to this.

"Beau, I need to ask you. Is this why you've seemed kind of distant lately?"

"Distant? I don't feel I've been that way."

"It just seems . . . You've had dinners pop up out of the blue a few times lately. And there was that whole business about you taking a different flight. I've started to wonder what's going on."

"'What's going on'?"

"Yeah, is there something I should be worried about?"

"Are you asking if I'm *cheating* on you?"

That hadn't been where I was going, but he had my attention now.

"*Are* you?"

"God, Bailey, how could you say that? I would never sneak around like that."

"You slept with that girl in Turkey."

"Yes, but you and I weren't exclusive then. If I've seemed distracted lately, I'm sure it's because of work. It's been crazier than I'd like."

"Okay," I said, relieved. I would have to take him at his word and remind myself that Beau had always seemed too secure and direct to try to deceive me. Yet still, the overall conversation had left me feeling unsettled. I reached up and massaged my temples.

"Bailey, we can't do this anymore tonight," Beau said. "You aren't well, and this isn't helping. All I ask is that you consider what I said, okay? Not change what you do, but at least consider the type of stories you go after."

"All right, I'll think about it." On one level I felt I owed him that. I would be worried about him, too, if his film work placed him in jeopardy. But I disliked what he'd said about me not knowing when to stop, and I hated the idea of putting restrictions on myself. What was I supposed to do? Start writing crime stories about people who littered or jaywalked or hunted deer and squirrel without a license?

I took a bath as Beau cleaned up, with my left arm draped over the edge of the tub. As I soaked in the sudsy water, with Maria Callas singing from my iPod, I found myself wondering if there was any chance that Beau's Bailey-is-a thrill-seeker theory was correct, that I had a special kind of sonar for stories that would lead to harrowing situations because I derived a rush from being in the mix. And yet it just didn't make sense. I certainly had no history in that regard—I mean, for God's sake, my college sport had been intramural *volleyball*, and though I'd been spiked in the head plenty of times, I certainly hadn't *liked* it.

For the first time I asked myself if this could be a deal breaker between Beau and me. No, I couldn't allow that.

I crawled into bed at about ten, and Beau joined me moments later. Something told me sex would help reconnect us—it'd been at least a week since the last time—but there was no way for any kind of romp in my condition, and Beau knew that, too. I fell asleep almost instantly, but when I woke next I saw that I'd been out for only an hour or so. A noise must have stirred me awake, maybe city noises blaring from the street below. Next to me I could hear Beau breathe deeply. He was sleeping in just his boxer briefs and his naked arm was draped over my thigh.

I tried to fall back to sleep, but within minutes I knew it was a hopeless cause. I was too wound up—from both the conversation with Beau and the awful one earlier with Heather, which was still replaying in my mind. I slid out of bed and drifted into the kitchen, in search of a cold drink. I'd left my phone charging on the kitchen counter, and after noticing I'd missed a call, I realized that it was the ringtone that had probably roused me from sleep.

I picked up the phone and squinted at the screen. *Jillian.* Six minutes ago, at 11:20.

Late for a call. My heart skipped a beat at the thought that she might be in trouble. I hit redial.

"Hi," she answered. "Sorry for phoning so late."

"Not a problem," I said, easing the kitchen door closed so I wouldn't wake Beau. "How are you doing anyway? You've really been on my mind."

"I'm okay. The bigger question is how are *you?* Is your arm any better?"

"It's on the mend, yeah."

"Bailey, look, I'm so sorry. I'm sorry for things I said and for bolting like that. And for leaving you in the lurch."

"No harm done, Jillian. I'm just glad to hear your voice." Even if she wasn't interested in getting together in the city any time soon, at least we would now be on better terms.

"I was really upset and frustrated that day," she said.

"That's completely understandable. Being there was incredibly hard for you. Where are you now, by the way?"

"You were trying to find the killer," she said without answering my question. "You were getting close. And I was setting up roadblocks."

I felt a warning light start to blink in the very back of my brain. It was because of the way she'd said roadblocks, with a certain emphasis.

"What do you mean?"

"I—I didn't tell you everything. I held something back. Something that might matter."

Oh boy.

"Do you want to tell me what it is now?"

"I can't. I mean not on the phone. . . . Bailey, please, will you come back?"

"To Dory?" That was a stupid question—of course I

knew what she meant—but I was buying myself a little time, processing the request.

"Yes. I'm still in Boston, but I can meet you there."

Though I already knew the answer, I didn't announce it right away. Maybe I was letting it sit for a few seconds in my mind, knowing that my response was destined to upset Beau.

"Okay," I said finally. "When?"

Chapter 17

By eleven the next morning I was in my car and bound once again for the Berkshires. The whole thing felt so weirdly like *Groundhog Day*. Eight days earlier I'd been barreling northeast along the same roads, dressed in the identical jeans and sandals.

Of course this time the pit in my stomach was even bigger than before, because by now I was aware of the *Hound of the Baskervilles*-type surprises the region had to offer. I would have to watch my back—and Jillian's—every single second.

During our call I'd actually tried to dissuade Jillian from returning as well, suggesting that if she felt un-comfortable sharing her revelation over the phone, she could do it via a Skype call with me, and then I'd head up to the Berkshires on my own. But she'd insisted on joining me, determined for us to speak in person.

Her plan was to rent a car in Boston and arrive late Saturday because she had an obligation to take care of before she could travel, but I told her I'd head up one day earlier. I didn't want to miss the opportunity to swing by the school while it was in session and try to coax Eleanor Mercandetti's contact information from the assistant principal.

Needless to say, things didn't go brilliantly with Beau on Friday morning. When, over breakfast, I confessed that Jillian had reached out late the night before and I'd decided to meet up with her again, he looked both stunned and confused, as if he half expected someone to jump out from behind a curtain and yell, "You've been punked!" Obviously he'd told himself that the concerns he'd expressed the night before had made more of a dent in my thinking.

"Beau, I feel a real responsibility to Jillian," I said. "Please try to understand."

"You mean, like the way you tried to understand *my* point of view on this, Bailey?"

"I *did* try to understand. I thought a lot about it in the tub last night, and I promise to consider it more when I'm home again. But I can't just drop this particular investigation. There's an important new lead involving this guy Denali—as well as other stuff cooking—and I feel we may be close to figuring out the truth."

I was smart enough not to add how much the idea of going back really scared me.

"Well, then I guess you have do what you have to do," he said, seemingly resigned.

When he kissed me good-bye on his way to the studio, his lips barely brushed mine. I knew the issue had to be readdressed, but that would have to wait until my return. I was sure the matter would weigh on me the entire time I was gone.

After Beau had taken off for work, I made a quick stop at the gym, where I spent a pathetic half hour on the stationary bike, reminding my muscles that they existed and had certain jobs to do in life. I was feeling better than yesterday, in part, I assumed, because I was a day further removed from the second rabies shot. Before picking up my car, I dropped a goody bag of gourmet food off for Landon, in thanks for his heroic rescue of me.

Once I was out of city traffic and on the Taconic, I mentally reviewed the to-do list I'd generated on the bike. In addition to stopping by the high school, it included paying a visit to Keith Denali; obtaining whatever update I could on Penny's death (without stepping into DA Bacon's line of sight); possibly showing up unannounced at Jocelyn's home, since she still hadn't returned my emails; and grabbing more face time with Trevor Hague. I'd texted him an invitation from the gym that morning, explaining that I'd been back in New York but was returning to the area and wanted to buy him a drink to show my appreciation. Because we'd established a bit of rapport that night in the ER, I thought I'd have a good crack at worming information about Kordas out of him. To say nothing of the fact that he was a suspect himself and I needed a better look.

And, of course, more than anything, I wanted to hear Jillian's big secret, the "something" she'd held back that "mattered." I couldn't help but wonder if it related to the accusation John Denali had made years ago. She might have known there was an issue with her father and hadn't had the stomach to share it with me previously.

Much to my frustration, it ended up being close to three by the time I finally reached the area, thanks in part to several painfully slow-moving tractors on the last stretch of hilly, rural road. Rather than drop my bags at the inn—for security reasons, I'd picked a different one this time, one in the town of Cheswick—I drove directly to the high school, fearful that this late on a Friday afternoon, no one would be around. At first glance my fears seemed to be confirmed. There were only four cars and a couple of buses in the lot.

Thankfully the school was open. Gramps was no-where in sight, but I could hear rustling coming from one of the three administrative offices behind the counter. As I took a step closer, my gaze was tugged to the left. A shrine of sorts had been set up to Penny Niles. There was a wooden stand with a framed color photo of her with several students, a large bouquet of white flowers, and a card that read *In Loving Memory.* It felt as if my heart had been pinched.

"Can I help you?" a voice said. I turned and dis-covered a woman of about fifty with short gray hair eyeing me from the other side of the counter. I realized I might be in luck.

"Hi, I'm Bailey Weggins and I'm looking for Mrs. Campbell, the assistant principal."

"I'm Linda Campbell. What can I do for you?'

"So sorry to barge in this late in the day but I'm helping a former student from here write a memoir, and we've been trying to track down Eleanor Mercan-detti for an interview. I'm hoping you have contact info for her."

I'd delivered my little spiel in the most upbeat "this is a perfectly harmless request" tone of voice possible, and so I was surprised when the woman's eyes narrowed suspiciously.

"Is something going on?" she asked bluntly.

"Going on? I'm not sure what you mean."

"Why are you asking that question?" She didn't look at all happy.

"The former student I'm helping was a big fan of Mrs. Mercandetti and we'd loved to touch base with her for the book."

"You're the second person in a week to ask me about a principal who left fifteen years ago. If I didn't know any better, I'd say that was pretty odd."

She had to be talking about Penny, which meant my hunch last week had been correct. After my visit to her home, Penny had tried to hunt down Mercandetti.

"Oh, yes, I'm sure it seems like a weird coincidence," I said, keeping my tone light. "But actually, the two requests are probably connected. I spoke to Penny Niles last week, hoping she had a number for Mrs. Mercandetti. I assume she was the one who called you, trying to help me out. By the way, I'm terribly sorry for your loss."

"Yes, it was Penny who inquired," Campbell said, her body still defensively stiff. "She called me at home for it. But she said she was trying to reach Mrs. Mercandetti herself."

"Probably just to ask her if it was okay to release the

contact info to me. Were you able to provide her with a number?"

Campbell leveled her gaze at me, assessing.

"I really don't feel comfortable discussing that call," she said. "Are you aware that Penny Niles was *murdered*?"

"Yes, I heard. I was really upset to learn that."

"If you don't mind, I really need to lock up now."

"Of course. But I'd love a number for Mrs. Mercandetti before I leave. I hear she moved to California."

The prompt didn't work. Campbell pressed her lips together, almost like a little kid determined not to spill the beans.

"I'm not at liberty to provide contact info for Mrs. Mercandetti," she said after a moment. "Regardless of whether I have it."

Tough to translate whether the number was in her possession or not. If the former, she'd probably had no problems divulging it to Penny when she called.

"Can you tell me who I should speak to then?"

"The principal. But unfortunately, he's on vacation until a week from Monday."

"In that case, here's my card," I said, drawing one from my bag and placing it on the counter, since Campbell made no move to accept it. "Could you ask him to give me a call when he returns?"

She nodded without picking up the card. "Now if you'll excuse me."

"Of course. Have a good day."

Linda Campbell had done squat to improve my mood. I still had no leads on Mercandetti, and my next chance at securing it was over a week away.

I did, however, have one key piece of information in my pocket now. Penny had clearly felt an urgent need to connect with Mercandetti. Since it was possible that Campbell had been able to provide Penny with the phone number, it could also mean that the call had set off a chain of events that culminated in the staged hanging. I wondered if Mercandetti had played a direct role in Penny's death.

I'd almost allowed myself to become convinced that Penny's death was indeed the end result of a burglary and that I may have even read her wrong during the interview. But now it seemed obvious that there had been a serious issue at the school, one both she and Mercandetti were aware of, and maybe entangled in.

When I checked my phone in the car, I found that Trevor Hague had responded to my text about a meet-up.

Trevor: How about tomorrow at around 6?

I was glad he was game, but I didn't want to wait that long. I wrote back.

Me: Not sure how many days I'll be here. Could u do tonight? I'm buying.

I was halfway to the new inn when he responded.

Trevor: Sure. Will have to be 7. Shall I pick u up?

Needless to say, I wasn't going to let him find out where I was staying. Besides, I had my own idea for a meet-up location. When I'd last been in Dory, I'd noticed a wine bar called Pag's, attached to a restaurant called Paganini's, and that struck me as the perfect place for our rendezvous. I was more than curious to learn how Hague handled himself just a mile from the Lowe house.

Me: Pag's wine bar?

His response to my suggestion came two minutes later.

Trevor: Sure. See u then.

He hadn't flinched.

I picked up a coffee at Starbucks and then made my way to the Dragonfly Inn. After checking in with Mary, the innkeeper, I lugged my bag to my room. It turned out to be spacious and like the last inn, mercifully free of tchotchkes and cutesy wall hangings—unless you counted the print of a cherub riding a dragonfly as if it were a pony. I kicked off my sandals, flopped on the bed, and considered how I was going to play the situation with Hague. This would be my chance to really evaluate him, which had been tough to do when I was writhing in pain.

Was Hague actually the one who set the dog on me? Kordas could have told him I was driving to the site that day, allowing for Hague to arrange the attack, though the more I'd thought since Sunday, the less likely Hague's involvement seemed. It was hard to imagine that he could have spied on me from the woods, unleashed the dog after I was out of the car, and then skedaddled back to the cluster of large luxury houses in time to be picked up by Bruce.

Of course, even if he wasn't responsible for the dog attack, he still might have murdered the Lowes. Tonight I'd need to steer the conversation around to his dismissal sixteen years ago, though I couldn't appear threatening with my questions.

I freshened up and changed, slipping on a navy-blue DVF wrap dress I'd tossed into my bag. After all, there might be an advantage to being in something more presentable than jeans. Before leaving the inn, I googled directions to Keith Denali's home. Though I had no intention of paying him a visit tonight, I wanted to do a drive-by if time allowed.

I ended up running late and Trevor was already at Pag's, sitting at a small table in the back, near a fireplace decommissioned for the summer. The place was more of a wine bar and tavern blend, with lots of brick and dark wood paneling, a few red leather banquettes, and a couple of wine barrels meant to be used for extra tables.

"I almost didn't recognize you," Trevor said, rising from the table and, to my surprise, brushing my cheek with his lips. He was dressed in business casual—black pants, a rust-colored belt, and a tightly fitted, button-down lavender shirt with the sleeves rolled to the elbows. Though he definitely was on the pale side—and his almost see-through blue eyes accentuated that factor—he was what many women would consider an attractive guy.

"Is that good or bad?" I asked.

"Good. You were pretty beat up the last time I saw you—through no fault of your own."

"That's for sure. By the way, thanks for being so accommodating with your schedule."

He flagged down the waiter and asked what I'd like. He had a glass of red in front of him—"The Stag's Leap Cabernet," he said—so I ordered the same. Now that I was no longer in a haze of pain and Trevor's clothes weren't smeared with my blood, I could see that he had an elite, posh air, like some of the guys I'd met at Brown, particularly the ones who'd gone to boarding school. I recalled Jillian saying that his mother, Lynne, had been left millions by her first husband.

"But hey, remember, this is my treat, okay?" I said. "I owe you big-time."

"If you insist. . . . So tell me, how are you doing? When you said in your text that you were better, I wasn't sure if that was the truth or just you being a real trouper."

"I won't lie, it hasn't been a fun recovery. Though it could have been much worse if you guys hadn't come when you did."

"Well, I'm glad Bruce called and offered to give me a lift. I don't think one person could have subdued that dog on his own."

"Other people must have made the same mistake I did, right?"

"Which mistake is that?"

"Showing up at the town houses rather than those big single-family homes?" I said, watching his expression.

"I think if they had, Bruce would have been clearer with you. Anyone working on the site would know the difference, so he probably didn't realize how confusing it would be to an outsider."

Or perhaps Trevor Hague felt a need to cover for his boss and stepfather.

"Did you ever learn anything about the dog, where it came from?"

At that moment a cluster of people burst in the door of the bar and Hague glanced over in their direction, either distracted by their loud chatter or looking for an excuse to momentarily remove those translucent eyes from my inspection.

"Nothing," he said, turning back to me. "I asked around, but no one claimed to know anything about guard dogs being used in the area. I thought *you* might have heard something."

"Me?"

"Right. I assumed that was why you were back in town. Checking out what the authorities found."

"Actually no. I'm following up on a few loose ends for the memoir."

"Ah, the memoir. You must be focusing on Jillian's years in Dory."

"Yes and no. Mainly we want to concentrate on the new life she built for herself, but we have to address the past, too."

"'What's past is prologue'?"

"Yes. To some degree."

"Though, of course that phrase has more than one interpretation. People today use it to mean the past sets the stage for the present and future, but that's not necessarily what Shakespeare was going for in *The Tempest*."

"What do you think Antonio meant then?"

"You know the play?" he said.

"Well I couldn't give a TED Talk on it, but I've seen it a few times. So?"

He rubbed his chin lightly with his pale fingers. "I think Antonio was saying that what comes before doesn't have to matter. There's a new future ahead."

"Am I looking at a fellow English major or just someone who loves the Bard?"

"Actually, I studied theater in college."

"Oh, nice. Did you ever give acting a try?"

"No. I spent a few months after college trudging around New York, trying to land an agent, and then went home with my tail between my legs. In all honesty, I was pretty much a fuckup for years, and had no real clue what I wanted out of life. My father died when I was sixteen, and it threw me an utter curve ball."

Good, he was opening the door about his past, which meant it would be easier to direct him to that February before the murders.

"How did you finally figure things out? I mean, you certainly don't come across as a fuckup *now*."

"That's nice of you to say. I left here for a long stretch. I traveled, tried a lot of different things on for size. I studied Buddhism. I worked as a carpenter. I lived in New Zealand for a while, herding sheep."

I was about to chuckle about the sheepherding but caught myself when I saw that he was speaking in total earnestness about his self-discovery years.

"Sounds like a great journey."

"It was."

"Someone told me that you worked for Carl and Bruce years ago. Where did that fit in the scheme of things?"

"That was the winter after I'd tried acting. I was there all of five weeks before they canned me."

"I'm sure it was a tough situation," I said. "Working for your stepfather."

"Yeah, it wasn't pretty. My mother pressured him into hiring me, and he clearly regretted it."

"Maybe it was Carl Lowe who pushed him to fire you," I said. I gave a little shrug as I said it, keeping my vibe casual, but watching him intently.

"I can guarantee you that I didn't dazzle C.J., but he actually seemed willing to give me more time. I never had a beef with him about it."

So no hard feelings about Carl Lowe. Could I believe him?

"Then what happened?"

"Zorba made the call. Claimed that I lacked the motivation to pull off the job. And he was right, of course."

"Bruce is Greek?" I'd figured as much from his last name but the Zorba comment had been a dig. "Was he born there?"

"Yes, but he moved here with his family shortly after birth. Grew up in Worcester, Mass, and worked his way up from next to nothing."

His tone gave zero away, but if I'd had to guess whether his underlying emotion was admiration or disdain, I'd pick the latter.

"And now you're working for him again? How's that going?"

"Not *for*. I have a kitchen-design business that's pretty successful, and his company brought me in to do the kitchens in the new development. To be honest, I don't love the arrangement, but I felt I had to say yes."

"Because of the business?"

"Because of my mother." He let his fingers graze his chin again. "She's getting older now, and I like to keep an eye on her. And how her money's being spent."

Okay, wow.

"Sounds like you might have concerns about Bruce."

"Are we speaking off the record?"

"Of course."

"Then the answer is I do. My father left a substantial fortune. My share's protected, but I don't like seeing my mother taken advantage of."

"Doesn't Bruce make plenty of money from his own company?"

"It took a long time to recover from the last recession, and my mother was tapped as an investor. And besides, no matter how well Lowe/Kordas Development has done—even during the days Carl was there—it was never going to be able to provide enough to fund the life Bruce Kordas envisioned for himself."

In other words, Bruce Kordas likely married for money. I thought of his wife, so much older. I thought of the house, with its fancy paintings, in a whole other league than the Lowe home. I also wondered why

Trevor was so willing to air his family's dirty laundry. He may have liked the chance to vent—or he could be using me for a purpose I couldn't identify yet.

"Do you think Carl was happy with Bruce?"

"You mean as a business partner? Why do you ask?"

"Someone mentioned in one of my interviews about the family that there may have been issues between them. Did you notice anything?"

"I never saw them come to any verbal blows during the weeks I was there, but they certainly didn't seem very friendly toward each other."

Interesting. And not unlike what Heather had shared. No huge problem between the two men, and yet a noticeable distance.

"So maybe the bloom was off the rose."

"I wouldn't go that far. At times, though, Carl seemed to be studying Bruce, trying to read him."

"Any idea why?"

"No. I was stoned a lot then, so maybe it was only the pot talking, making me paranoid. There was one occasion, though—I don't know, a week or two after I started—when I walked into Bruce's office and I caught Carl going through Bruce's cell phone. Or at least that's what it seemed like. Carl made up an excuse, said he was trying to find a client's deets."

So Carl was checking up on Kordas. He might have

thought his young partner was up to something—anything from hatching a plan to go out on his own or syphoning off funds.

"What about Carl personally? Did he seem like an okay guy to you?"

"Sounds like you're interested in more than Jillian Lowe's personal history."

"Well, when you're writing a memoir, family plays a huge role. As does everything that happens to that family."

"So you're interested in the murders, too, I take it."

"That certainly has to be factored in. I supposed you've heard Dylan Fender was in the process of being cleared. Any suspicions about who the real killer might be?"

"None whatsoever. What about you? You're a crime writer. You must have a few ideas."

He'd done his homework.

I shrugged. "I really don't know enough to speculate."

"Must be an exciting job, though. Writing about crime."

"Yes, it certainly can be."

He glanced at his watch. "Look, I think we've exhausted all the Dory gossip available. What about grabbing a bite to eat—my treat this time—and we can focus on more interesting subject matter? The food is actually quite good at the restaurant here, the one next door."

Jeez, he was actually asking me to dinner, and it seemed to be in a date-y kind of way. I should have stayed in my jeans and not bothered with the lip gloss. Since he was done talking about subjects that held any urgency for me, dinner would add nothing to my research, and I certainly didn't want to give him the idea that I was in the market for a man. Besides, if he *was* the killer—or the person who'd set the dog on me—I wasn't going to take any chances. Being with him after dark, even in a restaurant, felt potentially risky.

"That's so nice of you, Trevor, but I'm afraid I have another appointment tonight."

"Well, if you do end up staying at least another day, perhaps tomorrow night then."

He said it almost as an afterthought, like someone finding a brochure on his desk right before you leave the room and passing it along in case you might be vaguely interested. But there was rigidity to his body that suggested he was eager for a yes.

I raised my hand for the waiter and gave the universal sign for the check.

"Can I let you know?" I said. "If I end up staying,

my schedule's going to be packed, and I won't have much free time."

He jutted his chin out just enough to make me sense I'd annoyed him with my lack of interest. What did the guy think, that I owed him a date in exchange for his dog-bite intervention?

Though I tried to act friendly enough as I paid the bill, the minutes that followed were awkward. Hague barely said a word as we exited the bar.

"Well, this is me," I said, nodding toward my car as we stepped onto the sidewalk. I'd managed to find a parking spot right in front of Pag's. "Are you parked nearby?"

"In the lot out back."

"Trevor, thanks again for everything. I can't tell you how much I appreciate all you did."

"No problem. It wasn't that big of a deal."

His whole manner toward me had cooled. Had the guy never been turned down for dinner before?

"To me it was. I can't bear to think of what would have happened if you hadn't been there that day." I was floundering a bit now, trying to smooth over the moment.

"I guess you'll have to be more careful in the future."

What was *that* supposed to mean? I could have hardly anticipated that a mad hound would shoot out of the woods and attempt to sever my arm from my body.

"I'm not following."

"Just watch your back. You may find out that wasn't the only nasty dog in town. . . . Good evening."

The hairs on the back of my neck shot up as I watched him turn and saunter away, rounding the building toward the parking lot. Had that been nothing more than his bruised male ego talking?

Or had he just threatened me?

Chapter 18

As I pulled away in my car a couple of minutes later, I kept my eye on the rearview mirror, making sure there wasn't a vehicle close behind. Hague's last statement *had* seemed vaguely threatening. And I didn't like the way his whole mood had shifted when I'd declined his invite, suggesting someone who was thin-skinned and easily miffed. He claimed he'd had no hard feelings toward Carl Lowe, but that might not be the case.

My mind lingered on the comment he'd made about the scene from *The Tempest*, interpreting Antonio's line to mean not that the past sets the stage for the future, but that the past doesn't have to matter. It's over and done with, and a bold and exciting future awaits. Interesting, too, to consider the context in which Antonio delivers the line. He's trying to convince Sebastian to murder his brother so Sebastian can be king.

Perhaps Hague had once embraced the same philosophy as Antonio. He murdered a family and then sailed off to herd sheep and start fresh. The thought made me shudder.

Spotting a couple of now familiar markers on the way out of town, I realized that I wasn't far from the fried-clam place I'd stopped by once before, and I made a brief detour for an order to go. Back in the car, I programmed Keith Denali's address into the GPS and took off with the aluminum container of clams nestled beside me. There was still light in the sky, and I wanted to check out his residence, since I had the chance. Houses always told you plenty of stuff about the people who lived in them.

East Lyle turned out to be less of a town than a township, with barely more than a post office on the main drag. It lacked the touristy charm of some of the other Berkshire towns I'd visited, and my guess was that the residents didn't care one iota. After making a right past the post office, I found myself on a quiet, winding road. Though it had probably been dotted with farms at one point, it now featured an eclectic mix of houses, none of them fancy and all built a fair distance from each other, set back from the road.

To reach Denali's I made one more turn, onto an even more rural stretch of road but with the same look and feel. Woods lined the back of these houses, and many had outbuildings along the side or to the rear.

"You have reached your destination," the GPS lady announced. I couldn't see a street number, so I had to assume she was correct, that the dingy yellow house on my right was what I was looking for.

I pulled the car onto the far shoulder, killed the engine, and leaned into the passenger seat, staring out at the house. No car in the driveway. Maybe Denali wasn't back from work yet—or he'd gone out for a bite—which would give me time to absorb the scene.

I stepped out of the car and into the warm early evening. The sky was as soft as an old piece of cloth and bleached of color, though it wouldn't be dark for a while. There was an earthy, grassy scent in the air and from somewhere nearby I heard a tractor hum, its rider clearly using the waning daylight to finish the task.

I settled my gaze on the house and studied it. It didn't take much trouble to conclude that the person who lived here either lacked dough or energy, or both. The paint was peeling, the porch sagged, and the front lawn was almost totally bald. There was also a fair amount of junk stacked and scattered around each side of the house—car parts, rusted aluminum lawn furniture, a row boat, old bikes.

No sign of kids. My gut told me that Denali also didn't have a wife or girlfriend living with him. If your guy was a hoarder, there probably wasn't a lot you could do about it, but I just wasn't picking up any female presence. Beyond that, the overriding vibe was sad. Which you might expect from a guy still possibly dealing with a horrible trauma from his childhood.

Of course, the most immediate question was whether this was also the house of someone gunning for me.

A sound startled me, and I whirled to my right to find a woman speed-walking up the road in my direction. I hadn't heard her coming over the hum of the tractor. She was about forty-five or so, her dark hair pushed back with a stretchy band, and she was wearing sweatpants topped by a T-shirt that read, *I don't make mistakes; I date them.*

"Can I help you?" she said, stopping in her tracks and catching a breath. There was nothing hostile, just concern, as if she assumed I might be having car trouble.

"Oh, thanks, yes. I was hoping to surprise an old friend of mine named Keith Denali. Do you happen to know if this is where he lives?"

"Yup," she said, though the mild surprise in her eyes suggested Denali didn't have a lot of visitors in wrap dresses and strappy sandals. "But you just missed him. He drove by while I was walking."

"Okay, I'll stop by tomorrow, I guess."

"Better make it late in the afternoon. He's in the shop on Saturday. I think he works till three."

"The shop?"

"His auto shop."

"Oh, right. So he's still doing that then."

"I guess you could always go by there tomorrow to see him. It's on Route 29, D and A Auto. Or you could wait around now because he'll probably be back in a little while. He always walks his dogs at night."

My heart skipped. The guy had dogs. *What kind?*

"Oh, gosh, I'm not a fan of dogs. They're little, I hope."

"No, but he keeps them out back, not in the house, so you don't have to worry."

"Shepherds?"

"Pardon me?"

"I was wondering if he had German shepherds. I don't mind those."

She narrowed her eyes, obviously curious about where I was going.

"I don't really know. They're just big."

Big and friendly? I wondered. Or big and terrifying?

"Okay, thanks for your help," I said, afraid she

might mention me to Denali if I pressed her with any more questions. And it sounded like the guy was due home shortly. "I'll swing by another time."

As she took off along the road again, pumping her arms as she walked, I jumped in the car and brought the Dragonfly Inn's address up on GPS. The route there involved returning the way I'd come. I started the engine and backed into Denali's driveway so I could turn around. I'd no sooner put the gear into drive and tapped the gas then the sound of barking dogs tore through the car.

I hit the brake and spun around in my seat. The dogs were nowhere in sight. Clearly, they were chained up out back or in some kind of kennel, and had reacted to the noise.

I hit the gas again and pulled out. The primitive part of my brain half expected the dogs to come tearing after the car, trying to chomp off my bumper with their teeth. Weirdly, my wound began to throb, as if hearing the growling had scared the bejesus out of it.

The fact that Denali owned snarling dogs was significant. Before I made any attempt to talk to the guy, I needed to figure out the type of dogs they actually were.

On the way home I took a small detour onto Route 29 and located D&A Auto. I'd actually been on the road before, though never paying close attention. The shop was closed up tight for the night. If I were going to pay Denali a visit, this would be a better place to do it than his house. More people around.

When I returned to the inn, I found a small gathering in the parlor, a reception for guests, it appeared, and as I passed through on my way to the staircase, Mary, the innkeeper, offered me a glass of wine.

"I'd love it," I said. After taking a single sip from the glass handed to me and nodding at a few guests, I snuck off to my room.

By this point, I felt as fried as the clams I'd bought—from the push-and-pull conversation with the assistant principal earlier, that weird final comment by Trevor Hague, and those angry dog sounds coming from behind Denali's. After stripping off my dress, I pulled on pj bottoms and a fresh T-shirt and polished off my dinner and wine. While eating, I jotted down notes in my composition book.

Then I called Beau. I knew he wasn't happy about my decision to restart the investigation, but he seemed to have accepted it, and I wanted to make sure there weren't any serious wrinkles.

"Hey," I said when he answered. "How's it going?"

"Pretty good. You make it up there without a hitch?"

"Yeah, a little more traffic this time and slow-moving farm vehicles, but other than that it was fine."

"Where are you now?"

"I'm at the inn, the Dragonfly. Jillian arrives late tomorrow."

"You getting some stuff handled before she arrives?"

"Yeah. I did a few interviews late today, and I turned up new info, which could be of value."

"Well, I hope it works out," was all he said. So he wasn't going to press for specifics, and since we'd established a fragile peace, maybe it was for the best.

"Where are you anyway?" I asked. "It sounds like you're outdoors."

"I'm up on the roof deck. It's a gorgeous night, so I came up with a half bottle of wine and a sandwich."

"Oh, that's nice," I said, realizing how glum I sounded. "Well, look, I better turn in, because I need to make an early start tomorrow. I'll call you at the end of the day? Or you call me."

"You bet."

"I love you, Beau."

"Yup, same here."

Beau usually said it in return, not some lame shadow response, so that was a little odd. Were we *okay*? It was one thing to keep the peace for now, but we certainly weren't going to fare well if we were always walking on eggshells with each other. I'd have killed for another glass of wine at the moment, but I doubted Mary would have liked me trooping downstairs in my jammies.

I turned in early as promised and woke before six the next day, feeling anxious. I had a lot on my plate. Plus, I would finally learn the secret Jillian had been so reluctant to share. My mind was constantly tempted to speculate—*Was it about abuse? Had she actually suspected a relationship between her mother and Jocelyn? Was there a serious issue regarding her family that she'd never shared with the cops?*—but I fought off the urge. Speculation wouldn't do me any good and would take up precious time.

Over coffee, I plotted out my morning. I wanted to pay Jocelyn a visit today in Dory, and I also needed to swing by a clinic for my next rabies vaccine. I'd located one online and made an appointment. Most pressing, though, was figuring out if Denali had a German shepherd in his mix of dogs. My only option, it seemed, was to return to his place on a reconnaissance mission.

A question nagged at me, though. Shepherds were a popular breed, and if I discovered one at Denali's, how would I tell if I was looking at the culprit? I could hardly swab him and see if he had a trace of my DNA left on his gums. I needed someone to help me make a knowledgeable assessment.

Blake.

Though I had Mamie's cell number, I had nothing for Blake, so I found the vet clinic number online and left a message on voice mail asking Dr. Allard to call me as soon as he arrived.

Since it would be rude to arrive at Jocelyn's before nine on a Saturday, I dawdled over breakfast, using my laptop to search for Trevor Hague and Lynne Hague Kordas.

The website for Trevor's business popped up and it seemed impressive, though there was no way to measure its success. I found less on Lynne, only a few references to fund-raising efforts she took part in.

My first stop that day, before Jocelyn's, was at the clinic, on this side of Dory, for my shot. This injection stung less than the last.

Due to the location of the clinic, I ended up heading toward Dory on a road I hadn't traveled on before, a stretch featuring fast-food stores, retail outlets, and car dealerships. It gradually gave way to an area of older, more rustic-looking places that had obviously existed before all the recent development. I was about to make a right off the road, when I did a double take. At the corner was a cedar-sided, peak-roofed building with a sign that read TWO BOOTS TAVERN.

Two Boots. It took me a couple of seconds before I realized why the name was so familiar. It had appeared twice on Julia's credit card statement, right around the same time as a charge for J.Crew. I'd assumed it was another clothing store.

I'd already made the right before I saw the connection, so I found a spot to turn around, and then pulled into the front parking lot of the tavern. The place was closed right now, but according to a sign in the window, it would open for lunch at noon, serving the juiciest burgers on the planet.

I was only two miles from Dory at this point, which meant this must be the place where Julia had used her credit card in late March. At least twice. She'd clearly felt healthy enough by those dates to step out for a bite.

Jillian had indicated that her sister was totally housebound in late March and April, but that obviously hadn't been the case. Had she come here alone or with a friend in the area, a friend Jillian hadn't been aware of?

Perhaps she'd developed such a fierce case of cabin fever or was angry enough with her mother that she'd ignored medical advice. I remembered someone—maybe it was Kordas—saying that there was a point at which Julia was no longer contagious, so at least that hadn't been an issue.

I decided to come back to Two Boots later, though the chance of anyone remembering anything after all these years was extremely low.

I set out again for Dory. The London house turned out to be only a few blocks from where the Lowes had lived. There was a car in the driveway, suggesting that people were home. The potential fly in the ointment was big, burly Bob. He might do his best to ensure that Jocelyn and I didn't speak privately.

Jocelyn answered the door, dressed in a sleeveless dark red top, white capris, and jeweled sandals, and she seemed even more shocked to see me than I'd expected, as if I were the daughter she'd given up for adoption years ago who had finally arrived on her doorstep.

"What is it?" she asked bluntly before I could offer a hello.

"Good morning, Jocelyn, sorry to catch you by surprise. I was hoping you could spare a few more moments for me."

"I've told you absolutely everything I know. I don't have anything more to share."

"I actually have something to share with *you*. That's why I've been trying to get in touch."

Actually I had no plan to share anything with her but I wanted to wend my way to the subject of her and Claire. With any luck, I'd coax the truth from her.

"All right, come in, but I only have a few minutes."

"Is your husband around?"

"He ran out on an errand."

Good, we'd have a few minutes alone at least.

She directed me to the living room, not as grand as the one in the old Lowe house, but it was evident that the Londons lived comfortably. The room looked like someone had invested time in decorating it, but the colors were so subtle they barely registered, and the furniture seemed pushed back too far against the walls. It was hard to imagine anyone having intimate conversations in this room, let alone fun. Above the fireplace was an oil portrait of two girls in yellow dresses whom I assumed were the London daughters when they were young.

Jocelyn motioned for me to take a seat on the couch. She chose an armchair across from me, her butt barely touching the cushion.

"So what's going on?" she demanded.

"When I spoke to you last week, I mentioned that there might have been an issue at the school that had upset Julia. I don't think it was about the alpha moms. I believe what happened occurred closer in time to the murders, and may be significant. And to be honest, I'm not simply trying to help Jillian write a memoir. I'm helping her figure out who killed her family."

"Why didn't you say that to begin with?"

"Because initially we felt it was smarter to keep that under wraps. Are you familiar with the name Penny Niles?"

Jocelyn went totally still, which was saying a lot because she was, in general, so spare with her movements.

"The woman from the high school who was murdered?"

"Yes. I went to see her before she died, and though she didn't divulge any information, I had the sense there *had* been something at the school, and she was keeping it secret."

"Are you saying this secret is connected to her death? That there's some kind of *conspiracy?*"

"Not a conspiracy, no, but to be honest, I'm worried that someone may have decided to prevent her from revealing what she knew. Can you think of anything else regarding the school that might have caused difficulty for any of the Lowes?"

She seemed to think for a moment and then slowly shook her head.

"No, nothing. Like I told you, I was away the weeks before—before everything happened. The only thing I can recall was that Claire seemed agitated one day about Julia getting her driver's license. It's just coming back to me. Julia was home sick by then and she started lobbying hard for it."

That was twice now the subject had come up. I wondered why Claire had been so restrictive of Julia driving. Maybe there had still been a health issue to be concerned about.

"Did Claire share a lot about the kids with you?"

"Of course. Why wouldn't she?"

"You were her best friend, right?"

"If you want to put it in such a silly, schoolgirl way."

"Are there any other friends of hers I might be able to speak with? To ask about Claire's life?"

"No one who she was particularly close to."

I saw now that I could try to coax her until the cows came home, but it wasn't going to work. And speaking of coming home, Bob would probably blow in any minute. I decided to shift tactics and charge in. That might work better with her seemingly impenetrable manner.

"Just one more question, Jocelyn, and I hope you'll take it in the right light. If I'm going to help Jillian, I really have to understand what was going on in her family. Your friendship with Claire. Was it more than that?"

Her placid expression quickly morphed into a death stare.

"You've got a lot of nerve," she said.

"If you prefer, the answer can stay between the two of us. Jillian doesn't have to know."

"Get out," she said, rising from her chair. "Get out right now."

"Jocelyn, please, wouldn't Claire want us to do everything possible to find the killer?"

"You know nothing about Claire," she said. "Or about our relationship. I said get out."

The fierceness of her response might have reflected nothing more than anger at my impertinence, but I sensed something else—that she resented me for trying to tear off a lid she'd worked hard to secure. My gut told me she and Claire *had* been lovers—or at least Jocelyn had wanted them to be.

I rose quickly and made my way from the room. Jocelyn followed behind me, like a human cattle prod, and as soon as I was on the porch, I heard the door slam behind me.

As I reached the sidewalk, a second car swung into the driveway, fast and sure. I waited while Bob London extracted his large frame from the driver's seat, with a *Boston Globe* tucked under his left arm. He was dressed in brown slacks and a navy polo shirt that looked like it had required about four bolts of fabric.

"Well, Ms. Weggins, good morning," he said, a bushy dark eyebrow raised. Unlike his wife, he didn't seem stunned to see me, as if he'd pegged me as a snoopy girl and had expected I'd circle back before long.

"Bob, right?" I said, stepping forward. "Nice to see you again."

"Are you coming or going?" he asked.

"Just leaving. I wanted to check with your wife on a few more details."

"And are we done?"

"Done? Yes, I believe so."

"Good," he said, towering over me now. His breath blew hot, with a coffee-and-bacon smell, as if I'd ended up stuck by the exhaust fan of a local IHOP. Not a pleasant experience. "Because this really isn't fair to either my wife or myself. We spent a lot of time putting that tragedy behind us."

"Jillian appreciates that. But I'm sure you can appreciate her desire for answers."

Just over his shoulder I detected a curtain in the house parting a couple of inches and then dropping back into place.

"We all have to deal with things in our own way," he said. "Good day."

He started up the path to the house, and as happy as I was to have that breath off my cheeks, I wanted a better read on him.

"Before you go, can I ask you a crazy question?"

"What is it?" he said, rotating his big frame.

"I'm trying to track down someone who trains personal-protection dogs. Do you know anyone in the area who does that?"

He evaluated me, his jaw set and his eyes cold.

"Unfortunately, I'm not a dog person," he said. "I can't help you." He turned on his heels and resumed his trip up the path.

Pulling away in my car a minute later, I could still feel the residual force of Bob London's presence. He was the kind of guy who liked to be in control, who probably liked to control his wife, too, and didn't want anyone impinging on the world he'd constructed. My guess was that the idea of his wife falling in love with someone else, man or woman, would have worked him into a serious lather.

I checked my phone at a stoplight and saw that there was a return call from Blake. I pulled over on Main Street in Dory and rang him right back.

"Jillian texted Mamie to say you were both coming back up here," he said. "Is everything okay?"

"As of right now, yes. You still haven't heard anything about the dog, have you?"

"Nope, not a thing. I actually checked in with animal control again this morning. And nothing from the vets I asked. No one's seen a dog fitting that description."

"Well, there's a small chance I might have found it."

"*Where?* Who does it belong to?"

"It may be in an outdoor kennel in someone's backyard—about twenty minutes from your clinic. I'm not sure yet if there's a shepherd in the mix but I *heard* the dogs and they sound mean."

"Is this person connected to the case somehow?"

"Maybe. His family might have had a reason to be seriously upset with Carl Lowe."

"Does Jillian know about this yet?"

"No, and I definitely don't want to say anything at this point. . . . I know this is a lot to ask, but would you be willing to come with me?"

"To check out the *dog?*" he said, clearly stunned by the request.

"Yes. If we find a shepherd there, you'd be better able than me to tell if it had been trained to attack."

"Wow. Um, does this mean we'll be trespassing?"

"Yes, but it's the only way for me to figure it out."

I heard him sigh nervously. I *was* asking a lot of him. Hopefully his desire to help Jillian would persuade him.

"I could probably sneak away, but not until at least one," he said. "I could meet you there around one thirty."

That would still give us plenty of time. I provided

him with directions and told him to park his car on the road just north of the house and that I'd see him at one thirty. Afterward I called the number for the auto shop. Someone answered "D and A Auto. Denali."

"Sorry, wrong number," I said. Good, Keith was definitely working today.

I checked my watch. It was close to noon. I drove back to Two Boots, and while sitting in the parking lot, jotted down notes from my brief talks with each of the Londons.

Once the tavern opened, I grabbed a spot at the bar. After ordering a Caesar salad that had croutons hard enough to pave a road with, I nodded toward the bartender. I asked whether he knew if anyone on staff had worked here sixteen years ago or longer. He didn't fit the bill himself, since he was probably no older than me.

The guy snorted, "Don't think so. I mean, Gina's been here the longest but I think that's been only five or six years."

"You're sure?"

"Yeah . . . Well, I mean, unless you count the owner, Jerry. He's had the place over twenty-five years."

Duh.

"Great, is he here?"

"No, but he comes on at eight. He's tending bar to-night."

I would swing by later, after I'd met up with Jillian.

By the time I was in my car again, retracing the route to Denali's, my stomach was twisting. Nothing about the plan for this afternoon appealed to me—not the snarling dogs, not trespassing on someone's property, and certainly not the possibility of meeting up with a man who might really have it out for me. See, Beau, I thought, I'm *not* a danger lover.

I pulled past the house and parked where I'd told Blake to meet me. One thirty came and went, and as each minute passed, I could feel my stomach churning even more. Finally a black SUV materialized in my rearview mirror and nosed in front of me. As we slid out of our vehicles simultaneously, I saw Blake look anxiously around. He'd thrown on a lightweight jacket over his green scrubs, obviously, on this warm of a day, to make his uniform less of a beacon.

"Thanks so much for this," I said in greeting. "I hope it isn't too uncomfortable for you."

"No, happy to help," Blake said, though he looked ready to jump out of his skin. "Who's the owner any-way?"

"Someone whose father was once in a rage about

Carl Lowe. But as I said, I haven't filled Jillian in, so don't say anything to her, okay?"

He nodded solemnly.

"Let's get this over with, and then I can explain more later."

We jogged up the driveway, both of us swiveling our heads as we moved, casing the area. When we were three-quarters of the way up, the barking began and it set my nerves on edge.

"Stay behind me, okay?" Blake said. Seconds later we found ourselves in a shabby backyard with an outdoor kennel—a small building, actually, made of faded red wood, with five separate chain-link compartments running along the front. At the rear of each one was a doggie door leading into the enclosed structure.

Four dogs were in the compartments, their heads snapping back with each bark, and as soon as they spotted us, they lunged forward, practically mounting the chain link. I jumped so high I was nearly airborne.

I spun around to make sure no one was charging out of the back of the house. The place definitely looked empty for the moment. And thankfully there was no sign of a security camera. When I turned back around, Blake was stepping closer to the dogs, which made their barking even louder and crazier. They were all some type of retriever, I realized.

"Hey, hey, easy now," Blake said, his voice low and almost hypnotic. "Come on, nice and easy."

Within a couple of seconds, they'd taken it down to a low, warning growl. From his pocket Blake scooped out a bunch of bone-shaped dog biscuits and tossed one at the feet of each dog. They pounced on the treats and not only stopped their barking but also began to wag their tails.

Blake glanced toward me, his handsome mouth scrunched in uncertainly. "I don't know for sure," he said, "but I'd say they're nothing more than house pets that live outside. Not protection dogs."

"Where's the fifth one, though?" I said, nodding toward the empty compartment.

In unison we searched the area with our eyes. For the first time I noticed hints of other outbuildings— the peaked roof of one through the back trees, and the edge of another behind the kennel.

"Good question," he said. "Should we look around?"

I glanced at my watch. "Yes, okay, but let's split up to save time. Why don't you go left and I'll go right."

Blake tossed a few more biscuits in for the dogs and then we separated. As I headed around the kennel, I saw that the small structure behind it was a toolshed, its door hanging open by one hinge. Cautiously I stuck my head inside. There was enough daylight seeping through for me to make out the shape of old rakes and shovels, broken clay pots, and an ancient rotator lawn mower.

After pulling my head out, I circumvented the shed. Directly behind it were the woods, though to my right were farm fields and farther beyond that a neighbor's large gray barn. I was about to head back to the kennel when a brief shout pierced the air. Followed by the sound of what seemed to be something bouncing on the ground. And footsteps.

My heart threw itself against my rib cage, like one of those dogs against the metal cage.

"Blake?" I called out. No answer. Keeping my eyes peeled, I hurried to the front of the kennel. The dogs emitted low growls.

"Blake," I called again. Still no answer. Not good.

I tore around the kennel and then straight toward the other outbuilding, the one Blake had set out for. This one seemed to be a work shed as well, but larger than the one I'd inspected. Cautiously I made my way around to the back. That's when I saw him.

Blake was kneeling in the dirt, his back to me and

his body sagged low. He squeezed his head between his hands.

"Blake, what happened?" I yelled, racing toward him.

His only response was a moan. As I reached him, I saw that one of his hands was smeared with bright red blood.

Chapter 19

I squatted down, grasping Blake's shoulders from behind.

"Blake, what is it. *Tell* me."

"I—my head. It hurts like hell."

"Do you need a doctor?"

"No, no . . . I'm okay, I think." He shifted back on his haunches, lowered his hands, and slowly twisted his head toward me, his face white. With his hands no longer on his head, I could see that a section of dark blond hair on the back of his head—on the lower right—was wet with blood.

"What happened?"

He'd started to raise a hand to his head again but then let it drop by his side as his brow wrinkled in worry.

"Someone hit me, I think—from behind. Damn."

I spun around, anxiously scanning the area. The footsteps I'd heard must have been the attacker running off. There was no sign now of anyone, and the house looked as battened down as it had a few minutes ago.

"Did you see the person?"

"No. Didn't even hear him come up on me."

"Someone shouted. Was that him?"

"No, I think that was me. When I felt the blow."

"Gosh, Blake, I'm so sorry. We need to get out of here. Can you make it up?"

"Yes, just give me a hand, okay?"

I offered my arm for support, and he struggled into a standing position. As I began to guide him toward the driveway, my gaze fell on a length of a two-by-four that appeared to have been flung a few feet away. From a distance I thought I could make out a smear of blood on the end, but I didn't want to take the time for a closer inspection.

We made for the driveway, with Blake's steps growing steadier as we moved. I stayed super vigilant, fearful of someone springing out of hiding, but there was no sign of anyone. The dogs remained quiet but alert, hopeful perhaps for more biscuits.

"Blake, you'll need to come with me," I said when we reached the road. "There's no way you can drive."

"No, I have to. I'm not going to leave my car here."

"I'll drive it then and someone can bring me back for mine."

"I honestly think I'm fine now. Why don't I try driving for a stretch, with you following, and see how I do."

"But only for a half a mile or so, agreed?"

As soon as he was in his car, I jumped into mine and tailed him as he pulled away. We were heading in the opposite direction from the main road where we'd come from, but I assumed Blake knew how to return to the clinic going this way. About a mile down the road, just as I was beginning to worry why he wasn't stopping, he pulled into the dirt parking lot of a small commercial apple orchard, its gates locked. I followed suit.

"How do you feel now?" I asked once I'd bolted out of my car and reached his. He'd rolled down the window and was dabbing at the back of his head with a paper napkin.

"I'm all right. It mostly knocked the wind out of me. What about *you*? I didn't even ask."

"I never encountered anyone. I just heard a shout and footsteps after that. And you saw nothing, not even a glimpse of clothing?"

"Nothing, though the guy couldn't have been very

tall. He only managed to whack me on the side of the head. Do you think it was the person who lives there?"

"Maybe. Or a pal of his watching the place." I wondered if the "I date mistakes" walker had alerted Denali to my presence yesterday, and since he had to work today, he'd recruited another neighbor to keep an eye on the property. If the neighbor had been expecting *me*, he may have been seriously thrown off to discover Blake in the backyard.

"I still don't understand. Why would the owner have released a dog on you? Do you think he killed the Lowes?"

"There could be a definite connection to the case, but I don't want to go into it until I know more."

"By the way," Blake said. "I looked into the enclosed part of the kennel. No sign of a fifth dog."

But there could have been one over a week ago. A dog that was now seriously incapacitated and couldn't be left in the backyard.

"I better split," he added. "I need to be back at the clinic."

"Blake, I'm really sorry about this," I told him again. "But I'm glad we came. I may be on to something."

He nodded halfheartedly. "I'm happy to help." Though he clearly wasn't thrilled with the outcome.

"I'll follow you to the clinic," I said. "I want to be sure you're okay."

"That's really not necessary, Bailey."

"Look, you know as well as I do that it's important to keep an eye on a head injury."

"All right, but if we run into Mamie, don't mention this to her. I didn't tell her I was helping you, and she'll be totally freaked."

I agreed and jogged back to my car. Blake's command of the road seemed perfectly normal, though I noticed that he never went above the speed limit. When we reached the clinic parking lot, I slipped out of my car once more to double-check on him.

"No lasting damage," he said, stripping off his jacket and tossing it into backseat. "If Mamie notices the egg on my head, I'll tell her I bumped it somewhere."

"Are you sure she won't understand if you fess up to her. I can explain I implored you to go with me."

"It's not that she wouldn't understand," he said, turning back to me. I was eye to eye with the V at the top of his uniform and the blond chest hairs poking out. "This whole thing with Jillian has her really worried, especially after the dog incident. She's scared for you and Jillian, and to be honest, she's afraid of us ending up in the bull's-eye as well. Today would only ratchet up her fears."

"I guess she isn't too happy about Jillian and me blowing back into town."

He exhaled loudly. "She wants the best for Jillian, of course, but she doesn't think it's smart for you two to be playing what she calls Holmes and Watson."

I suspected she was also worried about putting her husband in close proximity again with her old BFF.

"Do you agree with her?"

"Frankly, yes. Regardless of whether Dylan was guilty, this is a matter for the police to handle. In fact, Mamie even suggested we go to the cops ourselves and fill them in."

Bad idea. At this point there wasn't enough evidence to prompt them to become more engaged, and they'd be none too pleased to learn I'd been digging around.

"I've managed to discourage her for now," Blake added, clearly reading the consternation on my face. "Because I don't want to interfere with what you're doing. But I can't hold her off forever."

"I appreciate that. I absolutely plan to go to the cops when we have enough to give them."

"Things may move slowly here initially, but I'm sure that eventually the police will take action." He glanced at his watch. "I'd better go. I've got a really sick corgi I'm supposed to be attending to and I'm already running behind."

His good-bye was friendly enough, yet I wondered how long that would last if I kept up my so-called Sherlocking. I felt more than a twinge of guilt for having urged *him* to play Watson today. I'd not only put him in danger but also in a position requiring he lie to Mamie. I glanced at my own watch. If I hurried, I had just enough time to reach D&A Auto before it was the supposed time for Denali to split. I wanted to check him out, see if he was actually working today and determine if there was a way to come face-to-face without putting myself in any jeopardy.

I took off at a clip, and drove past the auto shop just far enough to pull into the parking lot of the liquor store next door. This way I could survey the scene briefly before going over there.

The shop was housed in a slightly scruffy-looking building and was clearly a mom-and-pop operation rather than one of those huge chains you found in suburban sprawl. It consisted of a small office with a single bay for cars on one side and three bays on the other. Two men stood in front of the building, and though I couldn't make out their faces, I could see that they were both in short-sleeved navy shirts, which I figured was probably a uniform.

From my glove compartment, I withdrew an old but powerful pair of binoculars. They'd once belonged to my father, used mostly for bird-watching, and my mother had passed them on to me because she knew how much I'd loved the Sunday treks he'd taken me on in the woods. Though I wasn't much of a birder yet, I hoped to be one day, and I never used the glasses without thinking of his sturdy hands on them.

With the lens focused, I confirmed that the men, who were about the same height and build, were in matching shirts, which suggested that they both worked at the shop. That meant that when I dropped by, I at least wouldn't be alone with Denali. There was a name patch on each shirt, but the lettering was indistinguishable from this distance.

It was now 2:46. I had fourteen minutes to drive over there and get a read on Denali—and to see if his face betrayed the fact that he knew who I was and had probably been tailing me.

As I restarted the engine, one of the men entered the bay and the other slipped into the office, only to emerge thirty seconds later and make his way to a red four-door parked along the side of the building nearest to me. I had the feeling that this was Denali and he was splitting early for the day. There was no way I'd be able to make it over there in time—and I wouldn't have another shot until Monday.

I took the chance, at least, to study him. He appeared to be in his late twenties, which fit with what I knew about him. He had a boyish face and lanky, sand-colored hair. The notion that Carl Lowe could have abused him sickened me.

The guy swung open the car door but didn't climb inside. Instead, he snatched something on the dashboard, which turned out to be a pack of cigarettes, and lit up. His deep-set eyes, I noticed, had a peculiar sadness to them. For a couple of moments, he leaned against the door in the sun and smoked, alternating between watching the cars whizzing along the road and studying the cigarette in his fist. Maybe, I thought, I still had time.

But then he flicked the butt across the lot, slid into the front, and gunned the engine.

I fired up my own engine, backed out of the spot, and approached the entrance of the lot. I watched as the red car pulled out, and I allowed a car already on the road to close in on it before pulling out myself. Five minutes later the red car made a turn, and as I followed, it swung onto the road Denali lived on. It had to be him.

I didn't make the turn myself, just kept driving straight, and eventually found a café in Cheswick, not far from the Dragonfly Inn. After grabbing a table on the side porch, I ordered a cappuccino and flipped open my composition notebook, jotting down my most recent observations.

The Denali stuff was important, but I couldn't become too sidetracked. There was Kordas to think of still, and Hague. And Bob London. And then there was whatever bombshell Jillian planned to drop at my feet. She had said it *mattered.* I ordered a second cappuccino and lingered at the table for over an hour.

As I was paying the bill, I noticed that Jillian had texted earlier to say she was planning to arrive by seven. I picked up a bottle of wine and a few sandwiches on my return to the Dragonfly, figuring she'd be hungry when she arrived and we could park ourselves somewhere at the inn and catch up. I unpacked and took a shower to help me unwind. I was settling down at the desk in the room when I heard a light tapping on the door. I froze on alert. Maybe it was housekeeping, wanting to turn the bed down for the night.

"Yes?" I called out.

"Bailey, it's Jillian."

"Oh, wow, I wasn't expecting you this soon," I exclaimed, throwing open the door. We hugged hello and she stepped into the room. She was wearing a white V-neck T-shirt, jeans, and a pair of sneakers, and her face was free of makeup.

"I ended up making better time than I'd thought,"

she said. "Gosh, it's really good to see you, Bailey. How's your arm?"

I raised it in the air.

"Much better. I still need to wear a gauze bandage every day, but that's mainly to prevent anything from rubbing against it—and to make sure people don't gag at the sight."

"Are you done with the rabies shots?"

"I still need one more but not for a week. Tell me about you. How was Boston?"

"Good. I caught up with some friends from there."

"Was it tough to come back here?"

I really didn't have to ask the question. Though she looked lovely, her skin clear and her eyes that magnetic deep blue, her tension was almost palpable, as if there was something pulsing very lightly beneath her skin.

"I won't lie. I'm nervous, as I'm sure you are, too. And just being here is painful. When you and I drove up from the city, we didn't pass a single sign for Dory. We were always far enough away from it. But coming from Boston, it was unavoidable. I saw this sign that read 'Dory, population: 1,947,' and it made me want to weep. I kept thinking about the four that were no longer there."

"Oh, Jillian," I said. I stepped forward and hugged

her. "I can't imagine what it's been like for you. Then or now."

"I know they say that grief subsides over time," she said, "but in some ways it gets worse and worse. Because it finally sinks in that you will never ever see them again. Ever."

"Like I told you, you don't have to stay. I can handle this on my own."

"No, I want to be here."

"Well, how about some food? I happen to have two mouthwatering turkey sandwiches and a bottle of Cabernet."

"Nothing has ever sounded so appealing."

I poured us each a glass of wine and we ended up using the desk as a table for two by dragging a straight-back chair over from across the room. I wasn't going to press about the secret. I knew that would come when Jillian was ready.

"What you mentioned about grief?" I said, as I unwrapped the sandwiches, "I remember that from my father dying. It does get worse. And people keep wanting you to reassure them that you're better."

"That's one of the problems with Mamie," Jillian said. "I feel she's constantly searching for that reassurance. That I'm all better now. When I was shadowing at the clinic, she always seemed to be watching me, monitoring my mood."

"Not easy to deal with, I'm sure."

She took a long sip of wine.

"You were right about Blake, by the way. I *was* flirting with him. I think it's because it felt nice to be myself around him. He didn't seem to mind if I was gloomy, though in hindsight I realize it was probably disinterest. He's totally devoted to Mamie."

"Have you spoken to her since then?" Blake had said something about them hearing from Jillian, but I had no intention of mentioning that I'd played detective with him. I didn't want her to know about Denali unless there was a legitimate reason.

"I called when I hit Boston to say thanks for everything. She sounded okay, but a little cool. Like she was happy to have me gone, and I texted to say I was coming back."

"Give it time."

I topped off Jillian's wine, noticing she'd only nibbled at her sandwich. She touched the hollow space on her neck and then looked off, sighing.

"What is it?" I asked.

"I don't think I can think straight until I say what I promised to tell you. The thing I brought up on the phone . . ."

"Of course. I've been eager to hear."

The word *eager* barely covered it.

"I wasn't totally straight with you when I had that hissy fit on Monday," she said. "Yes, the dog attack freaked me out, but part of the reason I was so upset was because you were circling an issue I felt really anxious about. I didn't know how to confide in you."

"I promise not to pass any judgment, Jillian," I said. "It may have seemed like I was doing that about Blake, but I wasn't. I was simply concerned about how that could affect the situation."

"Understood. I—it's hard to even spit it out."

"Don't be embarrassed, okay?"

"It's more than embarrassment. It's shame and fear, too . . . I need you to know that I had a pretty intense flirtation with Bruce Kordas."

It actually took me a couple of seconds to process the comment, as if my brain couldn't override the message flashing, *Does not compute.* Jillian and Kordas. I could barely picture it. And yet on the one hand, I could. A beautiful, impressionable college student; a charming and seductive older man.

"When?" I asked finally.

Jillian took another long slug of wine, as slivers of memory reconfigured into a pattern for me: Jillian reaching out by phone to Kordas before I had the chance; her sudden distraction when I described my meeting with him. Her behavior made sense in hindsight.

"That January. The winter before everything happened. When I was home for vacation, one of the clerks in my father's office came down with the flu and I offered to fill in. Remember how we had a whole month off for Christmas? It rained instead of snowed, so the skiing was bad around here, and I was bored out of my mind. Besides, I was still moping over being sort of ghosted by a guy at school in early December."

Heather, of course, had mentioned Jillian filling in at the office, but it had seemed irrelevant at the time.

"Define flirtation for me," I said.

"We never had sex, but we spent hours making out in his car with half our clothes off."

"Okay," I said, trying not to let my face read as judgmental. And I wasn't. I was glad she'd told me this. "Thanks so much for filling me in. . . . Do you think your father ever found out?"

She shook her head woefully.

"No, not definitively but—but I think he might have suspected it. One time in January, right before I went back to school, Bruce drove my father to a site they were working on and my father found my scarf in the car. Bruce said he had to scramble and come up with a story about running into me somewhere and giving me a lift. But I think my father was suspicious afterward."

That might explain Carl's sudden coolness toward Kordas. And also why Hague found him snooping on Bruce's phone.

"And," she added. "I think Julia had her suspicions—she could read me like a book sometimes—but I didn't dare tell her. She had a way of running to Mommy with private stuff."

"Did you continue to see Bruce after the break was over?"

Jillian threw up her hands, stood, and began to pace. "For a little bit. He came down to Providence one day and took me to lunch, and he wanted to book a hotel room but I made an excuse. I know this sounds selfish and horrible, but I didn't really have all that much interest in him anymore. Like I said, it had been mostly out of boredom and my need to pump myself up. I'm still ashamed all these years later."

"Did you blow him off after that?"

"I tried. But—but he kept calling me. And emailing. It was like he was suddenly *obsessed* with me."

"What do you mean by *obsessed*?" My pulse was moving like a bullet train. A fling was one thing. Someone obsessed was a whole other deal.

"He just wouldn't give up. He even sent flowers to my dorm room."

"Was he looking for more than a fling?"

"I seriously doubt it. All he really wanted was to get in my pants, and I could tell he was sick of being turned down."

"Jillian, did he ever say anything threatening to you?"

She let out a low wail, so unexpected and mournful-sounding it made my heart skip in surprise.

"I know why you're asking," she exclaimed. "And after they all died, I kept asking myself if I'd made him so mad that he did it. That it was somehow my fault. I was sick with relief when the cops arrested Dylan."

Her eyes welled with tears.

"Oh God," she said. "I make a mess of everything."

"Jillian, that's not true. We all do seriously dumb shit in our twenties. I married a compulsive gambler who hocked all the jewelry my grandmother had given me and lied about absolutely everything."

"But what if this was worse than stolen jewelry? Even after I heard from the innocence group, I told myself it couldn't be Bruce. But ever since you were attacked on his site, I've kept wondering if it *was* him."

"I need to ask you again. Did he ever say anything threatening?"

"Not threatening," she said, sinking back into the

chair. "But on the last call we had, he sounded really pissed."

"And when was that?"

"March, I think. He called to see if I might be coming home for any kind of spring break, and I told him that my parents didn't want me around Julia, just in case she was still contagious. He said he wanted to drive to Providence again, and I made up a totally lame excuse. The last words he ever said to me were 'You're just a little game player, aren't you?'"

"How was he at the funeral?"

"I steered totally clear of him."

"And what about when you called him last week?"

"Cool as a fucking cucumber. I hated talking to him, but I wanted to test the waters before you spoke to him."

"Okay, look, I know this is torturing you, but you need to let it go. I'm not saying Kordas isn't responsible for what happened—maybe there was a motive related to his business dealings with your dad that we don't know about. But I doubt he would have killed your family because you wouldn't sleep with him. Being pissed isn't the same as a homicidal rage. Besides, even if he'd gone psycho because you cockteased the hell out of him, he would have directed it *your* way, not toward your parents and siblings."

She let out a long breath and wiped away her tears. "Okay," she said finally. "I'll just keep telling myself that."

We finished our sandwiches then, mostly in silence. Jillian seemed to need time to pull herself together again, and I kept processing the info, mentally going over my earlier encounters with Kordas, and viewing them from this new perspective, trying to decide if they needed to be reinterpreted.

Eventually Jillian announced she was going to turn in and read. I walked her down the hall to room seven, said good night, and returned to my room to grab my purse and car key. It was now close to eight and time to head back to Two Boots.

The place was only half-full, but the music was pounding and there was already electricity in the air. It was Saturday night, after all, and it looked like the kind of place that jumped on weekends. I strode toward the bar, where there were a dozen beer drinkers watching a baseball game on mute. The bartender was about fifty and potbellied, with thick dark brows and a receding hairline.

"Evening," he said. "What can I get you?"

"Are you Jerry, the owner?"

He smiled, flashing some yellowed teeth. "Depends on who's asking."

I ran through my prepared spiel: Working on a memoir with Jillian Lowe. Her family was murdered sixteen years ago. Jillian wanted to retrace her sister Julia's steps during the last weeks of her life.

"Wow," he said, hooking his thumbs into the waistband of his saggy jeans. "It's been a while since I heard those names."

"So you were familiar with the girls?"

"Oh, sure. Couldn't serve them yet, but they'd sit at a table with friends. Have a burger. That guy should have been burned at the stake."

He clearly hadn't heard the latest about Dylan.

"We have reason to believe that Julia was here a few times before she died. By any chance do you remember that?"

"I do, actually. Well, one time at least. About two or three weeks before the murders. I probably wouldn't recall it if she hadn't died so soon afterward, but because of that, it's been seared in my memory."

I could feel the spike in adrenaline. So Julia *had* come here, despite the fact that she was supposed to be recovering at home.

"Who was she with? Anyone you know?"

"She was alone. Sat at the bar here and had something to eat. Said she was taking the term off. It was late, I remember, because the crowd had thinned out.

After the murders, I jotted it down in case the cops ever asked. But they never came by."

Was it simply a case of cabin fever that had propelled Julia out of the house that night? And I had an even trickier question now: How had she managed to get here on her own? She didn't drive, after all.

"Is it possible she came in with someone and they split up inside?"

"Hold on for a second, okay?"

He cocked his chin toward a customer who'd just slid onto a barstool and moseyed down there, then pulled a draft beer for the guy without him having to ask.

A minute later he was back, scratching his head.

"Not that I recall. Why not ask her sister? Maybe she would know."

"Jillian? She was at away at college then."

"Well, not that week. She came in, too, one night."

Chapter 20

It seemed at that moment as if the ground had buckled under my feet, and instinctively I touched the bar, as if subconsciously I was afraid that if I didn't grab hold, I'd be knocked on my ass. My heart was beating faster, starting to race really, like it had been startled by a gong.

He had to be wrong. Jillian would have mentioned that she was in the Dory area that close to the murders. She'd actually told me that she'd avoided going home in March because Julia might still be contagious.

"Jerry, this is very helpful," I said. "But could you be mistaken about Jillian? She wouldn't have been on any kind of college break then, so I don't think it could have been her you saw."

"Nope, I'm positive. It was a few nights after Julia

was in, and I remember being surprised that they were both home. And, of course, you don't forget a girl who looked like Jillian. I called out to her and she said hello back, but then she wandered into the other room, where the crowd and the band were."

"And she was alone? Jillian?"

He shrugged. "There may have been someone with her but I don't recall. I thought she might be looking for her sister."

A thought wormed its way into my brain, and it wasn't a very nice one.

"By any chance do you remember if a man named Bruce Kordas was here that night? He's a real estate developer—slim, handsome?"

I was wondering if Jillian had come only partially clean with me earlier. Maybe she *had* come home, but to see Kordas, holing up somewhere other than her family's house.

"Never heard of the guy. Look, sorry, but I've got customers chomping at the bit."

I thanked him for his help and slid a business card across the bar surface, asking that he reach out if anything else occurred to him.

"I thought you were a writer," he said, dropping the card in his shirt pocket. "You sound more like one of those private-dick types."

"Just trying to be thorough," I told him.

I snaked my way through the swelling crowd and spilled out into the hot summer night. Up until a few minutes before, my latest rabies vaccine hadn't made much of an impression, but I was starting to detect an intensified achiness in my limbs, and a distant but determined pounding in my head.

My Jeep was parked close to the front, and after slipping inside, I foraged around in my purse until I scored two lint-covered acetaminophen, swallowing them down with the tepid remains from a water bottle. I rolled down the driver's window, hoping for a breeze, and started to unpack what I'd just heard in Two Boots.

Sixteen years was a really long time, and Jerry could have remembered all wrong—or perhaps out of sequence. Julia was clearly on the premises during that period—her credit card statement proved it—but he might be confused about Jillian. She may have been in the bar over the long Christmas vacation and Jerry's brain had shuffled snippets of memories into a narrative that bore only partial resemblance to the truth. Recent research had proven just how incredibly faulty our memories can be, even when we're positive stuff occurred in a certain way and certain order.

I couldn't, however, simply blow off what the guy

was saying. There was the chance that he *was* remembering correctly. So the question was: If Jillian *had* been in Two Boots when Jerry claimed she was, why had she left Brown at that time—and why hadn't she shared that?

It was disturbing to think she might have lied or misled me. I couldn't imagine what the reason would be. Did she have *other* secrets than the one she'd confessed earlier?

The only shot I had of finding out the truth would be by asking Jillian directly. Which might lead to its own set of problems. If I came across as distrusting of her, it could make things bumpy between us again.

A burst of laughter from outside the car broke my concentration and forced my attention toward the front of the tavern. A cluster of millennials had gathered there, three guys and a couple of women, smoking and talking, sometimes snapping their heads back in laughter.

After a minute, one of the women flicked her cigarette butt across the parking lot, gave the group the back of her hand as a wave, and strode toward the entrance. As I watched her saunter inside, I imagined Jillian slipping through that same door sixteen years ago. Of course, it would have been cooler then. She would have been dressed in more than jean shorts and a sexy top like this girl.

It came to me then, like a thunderbolt. In my mind's eye I could suddenly see the photo of Jillian I'd stumbled upon when I'd ferreted through Julia's belongings in the plastic tub. She'd been standing in front of a dark building, which, if I remembered correctly, was sided with brown cedar shingles. It might very well have been Two Boots Tavern.

I jumped out of the car and used my phone to snap a photo of the exterior of the building, ignoring the smokers' curious gazes. Finished, I drove toward the inn as fast as the winding roads allowed. After pulling into the parking lot, I tugged the tub with Julia's belongings out of the trunk and lugged it to my room.

It took only a short amount of rifling to locate the photo again. I held it in one hand and my phone in the other, letting my eyes dodge back and forth between the two images. The building Jillian had been leaning against featured the same brown shingles, and to her right was a sliver of what appeared to be a metal railing, just like the railing along the stoop in front of Two Boots. Jillian's outfit—jeans and a black leather jacket—suggested the time of year easily could have been late March.

Jillian must have given the photo to Julia. Or Julia might have even taken the shot of her sister after meeting up with—or bumping into—her at the tavern.

It was starting to look like Jillian had indeed misled me. I wasn't happy about it.

I tossed the photo back into the tub and began to pace. Surely the cops investigating the murders years ago had checked on Jillian's whereabouts, not only on the night of the murders but during the days beforehand.

I realized at that moment that I wouldn't be able to sleep until I heard Jillian's version of events. It wasn't quite ten yet, so she might still be reading. I hurried to room seven and tapped lightly on the door.

"Jillian, it's just me," I called out, not wanting to alarm her. "Are you still up?"

"Yeah, hold on," I heard her say. Thirty seconds later she opened the door, a sweater tossed on over a camisole and cotton tap pants. "Is everything okay?"

"Yes, no worries. There's just something I need to ask you about."

"Sure," she said, motioning me in.

I slipped into the room and she shut the door behind us. Though she'd checked in only a short time ago, the space already looked lived in. Clothes were tossed here and there, a splayed iPad case poked out from the folds of the rumpled bedding, and a candle was burning on the dresser, filling the room with the scent of lavender. I figured the candle must be an inn no-no, but I wasn't about to play fire marshal.

I moseyed across the room and rested my butt on the edge of the desk. I'd been so desperate to hear her take on Jerry's revelation that I hadn't worked out exactly how I would ask, and I needed to buy myself a little time to do that. The last thing I wanted was to put her on the defensive or piss her off again.

"Ah, I see they've adequately represented the dragonfly in your room as well," I said, pointing. There was a series of metal ones snaking up the outside edge of the window frame.

"I'm just glad I dig insects. You sure everything is okay?"

"Yeah, like I said, a question popped up and I wanted to run it by you."

"Shoot." She settled on the bed, tugging the cardigan tighter around her, almost protectively.

"You know the bar Two Boots, right?" I asked.

"Of course," she said. "That was always a big hangout, though the owner knew my age so I could never drink there, even with a fake ID. Why do you ask?"

She'd narrowed her eyes quizzically but nothing about her manner suggested I was on forbidden terrain.

"It turned up a couple of times on Julia's credit card statement from March—toward the end of the month. At first I thought it was a clothing store, but then yesterday I happened to drive by and put two and two together. I stopped by there tonight and talked to the owner, Jerry. He actually remembers Julia being there once that March."

"Really? That's kind of weird."

"You mean because she was supposed to be housebound when she was home?"

"Uh-huh."

"And still contagious?"

"Well, on that front, I think it might have been okay for her to be in public. She told me at one point that she'd had follow-up tests done, and she wasn't contagious anymore. Maybe she was going stir-crazy and needed to get out, even if she didn't feel so great."

I noted that Jillian had yet to volunteer a remark like, *Gee, I was at Two Boots that week and never saw her.*

"That's what I figured, too."

"Does it even matter that she went there?"

"I think it's important to examine what she was doing during late March and early April."

"Even minutia like going someplace for a burger?" Her words were tinged with frustration.

"Yes, we want to know everyplace she went and

who she came into contact with. Because something triggered someone to do the unthinkable to your family, and we need to figure out if that trigger was related to Julia."

It had come out more forcibly than I'd intended, and I prayed my words hadn't pained her. But I needed her to finally understand this, to know that minutia mattered, even the seemingly dumb stuff—and that if details were kept from me, I was operating with a handicap.

"Okay."

"You mentioned a while back that Julia was kind of a loner and didn't have many friends at home. And Jerry thought she'd come in alone. But I'm wondering if out of boredom, she'd looked someone up while she was home. They might have gone to Two Boots together but didn't hang with each other once they arrived."

"There were a couple of kids from high school she was friendly enough with, but they would have been away at college then. Mamie was around—she went to a community college in Pittsfield—but she and Jules didn't really know each other."

"This is a real stretch, but is there any chance she could have gone with Trevor Hague? He was in the area then, he might have been nursing a nasty grudge toward your father, and it's possible he tried to ingratiate himself with Julia."

"No way. Like I said, he creeped her out. And one thing to keep in mind is that Jules wouldn't have hesitated to go someplace on her own. She did a lot of that."

"But Julia didn't drive," I reminded her.

She scrunched her face, thinking. "Maybe my mother dropped her off that night." A pause. "No, wait, that wouldn't have happened. If Jules was still the least bit sick—and apparently she was—my mother wouldn't have let her go out at night."

"So at the very least, she would have had to figure a way to sneak out of the house without it being noticed. Jerry indicated she was there on the late side."

Jillian nodded, as if putting pieces together.

"It might not have been hard. My parents went to bed early. And Jules told me on the phone that they'd let her commandeer the couch in the library so she wouldn't have to be stuck in bed in her room all day. She even slept there some nights."

The room she'd been killed in. I could see it in my mind as if I were still standing there. The wood-paneled walls and endless bookshelves.

"So if she was downstairs already, she wouldn't have had to worry about creaking stairs waking up your parents. And there were two charges for Two Boots on her credit card, so she clearly went out more than once."

Since I didn't have access to the credit card statement

for April, I had no idea how many more times she may have stopped by the tavern after those two occasions.

"There's—there's something else I'm remembering, from over Christmas," Jillian said. Her expression had suddenly clouded. "Julia's break started earlier than mine, and after I was home, she confessed that she'd taken my mom's car out one night after my parents were in bed. It made me nuts, and I begged her not to do it again."

"Then she *did* have a way to get to Two Boots on her own."

If Julia had gone out alone, she might have met someone, someone who seemed harmless but wasn't and had followed her home. Talked his way in.

"God," Jillian said, groaning. "Why couldn't she have waited a few more months, till she had her license? If it's true she was driving that spring, she could have gotten into a shitload of trouble. Or even been hurt."

A second later she winced, clearly recognizing the awful irony of her last comment. Julia had died anyway.

I shoved off from the desk and crossed to the bed, sitting down beside her.

"In all the craziness after Penny died, I forgot to mention something she told me about you. That you always watched out for Julia in the most amazing way."

"I probably irritated her at times by being over-protective. I've sometimes wondered if it was a way of overcompensating for needing more attention from my mom than she could give. . . . Gosh, sorry to sound so maudlin."

"Don't be silly. I want you to feel comfortable sharing everything with me. There—there's actually one more thing I wanted to ask you about before I turn in. When I was talking to Jerry, he said he saw you at the Two Boots as well—the same week Julia was there."

"*What?*"

"Were you home around that time?"

"Home? No, of course not."

"Could you have driven back to Dory for a day or two and just not remember? In Julia's belongings, there's a photo of you that I'm pretty sure was taken in front of Two Boots."

"I'd surely remember if I was home around then. The picture was probably from the previous summer. Or over Christmas. I generally went there a few times during vacation."

"Right . . . Well, why don't I let you get back to reading?"

"Good night," she said glumly. "See you tomorrow."

As soon as I was back in my room, I made an instant beeline for the desk and picked up the photo I'd tossed there. Jillian's leather jacket was unzipped and she didn't seem to be dressed warmly enough for the shot to have been taken over a Christmas break. And the jacket, jeans, and suede booties hardly screamed long, hot summer.

Had Jillian just lied to me? I wondered. Nothing about her body language had suggested deception, and yet I knew that was no guarantee. Ear tugging, nose scratching, and eye shifting are supposed to be unintentional trademarks of liars, but many people fabricate without any kind of tell. For two and a half years I lived with a man who lied as easily as he hummed in the shower and I never had a clue—that is, until the bookies started circling.

While I'd been gone I'd left the AC unit running, but I flipped it off now and raised the window shade and sash, eager for the breeze I'd noticed in Jillian's room. The achiness that had begun to kick in earlier had retreated for now. I stripped off my clothes, letting them drop to the floor, and slid between the sheets.

I was sure I'd have trouble falling asleep, but from sheer mental exhaustion, my brain gave up the fight quickly. Seconds after lying my head on the pillow, I felt myself drifting off.

And then—I had no clue how much later—I was awake, with my heart thrumming so hard I could hear it pinging against the mattress.

Someone had whispered in my ear.

I flung myself over on my back and jerked upward. My fists were clenched in fear.

"Jillian?" I called out, my words nearly strangled. Was it *her*? No, it couldn't be. I'd locked my door. I peered through the darkness but couldn't make out anything other than the hulking shapes of furniture.

Desperately I fumbled for the lamp on the bedside table, finally forcing my fingers to the switch.

The illumination from the lamp wasn't much, though it was enough for me to view the corners of the room. I was alone. I must have heard someone whispering in a dream. And yet it had seemed so real, so vivid. I peered at the digital clock on the bedside table. 1:17.

A second later a noise reached into the room through the screen on the window. It was from a car moving slowly outside, crunching gravel. *That* was the sound, I realized, that had penetrated my dream, disguised as a whisper. Was it guests returning to the inn after a night out? I kicked my feet out of the sheets and covered the distance to the window, the one that faced onto the parking lot. I pulled aside the gauzy curtain.

I couldn't see the car from where I was. But as the crunching noises grew fainter, I realized the vehicle was actually *exiting* the lot, headed toward the street.

There was a bounce sound as the car took the curb, followed moments later by the light growl from the engine accelerating now that it was on the street. So it *hadn't* been guests returning from a late evening.

I backed up to the bed. Who would be *leaving* the inn at this hour? Not a staff person surely. When I'd checked in, Mary had explained that no one was on duty after midnight, so if there was any kind of emergency, guests needed to tap on the door to her small apartment at the rear of the house.

I crawled back into bed, sitting for a while with my torso propped against the headboard, trying to decide how concerned I should be about the car. Perhaps one of the guests had entertained a late-night visitor who had just departed.

Or had someone been spying on Jillian or me? I'd let no one know where Jillian and I were staying. Had *she* kept our whereabouts under wraps this time?

I turned off the light finally, but lay awake for a while, listening carefully for sounds—both from outside and within the building, along the corridor. It took forever to finally drift off to sleep again.

I was up by seven, still feeling jittery. After dressing, I went downstairs and from the breakfast buffet, took a plate of raspberries and a couple tiny muffins out to one of the wrought-iron tables in the yard. I felt achier this morning than I had the night before, but thankfully I wasn't experiencing the full-blown misery the earlier shots had led to.

As I was halfway through my second cup of coffee, writing questions to myself in my composition book, Jillian came traipsing across the bright green lawn, empty-handed.

"No breakfast?" I asked as she approached.

"Maybe later. Have you got a minute to talk now?"

"Of course." She looked agitated. "Is something the matter?"

"When you came to my room last night and told me what Jerry said, were you trying to make a point?"

"A point?"

"I've been thinking about the conversation and it seemed as if you were hinting at something, saying it between the lines."

Oh boy. I'd questioned her honesty, or at least her memory, and it annoyed her, just as I'd feared I might.

"Jerry had seemed really adamant and I had to ask. I wondered if you'd come home one night in March and just not recalled it."

"And that maybe I'd come home *another* night and murdered my entire family, right?"

My breath caught in my chest.

"Jillian, of course not. That's not why I pushed

about it. If you *had* been home, there might have been something you saw that week that was important. Like I said, I'm simply trying to piece events together and make sense of everything. We have to trust each other, even if the questions are sometimes difficult."

She relaxed her shoulders a little, as if my response had partially mollified her.

"I'd never think that, *ever*," I said.

I *hadn't* thought it, not in one coldhearted statement at the center of my brain, but I knew the idea had been a vague form on the edges, threatening to take shape. Family members were always the first suspects in a domestic homicide. Young women sometimes *did* murder family members. Or they persuaded a boyfriend to do the dirty work. But surely the police had ruled her out.

"Okay," she said.

"What I *do* think is that we need to figure out if Julia was hanging with anyone during late March or early April. If she was, this person is worth talking to."

She nodded, exhaling. She still didn't look too happy with me. At that moment my phone rang from the table, an interruption I couldn't help but be grateful for, though the number wasn't one I recognized.

"Let me get this, okay?" I said. "In case it's important."

"Is this Bailey Weggins?" a voice asked after I offered a quick hello. It was a woman, on the older side, I thought, but beyond that I had no idea who it might be.

"Yes, it is—can I help you?"

"I believe you wanted to speak to me."

"Who is this, please?"

"It's Eleanor Mercandetti."

Finally. I couldn't believe it.

"Mrs. Mercandetti," I said, mainly for Jillian's benefit, so she'd know who I was talking to. "Thank you so much for getting in touch. I'm eager to ask you a few questions. Do you have time now?"

A short pause and I thought the call might have been dropped. By now Jillian's eyes had widened in surprise.

"Not on the phone," Mercandetti said into the silence. "We need to meet in person."

Okay, wow, I thought. Clearly what she had to share was a doozy.

"Where do I find you?"

"I'm in Litchfield, Connecticut, not far from the border to Massachusetts. If you're still in the Berkshires, I'm about an hour away."

"Just name the time and the place."

"One hour then?"

"Um, all right," I said, rapidly processing the request. "Though can we say an hour and ten?"

"Fine. There's a small green in the center of town. I'll be on a bench. I'll have a red cotton sweater on."

"All right, I'll be there."

"If Jillian's with you, please bring her. It's important that I speak to her."

"Yes, I'll bring her."

Signing off, I let out a breath slowly.

"What's going on?" Jillian demanded.

"I guess you heard—that was your former principal. She wants to meet in an hour. And she wants you to come, too."

As I stuffed the notebook and pen into my bag, I filled Jillian in on the brief call.

"Should I go?" she asked, clearly unsettled.

"Yes, if you're up to it. She may be more forthcoming if you're there. She clearly has something big to share."

Seven minutes later we were in the car and headed southwest. I was vaguely familiar with the area we were heading to because my former boss, Cat Jones from *Gloss*, had a weekend home around there. Like the Berkshire towns I'd been traipsing through over the past days, that region of Connecticut had plenty of affluent weekenders in the population mix.

Jillian and I didn't speak much during the drive. I'm sure she realized as much as I did that it was pointless to speculate about what Mercandetti would divulge when we were just an hour away from hearing it.

We found the green easily enough, with a white, steepled church set behind it. We were no sooner out of the car than I spotted a blur of red on a bench on the far side of the green. We hurried in that direction, as if both of us feared the woman sitting there might be in danger of vanishing before our eyes.

Mercandetti was younger than I expected, perhaps in her late sixties, which indicated she must have retired early. She was attractive, what you might call handsome, with short black hair nicely styled and an erect bearing. She had her hands folded in her lap and seemed to be studying the grass off to her right. At the sound of our footsteps, she glanced in our direction.

For a moment, nothing registered on her face, and then her lips parted.

"Jillian," she said, drawing out the name as if haunted by it.

"Hello, Mrs. Mercandetti." Jillian stepped forward and awkwardly shook her former principal's hand.

"Please," Mercandetti said. "Please, sit down."

I let Jillian grab the spot next to Mercandetti. I took a moment to introduce myself, though Mercandetti could barely tear her eyes away from Jillian.

"It's wonderful to see you after all this time," she told her.

"You live here? In Litchfield?" Jillian said.

"Yes, I was out in California for about a decade, but I moved back after my husband died. I missed the area so much . . . But enough about that. I heard you were concerned about something your sister found out years ago but you have no idea what it is. I'm going to tell you."

As my heart skipped, I saw Jillian stiffen, fearful over what was coming next.

"Is it about her?" she asked. "About Julia?"

"Yes, partly. But it's also about you." Mercandetti's eyes were now brimming with tears.

"*Me?*" Jillian said.

"There's something your mother kept from you, though not out of anything other than her fierce devotion as a mother. I hope you can understand that."

"*What?* What is it?"

"You and Julia. You were identical twins."

Chapter 21

I t took a couple of seconds for Mercandetti's words to sink in. Once they did, my jaw slackened in utter surprise, and yet another part of my brain seemed to nod in slow motion, as if a puzzle I didn't even know was a puzzle was being solved before my eyes.

Jillian and Julia. Sisters who were each so smart and so musical. Who both loved science. Whose physical resemblance had seemed striking to me now that Jillian's hair was no longer blond.

I turned to Jillian and laid my hand over hers, hoping to comfort her.

For a moment she didn't speak. Even through the amber lenses of her sunglasses, I could see the distress in her eyes.

"What do you *mean?*" she said finally, her voice

hoarse. "How could she be my twin? I'm *older*. A year older."

"Your parents lied to Julia about her birthdate," Mercandetti said. "It was the same as yours. Jillian, it breaks my heart to tell you this."

"By why would they lie like that?" Jillian implored. *"Why?"*

Mercandetti lifted her eyes upward, searching for words, I assumed. "As I said, your mother had the best intentions. She loved you both so much. But due to her illness, your sister was underweight and frail for some time, as well as lagging in emotional maturity, and your mother hated the idea of her growing up in stark comparison to you."

"So she did it for *Julia's* sake?" Jillian spat out bitterly.

"No, for *both* of you. She didn't want you to feel guilty or to be burdened in any way. She knew it would be easier for both of you if Julia were your younger sister."

"When did this begin?" I interjected. "When the Lowes moved here from Virginia?"

"Yes," Mercandetti said, not removing her gaze from Jillian. "And I always assumed that was a big part of why your parents moved. I don't think I would have gone along with the scheme if Claire had simply arrived at the school on the day of enrollment and announced she wanted me to hatch this plan with her. But she said the family had been in the area for a half year already and that everyone at the preschool believed you and Julia were a year apart, and it would be traumatic for you both to be told otherwise. I didn't want to create any issues for the girls, so I kept the secret."

"But somehow Julia found out," I said.

"Yes. Your mother had always planned to inform the two of you, but she kept putting it off. And, of course, over time it became even harder. And then it was too late."

"*How?*" Jillian demanded. "How did Jules find out?"

Mercandetti bit her lip, clearly agonized. "From what your mother told me, your sister had begun to have suspicions over that last Christmas. I'm not sure why. But it came to a head when she was home from school and wanted to pursue getting a driver's license. She apparently had been badgering your parents and didn't understand why your mother was setting up roadblocks. Your mother had managed to doctor Julia's birth date on a few things but she wasn't going to be able to pull it off for the permit application. Finally, Julia decided to put things in motion herself. She went hunting for her birth certificate, found it, and saw the real date. Your mother came by to tell me what had happened. Julia was furious with her and angry with me, too, because she knew I'd been in on the deception."

Jillian leaned forward, grabbing her head in her hands and squeezing hard.

"But Jules would have told me," she muttered, her eyes cast downward. "She wouldn't have kept this from me."

"As angry as your sister was, she apparently agreed to let your mother be the one to share the news with you."

"When? When was she going to tell me?"

"Your mother was going to drive to see you at school that spring so she could do it face-to-face. But she obviously never had the chance."

Jillian shot straight up again and pivoted toward Mercandetti, her blue eyes flashing anger. "But why didn't *you* tell me—after they were all dead?"

"I considered it, Jillian. Please believe me, I did. But I was afraid it would cause you to suffer even more. You might resent your mother . . . And then Penny called."

Mercandetti glanced toward me now. "She told me you were asking questions. That you'd said Jillian knew her sister and mother had been arguing about something related to the principal but she didn't know what." She turned again to Jillian. "I couldn't let you be tortured by that mystery."

For a few moments Jillian sat listlessly, saying nothing, and then without warning she launched herself off the bench. She crossed her arms and swept her gaze across the green, as if there was something out there that would reconfigure everything she'd just learned into a better, more palatable truth. But all that lay ahead was a cluster of kids scrambling over a pockmarked cannon, probably from the Revolution. She looked back at Mercandetti.

"Is there anything else I should be aware of?" she asked bluntly.

"No, that's all of it, as far as I know. Jillian, please, can you ever accept my apology?"

"You're not the one to blame." She turned to me. "Bailey, I—I want to go back to the car."

"Of course. But would you mind giving me a few more minutes with Mrs. Mercandetti? I promise I won't be long."

As Jillian nodded solemnly, I dug my car key from my purse and passed it to her. I watched as she began to retrace her steps across the green. I couldn't even imagine the anguish she was feeling over this news. I wanted to comfort her, but there were answers I needed before I split.

"Mrs. Mercandetti—" I said, sliding a little closer on the bench now that Jillian had vacated her space.

"Please, call me Eleanor."

"Eleanor, talk to me about Penny. I take it she called you right after I left her house."

"She said you'd been there a couple of hours earlier. We'd lost touch over the years and she had to track down my number through Linda Campbell, the assistant principal."

"Penny seemed pretty shaken when I spoke to her. Was she nervous Jillian might learn the truth?"

"She *was* shaken, yes. But neither one of us wanted to keep the information under wraps any longer. I told her I'd call the number you left and would arrange to speak to Jillian."

"But you didn't."

"Not then, no. I'd barely had time to think about it when I heard Penny had been murdered. I was very distraught, and I put off reaching out to you. When Linda called, saying you'd been at the school, it was the push I needed."

"Did anyone besides you and Penny know the truth about the girls?"

"At the school, not a soul. I only took Penny into my confidence because her job often entailed going into files and records, and I didn't want to risk having her stumble on the information one day and blurt it out to anyone."

"Would she have discussed the situation with anyone besides you after I left her house?"

The question clearly caught her by surprise.

"Goodness, no. What reason would she have?"

I weighed my next words carefully before speaking them. "Eleanor, I don't want to alarm you, but I've been concerned that Penny's death might not be related to a burglary. That it could have something to do with this secret."

"Dear God." Mercandetti pressed a hand to her breast.

"I haven't an ounce of proof. But it seems bizarrely coincidental that she would have been killed mere hours after I spoke to her."

"What motive could there be? It's not like anyone would be harmed by the fact that the girls were twins."

She had a point, a good one. For days I'd been fixated on the idea that Penny had been sitting on a potentially explosive secret, perhaps one involving sexual abuse, and that someone had murdered her so it wouldn't surface. The actual truth, though painful for Jillian to learn, was pretty tame.

"From what you know, could that information have rocked *anyone's* boat?"

Mercandetti shook her head. "No, not anyone I can imagine—other than Jillian, of course. Claire mentioned the day she came to see me that the situation had put a strain on her marriage, that her husband went along with the scheme and then always regretted doing so. But that could hardly play a role now."

"Speaking of Jillian, I better find her and see if I can help in any way. Eleanor, do me a favor, will you? For the time being, please be cautious. As you said, it doesn't sound like Penny's murder could be related to this, but my gut keeps telling me it might be."

"You're scaring me."

"I know, and I'm sorry, but I want you to be safe."

We rose in unison from the bench. She was tall, at least five foot eleven.

"Maybe I don't deserve to be a hundred percent safe," she said. "For being part of that terrible hoax."

"Claire pressured you. And you were clearly doing what you thought was right."

She offered a sad shrug that didn't quite fit with her elegant stature.

"Do you know, it's why I left the school the following year. Why I retired early and moved away for so long."

"Because you felt guilty for being in on the deception?"

"Yes, but it was more than that. I'd enabled the family to be secretive, and perhaps a secret had played a part in their deaths. I felt too guilty to be around here anymore."

She could be right. If the Lowes were good at keeping secrets, there may have been others besides the one I'd just discovered—a secret about Claire and Jocelyn, for instance, or Carl being a predator, or troubles with Bruce in the business.

I shook Eleanor's hand, thanked her for meeting with us, and promised to keep her abreast if I learned anything more about Penny's murder.

Back at the car, I found Jillian sitting in the passenger seat, staring glumly out the front window, her face wet with tears.

"Hey," I said. "How about grabbing something to eat or drink in town here?"

"Thanks, Bailey, but I'd rather go back. I feel the urge to curl up into a fetal position and stay there for a few weeks."

"Jillian, I know you must feel horrible about this. But I'm sure Mrs. Mercandetti was right—your mother was only trying to protect you as best she could."

"It would be nice to believe that, but it all really seems to be about *Julia*."

"You know, a few years back, I had a gig as a contributing writer for *Gloss* magazine, and I did a few human-interest articles for them as well as crime pieces.

I wrote a story once about the way identical twins com-
municate with each other, and there was a family I
interviewed in which one of the twins—two boys—had
been badly burned in a freak accident. And as hard as
it was for the twin who was scarred, I think it was even
worse for the uninjured one. He was absolutely *stricken*
with guilt—though he'd had nothing to do with the
accident. That guilt sabotaged his confidence. Your
mother must have dreaded the idea of something like
that happening to you."

She didn't say anything, and I figured she wanted to
be alone with her thoughts, so I started up the car.

Ten minutes later, as we rolled through farmland on
our way back to the Berkshires, she finally spoke.

"I appreciate what you said about those twins, Bailey. And—and as awful as this is, I'm glad I found out."

"Are you?" I had been wondering about that, my
stomach tight with worry. I'd pushed and pushed to
learn this secret and all it had done was leave Jillian in
even greater turmoil.

"Uh-huh. Remember what I told you on the deck
that night, how I'd always felt a weird restlessness, a
yearning? Maybe this is why. I was missing my twin—
though she was there all the time."

"That could very well be the case. As you think
back, did you ever have any kind of inkling?"

"No, never. Jules was pretty scrawny in high school, and that would have kept our faces from looking identical. Though I remember someone once saying that we both had our mother's blue eyes, and I think I noticed then that our eyes *were* a lot alike, both the color and how they were set kind of far apart. But you'd expect that for sisters."

"Julia's college roommate mentioned on the phone that she'd gained some weight during the school year. That probably played a role in her starting to see the resemblance."

Jillian let out a ragged sigh. "But what happened over *Christmas*? Mrs. Mercandetti said that's when she became suspicious."

"Unfortunately, we may never know."

Jillian leaned her head against the window and closed her eyes. In a few minutes, her breathing grew deeper and I realized she'd fallen asleep. I did my best to concentrate on the winding two-lane road, but mostly I drove on autopilot, my mind rehashing the revelation from earlier and what it might mean.

I'd be lying if I didn't admit that a small part of me felt oddly excited about the discovery. I'd had a hunch that the argument between Claire and Julia was significant, and I'd been right. I took no pleasure from

Jillian's misery, but it was good to know that I could trust my gut.

On the other hand, I wondered if I'd been a fool not to have guessed the truth, which made such sense in hindsight. It was a little like having a sleazy, disgruntled bookie come up to you on the street and announce that your husband owes him seventy-five thousand dollars, and then suddenly realizing why all your jewelry is missing and his cell phone pings throughout the night.

But some lies are just too good to see, even in plain daylight. My bet was that Jocelyn had never guessed or been given the information. It was a secret Claire had been unwilling to share with anyone who didn't need to know.

As stunning as Mercandetti's observation had been, however, it didn't seem to explain why Penny Niles was strangled or, for that matter, why Jillian's entire family was brutally stabbed to death.

I needed to put myself back on track. I needed to find out more about Kordas and Hague and Bob London, and whether Julia might have struck up an acquaintance with someone during one of her stops at Two Boots. And tomorrow I would drive by D&A Auto once it opened and try to have a conversation with Keith Denali.

Jillian stirred as we were nearing the inn.

"Do you want to stop for lunch someplace?" I asked. "There are a couple of cute spots around here, if you don't mind kale or quinoa."

"Thanks, but I'm just going to hang in my room."

"Understood. And you're sure you don't want to go back to New York or Boston?"

"Pretty sure. I definitely don't feel up to traveling today."

"All right . . . Do you plan to see Mamie and Blake on this trip?"

"I told them I was coming back and that I'd call them when I arrived—but I haven't done that yet."

"And you haven't mentioned the visit to anyone, have you? Or where we're staying?"

I was recalling the car last night, the stealthy crunch of tires on gravel, my concern that someone had eyes on the inn.

"No, I was a slow learner on that front," Jillian said, "but it finally stuck."

We'd arrived at the inn now and, rather than pull into the lot, I parked directly in front. I hugged her good-bye and watched as she walked up the blue slate path.

As soon as the front door closed behind her, I phoned Candace and asked if I could take her to lunch on short notice. After such an emotional morning, I was craving her company.

"Come *here*," she said. "I already have lunch started."

"You sure?"

"Absolutely."

On the drive to her house, I took a short detour and drove by the address I'd googled for Trevor Hague's kitchen showroom, Hague Designs. It was sleek and attractive, set among several upscale-looking businesses not far from Dory, and, of course, closed today, since it was Sunday. I don't know what good came from eyeballing it. Was I expecting a sign that read, "We design luxury kitchens *and* keep a pack of personal-protection dogs in the back." But at least it confirmed that he had his own business, which on the surface, at least, appeared successful enough.

"Twice in one month, how lucky can I be?" Candace exclaimed as I stood on her threshold minutes later.

"I've come bearing gifts," I said, handing over a shopping bag. I'd bought her a selection of gourmet food items at the same time I'd picked up the ones for Landon.

She took a peek inside. "How sweet of you. . . . Come in, come in. Lunch is already on the table."

I trailed her through the house to the kitchen. She

was dressed in another one of her long, flowy skirts, this one bright red, and she'd added a little product to her cropped hair, spiking it up in the front in a fun, feisty way. Her cheeks were rosy. It looked like she'd spent time outdoors since I'd last visited.

"I've made a salad Niçoise, by the way. You're not allergic to tuna, are you?"

"No, just peanuts. But I hate mooching another meal off you."

"It's my pleasure, sweetie, and I want to hear what's going on. . . . My goodness, what's the bandage on your arm for?"

"Oh, a long story. I'll tell you over lunch."

I knew I could trust Candace, but it didn't feel appropriate for me to divulge anything personal about the Lowes to her, like the twin revelation. So over salad I offered only the broad outlines of events since I'd seen her: the dog bite; my brief sojourn back to New York; my return for a new round of interviews, still hoping to determine who'd had enough rage to kill four people.

"Is there any chance it was simply one of those horrible home invasions?" Candace asked as I wound down my recap.

"It doesn't seem that way. Because the security company records indicated that the alarm was deactivated around eleven that night by someone inside the house, which had to have been Julia, since she was apparently downstairs then. She must have known the person."

As I twirled the melting ice around in my glass of iced tea, a thought resurfaced, one I'd toyed with when I was talking to Jillian about Two Boots. Julia's trips to the tavern might have played a role in her death. Maybe she'd gone on another secret sojourn the night of the murders and come into contact with a predator who later tailed her home, which wouldn't have been difficult, since she was such an inexperienced driver. But why would she have let him into the house?

What if it hadn't been a stranger who followed her but someone familiar who she'd bumped into at Two Boots? Someone she didn't know was dangerous. They may have briefly chatted. He could have shown up at the house after she was home and called through the window glass that he had something she'd dropped or left behind.

And yet that didn't make sense, either. If she'd de-activated the alarm twice that night, once to sneak out and then another time to let someone into the house, the cops would have been all over that.

"Do you have any ideas who it might have been?" Candace asked.

"I'm working on a few theories. Until this morning

I thought that the murders might have been related to a secret that had been kept hidden for years, but that looks like a dead end now."

"There wasn't a secret after all?"

"No, there *was* a secret—and a real whopper—but I don't think it would have triggered anyone to kill the Lowes."

Candace sighed as she collected our plates, waving off my attempts to help.

"Families keep secrets in order to protect one another," she said. "But they generally only make things worse in the end."

I sat very still for a moment. Her words had felt loaded, as if they had to do with more than the Lowes.

"Candace, there's a question I need to ask you," I said. "Why didn't you tell my mother you'd been ill?"

"Oh, sweetie, I barely told a soul. I tend to be private about these kinds of thing." She was sliding plates into the dishwasher, her back to me, and I couldn't read her face. But her words had sounded stilted and inauthentic.

"It's more than that, though. You and my mom. There's been a certain coolness between you guys for a long time, and I've never understood why."

I saw her shoulders sag, and she slowly turned to face me. Her expression was stricken.

"Bailey, I respect your mother so much, but I don't seem to be one of her favorite people."

The lack of warmth between them had always concerned me, and I could see now that it was a source of sadness for Candace.

"But why not? My dad adored you."

"It's complicated. I'm not sure you really want to hear about it."

"I *do*," I said. I might have been remembering incorrectly, but the coolness seemed to have started after my father died. I'd noticed it at family events ever since. Had there been a falling-out related to my father's death?

Candace returned to the table and slowly lowered herself into her chair.

"Maybe I should tell you. If it's something you've noticed and always wondered about, I don't want you to be troubled by it."

Candace's words eerily echoed one of the comments Mercandetti had uttered this morning before breaking her news. She was starting to scare me a little.

"And it may shed valuable light for you," she added. "Help you understand things about your family."

Oy. I hoped this wasn't going to end up being a "Luke, I am your father" moment, the kind of awful bombshell that had been dropped at Jillian's feet this morning.

"Yes, I'm a big girl. I can handle it."

"About a half year before your father passed, he came to stay with me here for three and a half weeks."

I found myself squinting instinctively as I paged through my memory to the year I was twelve. My father had traveled for work, but off the top of my head I couldn't recall him ever being gone that long.

"Were you sick back then, too?"

"No, no. He came for his own reasons. To get away."

"From *us?*

"Your mother."

My stomach lurched.

"Are you saying my parents were briefly separated?"

"*Separated* is too strong a word, but your father told me he needed a break. As you know, your dad was a very thoughtful man and also very introspective. On occasion he felt as if the world was too much for him. Usually a good hike in the woods would solve the problem. But I think this time he was going through a minor midlife crisis, experiencing a real ennui, and it triggered a need for more remedial measures."

In some ways it felt as if she was talking about an-other person, because my father had mostly seemed so present and centered, and yet on a level her words rang true. On a few occasions I'd definitely had glimpses of a man who needed to retreat.

"But why didn't he just shut himself up in his study? Why did he have to leave my mother? I'm sure it must have really hurt her."

"Your father was crazy about your mother, but they were very different. She's so outgoing and personable. I think at times he felt overwhelmed by her. He didn't actually say very much to me about it. Just that he was craving a break, a chance to spend a lot of time alone. I barely saw him when he was here."

It pained me to think of what my mom had gone through, worried sick about how she fit into the midlife blip and probably wondering if he was actually coming back. And it pained me to think of my dad, too. His feeling that the world was too much.

"I hope you're not sorry I told you," Candace said. She laid a hand over one of mine, just as I'd done to Jillian.

"It's unsettling to hear, but I agree with you. It's better to know why things are the way they are. But what about this made my mother change toward *you*?"

"She always suspected I'd urged him to come stay with me, which wasn't the case at all. If your father had called and asked, I would have discouraged the whole idea. But he just showed up at the door one day, and I couldn't turn him away."

I chewed on my thumb, discombobulated.

"Did my parents patch things up when he returned home?" I asked, my voice catching as I spoke. "Were they okay when he died?"

"Yes, I believe so. Though your father was always a bit of a mystery to your mom. I know that frustrated her."

Omigod, talk about *echoes*. It was the refrain I was constantly saying in my mind about Beau.

"Bailey, are you sure it was okay to tell you?" Candace asked.

"Definitely, it helps in more ways than you know. Now, you're going to stay at the table, and *I'm* going to fix the coffee."

Later, after coffee and cookies and Candace seeing me to the door, I sat for a few minutes in my car before starting it, still digesting what I'd learned. I felt so sad thinking of the hiccup that had occurred in my parents' marriage, and prayed it hadn't tainted their last months together. And I also couldn't stop wondering:

Was I attracted to Beau in part because his sense of mystery reminded me of my father? Did I need to cut him some slack because my concerns weren't so much about things he did, just who he was?

As preoccupied as I was with these thoughts, there was a task I needed to take care of before returning to the inn—and that was drive by the Lowe house once more. Something had been niggling at my brain and instinct told me being in Dory might help the thought finally surface.

When I arrived at the house, I noticed the "for sale" sign still up, being jostled on its chains by a hot breeze. I sat quietly in the car, hoping for a revelation. I recalled standing at the foot of the stairs and imagining Claire lying dead there. And also standing on the threshold of the library, picturing Julia's bloodied corpse. Julia, with the most stab wounds of them all. The elusive thought felt hopelessly out of reach. Maybe I was too churned up from my visit with Candace.

On the way back to the inn, I stopped at a couple of small roadside markets and picked up items for dinner. Emerging from the last store, I noticed that dark clouds were hunched on the western horizon, as if biding their time before setting out.

The first floor of the inn was empty when I returned, with no sign even of the innkeeper, Mary. It was Sunday, of course, and the weekenders had cleared out by now.

I grabbed my notebook as soon as I was settled back in my room, but before I could even open it, I felt over-whelmed by both achiness and a weird malaise, which had snuck up on me since leaving Candace's. I flopped on the bed and closed my eyes.

When I woke up almost two hours later, my eyelids were nearly glued together and my brain was foggy. I quickly texted Jillian, who had cell service here.

Me: You okay? Want to have dinner in the yard at 7? I have food.
Jillian: Doing better. Yes, 7, great. Pick you up.

I took a quick shower in order to defog, wound fresh gauze around my arm, and made a few more notes. I tried to conjure up ways to learn more about Julia's activities during the last weeks of her life, but I kept coming up empty.

As promised, Jillian arrived at seven. She definitely looked better than this morning, her face all composed again.

"You really okay?" I asked.

"Yeah, though I keep ricocheting between telling myself that my mother loved me fiercely and then wondering how she could have ever done what she did. . . . Do you need me to carry anything?"

"Just the wine and Perrier—they're on the desk. I'll grab the food from the fridge."

"I owe you for all this food you've been buying," she said as she closed the gap to the desk.

"Don't worry about it." I glanced over to smile at her and noticed that her gaze had fallen to the open tub of Julia's belongings sitting on the floor next to the desk. Her perfectly smooth brow wrinkled in confusion, and I realized that I should have replaced the lid earlier.

"What's this?" she asked, withdrawing an item from the tub. It was the photo, the one of her in front of Two Boots.

"That's the picture I mentioned last night, the one of you that Julia kept. There's a pushpin hole at the top, so she must have hung it on her bulletin board. Which shows how much she adored you."

Jillian kept staring.

"What?" I asked.

"It's—This isn't me."

"Wait, what do you mean?" I said, crossing the room to her. "Who else would it be?"

But even as I asked the question, I sensed the answer computing in my brain and a chill crept up my spine.

"It's Julia," Jillian said, her voice tight with shock. "She'd done her hair so she looked just like me."

Chapter 22

Are you absolutely sure it's not you?" I urged. "Maybe you're just not remembering right."

"No, those aren't my clothes. The leather jacket was hers, I'm sure of it. I never had one."

"Had she ever worn her hair like this before? This color or style?"

"After I went blond junior year in high school, she had highlights put in, I think partly because of me. But she didn't keep them."

"So this look was totally out of the ordinary for her?"

"Yes, it's like she was trying to *imitate* me. The color is exactly like mine was, and she's wearing the part to the side like mine. Hers was always in the middle."

"Oh God," I said, my mind racing. I recalled what Jerry had said about Jillian striding through Two Boots a few nights after Julia had been there. How he'd called out to her and that Jillian had acknowledged the greeting.

"What is it?"

"I'm wondering if she was doing more than wearing her hair like you. Maybe she was actually passing herself off as you."

If Julia had allowed people in the area to think she was Jillian, it presented a scenario different than any I'd toyed with in my mind—that the killer might have been after *Jillian*.

"But why would she do that?" Jillian pleaded.

"Jillian, I have to ask you. Who identified your family's bodies? Was it your father's secretary, do you know? Or maybe Jocelyn?"

"No, it was me," she said, her voice grim. "I wanted to see them one last time. But the police only let me look at photographs. And—and I remember that everyone had these blue cloths draped around their faces, so there was no hair to see."

"And the caskets were closed at the service?"

"Yes."

"So as far as we know, Julia was blond at the time of her death."

"But not at Christmas." Jillian grabbed her head with both hands and squeezed. "She went back to school before me and her hair was definitely brown then."

"I think there was actually a fairly short window when she was blond—maybe a few weeks. We know from Jerry that she showed up at Two Boots as a brunette a few weeks before her death. She sat at the bar and had something to eat. And then according to him, *you* showed up a couple of nights later. Which means she colored her hair that week. There was a second charge on her credit card statement, so she was definitely there at least twice."

"I still can't believe Jules would do that. What was she trying to prove?"

"Maybe she'd just figured out the twin thing and wanted to test how much you really looked alike, see if people could tell you apart. . . . But, Jillian, regardless of her intentions, this changes things."

"You mean, even if she wasn't out-and-out pretending to be me that night, someone could have assumed I was home. And they came to the house that night to kill me, not her."

"Yes. I know this must be horrible to face, but it could put us closer to figuring out who the killer is."

She began to cry, not just tears streaming down her face but gut-wrenching sobs that made her torso heave. I put my arms around her, patting her back.

"It's my fault," she said, her words choked by her sobs.

"Jillian, I'm not going to let you blame yourself for this. What we need to do instead is focus on possible suspects. People who might have wanted you dead."

"*Kordas,*" she said, breaking out of the hug. "It's got to be Kordas. You said before that if he ended up in a rage because I rejected him, he would have directed it at me, not my family. Well, now we know he could have thought I was home in Dory."

"Do you know if he ever went to Two Boots?"

She shook her head in disgust. "No, that kind of place would be beneath him. But maybe he drove by our house one day and got a glimpse of the new Julia."

And of course it was Kordas who'd lured me to Foxcroft and gave me directions that mistakenly sent me to the town house part of the development.

"True."

"So now what?" Jillian said. She used the back of her hand to wipe away her tears.

"Um, let me think for a bit, okay. Kordas is a key suspect now, but we also have to consider other possibilities."

"What do you mean?"

"There may have been someone else who wanted you dead. Or it may not relate to you at *all.* I'm actually pursuing a couple of other leads that I can talk to you about later."

That was a conversation that I needed to postpone until I had absolute proof on either front: about her mother and Jocelyn, and about her father and Keith Denali.

"So we just sit on this for now?"

"No, it's too urgent to sit on. But I have to decide on the best course of action. Why don't we take our food down to the garden and as soon as we're done eating, I'll come up with a plan?"

"Listen, would you mind if I brought my food to my room and had it later? I'm not in the mood to eat right now."

"Of course."

She made a plate of hummus, cheese, and bread, and we agreed to speak first thing in the morning over coffee.

"Do one thing for me, okay?" I said as Jillian prepared to leave. "I want you to think about your life back then and whether there might have been someone—besides Bruce Kordas—who was fixated on you or really pissed off, and could have become enraged."

She nodded somberly and left.

As soon as she departed, I lugged the wine and food to the garden, which I had to myself, unless I counted a group of goldfinches darting around the birdfeeder. I would have liked company for dinner, but eating alone at least gave me a chance to mull the situation over without interruption.

I started by thinking about Kordas. He was the ultimate cool customer, but there might be another side of him he mostly kept hidden. As I told Jillian, however, I had to think *beyond* Kordas as well. I had to consider other people who might have wanted to hurt her, as well as people who might have hated another member of her family. Like Keith Denali.

As I picked at my food, I made two decisions. Tomorrow, I was going to call Mamie. Blake wouldn't be happy, but she was an ideal source for the info I needed. According to Jillian, she attended community college in the area, and she might be aware of anyone who'd been around that April and had harbored animosity toward Jillian or, on the other hand, had been weirdly enchanted with her. Mamie might recall someone even if Jillian didn't.

And I was going to bring the cops into the loop, with Jillian's permission, of course. It would have been useless to inform them about some of the stuff I'd turned up earlier. There wasn't enough of a critical mass to capture their attention. But now there *was*. They needed to know that Julia might have been pretending to be Jillian, which could point to other suspects, and that Kordas once had the hots for Jillian and had eventually been rebuffed by her.

Detective Maynard struck me as the person to approach. He had seemed smart and fair, and though I had no reason to believe he had any direct involvement in the supposed re-investigation of the Lowe case, I could start with him as a point person.

I splashed more wine in my glass—it had been that kind of twenty-four hours—when my eyes were drawn to a flash of light through the fir trees to my left, and two seconds later I heard the first deep rumbles of thunder. I quickly packed up my stuff and bolted across the yard, reaching the screened porch the same moment fat, determined raindrops began spattering the grass.

Stepping into the main part of the house, I ran into the innkeeper, Mary, lowering the windows in the parlor. We wished each other a good evening, and as I headed for the stairs, I caught myself and turned back to her.

"Mary, I'm curious," I said. "I heard a car leaving the parking lot after one o'clock this morning. Any idea who might have been visiting here so late?"

She hesitated before answering. "It must have been a car from the house next door," she said. "The wife is a doctor, and she's sometimes on call."

Her brows had knitted during the pause before she'd spoken, and I sensed my question had confused her. And that her answer had been a wild grab for an explanation that wouldn't alarm a guest. There was no way the sound had come from the house next door. I wondered again if someone might be keeping tabs on Jillian and me. And yet neither of us had told anyone where we were staying, and after so many hours checking my rearview mirror while driving, I was sure I hadn't been tailed.

Beau phoned as I was sticking the leftover food in the fridge in my room.

"Hey, you beat me to the punch," I said. "I just ran inside to escape a thunderstorm."

"How's it going otherwise? Did you have your third rabies shot?"

"Yes, and I'm a little achy, but it's almost been too crazy here to notice. Are you ready for a few bombshells that I uncovered this weekend?" He said he was, and I shared the news about Jillian and Kordas, the girls being twins, and Julia sneaking out as Jillian.

"My god, how incredible. How could the mother have done that?"

"She probably had the best of intentions but didn't think hard enough about how it might all play out in the girls' future."

"So what happens from here?"

"Still researching possible suspects, but now factoring in people who might have wanted Jillian dead as well."

"Bailey, you have to be careful of this Kordas dude."

"I know, and you'll be happy to hear I'm going to reach out to the cops tomorrow and take them up to speed on this. Hopefully this will be enough to make them really want to examine the case again."

"Glad to hear it."

I was tempted to divulge what I'd learned from Candace about my father but decided to hold off until I'd processed the news more, and what it meant for me in relation to Beau.

We chatted for the next few minutes and signed off with a warm "I love you" to each other. There was an ease to the last part of the conversation that relieved me. Beau was clearly trying, doing his best to understand my motives for coming here. And I was trying, too. No major sins of omission this time.

Though it was only eight o'clock, it seemed later because of how dark the sky was, and I took that as a prompt to undress for the night and crawl under the covers with my iPad. By now the rain was pounding on the roof and thunder rolled through the room.

Mercifully the lights never went out—wouldn't that

have added to the fun?—but the storm intensified my sense of dread. There'd been so much to contend with over the past twenty-four hours, and probably more to come. Though the police might begrudgingly welcome the information about Jillian, they would surely chew me out for playing detective. Also on the no-fun list: coming face-to-face with Denali tomorrow. I was going to have to play that somewhat by ear. If he seemed at all threatening when I showed up at the auto shop, I might have to beat a fast retreat and devise a plan B.

I had the breakfast room to myself when I went downstairs the next morning, though Jillian arrived ten minutes later. There were blue-gray circles under her eyes, and her usually creamy skin had a few rough red patches. She was obviously being tortured by the possibility that she'd been the killer's primary target.

"You survive the storm okay?" I asked.

"I barely slept, but it wasn't the storm's fault. . . . Tell me, did you come up with a plan? For what we should do next?"

"Yes, and it really needs your blessing." I shared my decision to talk to the police.

"You'll tell them about me and Julia?" she said.

"Uh-huh. And I think it's also critical for them to

know about you and Kordas. I'll start the ball rolling but then they'll want to speak with you, too."

She cringed. "I'm so ashamed to admit what I did."

"You were twenty years old. If anyone should be ashamed, it should be Kordas. He was older and married. And the police, well, they should be ashamed for not being more thorough the first time they investigated. For quickly deciding on Dylan Fender as the number one suspect and then making all the pieces fit."

"Do you think Bruce could have really done it?"

"I still have a few other leads to pursue, but we can't ignore Bruce. We need to call the cops today."

"All right," she said. She looked off across the yard, staring at something I couldn't see. "Bailey, I'm so grateful you came back. It all hurts so much, but we may finally know the truth."

"I hope so."

By the time Jillian left the table, it was after eight, and a sane enough hour to try Mamie. Based on what I knew about their schedule, she and Blake would already be at the clinic.

"Hi, Bailey," she said in greeting. "I hear you're back in the area." She sounded friendly enough, which was Mamie's style, but she was hardly gushing about me turning up again.

"Have you spoken to Jillian?" I asked.

"Not for a few days, but I'm sure I'll see her once she's in town. Are you feeling better?"

"Yes, thanks for asking. Much."

"I know you've seen Blake, of course."

Oh boy. I'd been busted somehow.

"Um, right."

"He told me about going to that man's house with you, and getting accosted. He didn't want me to find out, but I could tell something was eating at him and I finally wormed it out of him."

"I'm so sorry about that Mamie. I—"

"I hope this doesn't make me sound selfish, Bailey, because I care about Jillian. And I care about you, too. And if someone went to prison who shouldn't have, well that's awful. But Blake and I *live* here. We don't get to leave town in a few days like you. And we can't put our lives or our business in jeopardy."

"I understand that, Mamie, I really do. Here's the deal. I could use your help on one more matter, but it won't involve anything more than a quick conversation between the two of us."

She hesitated before answering. "A conversation about what?"

"I want to ask you a few questions, mostly about

Jillian. Do you have a minute now? We can do it over the phone."

"I guess, if that's all it is. I'm not actually at work this morning. I'm going in a little later today."

"Okay, good. Like I said, I'll be quick. Jillian mentioned to me that you attended a community college in the area. Is that right?"

"Yes, I earned my associate's degree in Pittsfield. But what does that have to do with anything?"

"I'm thinking that you may have been aware of things going on in the area when the Lowes were killed. People who were in the vicinity at the time."

"You mean who might have killed them? I was here, but like I told you, I never knew the rest of the Lowes that well. When I heard the news, I had no clue who could have done it."

"I'm actually thinking about Jillian. To your knowledge, was there anyone who lived in the area who had it out for her? Someone nursing a grudge, for instance."

"*Jillian?* You think someone killed her family as some kind of revenge? How horrible."

"No, not that," I said. I picked my words before I spoke next, hoping to avoid giving too much away. "We've just discovered that Julia dyed her hair blond when she was home with mono, and there's a chance that someone saw her and thought Jillian was in town instead."

"Oh, wow," she said. I could hear the shock in her voice. "But Julia was always so skinny. They really didn't look very much alike."

"Julia filled out in college, and I've already spoken to one person who saw her and assumed it was Jillian. So I'm trying to figure out if there was anyone around then—someone who hadn't gone off to college or was attending school locally—who might have been really angry at Jillian. Or perhaps even obsessed."

She exhaled loud enough for me to hear.

"That's so scary. But—I don't know. I mean—"

She hesitated. One second. Two. Three. I stayed with the silence, waiting for Mamie to fill it.

"The thing about Jillian," she said finally, "and I don't mean this the wrong way, but she was always really confident and at ease in her skin. Other girls could be so needy compared to her. And I think it drove some people crazy. Both men and women."

"Anyone in particular come to mind?"

"Wouldn't Jillian know better than me?"

"She may have been oblivious."

Another pause, just as long as the earlier one.

"I'm not sure if I should be telling you this," she said. "But I think Jillian was seeing someone local over

Christmas vacation, the Christmas before everyone died. She didn't have much time to do stuff with me, and when I pressed her about why at the time, she was kind of secretive."

Kordas.

"Maybe you should check that out," she added.

"Okay, thanks. I'll find a way to ask her about it without saying where it came from."

"I appreciate that. I hate to rush you, Bailey, but I need to get back to what I was doing."

"Of course. Thanks so much for your help. And just so you're aware, I'm working with the police now, keeping them posted."

I wanted to be sure she didn't beat me to the punch.

I sat for a few minutes afterward, replaying the conversation. I wondered if Mamie knew more than she'd let on, that she'd heard rumors specifically about Jillian and Kordas back then but preferred that Jillian be the one to tell me. It didn't matter in the end. Kordas was already a contender.

I called Detective Maynard next, and, reaching only his voice mail, left a message saying I had information that I needed to share with him as soon as possible.

Twenty minutes later I was on my way to D&A Auto, knowing it had opened at 8:00 a.m. My stomach was churning big-time. Regardless of what I'd recently learned, I still considered John Denali a viable suspect in the Lowe murders, and Keith may or may not have been attempting to protect his father's name by trying to scare me off the case. He could have set the dog on me. He could have bashed Blake in the head. I needed to keep my guard fully up today. This interaction would be in a different league than scoping out the guy through binoculars.

Last night I'd drummed up a decent reason for dropping by the auto shop. My passenger door had a nice little ding in it, courtesy of a New York City yellow cab, and I planned to ask for an estimate and time frame for having it repaired. That should provide me with a chance to take a read on Denali. See how he reacted to me.

He was definitely on duty today. I could see his red car in the lot as I pulled in. I parked and strode toward the entrance to the office. A buzzer sounded on the door when I opened it, jangling my nerves even more.

There were two employees currently holding down the fort. An older dude stood behind the counter, just idling, it seemed, or maybe attempting to channel the spirit of the deer buck whose head had been mounted and hung directly above him.

The other guy sat on a badly stained blue sectional sofa with his long, lank hair tucked behind his ears.

Denali. And he was murmuring into a cell phone. Unfortunately this meant I'd be obligated to deal with the other dude about my car—at least initially—until I could figure out a way to connect with Denali.

"Help you?" the older guy asked above the pulsing whir of the AC. I was sure he was already sizing me up as a chick who probably knew squat about cars. I stepped closer to the counter, and as I did, I sensed Denali's eyes on my back.

"Yes, thanks. I've got a small ding in my front passenger door and I'd love an estimate for having it repaired."

"Why don't I take a look," he said, pushing off from the counter and coming around in front. I noticed that the name on his shirt was Gus. He opened the door and motioned for me to precede him. As I exited the shop, I continued to feel Denali's eyes on me. Was it because the woman he'd been stalking for days was now right here in his shop, or did he simply like how my legs looked in a jean skirt?

Gus spotted the small ding immediately, as if he had a nose for them.

"That's not going to be too complicated of a job," he said, arms akimbo. "Why don't we say one hundred and forty dollars? It'll look like brand new when we're done."

"How long will I have to leave the car for?"

"Oh, there's no need to leave it. We do something called paintless dent removal. No sanding, no filling. It'll take less than an hour."

Should I go along with it? I wondered. If I hung around, I might have a chance to interact with Denali once he was off the phone. Though maybe a better option would be to say I'd think about it and return later, hoping for a shot at actually being waited on by Denali himself.

"Hmm," I said, buying myself a few seconds. "You can do it right now?"

A movement caught my attention, and I looked up to see the office door swing open and Denali step onto the threshold. He leaned a shoulder against the doorframe and stared hard at me, his eyes practically gripping mine. He *knew* me; it was clear. And more than that, the scowl on his boyish face suggested he wasn't a fan. Gus glanced over, curious. He could tell something was going on but was clueless.

Now what? Should I try to interact with Denali?

"Which one of you is D, and which one is A?" I blurted out.

"Huh?" Gus said.

"D and A Auto. Who's who?"

"I just work here," Gus said. He raised his chin

toward the door. "But Keith there is one of the owners. Keith Denali."

At that moment Denali turned on his heels and reentered the shop, letting the door slam behind him. Now that it was pretty clear he'd probably had me in his sights, it didn't seem smart to follow him and have a confrontation. What I needed to do was retreat and determine my next steps.

"Um, I'll think about it, okay?" I said, turning back to Gus, who now looked totally confused.

He scoffed lightly. "What, you don't like the price?"

"It's not that. I don't have a full hour right now. But I'll be back."

"Okay, whatever floats your boat," he said.

I jumped in my car and took off, my stomach in knots. This added a new wrinkle to everything. The hostility in Denali's eyes suggested he could very well have been the one who turned the dog loose on me and attacked Blake from behind. What other explanation could there be? You don't shoot a look like that at a potential customer.

Maybe his father really *was* the Lowes' killer and Denali wanted me out of Massachusetts no matter what it took. Which would mean that Jillian and Julia being twins was nothing more than a heartbreaking secret instead of a catalyst for murder, and that Kordas was innocent, and Penny had died during a break-in. God, my head was spinning.

And if this theory was the right one, how would I ever admit to Jillian that her father might have been a pedophile?

What I needed to do was return to the inn and wait for Maynard to call. I would have to share what I knew about Denali, too.

The road forked and I bore left, headed, from memory, down a road in the direction of Cheswick.

Lost in my thoughts, I heard the noise before I even saw the source. It was the sound of a car engine being gunned, coming up behind me. *Asshole*, I thought. My eyes cut to the rearview mirror. A red car was roaring up behind me, fast as a bat.

Denali. My heart leapt, and I hit the gas, trying to put distance between us.

He accelerated. He was practically riding my bumper now, the image of his car exploding onto my mirror. I had no freaking clue what to do. We were at least three miles from a town.

I accelerated again myself, gripping the wheel as tight as I could. Suddenly Denali jerked his own wheel and pulled out from behind me into the other lane, aligning his car with mine.

Instinctively I tapped the brakes lightly, terrified of

someone barreling toward us. But Denali slowed, too, and nosed his car closer to mine. I could almost taste the terror coursing through me. I veered a few inches to the right, trying to keep him from ramming into me.

For a second I thought he was finally going to pass, but he edged even nearer, so close I had no choice but to ease the wheel farther to the right.

And then, before I could control it, I was off the road, plowing into a trench. I hit the brakes and my head jerked forward as if someone had punched me in the back of the skull.

Chapter 23

The nosedive knocked the wind out of me, though it wasn't strong enough to deploy the airbag. I grabbed a breath, tried to get my bearings. I didn't think I'd been injured.

I peered through the front window. The ditch wasn't deep, and I could see ahead on the road. Denali had halted not far ahead. Adrenaline surged through me. I shot out my left arm and hit the button to lock all four doors.

My purse had been on the front seat, but it must have flown off when I bounced into the ditch. As I frantically rooted around the floor, I heard a motor being gunned. I cocked my head up. Denali's car was plowing back toward me in reverse. I gasped in shock, bracing for impact. The car stopped just inches away.

I pressed on the horn and kept my hand there, praying someone would hear and come running. The blaring sound pierced the air, but did nothing to deter Denali. He was out of his car now and charging toward me. I groped on the floor again for my purse, grasped leather, and upended it, spilling the contents onto the seat.

Denali yanked the driver's door handle but it didn't budge. I had my phone now, my finger hovering above the nine. But before I could tap the numbers, Denali had flung open the rear door and bolted into the backseat, reeking of sweat and grease.

"Get away from me," I yelled, twisting just enough to see him. In my panic, I must have hit the button for only the front door locks.

"Oh, that's rich," he said, panting. "You need to get the fuck away from *me*."

"I've called the police," I lied. "They're coming." What I needed was another car to drive by so I could flag it down.

"Good. Then you can explain to them what the hell you've been up to."

That didn't make any sense.

"Get out of my car," I said. "Get out *now*."

He raked a hand through his hair. "What the fuck do you want with me? What were you doing with my dogs?"

"So you were there that day? You hit my friend with a plank."

"What are you *talking* about? I wasn't anywhere near there. I saw you on the security camera."

"I didn't see any camera."

"You think I'm stupid enough to advertise it? I saw you and your buddy. And then you had the nerve to walk into my shop today."

His comments and questions weren't tracking with the assumptions I'd made. I gulped air and tried to pull my thoughts together.

"Wait, are you saying that you don't know who I am, that you never saw me until I showed up in your backyard?"

He scooted over in the seat, giving himself a better view of me.

"Lady, I have no freaking clue who you are. All I know is that you and that buddy of yours were prowling around my property, messing with my dogs."

I could read frustration on his face as much as anger.

"Okay, hold on a second," I said. "I think there's been a misunderstanding."

"Yeah, I'll say. I feel like I'm being stalked."

At that moment a car moseyed up the road, at no more than thirty miles an hour. This was my chance to yell for help, but my gut told me I could sort this out on my own. And I would have a chance to quiz Denali.

"I came to your house because I thought one of your dogs had attacked me." I stuck up my arm with the bandage on it. "Are you saying that didn't happen?"

"*What?* Where?"

"At a construction site about twenty miles from here."

"Are you nuts? My dogs don't bite, and they haven't been near any construction site. I never let them run loose."

"What about the empty kennel?"

"That was Lucky. He died six months ago."

"When you looked at the tape, did you see someone hit my friend with a two-by-four? He was by one of the outbuildings behind the kennel."

"You're saying someone *else* was on the property? No, I don't have a camera back there."

"Could—?"

"It's time you started answering *my* questions. Why would you think I sicced one of my dogs on you?"

I considered whether it would be smart to come clean with him, here in the middle of nowhere. I decided to go for it.

"I thought you might be trying to scare me away from the area."

"And why the hell would I do that?"

"Because I'm a friend of Jillian Lowe, and I'm try-ing to figure out who killed her family."

Denali slouched back against the seat and folded his arms across his chest, the muscles in his face finally slackening.

"Well, I was about twelve years old when that hap-pened, so I hope you're not suggesting *I* had something to do with it."

"No . . . But could your father have?"

"My *father*? Each of your questions is crazier than the next. Mr. Lowe was my *scoutmaster*, but we barely knew the guy. Why in the world would my father want him and his family dead?"

"Because Carl abused you. Or at least your father thought he did. He came to Carl's office shortly before he died and confronted him."

Denali's body stiffened and I held my breath, desper-ate to hear his response. But it wasn't what I expected. He pressed the pads of his hands hard against his eyes and sobbed just once, but enough for me to hear the despair. I felt as if I was staring at a little boy, and my heart ached thinking of the hell he'd experienced.

"Keith, I'm sorry to upset you this way," I said. "Have you ever talked to anyone about this, received any kind of help?"

"Christ, are you saying my father did it?" he said, ignoring my question. "That he killed them all?" He dropped his hands from his face and let them slap against his work pants. His brown eyes glistened with tears. "And—I thought they had the murderer. The neighbor."

"It looks like he was wrongly convicted. There's no evidence I know of pointing to your father, but because he was so angry with Carl, I wanted to learn more about it. Do—do you think it's possible?"

"Well if he did," he said, his voice choked, "he had the wrong man."

"What do you mean?" I asked and held my breath again.

"It wasn't Carl Lowe. My parents knew something was up because the doctor spotted the signs. I was too scared to tell them who, and so my father obviously made a bad guess. It was my fucking *uncle* who did it. My mother's younger brother."

I felt the strangest mix of emotions push through me—unbearable sadness for Keith Denali, utter relief that the abuser hadn't been Jillian's father, and then guilt from finding any solace in Denali's revelation.

"Keith, I'm so sorry for what you went through. And now that we've spoken, I have serious doubts that your dad could have done it. I'm pretty sure someone's been after me since I arrived here, and since it wasn't you, it has to be the killer."

"And now you're going to steer fucking clear of me, right?" He sounded defiant again, and I wondered if he regretted exposing his vulnerability mere moments ago.

"Yes, I promise."

Another car approached from behind and before I knew it, Denali had jumped from the backseat. He waved off the driver, in a gesture that said he didn't need help and then stuck his head back in the car.

"You're not in that deep. I think I can push you out. Once you start the engine, you'll need to jerk the wheel to the left."

"Keith—" There was more I wanted to say, an offer of help, perhaps, but he slammed the door before I had the chance.

It took a few minutes of rocking and pushing before my car spit out from the ditch. As I advanced down the road, I waved into my rearview mirror, but Denali kept his head bowed, growing smaller and smaller as he trudged toward his car.

I drove for a bit, too unsettled to bother with GPS, and finally ended up by chance in Dory. I needed to decompress before heading back to the inn. I nabbed a parking spot and traveled by foot the block to the café/bookstore where I'd met Jocelyn. After choosing a table in the back garden, I ordered a cup of chamomile tea, knowing that the last thing I needed right now was caffeine. When it arrived, I popped two ibuprofen, since my neck muscles were starting to ache from whiplash.

What a freaking morning. And yet as unnerving as events had been, I'd made progress. I'd eliminated a suspect. But I still didn't have the answer I needed.

And I still hadn't heard from Maynard, I realized. I double-checked my phone. Nothing. There was, however, a text from Jillian.

Jillian: Bailey, I took a drive. I'll be careful. Just needed to get out. And thanks again. For pushing.

I understood her desire to escape the room, but it worried me to think of her out and about, and someone possibly following her. With John Denali no longer on my suspect list, the killer felt suddenly close, closer than ever before.

I drained the last of my tea in two gulps. As I set the cup in the saucer, my gaze fell onto the menu still lying on the table. *Since 1991*, it read. The Lowes must have come here at times, I realized. Claire for coffee with Jocelyn, and the girls for muffins perhaps, after school or on Saturdays, walking down from the house on their own. It was only a few short blocks from where I was sitting.

I closed my eyes and pictured the house again in my mind. The family moving around it, eating meals at the kitchen counter, lounging on the screened porch, reading in the morning room.

I imagined Julia specifically, trying to picture her on the night of the murders. I'd already decided that she must not have snuck out that night, or the police would have seen that the security system had been disarmed earlier, too.

It seemed most likely that she'd been home all night. At some point her parents and brother had gone to bed but Julia hadn't. According to Jillian, she was dressed in street clothes. And then, at around eleven, someone had come to the door. Julia had clearly heard the knock or the sound of the doorbell, so she'd probably still been downstairs when the person arrived. Perhaps it was one of the nights she planned to sleep on the couch in the library.

A thought snagged on a part of my brain, something that had been just out of grasp the past couple of days. The couch I'd seen in the library—which probably had been staged by the real estate agent—was actually a love seat, set just inside the door. And too small to sleep on. A regular-size couch wouldn't have fit in that space. So when the Lowes had lived in the house, the sofa was obviously in another part of the room.

I opened my phone to the photos I'd snapped of the library. The only spot a regular-size sofa could have been situated was on the far side of the room—between two windows—a detail I could confirm later with Jillian. That meant the Lowes' sofa would have been a long way from the door.

And that fact was significant.

I flagged down the waitress and quickly paid my bill. I needed to hightail it back to the inn and my laptop, to the stories I'd bookmarked about the crime. Many of them had mentioned the rooms in which the victims were found—after all, that kind of gruesome detail made the story even more salacious—but there was one story, I was sure of it, that featured diagrams of the rooms where the victims had been found and the exact spot for each body.

There was no sign of Jillian's car in the small inn parking lot, so I texted her:

Me: Where are you?

A text came in from her as I was bolting up the stairs to the second floor of the inn.

Jillian: Still out. Will text you when I'm back.

Once I was in my room, it took a while, but eventually I found the diagram. It was featured in one of the more extensive articles about the crime. Julia's body, the piece confirmed, was discovered "lying in front of the couch in the library, a room off the large center hall." According to the diagram, the sofa was between those two windows on the far side of the room.

When I thought the couch had been positioned just inside the door of the library, I'd assumed that Julia had died there because she'd staggered into the room when attacked or because she'd spoken briefly to the killer before she realized the horror that was in store.

But this changed things. If she was stabbed that far across the room, it suggested she had stepped into the room for more than a moment, that she might actually have been having a *conversation* in the library before she was killed. A conversation she didn't want her parents to overhear.

Surely it couldn't have been Bob London or some other acquaintance of her parents. What would she have to say to someone like that? It wouldn't have been

Trevor, either. She disliked him. It would only have been someone she knew well. Or *Jillian* knew really well. Like Kordas.

My pulse was racing now. I had to talk to Kordas again. But not alone. And not out at a mostly deserted construction site. If he'd set me up for a dog mauling, he would have other tricks up his sleeve. I dug my phone from my purse and tried his number.

Voice mail.

"Hey, Bruce," I said. "Could you spare fifteen minutes for me? I mentioned last week that I had a few more questions and unfortunately I never had the chance to ask them."

I spent the next couple of hours in a holding pattern. Waiting to hear from both Maynard and Kordas, more and more irritated that Maynard hadn't deigned to return my call yet. There was also no sign of Jillian, and she didn't answer my latest text.

Finally, at 4:07, my marimba ringtone rippled through the silence of the room. I jerked at the sound. As I grabbed my phone, I saw Maynard's name on the screen.

"Ms. Weggins," he said, his tone as blunt as the back of a shovelhead. Gee, what had happened to all that cowboy charm?

"Yes, hi, thanks for calling me back. As I said in my

message, I have important information related to the Lowe murders."

"Weren't you distinctly told not to meddle in our police investigation?"

I had to bite my tongue and resist saying I hadn't encountered any signs there *was* an active investigation.

"I actually turned up this info while doing research for the memoir. I have reason to believe that at least a few people were under the false impression that Jillian Lowe was back in Dory the night of the murders, which opens up the possibility of other suspects. I'd like to share what I learned with you as soon as possible."

I heard a frustrated sigh from the other end.

"Tell me what you've got."

"I'd really prefer to do it in person." I knew my chances of making a strong case—and explaining myself—would be better if I handled this face-to-face.

I could sense him thinking it over.

"Okay, okay," he said at last. I heard the tap of computer keys, Maynard probably checking his schedule. "Why don't we say three o'clock tomorrow? We can meet where we spoke the last time."

"*Tomorrow?* Detective Maynard, I know you must be busy, but is there any chance you can squeeze me in today? The information I have is pretty serious."

Big sigh. Another pause. "I can't promise anything,

but let me see what I can do. It won't just be me. We'll need to include someone directly involved with the case."

"All right, I'll wait for your call."

When my mobile rang five minutes later I figured it was Maynard circling back, but another number, a vaguely familiar one, flashed on the screen.

"Bailey, it's Blake Allard. Where are you right now?" There was a scary urgency to his voice.

"In my room. *Why?*"

"Is Jillian back in the area yet?"

"She's back, yes." An alarm began to blare in my head. "Is everything okay?"

"I need to tell you something, but I don't want Jillian to know yet. Are you free to talk now?"

"Yeah, I'm alone. Tell me, please."

"I think I've found the dog—the one that attacked you."

My pulse went into overdrive, like a car shooting off a cliff. *"Where?"*

"Right here in the clinic—in one of the kennels downstairs. He's a shepherd, mostly black, the way you described, and he's not doing great. Apparently he came in this afternoon and one of the other vets handled him. He was told the dog ended up tangled in a rope and choked himself. It just seems to fit."

"But who brought him?"

"Well, that's the hitch. Some local guy named Harry Adams, not anyone you've mentioned as a suspect. Look, I can't stay on, but I was thinking you could come by and take a look. See if he's the one."

"Sure, but I honestly don't know if I'd recognize the dog that did it." In my mind's eye all I could recall from that day was the hulk of glistening black fur lunging toward me, the snout, those horrible bared teeth.

"It's up to you. I just thought I should tell you."

"Of course. I want to see it. Now?"

"No, you need to wait until five thirty, when Mamie'll be gone. She saw the lump on my head the other day and managed to get the truth out of me—and then she read me the riot act. I promised I would steer clear, but I can't ignore the fact that this might be the dog."

"Thank you, Blake. I'll be there. And if the owner shows up between now and then, you shouldn't mention your suspicions."

"Don't worry. I'm not interested in being walloped by a two-by-four again."

"See you at five thirty."

I couldn't believe it. Things might finally be coming to a head.

As I started to toss the phone on the bed, I saw a text from Jillian.

Jillian: Heading up to my room to lie down for a bit. Meet for dinner at 7?

Relieved, I texted back.

Me: Perfect.

With any luck, I'd have news to share with her by then.

I had an hour to kill before heading for the clinic. I decided to wait and call Beau after I'd seen the dog and therefore might have more to report. Instead, I used the time to pace, knead my sore neck with my fingers, and attack a slew of unanswered emails, trying the whole time not to overly invest in what Blake had shared. It could easily be another dead end. But it might not be. If the dog being treated was the one that attacked me, it would be another important detail to share with Maynard, though by the time I left, he still hadn't returned my call.

There were only two cars in the parking lot of the clinic when I arrived, and as I rang the bell at the front,

I noticed a sign with the clinic hours, indicating it closed at five on Mondays. A minute passed before I finally heard footsteps.

"Hey," Blake said, tugging open the front door. He was dressed in his scrub bottoms, clogs, and a blue T-shirt that flattered his coloring, though he didn't seem like the kind of guy who worked that sort of thing. "Sorry for the delay. I was dealing with a patient."

"Has Mamie left yet?" I asked, my voice lowered.

"Yeah, about fifteen minutes ago. I hate keeping stuff from her, but I don't want to upset her for no reason. Or Jillian, either. You didn't tell her, did you?"

"No, I agree with you. Until we're sure, there's no point. Besides, we had our share of upsetting news this weekend."

"What's going on?"

"I think Jillian would probably want to fill you in herself. It's something about her family, something she never knew until now."

Blake narrowed his eyes, clearly curious, but he didn't push.

We'd stepped into the large reception area, still bright with lights, and made our way to the fake-stone check-in counter. To the left were shelves of cat and dog products available for sale. Blake cocked his head toward a room shooting off from the area behind the counter.

"Can we talk for a few minutes before I show you exhibit A? I want to discuss how this might play out. Plus, I have more info."

"Sure," I said, and followed him into a galleylike room lined with counters and cabinets, and featuring a fridge, sink, and a few stools. It looked like the kind of room that served as both a storage area and a spot for staff to wolf down lunch if they were short on time.

"Want some coffee?" he asked, nodding toward one of those coffee machines that used individual pods.

"Yes, actually I'm desperate for some, thanks. All I've had this afternoon is a cup of wildflowers stewed in hot water."

While he took a minute to prepare the coffee, I perused a bulletin board crowded with shots of happy cats and dogs, obviously patients of the clinic.

"So tell me what you learned," I said, as Blake handed me a ceramic mug of coffee.

"Okay, I checked with the girl who did the intake and this is interesting. She told me that, according to Adams, the dog had accidentally choked itself a week ago, which fits with the timeline."

"Wow. Any clue why he hadn't brought the dog in earlier?"

"He had some story about that. Said the dog seemed better at first and then grew progressively worse. I don't believe that. My bet is that he didn't want to come forward with the animal in case the cops were involved and were checking with clinics."

"Did he say it was a personal-protection dog?"

"No mention of that."

"And do you know anything more about the owner?"

"The assistant recognized him and said he runs a small carpentry business, makes cabinets mostly. That's the part that *doesn't* seem to fit."

I froze, my coffee mug poised in midair.

"But wait, it might," I said. "Kordas must need people to do cabinetry work inside the houses he builds. Maybe this guy freelances for him and Kordas paid him to set the dog on me."

Trevor Hague jumped to mind, too. He would need cabinetmakers for his kitchen business.

"I can't believe I didn't think of that," Blake said. He swiped a hand through his short blond hair. "Dumb."

"Don't be silly. This whole thing is crazy."

He stared into his coffee, his mouth scrunched. I sensed there was something he wanted to say but didn't know how to spit it out.

"You mentioned something else a minute ago," I said. "That you wanted to discuss how this will play out. I'm not sure I understand."

"Mamie feels for Jillian, but she wants us to stay out of this. Initially she intended for us to go to the cops, but after what happened on Saturday, she's changed her mind. I might have been attacked, but I was trespassing. If this is the dog, I have an obligation to report it. Still, I want to minimize exposure for the clinic—and for Mamie and me."

Was he really worried he'd end up in trouble about the dog, like it was on par with harboring the Unabomber?

"Blake, I wouldn't worry. I talked to the guy who owned the property and I'm sure he won't press any charges. In fact, it wasn't him who hit you. If the dog is here and the cops become involved, I'll help keep you out of it. It's not your fault he was brought to your clinic."

"Thanks. I'm guess I'm a better vet than a sleuth."

He set his mug on the counter, and I quickly finished my own.

"Why don't I take a look, okay?" I said, eager to get to the business at hand.

Blake shoved off from the counter. "Right, let's do it. And don't be nervous. He's been sedated and likely won't even bark."

"As long as he's in a titanium cage that's been welded shut with a blowtorch, I'll be okay, I think."

He laughed ruefully. "I hear you. I ended up with a bad bite early in my career and I know how much it can hurt."

He led me from the galley room and down a long hall that jutted out from reception. On the left we passed a room already darkened for the night, though there was enough light from the hall to illuminate the metal doors on a double row of kennels.

"Not in here?" I said.

"No, those are the post-op cats. The dogs are downstairs in the bigger facility."

We descended via the elevator to a sparkling-clean hallway, and Blake slowly opened a door in front of us. Despite his reassurance, my stomach had knotted at the prospect of seeing the dog. As soon as we stepped into the room, Blake reached for a wall switch and scooted up a light dimmer, keeping the illumination fairly low, though bright enough to see.

"There are about seven dogs in here, and we don't want to agitate them," Blake said in just above a whisper. "Let's keep our voices low."

I nodded in agreement.

We made our way along a wall with two rows of kennels, one set stacked on top of the other. Our presence set off whimpering in one of the cages, and Blake reached inside to gently stroke the snout of a Boston terrier. A dog whisperer, Jillian had called him, and that's what he seemed to be.

Finally, as we approached the far side of the room, Blake nodded toward a cage at the end of the top row.

"He's in that one," he whispered.

I gulped and stepped closer. The dog was out cold, lying on its side, but his head was near the front at least. It was a shepherd, as Blake had said, and yes, mostly black, though its front legs were tan and there was a bib of tan beneath his neck. *Maybe*, I thought. Maybe. But I wasn't sure.

"I—I don't know," I said, trying to keep my voice low.

"Take your time. He's not going anywhere."

"Um—" I touched a hand to my forehead. I felt hot suddenly, with my skin clammy.

"You okay?"

"Uh, yeah. It's just the latest rabies shot. The aches come and go."

"Yeah, they can make you pretty sick. We have to get them, too. Take a look at the dog again. What do you think?"

"I not sure—" I was mumbling now. I reached out and rested a hand on the metal door of the cage for support.

"Better not touch the kennel," Blake said. "Wait, are you sure you're okay?"

My head was spinning by this point. And my feet seemed to disappear. I felt my body sag, and then I was slumping to the floor as everything went black.

Chapter 24

I opened my eyes. It was dark, but there was light seeping in from someplace. From beneath a door? I was lying flat. On a bed, maybe.

My tongue seemed swollen, like it had outgrown my mouth. My pulse raced. And there was a pain in the middle of my forehead, huge and hot. It felt as if someone had plunged an ice pick between my eyes.

I started to see. Just a little. The outlines of shapes. Counters and cabinets. Some kind of IV machine.

I was in a *hospital*, I realized. Back in the ER maybe. But there was utter silence all around me. What had happened? I remembered being at the inn, pacing in my room. Nothing more.

My head. It was pounding. I tried to raise my hand,

to touch my scalp, but it refused to move. I jerked my arm. It was bound to the table somehow. And the other one was too. I struggled, trying to pull them free, but they wouldn't budge. My heart bolted upward in my chest. I'd been restrained.

Why? To prevent me from thrashing? My legs, I suddenly realized, were tied down, too. And the bed was hard, without a pad or mattress. The IV machine suddenly began to shimmer and move to the left.

"Please," I called out. "Someone, please help me."

My voice sounded faint to me, like the meow of a newly born cat.

Cat. The word dangled in my brain, teasing me.

I knew then. I wasn't in a hospital. I was in the *vet clinic*, strapped to an exam table.

Fear enveloped me, trapping the breath in my chest. I yanked my arms and legs, desperately trying to free them, but the restraints refused to give.

A door opened, and light poured in. A figure loomed on the threshold, backlit. Shimmering. I squinted, trying to make out his features, but they were a blur.

"Have you got a headache?"

Blake. I recognized his voice.

"Yeah, awful. Blake, what's going on?"

"It's from the Special K I gave you."

He stepped into the room and switched the lights on, low.

"Blake, please. Untie me. What do you mean Special K? What—what happened to me?"

"I put the Special K in your coffee. It's ketamine."

Ketamine. Despite how fuzzy my brain was, the name seemed familiar. A type of date-rape drug. A fresh surge of panic nearly electrified me.

"Don't worry," he said, clearly reading my eyes. "We use it all the time here. It's a sedative and an anesthetic."

I didn't understand. I tried to think, but my brain felt dense. Blake began to shimmer again. I squeezed my eyes shut for a second and opened them.

"Please, Blake, just—get me out of here."

"I can't, Bailey." He raked a hand through his hair, his expression bleak. "You've made a mess of things."

Fragments came to me. The dog. Descending in the elevator.

"Blake, I won't say anything about the dog. I promise."

"It's more than that. I'm trying to prevent you from wrecking my life. And Mamie's, too."

"But why would I do that?" I tried again to wiggle my legs, jerk them free, but it was hopeless.

"Butting in. Asking questions. You won't leave the

past where it belongs. You called Mamie today, even though I begged you to stay away from us. Telling her how Julia looked like Jillian."

He squeezed his head in his hands, as if tormented by his thoughts, needing to drive them away. He seemed so different now. Sad, almost numb. Had he become unhinged? I had to stay calm, not alarm him.

"Blake, I'll stop. I'll stop butting in. Just let me go, okay?"

He shook his head back and forth, back and forth.

"It's too late. You pushed too much. You pushed and you pushed and you pushed."

"It's not too late."

"It *is*. I killed them all."

I heard myself gasp, as if the sound was emanating from another person.

"Who? Who did you kill?"

"The Lowes," he whispered.

My limbs went slack with fear, melting into the table. No, it couldn't be true.

"The Lowes?"

"It was never my fault, though. *Ever*. I was a wreck. I'd done one of those short study-abroad programs in Brazil and I got freaking malaria. They gave me this shit called Lariam, which made me crazy. They call it mefloquine psychosis. It fucks you up and you can't think straight and you feel out of your body half the time."

I forced my brain to latch on to his words. It didn't make sense.

"I—I don't understand. You weren't even here. You went far away to school, in Wisconsin." I'd pulled the detail from somewhere, maybe the conversation with Mamie by the car that night.

"I dropped out that term once I realized I was sick, and I snuck home. My parents never even knew. They were in Florida until May."

"But—" My head had cleared a little, maybe from adrenaline, but I still didn't get it.

"I started seeing her." He let out a moan. "Why did I have to set *eyes* on her?"

"Julia?" Pieces were coming together. "You started seeing Julia."

"Not *Julia*. Jillian. Or at least that's what I was stupid enough to believe. All I wanted was to be with her again."

"Jillian told me you'd had only a few dates. That—that she was never your type."

"Oh, that's the script she wrote in her head back then so she wouldn't feel guilty. But she was the one blowing *me* off. I was completely in love with her."

"And Julia pretended to be her?"

"The first night I saw her, she walked across a bar in my direction, and when she saw how I reacted—that I thought she was Jillian—she just went with it. She told me she was home from Brown with mono but no longer infectious."

So Julia *had* passed as her sister. She'd fooled Blake. *Kept* fooling him.

"Did her parents know she was seeing you?"

He shook his head hard, squeezed his hands against each side of his torso, his arms akimbo. "I'd pick her up in my car late at night, around eleven, and bring her over to my house until four, five in the morning. Sometimes I'd go to her house instead. We'd have sex right there in the library."

My heart was pounding so hard I could hear it in my ears. I had to buy myself time. Figure out how to escape.

"When did you find out it wasn't Jillian?"

"That last day. On the phone, I'd brought up something from high school and I could tell it didn't ring a bell with her. I started to wonder. There were other things pawing at my mind, things that didn't make sense. I called Jillian's dorm at Brown and found out she was there. That's when I realized I'd been *conned*."

"Did Julia admit the truth?"

"That night I showed up at the house and confronted

her. And she *admitted* it. She said she was a twin, that her mother had hidden it. She figured it out because of Danny."

"Danny?"

"Over Christmas he'd walked into a room she was standing in and called her Jillian. She suddenly realized how much they actually looked alike. When she was home sick, she managed to get a copy of her birth certificate, and then she knew. She said she was furious with her mother, and the school, too.

"And then I asked her, 'What about *us?*' and—she *laughed*. She said it had been a game, a way to test whether she possessed all the supergirl powers Jillian had. She'd even been using a disposable phone to call me in case her mother snooped on her regular cell phone."

Humor him, I told myself. *Make it seem like I'm on his side.*

"It must have been awful to be tricked that way. It was unfair of her to play with you."

"It wasn't just her, it was the *drug.* That's what I'm trying to tell you. It made me *nuts.* I went into the kitchen for a glass of water and I saw the knife and I just grabbed it. And when I came back she gave me this little look, like I should find the whole thing as funny as she did, and I started stabbing and couldn't stop. And then I saw her mother on the landing. She just froze there, staring at the knife in my hand. I was up the stairs before she could move. And then—and then everyone else had to go, too. I took the knife and her phone and took off."

I tried to block the images from my mind, but they punched through. All that blood. The bodies. *Danny.* God, what would he do to *me?*

"Blake, if you were having a psychotic reaction from a drug you were prescribed, then you weren't really guilty. There's legal defense for it. I've covered cases like that."

He stopped his pacing and leveled his gaze at me, his eyes frantic now. "Oh yeah? And how do you think Mamie would react? How could she love someone who did that? And besides, it's too late for that now. I'm in too deep. You kept pushing. Asking everyone questions. I didn't have a choice."

Penny.

My blood turned icy, almost froze in my veins.

"Did you follow me to Penny Niles's house? Did you find out that I talked to her about the school?"

"I couldn't follow you when I was working, but I needed to know what you were up to. I put a dog tracker in your car. Jillian told Mamie that you wanted to find out why Julia was furious at the school and the principal, and I knew that it probably had to do with the twin thing. And that Niles woman might know the truth."

"And you followed me to the development site with that dog? And you came to the inn the other night."

He seemed to stare right through me, *shimmering*.

"I had to know what you were doing."

"Is that the dog that attacked me downstairs?"

"No, the one downstairs was never choked. The other dog—he's gone. He belonged to someone I know and I didn't dare keep him around."

He was killing anything that got in his way. I would be next.

"What are you going to do with me?"

"I don't know yet." Again, he squeezed his sides, as if pushing together his thoughts. "But something."

I saw Penny's body suddenly, hanging by a scarf from the door. Was that what he had in mind for me? I fought off the urge to retch.

"Please, Blake. We can make this right."

"I *did* make it right. I paid my dues. I came back and took care of my father, and I married Mamie, and I started this business, where all we do is help sick dogs and cats. And you've ruined everything I've built."

A shadow crossed the threshold. I twisted my neck so I could see.

Mamie was standing in the doorway. And to my

shock and relief she had a gun in her hand, pointing it at Blake. He jerked his head in her direction.

"Mamie, what are you doing here?" he demanded.

"You *murdered* them. I heard you."

"Mamie," he said, "give me the gun. I can explain."

"Mamie, don't give him the gun," I pleaded, lifting my head. "Keep the gun on him and call 911. We have to get the police here. *Please.*"

Blake reached out a hand, palm up, beckoning her.

"Don't move," Mamie ordered.

"Mamie."

"I said don't move."

With my head raised as high as I could lift it, I saw Blake's body thrust forward.

She fired. There was a crack like thunder, followed by a thud and then the sound of the shell popping from the gun and bouncing off the floor with a ping. Blake kept moving, though, a blur to my right, and then the sound of gunfire tore through the room again. Another thud, another pop, and blood sprayed from the back of Blake's head onto the cabinets. A second later, his body slumped and I heard him collapse on the floor.

"Mamie, put the gun on the counter and then untie me, okay?" I called out. "We need to call 911."

She lowered her arm but stood rooted in the doorway.

"Mamie, it's going to be okay, but we have to call the police."

Finally she set the gun on the counter, stepped toward the table, and tried to release me. Her eyes were glazed, and her hands were shaking so badly, she couldn't undo the restraints.

I instructed her to take her phone from her purse, dial 911, and hold the phone near my mouth. As soon as the operator answered, I blurted out the message. A man had been shot. We needed police and an ambulance. The operator assured me help was on the way.

"Mamie, you know CPR, right?" I said once the call was done. "Is there anything you can do for Blake, do you think?"

She shook her head hopelessly. I couldn't tell which question she was responding to.

"Can you stop the bleeding somehow?"

"No. He's—he's dead, I think." She began to cry, rocking her body back and forth. She'd just killed the man she loved and thought she knew. She fired the gun to save me.

I encouraged her to keep trying to undo the ties, but she didn't even seem to hear me.

For the next ten minutes we stayed where we were, Mamie crying, her head in her hands, and me trying to keep any eye on her from a prone position. Finally

I heard a cat screech from the kennel down the hall, and then there were footsteps, firm and steady. Two cops edged into the room with their guns drawn. They quickly tried to get a bead on the situation. Out of the corner of my eye, I saw one kneel to administer to Blake. The other asked Mamie and me if we were okay.

"I'm all right but she's in shock," I called out. "And there's a gun on the counter."

Commotion ensued, activity I couldn't always see, though I heard one cop use his radio to check on the ambulance. "He's bleeding out," he barked to the person on the other end. From somewhere outside came the wail of a siren, cutting through the night.

Mamie was led out of the room by one cop, and I heard the other moving around the floor, obviously dealing with Blake. It wasn't until the EMTs entered the room a few minutes later that one of the cops was able to undo me. As he led me on wobbly legs from the room, I twisted my neck, craning for a look at Blake. The EMTs were administering chest compressions and one of them was already smeared with blood. My gut told me Blake wouldn't survive. I'd seen the blood shoot out from his head.

I was guided to the far side of the reception area. There were two other cops there now, though no sign of Mamie anymore. I gave the fastest, clearest account I could manage—that Blake had drugged and restrained me because I was close to discovering that he had murdered the Lowes sixteen years ago. Mamie had become suspicious and showed up at the clinic, overheard what he said, and realized he was going to kill me. When Blake started to rush her, she fired.

Before I could even focus on what might happen next, two of the cops were escorting me in their patrol car to a hospital, the same medical center, it turned out, that I'd been to before. Was Blake here, too? I wondered, as we pulled up to the ER. Was he still alive, in surgery, and fighting for his life? And what about Mamie? I groaned out loud, overwhelmed by emotion. The Lowes all dying, and for what? And now I would be the one to tell Jillian.

One of the cops had located my purse for me before leaving the clinic, and after digging out my phone, I texted Jillian, telling her not to worry, that I was okay, but there had been a major development and I needed her to sit tight and wait for my return. I didn't want to break any of the news over the phone.

I texted Beau, too, to say I would call him later. Man, he was *so* not going to like this.

I was examined by a PA who also took a blood test. I explained that I could still feel the ketamine in my system and that not only was my thinking foggy but objects sometimes shimmered. She gave me something to counteract the effects of the drug.

When I was free to leave the ER, the cops explained that I would need to stop by the station to give a formal statement. I still felt wobbly but was eager to provide all the information I could. They transported me to a police station, a different one than the station I'd visited the night of Penny's murder. Maynard was there waiting, along with a few other detectives.

I related my story in a small interview room and was peppered with questions. The detectives, of course, were especially interested in Mamie's actions. I explained, as I had to the patrol cops earlier, that she had shot her husband in self-defense, saving both of us.

When the questions finally trailed off, I turned to Maynard. "Please, I have to know. Is Blake alive?"

He shook his head. "Died en route to the hospital."

"And Mamie? Is she okay?"

"Yes, she's been questioned and released. Her brother came to pick her up."

The cops offered to take me back to the inn, since the crime scene team needed to search my car for the dog tracker. Later, as I mounted the steps from the parlor, where only a single table lamp burned, I realized I was totally spent. I'd have to summon some deep reserve of energy and do my best to comfort Jillian once I shared the news with her.

I tapped lightly on her door and she opened it almost instantly, as if she'd been standing right behind it waiting. She was dressed in a terry-cloth robe that had the name of the inn embroidered on the front.

"I've been sick with worry," she said. "Where have you been all this time?"

I stepped into the room and closed the door behind me. "Let's sit down, okay?" I said, and motioned to the bed.

"Bailey? What the hell is going on?"

"Jillian, there's no easy way to say this, so I'm just going to blurt it all out." And then I told her. Blake had killed her family under the influence, he claimed, of an antimalarial drug. He'd kill Penny, too, and had drugged and tied me up at the clinic. Mamie had shot him dead and saved my life.

I figured she would cry, but though her face was contorted in anguish, she didn't shed a tear. She sat for a minute saying nothing, obviously trying to process it all.

"And was it because of *me*?" she asked finally. "Because he thought Julia was *me*?"

"He didn't kill her thinking it was you. He'd figured out the truth and was livid at her for faking him out."

I shared more details about my experience tonight and what Blake had divulged, including the part about how Danny had first set Julia to thinking by calling her Jillian's name. The nugget I excluded was the part about Julia claiming she was playing a game, trying to see if she had her sister's supergirl powers. That would only add, unnecessarily, to Jillian's pain and misery.

"I can't get my arms around it," she said, her voice weighted with despair. "No matter how many different ways I look at it. *Blake.* God, how could it be Blake?"

I'd flopped back on the bed by this point, lying flat on my back. "I'm inclined to believe what he said about the malaria drug. I've read about it, and I know it can make you crazy. Maybe if he hadn't experienced side effects, he would have let the whole thing go. Just gone home miffed at Julia."

He couldn't blame the drug, though, for what he did to Penny Niles. That was coldhearted, a murderer terrified of being found out.

"I feel *sick*," Jillian said. "I was *attracted* to him these past weeks."

"So was I. I don't mean sexually, but he seemed like such a good guy."

"And—did Mamie figure it out? Is that why she came to the clinic tonight?"

"I think she might have started to put it together when I talked to her earlier. I called to ask her the same question I'd asked you: Was there someone in the area that April who could have been fixated on you?"

"She knew he was home then?"

"Maybe not at the time. They weren't dating then. But at some point since they've been married, Blake must have told her about coming back here with malaria, figuring that with Dylan in prison, it wouldn't arouse any suspicions."

"Right."

"I actually wonder, though, if she first smelled something rotten when we were all in my room after the dog attack. Blake brought up the concept of personal-protection dogs, probably to make me even more anxious about the attack. She seemed to look at him oddly that day. At the time I thought it was because she worried there was something between the two of you, but maybe her wheels were already turning."

"Poor Mamie. What's going to happen to her?"

"If the police are comfortable with the self-defense explanation, she at least won't be arrested. Apparently her brother picked her up tonight."

"And Bailey, what about you?" she said. "Are you really okay?"

"It's like this weird kind of hangover. The shimmering's stopped at least. Things that aren't supposed to be moving are no longer doing it."

"I was so freaked when you didn't come back. The irony is that I tried to reach Mamie, to ask what she thought I should do, but my call was bumped to voice mail."

I propped myself up on an elbow.

"Did you say in your message that I was missing?"

"Yeah, and I needed her to call me back."

"Oh, wow. That must be why Mamie hightailed it to the clinic with a gun. She had already decided Blake might be guilty, and when she heard I was missing, she might have worried I was in danger. Jillian, you helped save my life."

She shrugged, offering a wan smile. "It's the least I could do. You found the killer."

"I didn't find him so much as flushed him out."

"No, you *found* him. . . . And what happens from here?"

"The cops will want to talk to you. And perhaps to me again."

I could tell from how her face sagged that she was wiped, too.

"I should let you get to bed," I said. "Are you sure you're going to be okay?"

"Yeah, I think so. What about you?"

"I'll be okay. I need to sleep. Will I see you at breakfast?"

"Yup, for sure."

We hugged good-bye and I trudged back to my room.

Despite how late it was, I called Beau, rousing him from sleep.

"Everything okay?" he asked groggily.

"Yeah, sorry not to call earlier, but things pretty much exploded up here. I'm fine, though. And so is Jillian."

"What? Tell me."

"No, go back to bed and I'll fill you in tomorrow."

"When will you call?"

"Actually, I'll see you in person," I said. "I'm coming home."

Chapter 25

I didn't make it back to Manhattan until about four o'clock the next day. There were too many loose ends that needed tying up—or as close to tying up as I could manage.

Despite how wiped I felt when I awoke at seven, I forced myself out of bed. My head was throbbing lightly, and my muscles ached, most likely from being drugged and hauled around the clinic unconscious, along with some residual effects from the most recent rabies vaccine.

And maybe some of it, I thought, was due simply from having been scared out of my mind.

The first thing I did, even before grabbing coffee, was check on Jillian, who seemed weary but was coping surprisingly well. The police, she said, had just phoned and requested to speak with her, and she'd agreed to appear at the station in about an hour. While we ate a quick breakfast, the police rang my cell as well, and asked for another meeting with me, which was no surprise. I was sure they were eager for me to go into greater detail than what my addled brain had been capable of the night before.

Since my car was still at the clinic, Jillian and I decided to show up at the station together. I'd wait for her, or she'd wait for me, and we'd swing by the clinic for my car afterward. I dreaded setting eyes on the place.

At the station, I ended up being called in before Jillian. Some new faces were on the scene this time, but also some familiar ones, including Detective Maynard, who was obviously reopening the Penny Niles murder investigation. And lo and behold, there was the lovely Belinda Bacon. The expression on her face when she saw me would have led you to believe I'd just vomited all over her suit.

Once again I described the horror show last night, doing a better job than I had previously. I had a vague recollection now of arriving at the clinic, chugging the coffee, and descending to the basement level, and I was pretty clear about the things Blake had said to me. The one black-hole part of the evening was from the time I slumped on the basement floor until I regained consciousness and found myself strapped on the exam table like a dog about to be neutered. I assumed Blake had lugged me to the first floor via the elevator. From what I'd pieced together, I'd been there for over an hour before coming to.

The detectives pressed me again about Mamie's actions. Was she in imminent danger, in fear of her life?

I didn't waiver. *Yes*, she had seemed in imminent danger. Her husband had rushed toward her, clearly to grab the gun away. She would have realized that he intended to kill me and probably her, as well.

In truth I'd begun to wonder in bed last night if *rush* was too strong a word. I'd been lying flat on my back at the time, struggling to see. I knew Blake had stepped forward, moved in Mamie's direction, but I wasn't a hundred percent certain her life was in *imminent* danger. Would he have actually killed her? What I *did* know for sure: I wasn't going to let Blake wreck Mamie's life any worse than he already had.

Bacon didn't ask many questions. Just listened. I'm sure she was considering the case against Blake, how proof of his guilt would be established. Right now they had only my word and Mamie's to go on. But within a few weeks, forensic evidence, as well as my blood test, would prove that I'd been drugged, and his DNA would be linked to not only the recently discovered blood sample from the Lowe house, but perhaps to the Penny Niles crime scene as well.

What I never admitted in the interview was the fact that I'd been digging up info about the murders. Everything that I recounted—talking to Penny, hunting for Mercandetti, meeting with Kordas—fit very loosely under the umbrella of researching Jillian's life story.

I was pretty sure, however, I didn't fool anyone in the room. They knew that I was a crime reporter and could easily surmise my real intentions. They didn't thank me for my efforts, but neither did they take me to task. Though I'm sure Bacon was sitting there thinking, *Memoir, my ass.*

When the interview finally wound down, I explained I was driving back to New York City but would be available by phone or email.

Please, I thought, don't force me back here any time soon.

Jillian was interviewed after me, and I cooled my heels in the waiting room of the station. As we drove away later, she admitted that it had been painful to discuss the murders, but there was plenty of satisfaction in knowing Bacon would now set Dylan's exoneration in motion.

When we reached the clinic parking lot, I shuddered involuntarily. It was closed for business today, and I wondered what would happen going forward. Hopefully Mamie would have the strength to carry on.

I said good-bye to Jillian, but we agreed to meet later for lunch. I wanted to swing by Candace's first. Before going into the house, I called Eleanor Mercandetti to tell her the news. I also phoned Keith Denali at the auto shop and assured him his father wasn't the man who murdered the Lowes.

"All right, thanks," he said, his voice joyless.

"I hope you don't mind me calling. I promised I would."

"That's okay. I was actually going to call you. You know, I looked at the video again. No one else ever came up the driveway, and there's no easy way to access my backyard. So I don't know who could have possibly snuck behind the kennel and hurt your friend."

In my drug-induced haze, I'd lost track of the incident. There'd been no attacker, of course. Blake had faked the injury, another attempt to scare me off and make sure he was never viewed suspiciously.

"Thank you, Keith," I said. "I wish you the best."

What I still didn't know was whether Blake had followed me to the storage facility. That might always remain a mystery.

Candace, it turned out, had just heard the news about Blake Allard's death and was desperate to talk to me. I quickly filled her in on what had transpired, playing down the danger I'd been in. I promised to come back to visit before another year had passed.

On my way out she confessed that she'd been fretting since my last visit that she'd divulged too much about my father.

"No, I'm glad you did," I told her. "It's always best to know the truth."

Brilliantly put, Bailey, I thought. I could probably get a job coming up with maxims for T-shirts that sell online for $7.99 each and start to pill after a second washing.

Sometimes, of course, it did help to know the truth. I'd been on a search for the truth for two weeks and the end result was that Dylan Fender's name would be cleared once and for all.

And yet other times the truth merely tossed you something ugly to contend with or left you hopelessly confused. That's why, if Jillian's father had been a pedophile, I never would have told her unless the information was a hundred percent relevant to the case. And it was why I wasn't going to mention the possibility that her mother and Jocelyn might have been lovers.

And what about Jillian? I wondered, as I drove to meet up with her again. How did she really feel knowing that she and Julia were twins? And that Julia had impersonated her, inadvertently triggering Blake's rage?

"It's better that I know," she reassured me when I asked at lunch. She said it had answered questions for her about the restlessness and yearning she'd experienced as a girl, and, of course, it led to the discovery of Blake's guilt.

We'd picked a famous and historic inn at the center of Blackbrook for our meal and were sitting outside in the garden. There were still circles under her eyes, but she seemed more relaxed, the muscles in her face less taut. She'd been in touch with the innocence group this morning, she said, and had filled them in. They would take things from here.

"And you're sure you're okay?" I asked.

"Yeah, more or less, though I'm still having so much trouble coming to terms that it was Blake. It's so horrible and at the same time surreal. And he'll never be punished."

"Though at least you won't have to come back here and go through the trauma of a trial or sentencing."

"Yeah, I guess that's consolation," she said grimly. "What about Mamie? You think she'll be arrested?"

"My guess is no. I was adamant about it being self-defense—but she does need a good lawyer to guide her through the next weeks."

"Maybe that's something I can help with. I've decided I'm going to stick around for a few days, try to be there for her."

"That's great of you, Jillian. You're a good friend."

"You're a good friend, too, Bailey. I owe you so much, more than I can ever express. I said I'd pay you and we have to figure out an amount."

"No way. I did it because I care about you."

"If you want to turn it into a book, you can, you know."

"Let me think about it, okay?" That idea had been stirring in the back of my mind, but I couldn't focus on the future until I'd fully unpacked all that had transpired over the past couple of weeks.

Later, at the inn, as I was tossing my roller bag into the Jeep, I asked Jillian if she had any inclination to drive through Dory before she left the area. I thought maybe she was finally ready to.

She shook her head. "No, I don't think so. I couldn't bear to see the house. Though the other day, when I took that drive? I went to their graves for the first time in years. I wanted to say something to Julia, after finding out that we were twins. To tell her that I'd always loved her in that way but didn't understand it."

Tears pricked my eyes.

"I'm so glad you were able to do that."

We hugged good-bye and promised to speak in a day or so once she had an update on Mamie.

When I'd texted Beau my ETA, he said he'd leave work early to meet me, but I told him not to rush, that I'd probably need a nap.

But that turned out to be an unattainable goal. Despite how good it felt to be home, I was too restless for a siesta. I took my second shower of the day, hoping it would both calm me and unclog my still slightly fuzzy brain. As I meandered around the bedroom with just a towel around my waist, I heard the front door open and then Beau was in the room, grinning.

"Well *that's* a sight for sore eyes."

"Hey, so great to see you." We embraced and kissed. It was really nice to have those arms around me. And yet at the same time I experienced a twinge of dread. I wasn't looking forward to telling him how close I'd come to losing my life. Was he going to be seriously pissed at me once I finished sharing my saga?

"You want to eat early tonight?" Beau asked. "I picked up food and a great bottle of French wine."

"Oh, that's fabulous," I said. Bad girls weren't served Bordeaux, were they? So at least I wasn't in deep shit yet.

An hour later, over pasta and a glass of sensationally good wine, I told him everything, sparing none of the grizzly details. When I reached the part about me strapped down on the dog table—how do you make *that* sound less appalling?—and Mamie firing the gun, he cringed. I quickly moved on to the wrap-up meeting with the police and my last conversation with Jillian.

For a few moments Beau appeared to be digesting all the details and giving nothing away by his expression. Finally, he exhaled loudly.

"God, Bailey, you must be so proud," he said. His brown eyes were now soft with affection. "What you did was incredible."

"Thank you," I said, touched by his words. It was only on the drive home, with the Berkshires in my rearview mirror, that I'd really allowed myself a pat on the back for my efforts. "I've had a sense of satisfaction with other stories, but never like this one. I guess it's because I finally redeemed myself with Jillian. And I cleared Dylan Fender's name."

"Will you turn it into a book?"

"Not sure. I think I want to, but I'm still mulling it over."

The conversation stalled.

"Beau," I said at last, "I appreciate what you said, though I have to admit that at the same time I dreaded telling you some of this stuff. And I don't think I have to explain why."

We were sitting at the table tonight, and he leaned back into his chair, setting his wineglass down at the same time.

"I'm not going to disguise my feelings, Bailey. When I consider what that vet had in store for you—and the thought of the dog mauling you last week—it terrifies me. But it seems expressing my concerns hasn't made any difference."

I shook my head.

"No, believe me, it's made a difference. I've thought a lot about your objections and I understand your fears. I've also thought about my own motivations."

"And?"

"I don't believe I am attracted to risk the way you think. I was terrified of Blake at the clinic, scared shitless. But I also know I hate it when there's a clear injustice in the world and it looks like it won't be fixed. These past weeks, all I could think about is that a poor guy died in prison for nothing, and the person who killed everyone in Jillian's family was still strutting around with no consequences. And I had do something."

I was worried that my comments came across as fraught and overblown, right up there with Scarlett O'Hara's "As God is my witness . . . I'll never be hungry again," but I meant it.

"I hear what you're saying, and I respect it. How is that going to help me the next time you go off on a story?"

"Look, I can assure you that as of right now, at least, I don't have any plans to help another friend. I'm under contract to write my next book, which might very well be about the Lowe murders, and if it is, there won't be anything to worry about. The guy who did it is dead now. This will be my year of living *non*-dangerously, okay?"

"Okay." I didn't hear much enthusiasm in his tone.

"Beau, is this going to drive a wedge between us?" I asked.

"I certainly don't want it to . . . And maybe it's not the thing I really should be talking to you about."

"What do you mean?" I said, confused.

"You know what you said the other day about feeling I'd been a little remote lately, and I brushed it off? That was fairly disingenuous on my part. I think I *have* been a little remote. I've put some distance between us."

The bottom dropped from my stomach. So there was something. But what?

"Have you been unhappy with the relationship?" I asked.

"God, no, Bailey," he said. "But—I think I've pulled away because I've sensed a remoteness from you lately."

"What?"

"It's hard to explain. I know you were a little gun-shy when we first decided to live together, but you seemed to get comfortable with it soon enough. Then somehow this winter you started to drift away a little. You talk about me as the mystery man, the guy who can't be read, and yet I don't know where your head is in regards to me."

"I'm not following at all." Was he really doing a pot, kettle thing to me? "How exactly am I a mystery?"

"You're removed at times. There are nights when you seem happier working at your old apartment instead of coming home for dinner. If I have to hang with my parents, you find any excuse not to join us. And you don't always come clean to me about crap that happens to you. I'm on kind of a need-to-know basis. It's as if you're—I don't know—pulling away."

What he said took me totally by surprise. Had I seemed remote? I thought of what Candace had revealed about my father and winced inside. Maybe I was even more like him than I realized.

"Beau, I may have done those things, but you need to know they're not reflective of my feelings. There's another explanation for most of that. Your mom doesn't like me, so I've tried to steer clear and not make it worse. I probably *have* been holed up at Ninth Street a lot, but it's been about me being under the gun trying to find a new book idea. And if I hold back info, it's because I've become worried about how you'll react. But none of that means I'm not crazy about you."

He studied me, his eyes holding mine.

"What do you want from our relationship, do you think?" he asked.

"Um, I want to be with you. I'd be unhappy—really unhappy—if it ended. . . . What about you?"

"Same page. But I guess I want to think ahead a little, too. When we moved in together, we talked about seeing where this took us. I don't want us to be standing still forever. I'd like to know where we're going."

I thought of me posing as his fiancée with the real estate agent. Was that what he had in mind?

"You mean make it less tentative, more of a commitment?"

"Yes. God, isn't it usually the woman making these kinds of statements?"

I laughed. "You're not talking about the *m* word are you?"

"I know the idea of marriage scares you sometimes, but I'd like there to be a bigger commitment than what we've got now. I'd like to at least talk about what our options are."

Okay, wow. I hadn't been prepared for this. His

comments were making me jittery, but at the same time I *liked* the sentiment behind them. Right now at least, I didn't want to think of life without Beau in it.

"Gee," I said, grinning, "you like me, you really like me."

"I haven't terrified you, have I?"

"No, not at all"—which actually wasn't a hundred percent true—"I mean, actually it does make me a little nervous, and maybe at times my remoteness is related to feeling anxious about a big commitment again, especially since the first time was such a bust. But that has nothing to do with you. And—and I'm definitely open to talking more on the subject."

"Good."

"Give me a couple of days to recover from the Berkshires and then let's see if we can hash out a plan."

I was in bed early that night, asleep quickly, and not surprisingly, I suppose, Jillian stepped into a dream I was having. She said something to me, though I couldn't make out what it was. I stirred from sleep and sat up straight in bed.

I'd give her a call tomorrow and see what was happening. I was praying this time she'd really be able to make a fresh start in life. Settle in a place. Find love. Be happy.

Would she and I be lifelong friends now? I couldn't be sure. An unmistakable bond certainly existed between us now, but that didn't mean she'd necessarily want to hang together. I might remind her too much of stuff she wanted far from her mind.

That would be sad for me. And yet I would at least have no regrets about our friendship. I'd kept my promise. I'd dug up the truth just as she'd hoped for. It wasn't everything, but it was what she'd asked me for.

Acknowledgments

First and foremost, I want to offer a huge thanks to my wonderful editor, Laura Brown. Laura, you're a dream to work with. And thank you to Mary Sasso of Harper Perennial for her marketing magic, and to Amy Baker, associate publisher of Harper Perennial, for being so supportive of my writing career. A big shout-out as well to my always amazing agent Sandy Dijkstra and her awesome team, particularly Elise Capron, Thao Lee, and Andrea Cavallaro.

This book seemed to involve even more research than usual and I want to express my deep gratitude to all those gave their time to me: Barbara Butcher, consultant for forensic and medicolegal investigations; Nathaniel White, attorney; Louis M. Freeman, attorney; Anne Pleshette Murphy; Kyle Ann Treadway; Jessica

Tarter; Tate Kelly; Paul Paganelli, M.D.; Will Valenza, police chief (ret.); Raymond Berke partner in Woodard and Berke Investigations and author of *6 More Dead*; Iain Holmes; Nancy Alhum, associate broker; Florence Nolan, M.D.; P. Dee Boersma; PhD; Tom De Vincentis, D.V.M.; and Jane Pucher of the Innocence Project.

About the Author

KATE WHITE, the former editor in chief of *Cosmopolitan* magazine, is the *New York Times* bestselling author of five psychological thrillers (*The Secrets You Keep, The Wrong Man, Eyes on You, The Sixes*, and *Hush*), as well as six other Bailey Weggins mysteries. White is also the author of several career books for women, including *I Shouldn't Be Telling You This: How to Ask for the Money, Snag the Promotion, and Create the Career You Deserve*, and the upcoming *The Gutsy Girl's Handbook* (April 2018). In addition, she is the editor of *The Mystery Writers of America Cookbook: Wickedly Good Meals and Desserts to Die For*. She lives in New York City. Read more about her at www.katewhite.com.

THE NEW LUXURY IN READING

We hope you enjoyed reading
our new, comfortable print size and found it
an experience you would like to repeat.

Well – you're in luck!

HarperLuxe offers the finest in fiction and
nonfiction books in this same larger print size and
paperback format. Light and easy to read, HarperLuxe
paperbacks are for book lovers who want to see
what they are reading without the strain.

For a full listing of titles and
new releases to come, please visit our website:

www.HarperLuxe.com